CAIRO GAMBIT

Also by S. W. Perry

THE JACKDAW SERIES

The Angel's Mark
The Serpent's Mark
The Saracen's Mark
The Heretic's Mark
The Rebel's Mark
The Sinner's Mark

NOVELS

Berlin Duet

CAIRO GAMBIT

S. W. PERRY

CORVUS

Published in hardback in Great Britain in 2025 by
Corvus, an imprint of Atlantic Books Ltd

10 9 8 7 6 5 4 3 2 1

A CIP catalogue record for this book is available from the British Library.

Hardback ISBN: 978 1 80546 064 0
Trade Paperback ISBN: 978 1 80546 488 4
E-book ISBN: 978 1 80546 065 7

Printed and bound by CPI (UK) Ltd, Croydon CR0 4YY

Corvus
An imprint of Atlantic Books Ltd
Ormond House
26–27 Boswell Street
London
WC1N 3JZ

www.atlantic-books.co.uk

Product safety EU representative: Authorised Rep Compliance
Ltd., Ground Floor, 71 Lower Baggot Street, Dublin,
D02 P593, Ireland. www.arccompliance.com

MIX
Paper | Supporting
responsible forestry
FSC
www.fsc.org   FSC® C013604

For Jane

One

Until the shooting, the only slaughter committed against the Nimrod Theatre had been confined to the review pages of the Cairo newspapers. A cosy but unimposing little auditorium off Kamil Street, The Nim, as its habitués preferred to call it, was known more for the brio of its productions than for their commercial success. Before that warm and otherwise agreeable Cairene night, an audience could rest safe in the knowledge that a pistol was nothing more lethal than a prop, that the shot that made them jump in their seats was merely a blank, the resulting blood comfortingly fake. But – as all theatre folk know only too well – even the best runs must come to an end some day.

The time of the attack, 10.27 p.m., was not in doubt, it being the solemn habit of the manager – an over-earnest young Egyptian named Moussa Bannoudi – to set the foyer clock in accordance with the start of Radio Cairo's early-evening news broadcast. That night it took a fatal ricochet, stopping the hands dead and thus precluding any debate.

Outside, beyond The Nim's Moorish archways, painted a lustrous red and gold in a European's imagining of a caliph's treasury, the city was taking its pleasures as it did on any other

I

night. In the adjacent Ezbekia Gardens, a slice of belle-époque Paris transported to Egypt, the street lamps threw their warm light into the groves of banyan and acacia trees. Friends and lovers strolled along the pathways, around the lake and over the little wrought-iron footbridge. At nearby Santi's a cosmopolitan mix of Egyptians, Lebanese, British and French queued noisily for a late table. In the Long Bar at Shepheard's Hotel, and on the floating nightclubs moored along the Nile, the lounge-lizards were hard at work. At the Kit-Kat Club, officers from the British garrison vied with smooth young men from King Farouk's court for the attention of the chorus girls. And at the Nimrod Theatre that evening's performance of *A Midsummer Night's Dream* – already dismissed by the theatre critic of *Al-Misri* as 'lacklustre' – had just drawn to a close. Behind the safety curtain, the cast were rushing to cleanse themselves of greasepaint and sweat. In the auditorium the house-lights were up and the audience was already pushing for the exits.

Awaiting them in the lane outside was a small squadron of taxis, from which issued a growing hysteria of waving arms and blaring motor horns, the usual Cairo method of attracting trade. The more romantically inclined could choose instead a hantour, a horse-drawn carriage – there were several for hire that night – whose drivers, clad in traditional *galabeyas*, sat cradling their long whips like fishermen at their rods. And while the Cairo police later took copious statements from them all, it was perhaps inevitable that their attention was focused more on those coming out of the theatre's lobby rather than on the four men who entered it.

They came from the direction of Ibrahim Pasha Square, or so the driver of the hantour nearest the entrance said later to a white-jacketed Cairo police constable while his horse munched from its nosebag. And there were three of them, not four. Not so, claimed a motor-cab driver. They came from across the Gardens, and they were five in number. They were European gangsters… they were Egyptian nationalists… they were Jews… they were the Four Horsemen of the Apocalypse and they came by tram…

While the shaken witnesses inside the foyer each had their own recollection and guarded it jealously, all agreed there had been no warning given. 'It wasn't as if they came in brandishing tommy guns like mobsters from Chicago,' said the redoubtable Madame Nasoul, who ran the front-of-house. And indeed had she been smoking one of her foul Kyriazi Frères, it is quite possible that in the resulting smokescreen no one could have described the assassins in any consistent detail at all.

'I thought they were waiting for someone,' Madame Nasoul told the fiercely moustachioed detective inspector who took her statement – *they* being four gentlemen in overcoats and fedoras. 'They came in over there,' she said, pointing at the left-hand brass-edged swing door that led to the street, 'maybe two minutes before the inner doors opened.' And then, turning, with an imperious sweep of her hand she gave the inspector a rapid visual tour of the foyer. Look up to the gallery, please, Inspector. Observe the ottoman couches, thoughtfully provided for those who need to sit while chatting during the interval, and where we laid out some of the wounded. Follow the curving red-carpeted stairs – admittedly a little worn, but do you know what carpet costs these days? – down to the ground floor and the box office – note the interesting arabesque lattice-front dating from the Khedive era – and finally to the stalls: one double door on each side, hidden away beneath the circle's overhang like the private booths in one of the naughtier clubs on Emad al-Din

Street. And, all the while, studiously ignoring the sticky pools of drying blood.

When the swing door first opened and the four men entered, Madam Nasoul had asked herself why anyone would wear an overcoat on such a warm night. But if her suspicions were aroused, it was only because she feared they might be gentlemen from the bank, come to serve a foreclosure notice, which – given the precarious nature of the Nimrod's financial health – was a constant possibility.

At first they did nothing very much at all. Adopting a nonchalance that, with hindsight, Madame Nasoul agreed should have provided a warning, they made a casual pretence of studying the various photographs on the lobby wall: portraits of some of those who had appeared at the Nimrod since its opening late in the previous century, when it had been known as the Karnak. Some of these faces were Egyptian, including Rose al-Youssef and Zaki Rostom, while the others belonged mostly to second-tier English repertory actors seeking relief and employment after the mildewed trials of end-of-the-pier stages and provincial boarding houses. If the four men found anything to excite them in this collection, they did not reveal it. Indeed, on later reflection Madam Nasoul thought they might have been using the glass to ensure their fedoras were pulled well down over their brows. She considered asking them if she might be of assistance. But by that time the departing audience was already streaming out of the auditorium. This diversion drew her away and may very well have saved her life.

It was over almost before anyone realized what was happening – a sudden fusillade of shots. Maybe ten. Some said more. Some said fewer. Those whom the bullets struck were mostly not in any position to count.

From the cab rank it sounded like little more than the back-firing of a motorcycle engine. But inside the confined space of the Nimrod's foyer, it had the deafening brutality of an artillery barrage.

It stopped almost as abruptly as it began. For a moment there was silence, the stunned quiet of incomprehension broken only by the wet slither of blood-soaked clothing on stone as people sought to crawl away from the danger, or from their own pain. Someone moaned, a deep groan of anguish rising from the depths of damaged flesh. Then the screaming started.

The swing doors all but flew off their ornate brass hinges as terrified people fled out into the street, causing the usually placid hantour horses to startle. Once freed from the theatre's interior, panic turned truth into wild speculation, and the four gunmen into twenty. In a dozen breathless exchanges it was declared, with absolute certainty, that the assassins were still inside, stalking at will through the auditorium; that they had accomplices in the street ready to take potshots; that they were on the roof or rampaging through the nearby Hotel Bristol; that at this very moment they were gunning down people at the Alhambra Music Hall.

In fact they had calmly disappeared into the Ezbekia Gardens before the cordite smoke dissipated, leaving their discarded overcoats and fedoras in a neat pile beneath a bush by the lake, there to be discovered at daybreak by the police.

Moussa Bannoudi and Madame Nasoul tended to the injured as best they could, joined by the braver members of the cast and the backstage crew courageous enough not to lock themselves into cupboards or the dressing rooms. By the time the first police officer arrived, the polished tiles of the lobby were a kaleidoscopic picture of bloody footprints. The constable, a gangly Sudanese boy of barely twenty in a white tunic and fez, took one look at the carnage and began blowing his whistle. He went on doing so until Madame Nasoul told him brusquely to take the wretched instrument outside because the noise wasn't helping anyone.

The death toll was less than the number of prostrate bodies might at first have suggested: six fatalities and eight wounded. Amongst them was an assistant master from the English School at Heliopolis. The English-language newspapers, while giving him a glowing obituary, referred to the Egyptian casualties – amongst whom were a doctor from the Kasr al-Ainy hospital and his wife – only as *locals*.

The attack was naturally the subject of much speculation and many column inches in the next day's newspapers and over the days that followed. *The Egyptian Gazette*, being English-owned, stated confidently that it was a terrorist outrage, staged by nationalists for whom the implementation of an Anglo-Egyptian treaty – committing Britain to eventually removing all her troops from the country – was progressing too slowly by half. The leader writer of *Al-Misri* suggested the assassins might have been supporters of Benito Mussolini, and the attack staged in revenge for British criticism of Italian atrocities in Abyssinia. A suggestion in the periodical *Raghaeb* that the shooting was a protest at Western debauchery held little water, if any. For the zealot with murderous intent there were far more inviting targets elsewhere in the city.

Despite the encouragement of Thomas Russell, the English commandant of the Cairo city police, known throughout Egypt as Russell Pasha, none of the detectives investigating the crime could establish any connection between the victims, other than that they had chosen to watch the play. Until, that is, it was noticed that one of them – the unfortunate assistant master from the English School – bore a passing resemblance to the owner of the Nimrod Theatre, one Archibald Nevendon.

Nevendon was already known to the police, but not because of any former criminality. He was an upstanding member of Cairo society, director of the Egyptian office of the Anglo-Levantine Oil Company. And he was the man who, single-handedly, had been keeping the Nimrod Theatre afloat since purchasing it as a barely going concern several years previously. Indeed, his photograph was amongst those on display in the lobby. It hung beside that of his late brother Nimrod, after whom the theatre was named.

And there, for the time being, the trail went cold. Because, on further investigation, it was swiftly determined that Archie Nevendon had not been seen at his office for several days. Nor had his usual haunts had so much as a sniff of him. He had apparently vanished off the face of the Earth like desert mist at sunrise.

Two

The black Humber saloon pulled off the lane and began to edge cautiously between the ivy-covered stone pillars that guarded the entrance to Bevern Lodge, a minor and gently mouldering estate in the folds of the Ashdown Forest, midway between the southern fringes of London and England's south coast. Watched by the young woman in tweeds and headscarf who, until a moment ago, had been standing in the shadow of an ancient beech tree beside the curving driveway, it came to a halt on the gravel barely ten yards away from her.

Driver: male, she noted. Single passenger beside him. Also male. Both middle-aged. Pencil moustaches lending a touch of severity to their otherwise forgettable faces. Creased lapels suggesting cheap off-the-peg suits. Eyes taking in far more than they were giving away.

Until she'd heard the engine, Primrose Nevendon had been topping up the ancient metal bird-feeder that her father had strung on a cord from the lowest bough when she'd been too small to reach it without being hoisted onto his shoulders. It was mid-April, and beyond the thick laurel hedge the forest was once again turning itself into a mix of Birnam Wood and grouse moor, somehow dropped by mistake into the downs of East Sussex. Fallow deer grazed amongst the stands of Scots pine.

On the sandy paths, adders basked in the spring sunshine. And beside Bevern's driveway, a perceptive young woman reached a conclusion: *policemen* – in anyone's language.

Prim lowered her arm, letting the paper bag of birdseed rest against her right knee, and waited in silent expectation while the car window wound down with the juddering squeak of rubber against glass.

'Bevern Lodge?' asked the car's passenger.

Primrose set down the bag of birdseed and came closer, stooping a little to bring her face nearer to his. 'I beg your pardon?'

'Is this Bevern Lodge, luv? Only there's no sign anywhere.'

Pulling the scarf knot away from her chin, Primrose gave a regretful smile. 'Sorry – *luv*. We had to take it down.'

'Something to hide, eh?' suggested the passenger almost flirtatiously, for by now he could see that this was not the sturdy and weathered countrywoman he'd anticipated. 'Being a bit naughty, are we?'

'People from the village kept throwing paint over it.'

The driver rested his hands on the steering wheel and spoke across his companion. 'From what we've heard about you lot, can't say I'm surprised.'

Primrose shrugged. 'If you've come here just to insult us, we can get that down at the Rose and Crown, thank you very much.'

The man in the passenger seat had a pencil sticking crookedly out of his breast pocket and the drooping eyes of someone who holds suspicion amongst the highest of human virtues. He rested one elbow on the window frame and let his head loll out as if he had no muscles in his neck. 'Now we've established we're in the right place,' he said, in a tone that suggested the missing sign and the young woman were co-conspirators in a crime as yet unnamed, 'are you Celestina Lombardi?'

'No. You want my mother,' Primrose said. 'I'm the daughter, Primrose – Prim to my friends. But I take it you're not here to be friendly.'

'And what precisely makes you think that, Miss Lombardi?'

'Oh, just a hunch,' she replied. 'And it's Nevendon, by the way – Prim Nevendon. I kept my father's name when they divorced.'

'Don't suppose you've seen him at all, recently?'

'Only if you consider 1924 recent,' Prim said, looking surprised. 'Why do you want to know?'

'I'm Detective Inspector Swinnell,' the man in the passenger seat said, answering a different question entirely. He glanced back into the motorcar. 'And this is Detective Sergeant Mullen.'

Mullen leaned forward to peer through the windscreen. 'Nice little place you've got here. Must have cost a bomb. Foreign money, was it?'

Prim Nevendon smiled sweetly. 'This can't be about my overdue library book; they'd have sent a superintendent at the very least.'

Swinnell didn't rise to her bait. 'Assuming that you've seen your *mother* since 1924, perhaps you could tell us where we might find her.'

'Up at the house,' Prim said. She pointed up the drive. 'Keep going and round the bend. You can't miss it.'

'What do we do when we get there?' enquired Mullen sarcastically. 'Ask the butler?'

'If we had a butler,' said Prim evenly, 'I wouldn't be standing here wasting my time talking to Dick Tracy and his sidekick, now would I?' She stepped back from the car. 'You're bound to bump into some of the Fraternity up there. They'll be able to help you. My guess is you'll find her in her pottery studio.'

'Her *pottery* studio,' said Swinnell archly, turning to his companion. 'Do you have a pottery studio in your semi in Dulwich by any chance, Sergeant Mullen?'

'Next to the indoor swimming pool, sir.'

Swinnell began to wind the window up, his shoulder revolving as he turned the handle, as if he was exercising an ache. He stopped halfway. 'You might want to follow us,' he suggested to Prim. 'After we've spoken to your mother, I dare say we'll be wanting a word or two with you, Miss Nevendon. Not planning to leave the country or anything of that nature, are we?'

Prim frowned. 'Why on earth would I want to do that?'

'Oh, it was just a thought. Rome… Berlin… somewhere of that nature.'

'I'm perfectly happy in East Sussex, thank you all the same, Detective Inspector,' Prim replied, but by then she was talking to the glass.

She heard Mullen put the Humber into gear. Could have offered me a lift, she thought as it disappeared amongst the trees. Perhaps the discourtesy was a punishment; they were policemen, after all. Maybe they'd guessed she was lying to them. Not about Archie, of course. But about being happy in East Sussex.

The Lodge was a rambling Tudor manor house built by a Sussex wool-merchant-turned-sea-wolf who'd made his fortune pirating New World silver from the Spanish. In the intervening centuries it had sagged into the landscape like a sandcastle in a slowly encroaching tide. It boasted a tithe barn, several priest-holes and a moat, now given over to daffodils and meadow flowers. Celestina Lombardi had inherited it from an English aunt, otherwise it might have been sold in the divorce. Now, under her often-dreamy and scatterbrained rule, it was home to a small, eclectic community of artists and third-tier philosophers, known amongst themselves as the Bevern Fraternity, and to the surrounding hamlets as 'that bunch of Eyeties up at the big house'.

Besides Celestina – who, as Prim had explained to the detective inspector, was mostly to be found in her potter's smock with her greying hair tucked into a poacher's hat – there were in fact only two members of direct Italian descent: Gianni, a shy young fellow whose slender hands were permanently stained by the ink from his efforts at screen-printing, and Mariana, who wrote poetry in the style of Boccaccio and affected the tragic air of a modern-day Ophelia, even when she was happy. The latest addition to the Fraternity was a German, Gertrude Bernbaum, a young artist who'd fled to England because the Nazis had pronounced her work degenerate and who was permanently worried sick for her parents, who couldn't get the right papers to leave Stuttgart. The rest were English to their roots – except for Angus. Angus was a would-be playwright. He'd never had anything performed in public, but he was always pestering Prim to do the set design for his next great project that was sure to wow. A friend of a friend of John Gielgud was even now championing his efforts – and had been for several months. He was sure to hear something soon.

And playing the role of big sister to them all, sometimes even to her mother, was Primrose. Or Prim to her friends, if they weren't police detectives. Prim Nevendon, twenty-four, daughter of Celestina and Archie, occupation – of sorts – freelance stage designer, with a few provincial successes to her name but nothing yet to hang a hat on, let alone a reputation. Almost, if not quite, single out of choice, because quite frankly the sort of boys one met these days – well, so far, they'd proved about as appealing as a wet weekend in Bognor. And, if she were being honest with herself, scared stiff for the future: hers and everybody else's. And who wouldn't be these days, what with that dreadful Mr Hitler in Germany ranting away like a lunatic?

Reaching the house, Prim saw the now-empty Humber parked outside. Its nearside front tyre was plonked just enough onto the verge to flatten some of the daffs she'd planted last year. Deliberate and wanton violence, she decided. Police brutality. Next thing we know, we'll be exactly like Germany, if we're not careful.

'These two gentlemen are police officers, darling.'

Celestina was sitting at her old potter's wheel, still wearing her poacher's hat, with her arms, her apron and the floor around splattered with a milky residue of liquid clay. Swinnell and Mullen stood with their backs to the single window, looking as though they'd stumbled upon a crime scene in which extreme violence had been committed with a sack full of flour and a hosepipe.

'I know,' Prim said. 'I met them on the drive.'

'They claim they're from the station in East Grinstead,' her mother said. 'I don't believe *that* for a moment. We know almost every policeman in the county by sight, don't we, Primmy? God knows, we've had them sitting in their motorcars out there in the lane long enough, taking note of who comes and who goes. Scribbling away in their notebooks. Probably got binoculars, too. What do you think we're going to do, Inspector Swinnell – raise a giant statue of Signor Mussolini on the lawn? Signal from the dovecote to submarines full of Nazi spies off Seaford?'

Swinnell could have been wearing a bulletproof vest beneath his jacket for all the damage her sarcasm did him. 'It's a matter of allegiances, Mrs Nev—' he paused, before correcting himself. 'Mrs Lombardi.'

'Allegiances? Don't be so bloody impertinent, Inspector. I'm a British citizen. I was born here.'

'What is all this about, please?' Prim asked.

Without waiting for Swinnell to speak, Celestina said, 'They're here because your father's gone missing again.'

The tone in her mother's voice was the one she always used when speaking of Archie: disinterest as a disguise for complete loathing. It always brought out the combative side of Prim's nature. Where her parents were concerned, she didn't believe in absolutes.

'You don't sound overly concerned, Mrs Lombardi,' said Mullen.

'Why would I be concerned? It's not as if he hasn't done it before.'

'I see,' Mullen replied, raising an eyebrow. He drew a notebook from his coat pocket and thumbed it open. 'Would you care to tell us about the previous occasions on which he has disappeared?'

'There was just the one.'

'And when would that have been?'

'February 1924. He walked out and never came back. Did us all a favour, to be honest.'

'What do you mean, *missing*?' Prim asked. 'Is he all right?'

Swinnell turned in her direction. 'All we know is that Mr Nevendon hasn't been seen either at his office or at his customary haunts for some time. I can't be more specific than that.'

'Have they checked the local cocaine dens, or the whorehouses?' Celestina enquired.

Swinnell's brows lifted. 'Should they have?'

'My ex-husband had the scruples of an alley cat, Detective. Only alley cats tend to be more reliable.'

'Mummy!'

Celestina opened her palms defensively. A trickle of watery clay ran down her right forearm and dripped onto her knee. 'It's the truth. That's what we're supposed to tell policemen, isn't it? Otherwise they might get out their rubber truncheons.'

'You're thinking of the Gestapo, madam,' Mullen said. 'We're from the East Sussex Constabulary.'

'There's a difference?' said Celestina archly.

Inspector Swinnell emitted a slow, official cough. 'We had been led to understand that Mr Nevendon was an upstanding member of the British community in Cairo. Are you suggesting he might have a secret life?'

Celestina's reply was laced with bitterness. 'Casanova was an author – but he's not exactly famous for his *books*, is he?'

Mullen's mouth suffered a brief spasm that was very nearly a smile. He turned to Prim. 'And what about you, Miss Nevendon? Do you remain in contact with your father?'

'Egypt isn't exactly on the doorstep, is it, Sergeant?'

'I'll take that as a "no" then.'

Prim felt her cheeks burn. How could she have been so transparent? And to a policeman at that. In what she had imagined was a pithy grown-up reply, she had exposed the quiet childhood ache she felt at the infrequency of Archie's correspondence. 'That's not at all what I meant,' she said, too quickly and far too defensively for her own liking. 'He sends me a card at Christmas, and on my birthday. He writes letters every now and then. We keep in touch.'

'Regularly?' asked Mullen.

'Not as much as I should like. At least not these days. He has a very important job. I imagine it makes heavy demands upon his time.'

'And in these cards and letters, has he ever indicated any fears he might have for his safety? No hint of why he might have taken it into his head to disappear?'

'Of course not.'

'Why "of course"?'

'Because if he had, I would have asked him how I might be of help,' Prim said, barely avoiding an accusing glance at Celestina.

'What about this theatre business he's involved in?' Swinnell asked.

'You mean the Nimrod?'

'Has he ever mentioned any troubles he might be experiencing on that front?'

'What do you mean by "troubles", Inspector?'

'Like impending bankruptcy.'

'The theatre is a tough business to make money in, Inspector,' said Prim. 'I don't suppose it's any different in Cairo.'

Mullen was writing in his notebook. Without looking up, he asked, 'What exactly is his connection with this theatre, Miss Nevendon? Is he one of your amateur dramaticals, by any chance? I only ask because the missus is very much into that sort of thing.'

'He owns it,' Prim said bluntly.

'Well, well. An *impresario*,' said Swinnell mockingly.

'Not really. It's another of his hobbies. Well, more than a hobby really.'

'More in what way?' asked Mullen.

Prim glanced at her mother, but Celestina seemed content to let her do the talking. 'Well, you see, it's named after his younger brother, my uncle Nimrod,' Prim said. 'My father purchased it after the Great War. They had both served on the staff of General Allenby during the campaign in the Middle East. They'd discovered the theatre when they were on leave.'

'Isn't it a bit unusual, purchasing a theatre – and in Cairo, of all places?' suggested Swinnell, as if Prim had been pitching a doubtful alibi.

'They do have theatres in other countries, Inspector,' she said. 'And Uncle Nim had an early ambition to run one. Granny G always said they were like a couple of young boys with a secret den to play make-believe in. Isn't that true, Mummy?'

Celestina shrugged. 'Grace may have said something like that.'

'Anyway, they found this rundown old place and decided to give it a new lease of life,' Prim went on. 'Saw themselves as a pair of regular D'Oyly Cartes, according to my grandmother.'

'May we have the address of this uncle, Mr Nimrod Nevendon?' Mullen asked.

'Certainly,' said Prim. 'Try the War Cemetery in Jerusalem. I can't tell you what plot.'

'Ah,' said Mullen with a wince. 'I see. Please forgive me, Miss Nevendon.'

'That's all right, Sergeant. You weren't to know. He died in late 1917, fighting in Palestine against the Turks. My father was heartbroken. He vowed to keep that theatre going in Nim's memory.'

Swinnell wrote briefly in his notebook, then placed the end of his pencil against his thin moustache and gave a little rub, as if it suddenly offended him and he wished to erase it. Or perhaps he was simply preparing himself for what he said next. 'I'm sorry to have to tell you, but there was shooting at the theatre a few days ago.'

Prim's hands flew to her mouth. 'Dear God, not Archie—'

'No, not your father,' Swinnell replied hurriedly. 'The attack happened after he'd gone missing. But the local police do believe it might have something to do with his disappearance.'

'A shooting – that's just awful,' Prim said, looking at Celestina, who simply shook her head as if to say: I could have told you things would come to this, one day.

'There were several fatalities,' said Swinnell in a matter-of-fact way. 'But your father was not amongst them.'

'Why would anyone *do* something like that?' Prim asked, appalled. 'That sort of thing only happens in Chicago.'

'Forgive me, Miss Nevendon,' Swinnell went on, 'but did your father ever speak of politics in his letters, by any chance? I'm thinking international politics. The present tensions in Europe, for instance.'

Celestina had suddenly found her voice again. 'If you mean Nazi Germany and Herr Hitler, Inspector, or Signor Mussolini in Italy, why don't you come out and say so? We've heard it all before.'

Swinnell turned towards her, almost as if he'd forgotten she was there. 'Mr Nevendon is – let us use the word *is* until we have cause to think otherwise – a senior director of Anglo-Levantine Oil. Is that not true?'

'Yes. He runs their Cairo office,' said Celestina. 'What of it?'

'Then I suspect your former husband must have access to all sorts of confidential information that would be of interest to a potential enemy in the event of war breaking out,' Swinnell went on. It sounded like a recitation, as though he was speaking someone else's lines. 'Take the new oil pipeline from the fields in Iraq to the terminal at Haifa in Palestine, for example. It was installed to supply the Royal Navy's Mediterranean Fleet. Then there's the strategic importance of the Suez Canal. I dare say Mr Nevendon would have inside knowledge of that, too.'

'My, they do teach you a lot in the police, don't they?' Celestina said archly. 'I didn't know the training was so encyclopaedic.'

Swinnell chewed her response and found it tasted unpleasant. 'I'm sure Mr Hitler would be only too happy to get his hands on information pertaining to such matters,' he said loftily.

Prim said, 'Are you suggesting Herr Hitler has kidnapped my father, Inspector? Isn't that a little far-fetched?'

'Certain people in authority are at this very moment considering the possibility,' Swinnell responded cryptically.

Prim gave him a teasing smile. 'I think you've been reading too much John Buchan in your lunch break at the police station.'

'There is another possibility of course,' Mullen piped up from the wings. 'Perhaps he's decided to go over of his own free will.'

'Go over? You mean *defect* – to the Nazis?' Prim said. 'That's preposterous. Archie would never do such a thing.'

'Who cares where he's gone?' Celestina murmured to herself. Then, to Swinnell, she added, 'If you find a body, I suggest interviewing the vultures. Ask them if they found a backbone on the carcass.'

'Mummy! That's horribly uncharitable,' Prim scolded. Facing Swinnell, she said, 'My parents had a bad divorce. She doesn't mean it.'

Celestina stood up and wiped her arms on her smock. 'I really would like to get back to work, if that's not obstructing you in your duties, or whatever you call it.'

Swinnell's manner hardened. 'One more thing, Mrs Lombardi. What exactly do you get up to here at Bevern Lodge, if I might be so bold as to ask?'

'What do you mean by "get up to"?' Celestina hissed, flapping her stained smock and reminding Prim of an angry goose. 'I think it's time you left, Detective Inspector,' she said. 'But for the record, neither I nor my daughter, nor anyone else here at the Fraternity is, or has ever been, an agent of a hostile power – whatever you or the ignorant bigots who throw paint over the entrance pillars like to claim. We're *artists*, that's all. We have no political affiliation to foreign governments, and we just want to be left in peace. There, you can write that down in your silly notebook.' She became tearful, although when Prim rushed to comfort her, she flapped a hand to wave her off. 'It's *unbearable*, all this innuendo. It's prejudice, that's what it is. Prejudice, pure and simple.'

Prim said sternly, 'I think my mother has made her point clearly enough, don't you? Good day, gentlemen. When you leave, please try not to destroy any more daffodils.'

Swinnell tucked his notebook and pencil inside his jacket, his face impassive. 'If you should happen to hear from your father, Miss Nevendon,' he said smoothly, 'perhaps you'd be good enough to telephone the police station at East Grinstead and ask for me by name. Can you do that for me?'

Prim agreed that she could. She escorted the two men to the hall and closed the door behind them. She thought of bolting it, but knew they'd hear the clank of the ancient lock and think her actions suspicious. So she went to the kitchen to put the kettle on.

When she returned to the studio, bearing a tea tray, her mother was at her potter's wheel, hunched over it like a murderer, gripping the spinning clay as if she intended to strangle it. Prim watched her for a while in silence. She was a fine artist when the temper wasn't on her. She'd once aspired to be another Clarice

Cliff, selling her brightly coloured wares to the best people in London stores. Somehow it had never quite become a reality. Now Celestina sold mostly to her friends, her only commercial outlet being a shop in the Brighton Lanes run by an ageing tenor and his young male friend – something else Prim suspected her mother blamed Archie for.

Clearing a space amidst the jumble of knives, coils of cutting wire, scrapers and coilers on a nearby table, Prim set down the tray. 'Surely you must be a little worried about him,' she ventured tentatively, pouring the tea the way Celestina liked: milk first and to hell with snobbery.

'They weren't from East Grinstead,' her mother replied without looking up. 'They were Special Branch. You could tell by the size of their feet. Why do they have to come here asking their impudent questions as if we were enemy agents?'

'I think they just want to know what's happened to Archie,' Prim said, taking a sip of tea. 'And to be honest, so do I. It might be something awful. He might be hurt, or – God forbid – worse.'

Celestina took her foot off the pedal and the wheel slowed to a halt. The clay gleamed wetly as though it had risen from the ocean, its gaping mouth desperate for air. She looked up at her daughter. 'You were only ten when he left, darling. You were too young to know about things. Your father is like bad clay. Too many impurities. Too many voids. Nothing good will ever be made of it.'

'That's not how I remember him,' Prim said, trying hard not to sound argumentative.

'Yes, well, that's you all over, Primmy. Too good to see the bad in people. Wait till you get hurt, then tell me if you still feel the same.' Celestina reached across to the tray and drank noisily from her teacup, something she had started doing years ago simply to annoy Archie's mother, Lady Grace Nevendon. Then she put her foot back on the pedal and her head went down again. The potter's wheel began to whir once more.

There was no point in pushing further, not when Celestina was in one of her emotional deep-freezes. So Prim left her mother to it and went outside to inspect the damage the Humber had done to the daffodils. Kneeling on the grass verge, she imagined herself eight years old again, trowel in hand, digging up the little clay effigies that Celestina had made specially for Archie to bury around the grounds, so that Prim could play the great archaeologist. It was the year Howard Carter had found King Tut – 1922. Two years before catastrophe came into her life in the form of her parents' divorce. She tried to imagine Archie beside her now, not as she had seen him last – a bald, stocky man with the weary look of a prizefighter on the downside of his career – but *then*. Young and vigorous. Wearing his flannel Oxford bags and cricket jumper, smelling of Bay Rum cologne and linseed oil. Telling her stories of how he and Uncle Nim had played the amateur archaeologists in the years before the Great War, brown-kneed in their cavernous shorts in some dusty Mesopotamian defile while they dug for the lost treasure of Gilgamesh and came home with nothing to show for it but blisters. A young father with dreams.

Lady Grace Nevendon – Granny G to the family – had long ago told Prim how, as a child, Nimrod had dreamed of opening a grand theatre in the West End, while Archie was going to run the Middle Eastern galleries of the British Museum. Neither ambition had been fulfilled. Like so many of their generation, the Great War had got in the way. Nim had died of gangrene in a Jerusalem hospital, courtesy of a fragment from a Turkish hand-grenade, while Archie had come home consumed with guilt for having failed to protect his little brother. Maybe that had been what had destroyed his marriage to Celestina – even as a child, Prim had suspected that. After a few years of itinerant prospecting in Africa and the East, Archie had ended up behind a desk at the Anglo-Levantine Oil Company in Cairo. What was the point of dreams, wondered Prim as she nipped off the daffs that had succumbed to the Humber's tyres, when even the brightest ones can be crushed by someone else's careless parking?

Larchford Farm lay a short way down the lane from Bevern Lodge. The farmer, John Hanslope, was barely fifty, but looked more like eighty. Gaunt and grey-faced, he wheezed almost as much as the ancient steam tractor he employed on his land. He had been gassed in the Great War. Now his son ran the business. Knowing to his cost where jingoism could lead, Mr Hanslope Senior had had his fill of it, which was probably why he was one of the few people in the Forest with any time for the members of the Bevern Fraternity. Before the divorce, he'd been a firm friend of Archie's. By the time Prim turned five, she could count every horse in the Larchford stables as a close friend, bursting into tears when Celestina told her she couldn't keep them in her bedroom. Now, when she wasn't in London, she would often ride out in the Forest on Mr Hanslope's spirited chestnut hunter, to clear her mind and put things in perspective. An hour after the two detectives had left, she was saddling up.

Riding alone along the skyline, with the heather readying to bloom on the slopes that rolled away towards the South Downs, she had already half-decided to go to Egypt. After all, what *was* there for her in either London or Bevern?

A relationship with a much older theatre director was coming to its natural end, with all the emotional jolting and teeth-jarring of a minor motorcar accident, leaving her with a choice: either roll on until the wheels fell off, or head straight for the nearest tree and be done with it.

Harold Armitage, twenty years her senior, had only ever been a fling, but a fling that had got a little complicated. It was like a Béarnaise sauce: great when it worked, only occasionally worth the effort. It was the one affair she'd kept hidden from her mother, because Prim was almost certain she'd be accused of seeking a surrogate for her missing father's love. On occasions, Celestina could be uncomfortably direct.

Riding through the pines at King's Standing, she saw a troop of Territorials resting after a run. They called to her with good-natured juvenility until their sergeant told them to button their lips. She waved at them and went on her way, down a sandy track, giving a wide birth to the adders coiled sleeping on the warming earth in the spring sunshine.

If the newspapers – and Mr Hanslope – were right, there could soon be another European war. She'd seen too many women of Celestina's generation condemned to a widow's life and never remarrying. Then there were the women who'd never even had the chance, the ones who held a dead lover's letters to their heart every night as the empty years ticked by. If the slaughter was going to repeat itself, there was no question of getting serious about someone when the last communication you received might be an official telegram that read: *Madam, it is my painful duty to inform you that a report has this day been received from the War Office…*

And if there was to be a war, wouldn't the theatres shut down? This time, or so the experts said, it would be a war unlike any other, a war of bombs dropped on civilians, of whole cities reduced to rubble. Her fledgling career would be amongst the first casualties.

Then there was the promise of Egypt itself – a pull, if any-thing was. Its history was as familiar to her as England's, thanks to Archie's tales of his adventures with Uncle Nim. Of its recent history she knew only what she had read in the newspapers and heard on the radio: that it had gained its independence in 1922, but that it still maintained strong ties with Britain, even permit-ting her troops to remain there to protect the vital Suez Canal. She'd read that the new young king, Farouk, was something of a playboy. That there was a nationalist movement that wanted all remains of Britain's involvement removed. Beyond that, little enough – except that Cairo was home to the Nimrod Theatre. She'd been dying to see it from the moment her father had first mentioned it in his letters.

Besides, it was her duty to help in the search for Archie. Her memories of him had eased the pain of his absence. She had clung to them jealously, using them as a shield whenever her school friends had unthinkingly paraded the virtues of their own all-too-corporeal fathers, whose motorcars, lined up on the school's drive, had marked out the span of each term like bookends. Archie was her father. She loved him. And now he might be in trouble. What sort of daughter would turn her back at the very moment he had most need of her? The very thought of it made Prim's cheeks burn.

If there was any doubt, Mr Hanslope's chestnut mare put paid to it. Somehow, or so it seemed, she had read her rider's thoughts. Because, without really being conscious of having done anything with her legs or the reins, Prim now realized that they were trotting back towards Larchford Farm. And her mind was made up.

———

'That's the most ludicrous thing I've ever heard in my life,' Celestina said later that evening when Prim delivered her bombshell.

The Fraternity had eaten together in the dining room, which they called 'the refectory' – because it sounded grand and they weren't – and were now occupied playing gin rummy in the drawing room. Out of a sense of duty, Prim had joined her mother in the library to hear a talk from the foreign secretary, Lord Halifax, about the responsibilities of Empire on the BBC National Programme.

'How do you propose to even get there?'

'The same way anyone gets to Cairo: by steamer.'

'Don't be ridiculous, Prim.'

'I'm being quite serious.'

Celestina switched off the radio set and perched on the arm of the sofa. 'Look, darling, you really do have to remember that I know all about your father and his little peccadilloes. Trust me, you'll be far too late to mop up whatever mess he's got himself into.'

'At least I have to try, don't I?'

Celestina ran a hand through her daughter's blonde hair. It was the sort of calming caress she hadn't used since Prim stopped falling off her tricycle. 'I know you were his little girl,' she said, 'and I hate to have to be brutal, but he's probably either floating in the Nile with some tart's bullet in his head or lying insensible in a hashish den. He might have fooled you and all those clever people at Anglo-Levantine Oil, but Archibald Nevendon never fooled me – at least not since I woke up one morning and smelled someone else's perfume on him.'

'I can go by aeroplane.'

'How will you do that? You don't have the money.'

'I've got a little bit put by from my last commission. I thought you might help with the rest.'

Celestina stared at her daughter as if she'd suggested they rob Martins Bank in Tunbridge Wells at gunpoint. 'Me? You want *me* to fund this insane idea of yours?'

'He's in trouble,' Prim pleaded. 'I know he is. I have to go.'

But Celestina was unmoved. 'Archie bloody Nevendon made his own bed a long time ago – several of them, as I know to my own humiliation only too well. He can lie in whichever one of them he chooses, as far as I'm concerned.'

'Surely, Mummy, you must care a *little* about what might have happened to him.'

'Must I?'

'You loved him, once upon a time.'

'Once upon a time I had a taste for pasta. Can't abide the stuff now. I have absolutely no interest in that wretched man, and no intention of funding your foolish jaunt to Egypt. Forget all about gadding off to Cairo, darling. If you're at a loss for something to do, why don't you let Angus take you down to a dance in Brighton? You know he likes you.'

'I'll find a way, Mummy. You can't stop me; I'm a grown woman of twenty-four.'

'Primrose, darling—'

Prim flinched. Her mother only ever called her by her full name when she was about to deliver a lecture.

'Far be it from me to insult your intelligence, but the nearest you've ever travelled to exotic parts is Brighton Pavilion. God alone knows what sort of trouble a young woman could get herself into in Egypt. What if you end up in a Bedouin harem or a white slave-market?'

'I don't think the Bedouin have harems, Mother. And Gertrude Bell managed all right, didn't she?'

Sensing defeat, Celestina changed tactics. 'Darling, I couldn't bear the thought of anything happening to you, so far away. I wouldn't be able to sleep at night for worrying.'

Prim, who had long ago learned to counter Celestina's appeals to her conscience with practicality, said, 'I'll speak to the Cairo police. I'll go to see Anglo-Levantine. Just being there, I can at least hope to hear some news. I'll talk to his friends, put advertisements in the newspapers...'

'I give up,' sighed Celestina, removing herself from the arm of the sofa and pouring herself a large measure of vermouth from the drinks cabinet, the Italian way – neat. 'Want one?' she asked.

Prim shook her head. 'I'll find the money somewhere else,' she said. 'And I'll be fine. Don't worry about me.'

Celestina downed half the glass in one take. 'Well, that's going to be easier said than done. But I suppose I can't stop you, can I?'

'Not really.'

'Do we bother with an argument, like the one we had when you went swanning off to Birmingham for that production of *Uncle Vanya*? I mean, Birmingham of all places, *really*, darling.'

'You know I don't like arguing, Mummy. But I've made up my mind.'

Celestina finished her vermouth in two more gulps and slapped the glass down on the cabinet. 'And *I* refuse to feel guilty for not indulging you in this insane plan.'

'I'd rather go with your blessing than without it.'

'We wouldn't have this problem if you were married, Primmy,' her mother said ruefully. 'There'd be someone to put his foot down.'

Prim looked at her mother from beneath a lowered brow. 'I'd like to see *someone* try.'

'I suppose your next stop will be to visit that dreadful woman in Knightsbridge.'

A daughterly smile from Prim – like the ones she used to give Celestina whenever her mother had seen through some childish evasion, or downright lie. 'If that's the only way to get to Cairo, I suppose I'll have to.'

The next morning Prim caught the slow train to London. She sat in a second-class compartment as if dressed for an interview, because Granny G – Archie's mother – maintained what she called 'standards'. The compartment was half-full, mostly bowler-hatted men heading to their anonymous drudgery in the City. Prim had enough space to place her bag beside her on the tartan seat, which was just fine because she didn't care to be overlooked.

As the pipe smoke hung in the air like the aftermath of an artillery duel, she took out her collection of Archie's letters and began to read through them. She knew the contents as well as an actor knows their lines. They were precious to her: all she had left of him to cling to.

The early ones, sent when she was a schoolgirl, were chatty – or as chatty as Archie's formal, businesslike demeanour could manage. The later ones bore the stiff, uncertain taciturnity of a man addressing a young woman he no longer really knew. Typed, not handwritten – he'd always had a jumpy, inconsistent scrawl – they seemed to her now like letters sent from another century.

Once she'd read them all again, she returned them to her bag. Then, taking out her fountain pen and a notepad, Prim wrote a brief letter to Harold Armitage:

Dear Harold,

Sorry to break it to you like this, but I'm sure you knew it was coming one way or the other. I think it's time to drop the curtain. A short run. We gave it our best. We had some good houses, and I'm sure you've had worse reviews. Sorry, but my heart's not in it.

Yours,

Prim

She folded the note into the envelope she'd brought for the purpose and settled back into her seat. Outside the carriage window, the soot-stained brickwork of Victoria hove into view.

Lady Grace Nevendon maintained a genteel but dwindling salon in an echoey apartment off Lennox Gardens, to the south of London's Brompton Road. Stuffed with outsized furniture salvaged from an impractical family pile somewhere in Gloucestershire, it had the feel of an over-filled antiques shop. Granny G was an elfin woman in her late seventies. Habitually dressed in a flowing silk kaftan and turban, she was the focus for a local coterie of third-tier female aristos too low down the social scale to find a welcome in Belgravia. They met twice a week, rain or shine, to drink Singapore Slings for lunch and lament the present travails of the world, drawn to Grace Nevendon as if she were the medium at an Edwardian séance.

'I know exactly why you've come, darling,' she said as Prim kissed her on the cheek and caught the dry scent of faded lavender, making her think of old flowers left too long in a church bereft of a congregation. 'I have a friend at the Foreign Office who telephoned me a few days ago.'

'Oh,' Prim replied as she hung up her coat. 'But you didn't think to call me?'

'You know how it is. Celestina might have answered. I do so hate unpleasantness on the line. Can't abide it.'

'Aren't you worried about him?'

'Of course I am, darling. But what can one do from Knightsbridge? I've spoken to a charming Major-General Russell in Cairo – he runs the police there. Took two days before the operators could make a decent connection, but he was as helpful as anything.'

'And did he have any news?' Prim asked as Granny G led her into the drawing room.

'Not really. My bet is that Archie's gone off on one of his little jaunts into the desert, digging up whatever it was he and darling Nim used to get so excited about when they were young.' And as if to prove her point, she gestured at the collection of framed photographs she kept on a mahogany drum-table in the window bay. Prim knew each one by heart: Nim and Archie as children, pretending to be archaeologists as they dug in a flowerbed with a trowel too large for their infant hands; Nim and Archie in their army uniforms, standing by the Jaffa Gate in Jerusalem; Nim and Archie reclining in wicker chairs on the terrace at Shepheard's in Cairo; Nim and Archie in sola topees and shorts, leaning into each other and grinning like loons against a background of ancient mud-brick walls. Her boys, forever frozen in the past. Their images had stood on this table for as long as Prim had been coming here, a huddle of tombstones in the graveyard of Grace Nevendon's memories.

'We had two police officers come to Bevern Lodge yesterday,' Prim said. 'Mummy thinks they were either Special Branch or from the government. They suggested Daddy might have taken what he knows about the oil fields out there and handed the information over to the Italians or the Germans.'

'That's ridiculous.'

'Exactly what we said.'

'Archie does have a venal side to him – I'm allowed to say that; I'm his mother. But he wouldn't sell secrets to countries that could become our enemies. He risked his life against the Germans in the last war.' A pause. 'His brother *gave* his.' She shook her little head. 'It's out of the question.'

Sherry schooner in hand, Prim went over to the collection of photographs. She picked up the one of her father and Uncle Nim standing amidst some ruins. There was no way of telling where the shot had been taken. It could have been Palestine, Iraq – Mesopotamia as it had been then – or Egypt. A handwritten note took up the place where a signature would have been, had it been a painting rather than a photograph: *TURQUOISE, 1913*. The year before she was born, Prim noted. While Celestina had been carrying her, Archie and Nim had been abroad on another madcap expedition to dig for treasures both men knew they would never find.

'I've told Mummy that I'm going to find a way to get out to Cairo to search for him,' she said, turning towards her grandmother. 'When I asked for her help, she refused point-blank.'

Grace Nevendon nodded in sympathy. 'Yes, well, I'm afraid that doesn't surprise me in the least. I know Archie was less than a gentleman in that marriage. I'd have thought Celestina might have got over it by now; I suppose that's down to the Latin temperament she inherited from her father.'

'So I've come to you instead.'

Granny G's moist eyes widened. 'You're asking for *my* assistance in getting to Cairo?'

'You're the only one who can help me.'

'Do you really think that's a good idea, darling?'

'Why not?'

'First, it's a long way. Second – it's Cairo.'

'Granny, it's a cosmopolitan city. Plenty of people go there. I've read about it in magazines.'

Grace looked doubtful. 'I know you theatre people like to think of yourself as frightfully modern, but *Egypt*? Come on.'

'I'm not a child, Granny. I'm not a naïve little girl. I can take care of myself. I've survived so far amongst a lot of hot-blooded actors and directors. It takes a fair bit to shock me, you know. Besides, if not me, then who else is going to look for him? You'd go, wouldn't you – if you could; if you thought he needed help?'

Grace Nevendon reached out and took the photo from Prim's hand. She looked at it for a moment, a thin smile on her face. Whether it was from the memories or the regrets, Prim couldn't tell. 'Yes, if I were younger, I suppose I would,' she agreed. She set the photo back in its place carefully, as though it were too delicate to survive much handling. 'If I were to help you – and I emphasize *if* – how do you plan to get there?'

Prim tried not to grin. 'Well, time is of the essence. The Imperial Airways flying boat service from Southampton to Africa stops at Alexandria. They lay on a train from there. I could be in Cairo within a day and a half of leaving England.'

Granny G allowed herself a sharp laugh of admiration. 'Good heavens, darling. What a modern world we live in.'

'But will you help me?'

'Your mother isn't going to forgive me for this, you do realize that?'

'And I wouldn't be able to forgive myself for abandoning Daddy in what might be his hour of need. At the very least I can represent the family with the authorities. If someone's there to keep up the pressure, they might work a little harder.'

'You're a sweet girl, Prim,' Grace said, as if she'd only just reached that conclusion. 'I'm sure Archie would be proud. But have you considered the possibility that he might have got himself into some sort of deep water? He's always been a very forthright sort of boy. Some people find him rather rich meat. He makes enemies easily.'

'He's still my father, Granny.'

Granny G refilled their glasses from the cut-crystal decanter. 'Chin-chin,' she said.

'Chin-chin, Granny,' Prim replied, desperate for an answer, but trying hard to hide it.

'What happens if you don't like what you find? Have you thought of that?'

'Honestly, I've never thought of Daddy as a saint. But if he's in trouble—'

Grace Nevendon set down her glass and took her grand-daughter's hands in hers. To Prim's surprise – followed swiftly by a sense of guilt that made her blush – they felt like cold, reptilian claws. It was like something from a fairy tale made to scare children, the clutch of an old crone warning her not to go deeper into the forest. She shook off the notion and gave Grace her best smile. 'I'll be fine,' she promised.

'Well then, I suppose I ought to fetch my cheque book.'

At the door, as she was leaving, Prim said, 'Oh, I almost forgot. I'd like you to look after these.' She reached into her bag and withdrew the wad of Archie's letters. Holding them out for Granny G to take, she added, 'Will you take care of them for me? I know it's silly, but I had the daftest notion that Celestina might have one of her angry episodes and burn them while I'm away. And they're really all I have left of him – apart from the memories.'

Moussa Bannoudi was about to cross Cairo's rue Bostane, near the Yugoslav Consulate, when the car pulled up a few paces ahead. He barely gave it a glance. He didn't recognize it, or the three men wearing Western clothes who lounged so casually in their seats. Nothing to do with him. They'd stopped for someone else. He kept walking.

When the three men stepped out to block his path, he still had no cause for concern. Indeed they waved at him, smiling, as if they knew him. He heard a cheerful 'As-salamu alaykum'. He smiled back and gave the expected reply, purely out of courtesy: 'Wa alaykumu s-salam'.

The punch to the solar plexus, discreet yet devastatingly professional, took the young manager of the Nimrod Theatre Company completely by surprise. He doubled up, unable even to grunt because suddenly there was no air in his lungs and his body seemed so filled with molten agony that it spilled into his eyeballs. All it took then was a shove. To anyone watching, he'd gone into the back seat of the car of his own free will. An ordinary street scene in Cairo: a man joins his friends for a pleasant bit of catching up. *Hi there, great to see you again. Where are we going?*

By the time the pain and nausea had subsided enough to allow Moussa the capacity for something approaching lucid thought, they were already weaving through the traffic at a positively dangerous speed.

Who were these men? Why had they used him so unjustly? He had no enemies that he knew of. Were they plainclothes policemen? Had they picked him up in a trawl for members of the Muslim Brotherhood or Young Egypt? He belonged to neither faction. If it was a random kidnap they had wasted their time; now that the Nimrod Theatre was dark, he was almost broke. Unable to answer his own questions, Moussa Bannoudi had no choice but to ask his assailants.

'Why have you done this to me? How have I offended?'

Receiving no reply, he crouched on the back seat and simply groaned, until a vicious cuff informed him that even this was offensive to their ears.

Until the shooting, Moussa's exposure to violence had been confined to playground fights. At university he had studied liberal arts with the intention of becoming a lawyer. But a visit to the theatre at the age of eighteen – a performance of Ahmed Shawqi's *The Death of Cleopatra* – had captivated him. He'd completed his studies because his family would have disowned him if he hadn't. But as soon as the ink was dry on his diploma he'd begged Nevendon Pasha – a friend of his father's – to give him a job: assistant stage manager. He'd taken to it as if the theatre was in his blood. Within two months Moussa had been appointed head of just about everything, but on a salary that even a Cairo water-seller would have turned his nose up at.

'Sorry, Moussa, old boy,' he could hear Nevendon Pasha telling him, though the voice was somewhat distorted by the throbbing of his heart and the whistling in his ears from where they'd cuffed him, 'things are a bit tight at present. Belly dancers and cabaret are all they want these days. Well, let them have them. That's not what we do at the Nimrod, is it? We keep the torch burning for the art. Let the flame die, we might as well all pack up and go home. But dear old Nim can't go home. He never got the chance. So it's up to us to do what we can to keep his flame alive.' Which was the boss's convoluted English way of saying a rise was out of the question.

Moussa, like the rest of the company, knew of the great Nimrod only in the way that Egyptians knew of Rameses: as a mighty force of ancient history, whose immortal spirit gave life and reason to each new day. Like the cartouche on the wall of a tomb, his name made up half of the brightly painted legend in English and Arabic over the theatre's entrance, arching above the neon outline of a winged bull. His true image hung in the Nimrod's lobby, his memory the eternal flame of their inspiration. And Nevendon Pasha – he wasn't a real pasha, but everyone in the company called him that, out of respect – was Nimrod's high priest, descending from his temple at Anglo-Levantine Oil twice a week to keep the dream alive and distribute beneficence to the faithful; in Moussa's case, at a meagre five Egyptian pounds per month.

But right now, for all his devotion, Moussa Bannoudi was coming to the rapid conclusion that five pounds a month wasn't anywhere near enough to compensate for finding himself centre-stage in a scene like this.

When they untied the rags from his eyes sometime later, Moussa knew he had guessed correctly. The time he had spent trussed up on the back seat of the car, plus the blind, stumbling slalom on foot with its abrupt changes in direction every few paces, arms pinned behind his back, all hinted at it. And now, as he drew in his surroundings by the dim light cast by an oil lamp hanging from the ceiling, he had the proof. They'd taken him into the Bulaq slums.

If he was wrong and this was a stage set – which he devoutly wished it might turn out to be – they'd got it down pat. In one corner stood an old lathe, all chipped green paint and oil stains. Against the walls, racks of miscellaneous ironwork that he couldn't identify, being an unmechanical sort of fellow. Shelves containing grinders, drills, hammers, lengths of pipe. A dirt floor beneath the stool he sat on. Everything filthy from use and smelling of motor grease. Even the lighting was spot on, a sick brownish-yellow. Threatening.

What was he meant to do? The men standing around him clearly expected something from him. Otherwise, why was he sitting on a stool in a Bulaq tool shop, his hands tied behind his back – they'd done that in the car – and the fear sour in the back of his throat? But how could he deliver his lines when they hadn't given him a script?

'Where is the Englishman, Never-don?'

Spoken in Arabic, they were the first words the men had uttered since they'd snatched him. They seemed to come from behind him, but if they were meant as a prompt, they were useless: he didn't know the play, let alone the part.

'I've no idea,' Moussa Bannoudi protested. 'No one's seen him since before... since before...' A terrible possibility occurred to him. Were these the gunmen who had attacked the theatre? 'I can't tell you anything,' he protested. 'And if this is about what happened at the Nim, I didn't see any faces – I promise you.'

Having thus improvised his lines in the best tradition of the thespian caught on the hop, Moussa waited for the man who had spoken to pick up his cue. *Thank you, you may go now. Sorry to have detained you.* But the man was still on the book – as actors like to say of a colleague who hasn't learned the script. 'You work for Never-don. You know where he is. Tell us, now.'

Moussa was about to protest at the inaccuracy of this assumption when the little workshop turned a brilliant orange, as though someone had thrown open an easterly window at sunrise. He was on the ground and his mouth was full of oily dirt even before the pain came crashing into his skull, making his eyes roll.

The man on his left – the one who had punched him hard on the side of his face – stooped over him. As if he had no mass to speak of, Moussa felt himself being lifted. The next minute he was back on the stool, swaying and trying hard not to be sick, ready to start pleading.

But the man who had asked the question seemed in no hurry to continue. Instead, he went to one of the shelves and returned with a chisel and mallet. Without speaking, he laid the razor-sharp edge of the chisel against the stool seat between Moussa's knees. He gave the chisel three taps with the mallet – nothing too hard, nothing showy. Just making the point.

Moussa watched as a skin-thin layer of wood curled up ahead of the chisel, almost transparent, as fine and delicate as parchment. Then the man who had hit him tore open the lower left leg of Moussa's trousers, exposing the kneecap. Moussa stared at the olive sheen of his own skin. He tried to swallow, but all the saliva in his mouth had burned off long ago.

'Now, Brother,' said the man as he laid the cold blade of the chisel gently against Moussa's kneecap, his face so close that Moussa could see that any hint of humanity had long since been drilled out of those dark-brown pupils, 'tell us – where is Never-don?'

Three

'Careful as you go, sir. Deck's a mite slippery and we don't want to start the journey with a dunking, do we?'

The uniformed Imperial Airways crew member stretched out a hand to assist the last passenger down into the motor launch, assuming him to be as lubberly as the rest. It was not yet five o'clock and an insipid sunrise was struggling to clear the grey waters of the Solent.

Harry Taverner, who had grown up on the River Dart and could sail close-hauled to the wind before he was ten years old, smiled his thanks, but did not take the offered hand. It was good, he thought, to have the smell of tar, marine paint and the sea in his nostrils once again. He'd forgotten how much he missed it. The motor caught with manic coughing, and the exhaust blew a belch of oily smoke across the well deck. Making his way between the stacked luggage, Harry paused, framed in the open door to the little saloon, where the other passengers sat on polished mahogany benches, eyes puffy from the early start, customers on a Cook's tour to somewhere they'd rather not be.

He had no idea what she looked like. At Broadway Buildings no one had been able to find a photograph of her. The only thing they'd come up with was a picture of her paternal grandmother, Lady Grace Nevendon, who'd been in the Service during the Great War. Maybe there will be a resemblance, they'd told him.

Not that Harry felt at his most observant this morning. A quick douse of the face in lukewarm water from the sink at the Southampton police station and a hasty brushing of his teeth had done little to refresh him. The night journey by road from London had been a torture, the springs and upholstery of the Hillman's rear seat designed to keep real sleep tantalizingly out of reach. His suit was crumpled and his joints ached abominably. He envied the passengers he was about to meet. They had travelled down on Imperial's special train from London the day before, spending a pleasant night in a hotel getting to know one another.

He had studied her father's meagre file in the car, mostly collated from War Office records and clippings from the *Oil & Gas Journal*. Someone in the office had thoughtfully included the most recently known image of Archie Nevendon: a grainy news photo from the *Palestine Post*, taken at the official opening of the Haifa terminal of the pipeline from Iraq. Even in the clear presence of fierce sunlight – note the sharp contrasts and shadows – he was wearing a suit. A big man. Imposing. One of a group: the clever bringers of future comforts, so long as the dividend was worth the investment. To Harry's mind, Archie Nevendon had looked like a thug.

But what would *she* look like, this daughter of innovation and industry, this child of tomorrow's men? Harry, who was supposedly on leave from a posting in Vienna and had seen there at first hand how some people pictured the future, had a pretty good idea: coldly efficient, streamlined, with an unwavering contempt for those who couldn't keep up.

He had been home from Austria barely two days when the telephone call had summoned him back to London for an appointment with Major Whitwell, head of the Middle East section. 'I understand it's asking a lot, middle of your leave and all that, but all we've got in Cairo at present is the head of station and a secretary. We need someone to fill the gap. Sorry, old boy, but that someone is you. We'll make it up to you – promise.'

Harry knew the score. For any young officer there was a probation period at the Service during which one had to play the lower-form boy, take the patronizing cold shoulders and the demeaning jobs, do the *yes-sir-no-sir* shuffle. Make any kind of fuss and he'd be on his way to a posting as assistant liaison officer (permanent) in Khartoum before he'd even begun to fight his corner.

'Don't go there thinking this is just a nursemaid job,' Whitwell had told him in that cavalry-regiment drawl of his. 'We need to find out if Miss Nevendon has been entirely honest with us about her missing father. I can't imagine she's decided to go to Cairo merely for the sunshine and sightseeing. She has what we might call "form", you see.'

'I can't think of a better posting, sir. Honestly.'

In other words, I'll take the shit and smile.

Harry looked around the little cabin at the passengers wrapped up against the early-morning chill. He counted fifteen of them, but only four women. Three of those were well beyond the age he'd been given. The fourth looked nothing like the coldly calculating daughter of a missing oil executive with pro-German tendencies that he'd imagined. Instead he saw an attractive woman about his own age, her fair hair tucked beneath a silk scarf. She had her hands folded in her lap. 'Demure' wasn't the right word. *Thoughtful* seemed a better choice. There was a brightness in her eyes that made him wonder if she'd chosen the subdued beige woollen day-suit, with its wide lapels, as a means of constraining an inner predilection for mutiny. Witness the way the jacket's single button was still done up at the midriff, even though her back was straight and her knees at a neat angle as if she were attending an interview for a job.

She was sitting at the end of a bench. To his satisfaction, there was space on the opposite row. As he took the spot, only a handful of the other passengers acknowledged his arrival. Primrose Nevendon was one of them, he was pleased to note. The rest maintained their English reserve, giving him at best a brief nod. That didn't trouble him; he was happy to be the outsider. More opportunity to concentrate on the woman. He felt the launch tremble as the engine powered up. With a gentle roll it pulled away from the jetty.

'Going all the way to Durban?' he enquired pleasantly.

She smiled. Now he could see she had a smooth, oval face with generous cheekbones, not at all angular. Her upper lip was longer than the bottom one, though not so plump. Large eyes, with flecks of gold in each grey iris. She looked as though she'd be good company. 'Only as far as Alexandria, I'm afraid,' she said. 'Then to Cairo. I understand there's a train.'

'That's a coincidence,' Harry observed, imagining himself connected to a lie-detector machine. 'That's my plan, too. Harry Taverner, British Council.'

'Primrose Nevendon,' she replied as they shook hands. 'Most people call me Prim.' That smile again: open and generous. 'And *please* don't make jokes about that. I've heard them all. I'm not prim at all. I drink and smoke and enjoy myself like normal people and I don't have a censorious nature.'

'I wouldn't dream of it,' he assured her. 'And I'm Harry.'

'The British Council – that sounds frightfully important. Are you a diplomat?'

'Nothing so grand, I'm afraid. We're cultural.'

'As opposed to uncouth, I suppose?'

He laughed at that. 'Bringing British arts and science to foreign parts, that sort of thing,' he explained. 'Waving the flag for our writers, artists and boffins. The Germans are doing it everywhere, when they're not building tanks. We thought we'd best do the same. We're thinking of opening an office in Cairo.'

'How wonderful.'

'That's not usually the reaction I get. Usually the eyes glaze over.'

'Not mine,' Prim protested. 'You see, I'm in the arts, too: stage design. My father supports a theatre in Cairo. That's why I'm going there.' It was the line she'd decided upon if anyone were to ask her what a single woman was doing, taking a flying boat to the Middle East.

'Oh, we're *all* for theatre,' Harry assured her. 'One of our leading industries. Even the Americans agree on that – though I was in Berlin recently and they're becoming very sniffy about some of the political stuff you can see on the London stage. They don't really do satire.'

She softened the angular poise a little. 'Who are your favourite playwrights? Mine are Patrick Hamilton for the grit, Noël Coward for the laughs.'

'To be honest with you, I'm really a behind-the-scenes man,' Harry said regretfully, as if it were a failing on his part. 'Sorting out offices and drawing up contracts. Stuff like that. But I'm with you all the way on Coward.'

'Did you catch his *Tonight at 8.30* at the Phoenix?'

'I was in Austria, I'm afraid,' Harry replied, as though confessing to a social misdemeanour.

'Germany *and* Austria. I say, you do get around. Is Berlin as awful as they say it is?'

Harry grinned again. 'It's great if you like a lot of marching up and down and shouting. They're very keen on that.'

The launch picked up speed, pushing into a slight swell. The prosperous-looking middle-aged couple next to Prim got up and went towards the bow for a better view.

'Well, at least we'll have something to talk about on the journey,' Prim whispered conspiratorially. 'They're mostly businessmen and plantation people on their way back to Africa. To be honest, I feared it was going to be a bit tiresome. You're lucky you missed dinner at the hotel last night – a lot of talk about international exchange rates and crop yields in Natal.'

'Thanks for the warning,' Harry said. 'I can never get my fill of crop yields in Natal.'

Prim turned to look out over the water. A hundred yards away lay the flying boat, silver-grey and sleek. The fluted rake of the hull where it met the water gave the machine an air of swiftness, even at rest. Forward from the high-set wing thrust four engine nacelles, each with a three-bladed propellor. At each wingtip, a float on struts supported her great span. At the bow, the cockpit windows curved smoothly down to a rounded nose, and Prim could imagine a giant mythical seabird at peace after a long flight across a vast ocean. Beneath the cockpit was her name, written large enough to read even from the approaching launch: *CELAENO*. And a little further along: *Imperial Airways, London*.

'A Greek goddess,' Prim heard one of the male passengers explain to his wife. 'One of the Pleiades, a wife of Poseidon.'

'Let's be grateful she's not called *Icarus*, dear,' the woman replied.

Prim turned back towards Harry Taverner. 'This is the first time I will have been aloft in an aeroplane since my father took me up at Shoreham. It was an Avro, about the size of that thing's wing-float. I was nine and frightened stiff.'

'They're very reliable these days,' Harry assured her. 'And these Empire Class are the very latest. They say it's better than riding in a Pullman railway carriage.'

The motor throttled back. The helmsman brought the launch deftly to a stop beside an open door in the flying boat's fuselage, close to the waterline. White-jacketed stewards assisted them over the doorsill and into the machine's belly. A notice on a bulkhead told them they were in the smoking lounge, a pleasant cabin with round windows, green trim on the walls and cream leather upholstery on the spacious seats. Looking to her right, Prim could see into a narrow galley of gleaming stainless steel, and beyond that to the after-cabins, all done out in the same trim. A steward was showing passengers to their seats. Another stood by with a silver tray on which was set an open bottle of champagne and a collection of flutes. For an instant, Prim felt a sense of shame at the luxury Grace Nevendon's largesse had bought her. But what alternative had there been? A steamer would have taken a fortnight.

'If it's not being too forward, shall we sit together?' Harry suggested. 'If you'd rather be alone, I quite understand. Just say the word.'

He wasn't by nature indecisive, far from it. But he needed Primrose Nevendon to think of him as merely pleasant company, nothing more. Someone she'd bumped into on an aeroplane and would most likely never see again. Frightening her off at the first hurdle wasn't part of the plan.

'No, that would be lovely,' she said, smiling. 'I can teach you all about British playwrights.'

They drank champagne and made small talk while the luggage was loaded. Then the door closed and the tender pulled away. Through the window Prim watched it go, its shape materializing from the shadow cast on the water by the expanse of wing. One after the other the four great engines roared into life, momentarily blocking her view of the water with swirling exhaust smoke. The *Celaeno* trembled like a racehorse in the starting gate. Then she began to move majestically out into the wide Solent. The sun had come up and was glinting on the surface of the water as they gathered pace. A sheet of spray plumed to the level of the window, glistening cream white and streaking the glass as if they were plunging through a waterfall. Now the noise of the engines was deafening. Prim wondered how on earth she and the attractive young man from the British Council sitting next to her were going to hear a word each other said between here and Egypt. It was like being in a speedboat, a sensation so exhilarating that Prim had to fight the sudden urge to grab his hand.

And then they were airborne. *Celaeno*'s shadow detached itself and fell away, shrinking, following them at an ever-growing distance until it was barely the width of Prim's wrist when she held her hand against the glass. The sound of the motors decreased a little. The machine swung abruptly to the left, tilting sharply so that Prim could see straight down to the tiny fields of the Isle of Wight. For a moment she found the sensation alarming. Then her stomach settled itself and she began to relax. She knew the schedule; in her enthusiasm she'd studied the timetable on the Imperial Airways train from Waterloo: five hours to Marseilles before a stop to refuel; then three hours to Rome; another stop

47

for fuel; three hours to Brindisi; refuel again; and then a further three hours to Athens and the promise of a few hours' proper rest in a hotel. Then – at daybreak tomorrow – the final five hours to Alexandria. After that, the other passengers would remain aboard, arriving in Durban almost three-and-a-half days after Prim herself would be safely in Cairo.

Glancing at the man beside her, she wondered quite how much of a coincidence his presence was. He hadn't been on the train from Waterloo. She hadn't seen him in the hotel last night. He'd just appeared out of nowhere. She thought about the two policemen who'd visited Bevern Lodge – the men Celestina was convinced were from Special Branch. Was he something to do with them? Could they have had her followed? Was the charming Mr Harry Taverner really who he said he was? You're getting suspicious in your old age, Prim told herself. He's merely an ordinary man, from the British Council; a pleasant companion to have for a long trip aboard a flying boat.

Suddenly, with a lurch, they were in cloud. Looking out of the window, she saw in her imagination her father's face. It was the Archie she remembered from her childhood. She tried to hold on to the image, but the turbulence made her stomach jitter. Or perhaps it wasn't the ride at all, but the currents of fear, hope and excitement all meeting deep inside her, swirling and cascading in an unsettling froth of emotion. There was the fear that something terrible had befallen him; the hope that, with her help, he might be saved; and the excitement that she herself could be instrumental in that salvation.

Had Archie felt the same unsettling confusion? she wondered, when, with Uncle Nim at his side, he had dug in the ancient earth in the hope that they would uncover some priceless artefact and make their reputations?

He never had, of course. But that didn't mean his daughter couldn't pull off the trick. Only this time the invaluable treasure lifted from oblivion would be Archie himself. Prim rather liked that idea. It had a pleasing symmetry.

She smiled at the prospect and peered out of the window, trying to hold on to his image. 'Hang on, I'm on my way,' she mouthed, raising her hand to the window and feeling the thrumming of the *Celaeno* through her fingertips.

But there was nothing to see out there – save for the milky-grey void and the raindrops streaming slantwise across the vibrating glass.

Four

It was early morning, the eastern sky a hazy orange, and Sir Miles Wedderburn Lampson was taking a pleasant ride through the lush grounds of the Gezira Sporting Club before the heat became oppressive. For the overworked colonial servant in need of relaxation, the club – set on a green island in the Nile – could hardly be bettered. It offered all the diversions of home: polo, golf, cricket, athletics, tennis… even a pack of hounds. On the pavilion veranda uniformed waiters in fezzes hovered attentively. Out on the pitches and greens, white-robed groundsmen knelt at their shears as if in prayer. Gardeners plucked and pruned as though they were expecting the imminent arrival of a band of fearsome lady judges from a county show. It was Hurlingham-on-Thames, only with guaranteed sunshine thrown in.

Lampson, an astute and seasoned diplomat in his late fifties, was British ambassador to the court of the newly crowned monarch, the eighteen-year-old King Farouk. Tall, broad-shouldered, jovial and balding, he was a familiar figure in Cairo's diplomatic community, towering above many of his colleagues. He had known Egypt as a colony and knew it now as an independent nation.

His companion on this morning's ride was another Englishman, for England still exerted some considerable power in the land, and the king, being young, required the guidance of experienced men. Major-General Thomas Russell was head of the Cairo police. Known throughout Egypt as Russell Pasha, he had tracked down drug smugglers in the Sinai, smashed prostitution gangs in the Bulaq slums and prosecuted countless cases of *thar* – blood-feud murders. He knew Cairo's underworld better than many of the Egyptian officers he commanded.

'I've really no appetite for scandal, Thomas. None whatsoever,' Lampson said as they rode together. 'Short of trying to sell hashish to Princess Fawzia at the Ras el-Tin Palace, I don't much care what that blighter Nevendon has gone and done. Just as long as it doesn't get into the newspapers.'

'We're not sure that he's gone and done anything, sir,' said Russell, whose taut features evidenced a ruthless efficiency. This morning he had forsaken his dark police uniform with silver epaulettes, fez and polished boots for a suit. But his posture in the saddle wouldn't have been out of place on Horse Guards Parade.

'Well, let's hope things stay that way,' the ambassador replied. 'I've enough on my plate without having to grovel to Farouk for some brouhaha Archie Nevendon has got himself entangled in.'

'If it was a scandal, Sir Miles, we would have caught a whisper of it by now. Someone somewhere would be trying to make money out of him. I'm quite sure of that.'

'What about a moonlight flit, an *affaire de cœur*?' suggested the ambassador.

'We considered that possibility naturally. Nevendon was apparently involved with the wife of a Lebanese businessman, but that all ended a year ago. We spoke to the ex-mistress – discreetly, of course.'

'And?'

'They remain friends.'

'What about the husband? There's a motive there, if you're looking for one.'

'Apparently both parties were content to live in what we might politely refer to as "unconventional liberty".'

'Sounds like our own dear Duke of Windsor,' Lampson said mischievously. 'And nothing since? No spurned mistress with homicidal inclinations? No vengeful chorus girl he's got in the family way?'

'From what we can tell, the only women to visit the Villa Narcisse arrived accompanied.'

'The villa *what?*'

'*Narcisse* – French for narcissus.'

'Sounds like a fancy whorehouse to me.'

'It's the villa that Anglo-Levantine give their Cairo director. We interviewed the housekeeper.'

'What about at work? Has he been chasing the secretaries? Run off with the petty cash?'

'Everything above board there, too, Sir Miles.'

The ambassador raised a hand from the reins to acknowledge someone he recognized. 'That shooting at the theatre he supports – any clues there?'

'Again, we haven't heard a squeak. Whoever the gunmen were, they were professionals. The clothes they left behind in the Ezbekia Gardens bore no identifying labels. Cheap local copies of European styles, from what we can tell. And by "local", I mean possibly Syrian or Lebanese. That leads us to think they may have come from outside Cairo. Perhaps even from beyond Egypt.'

'But you think Archie Nevendon was the target?'

Russell's mouth was so straight and narrow that it looked as if it had been drawn on his face with a ruler. Pursing his lips made it almost disappear. 'Even there I can't be sure. It may be mere coincidence that one of the victims bore a passing resemblance to our missing man.'

The ambassador flicked away a fly that had landed on his mount's neck. 'Jacqueline and I have had Nevendon round to the residence a few times, for bridge,' he said. 'A little rough around the edges for my liking, to be honest. Seemed taken with the idea of appeasing Herr Hitler. Very anti-war.'

'Probably because he lost his brother in the last one.'

'Is that so?' replied Lampson. 'Still, being anti-war isn't a crime, is it? If it were, we'd have to arrest the prime minister and the foreign secretary for starters.'

'The ex-wife's father was Italian,' Russell said.

Lampson looked down from his lofty vantage point, his bushy brows lifting slightly. 'As is my Jacqueline's father. What's your point, Thomas?'

'Oh, not mine, Sir Miles – London's. They're very twitchy about relationships with foreigners at the moment.' Catching the sudden lift of one of the ambassador's eyebrows, he added swiftly, 'Not yours, of course.'

'I gather you're not buying the notion of a defection?'

Russell shook his head. 'If Nevendon believed life would be better in Berlin or Rome, he could simply have bought himself a ticket on a steamer from Alexandria. No one was going to stop him. Besides, he might know a lot about our oil interests in the Middle East, but if the Germans wanted to make mischief with the Iraq–Haifa oil pipeline, all they have to do is pay the Palestinian Arabs to keep shooting holes in it and tapping off petroleum. They're doing that anyway.'

'Ah, Palestine,' said the ambassador wearily. 'I spoke to Sir Harold MacMichael, the high commissioner in Jerusalem, yesterday. Things are going from bad to worse there. The Palestinian Arabs are throwing bombs at us with increasing regularity; they're shooting Jews, and now the Jews are shooting back – when the Jews aren't shooting the Arabs, they're rioting because we've placed a limit on immigration; when the Arabs aren't murdering Jews, they're shooting each other in power struggles… More an unholy mess than a holy land, if you ask me.'

The two men rode on in silence for a while. Then Lampson went on, 'Mind you, if we're taking about anti-British sentiment, there's plenty of it right here in Egypt. Maybe that's behind Nevendon's disappearance.'

'You mean an abduction?'

'It's possible, isn't it?'

'We'd have heard something by now, Sir Miles.'

'Perhaps they've already killed him.'

'You don't assassinate someone for political motives and not leave the body in plain sight,' Russell said. 'Otherwise, what's the point?'

'I suppose not.'

'My own opinion, for what it's worth, is that Archibald Nevendon – for a reason I cannot yet determine – has made a deliberate effort to remove himself from public sight,' said Russell. 'We've checked the railway stations, the airport at Heliopolis, the docks at Alexandria and Port Said. I've sent officers further along the coast to Marsa Matruh and Sidi Barrani to ascertain if he departed from either. No one's had so much as a sniff of him. And to be honest with you, Sir Miles, I really don't have the resources to do much more.'

They were approaching the end of their ride. Ahead, grooms in white tunics waited to take their horses. Lampson said, 'My cloak-and-dagger man, Major Courtney, has appealed to London for help. The Secret Intelligence Service is sending a chap out as we speak.'

'Just the one?'

'It's all they can spare. Their eyes are firmly fixed upon Germany at present.'

'Well, in that case, let's hope they're not sending us the office tea-boy,' said Russell.

'And the daughter's coming out, too.'

'He's bringing his *family*?' queried Russell, his eyebrows arching.

'No, Thomas. I mean Nevendon's daughter.'

The groom stepped forwards to take the horses' reins. Russell prepared to dismount. 'Then let's hope she knows more about where her father's got to than we do,' he said as he swung out of the saddle. 'Otherwise, I'm afraid all we can do is wait for a body to turn up.'

Harry Taverner had been the saving of her. Without him, Prim reckoned, the flight would be torture: locked into a noisy metal tube with some of the most tedious people she had ever met. Three thousand feet over Paris she had visited the smoking lounge to get a better view from the larger windows, only to discover that the landowner was still mining his rich seam of fascinating information on Natal's crop yield to anyone who would listen. Approaching Corsica, the banker interrupted her view of the island by regaling everyone with his opinion of Chancellor Neville Chamberlain's economic policies in the light of German rearmament. At Rome, while they refuelled, the wife of a director of the Natal stock exchange had taken the opportunity of loudly expressing her approval of Mussolini's bombing of

Abyssinian villages: *Surely, my dear, you agree we need to show the lesser races who's in charge.* Over Corfu, with the sunlight glinting on the tranquil waters of the Ionian Sea, the owner of a chain of motorcar showrooms throughout the English Midlands had assured her that the Jews in Germany had brought their harsh treatment at the hands of Herr Hitler's supporters down upon themselves. It was like being trapped in the worst dinner party one could imagine.

Without Harry for a companion, Prim reckoned she'd have been pleading mitigating circumstances to the crime of murder, or searching for a parachute, long before the *Celaeno* reached Athens. As it was, he was a lifeline: a good-looking young man with wavy blond hair and a dimple on his chin. He had a quiet but easy sense of humour and he hadn't asked leading questions, which made her think that perhaps her earlier suspicions were unfounded. But what really set him apart, and made her warm to him, was that Harry Taverner appeared to be a man who knew when to shut up and leave her to look out of the window, or immerse herself in the book she'd brought along, *Gone with the Wind*. She hoped they'd keep in contact when they reached Cairo. It would be good to have at least one friend in an unfamiliar city.

And then, after their stopover in Athens, the American turned up.

'Say, it's real great to meet with you all. Mike Luzzatto! Real estate.'

They were standing on the quayside at Piraeus docks, waiting for the launch to sweep them away from the towering cranes and out to the *Celaeno*, when the taxi drew up and he climbed out. After long hours spent in the air, Prim's ears had only recently stopped ringing from the noise of the engines. When she'd woken, the hotel bedroom had had the silence of a grave about it, even though it was in the centre of Athens and the traffic flowing past had been unrelenting. Now Luzzatto's voice seemed unnaturally loud to her, though she couldn't be sure whether that was because her ears were still adjusting or whether he always spoke that way. The other passengers – apart from her and Harry – had by now formed into a clique. They responded to the greeting with all the warmth of golf-club stalwarts faced by an intruder on the eighteenth tee.

'And it's an equal pleasure to meet you too, Mr Luzzatto,' Prim said, matching his volume to make a point to the others. As she extended a hand for him to shake, she couldn't help admitting that Michael Luzzatto was going to make the remainder of the journey somewhat more interesting. Age about thirty, she guessed, muscular, tall and disgustingly handsome, with crinkly jet-black hair parted down the middle as if by a knife blade. A matinée idol in the flesh. Some idol, she thought. Some flesh.

Now that Prim had broken the ice, some of the other passengers had begun to take an interest in their new companion. 'Quite the explorer,' said the woman who'd earlier expressed her admiration for Italian excesses in Abyssinia. There was a flirtatiousness in her voice that Prim caught, but that her husband missed entirely.

'Beg your pardon, ma'am?'

The woman pointed to the single small suitcase the newcomer carried. It was covered in shipping-company labels. 'I can see you're a much-travelled man, Mr Luzzatto. But when you reach Durban, I fear you'll need a great deal more than you can fit in *there*.' She beamed invitingly at him. 'We have a *very* thriving social scene there. I can introduce you to all the right people.'

'That's real kind of you, and I thank you for it, said Luzzatto. 'But I'm going to Cairo, Egypt.'

'I didn't know there was any other Cairo,' replied the woman, clearly disappointed.

Luzzatto gifted her a brilliant white smile to admire. 'Why, yes, ma'am. Cairo, Illinois.'

'Well, Mrs Adendorp is right, then,' Prim said. 'You'd need more clothes there, too. I hear Illinois can sometimes get very chilly.'

Michael Luzzatto studied her for a moment, as though she'd spoken a language he couldn't recognize. 'I do believe you're making fun of me, Miss… Miss…'

'Primrose Nevendon,' she responded, suddenly feeling rather foolish. He might be eye-catching, but she could recall at least a dozen actors she'd met who fitted the mould. She'd found them mostly vapid or too egotistical to bear for more than five minutes. And forget romance. Either they collected women as less-blessed men collected cigarette cards, or they had no interest in the female sex at all. Even so, Prim found herself struggling not to stare.

'I think your husband is waiting for you to go aboard,' Luzzatto told her, glancing to where Harry Taverner was watching them from the launch.

'Oh, that's Harry,' she said, giving him a wave. 'He's just a friend. We met at Southampton.'

She took the boatman's offered hand and jumped down into the tender. As she took her seat, she felt a twinge of guilt. Too quick with the denial, my girl, she thought. Far too quick.

But when she replayed the scene in her mind, Prim couldn't recall even the slightest trace of jealousy in Harry Taverner's watchful gaze. Instead, he'd made her think of someone studying a blackboard in a lecture. As if he was taking notes for an exam he didn't want to fail.

Five

Prim woke before sunrise to the sound of the *adhan*, the haunting call to prayer echoing from the mosques around the Hotel National. It pulled her from a dream in which Archie had been guiding her through the exhibits at the British Museum, but whenever she had stopped to peer into a display case, the exhibits had crumbled into dust. Then, in one of the vast galleries, Archie too had disappeared, leaving her with an overpowering sadness that lingered when she opened her eyes in the unfamiliar darkness. Now she lay in the comfortable bed and let the rich, poetic a cappella of the chant wash over her. I've made it, she thought. I've crossed over from the familiar to the unknown. Whatever happens now, whatever I find – for good or ill – it will be utterly unlike the life I lived at Bevern Lodge. And that's worth a prayer of thanks in anyone's language.

She had chosen the National on the advice of the Imperial Airways staff at Alexandria. Less grand than the Semiramis or Shepheard's – which was fine by her, because she hadn't really come kitted out for cocktails and dancing – it was within walking distance of the Nimrod Theatre and the Anglo-Levantine office. It also charged a rate that she could justify to Granny G.

'No, no. Stay at Shepheard's,' Michael Luzzatto had pleaded when the train reached Cairo. 'That's where I'm staying. Best place in town, don't you agree, Harry, old man?'

That was indeed what he'd been told, Harry had confirmed. But as the British Council didn't run to such extravagance, and the embassy had a room set aside for him, he too declined.

'Then at least allow me to treat my new friends to a cocktail in the Long Bar before we all go our separate ways,' Luzzatto had insisted.

Taking him up on the offer, they had enjoyed the same small talk they'd made on the *Celaeno*, only without the deafening roar of aero-engines.

'If you ever need anything, just give me a call,' Harry had said when their shared taxi dropped Prim off at the National. The card he'd handed her was lying on the dressing table now. Maybe she would; maybe she wouldn't. There was only one man on her mind at present and, charming though he was, it wasn't Harry Taverner. It was her father.

Still tired from the journey, Prim closed her eyes again and dozed. When she came fully awake, daylight was spilling through the gap in the heavy mock-Louis XIV curtains. Going to the window, she drew them aside and looked out. It took a while for her eyes to adjust to the intense glare.

She recalled something her tutor at the London Theatre Studio had told her when she'd attended the set design course there last year. *Your task is to take the known and turn it into surprise. The audience must feel they've been transported somewhere fantastical, and yet at the same time comfortably familiar. It's a trick you must master.* Cairo, she could see, had mastered this in spades. Across the street, smart buildings that might have graced one of the better quarters in Paris filled her immediate view. Yet when she lowered her gaze she saw shop signs in Arabic as well as English, and men in voluminous robes jostling with others in business suits that wouldn't have looked out of place on Threadneedle Street. In London she'd been accustomed to men wearing bowler hats or workmen's caps. Here, they all seemed to be wearing fezzes, tarbooshes or embroidered skull-caps. Shiny black taxis steered their way around laden donkey carts. A tram went rumbling past, the passengers clinging to the running board. Directly beneath her balcony an Arab shoeshine boy squatted on the kerb, polishing the boots of a tall, imposing man in a flowing *galabeya,* a man whose face suggested to her – somewhat romantically – that he might just be a Nubian prince from the Thirteenth Dynasty.

And the brightness! It was as though every floodlight and follow-spot in a theatre had been switched on, solely for her. Then the scents of the street hit her: donkey dung, motorcar exhaust and overripe vegetables.

Turning back into the room, Prim went to the dressing table and read again the cable she'd received from her father's company, confirming that she could call upon them on her arrival. Slipping it into her handbag, she prepared herself to go down for break-fast. She was starving, and the last thing she wanted was to come over all light-headed in the meeting. She didn't know what sort of men they might be – she imagined the Texas oil barons she'd seen in the movies: all Stetsons and cheroots – but she didn't want them thinking that one night in Egypt had overwhelmed the sensitivities of an impressionable young Englishwoman from the Home Counties.

The Cairo offices of Anglo-Levantine Oil occupied an imposing four-storey block on the rue Khedive Ismail, complete with a uniformed flunkey who opened the brass-trimmed door to her, as if she were entering the Savoy for afternoon tea. Prim was shown into a panelled boardroom where two Egyptian men in their thirties sat behind a polished oval table that could have done service hosting the Admiralty Board. No Stetsons, no cheroots, she noted with a faint tinge of disappointment. Both men were smartly suited, with bright smiles beneath pencil moustaches. They rose as she entered, their manners impeccably London Season.

'My dear Miss Nevendon, how good of you to come,' said the taller, whose brown eyes gleamed with bonhomie. 'I'm Mr Gamil, and my colleague here is Mr el-Madani. We have the great honour of being Mr Nevendon's assistants. It is indeed a pleasure to meet his daughter. Would you care for tea?'

Prim smiled. *Somewhere fantastical, and yet at the same time comfortably familiar…* 'That would be wonderful. Thank you.'

A small silver hand-bell was wrung, and a male secretary was dispatched by a brisk command delivered in Arabic. The two men invited Prim to sit. They made small talk about her journey until the secretary returned with three glass cups of black tea, heavily sugared, with leaves of mint floating on the surface.

'I fear you have come a long way for little benefit, Miss Nevendon,' Gamil said as Prim sipped from her glass. 'We regret to inform you that the Cairo police have made little progress.' His smile was a wince of disappointment, as if a business deal had just fallen through.

'We don't want to give up hope – of course we don't,' said his colleague, his smooth face suddenly lined with a physician's bedside concern. 'But in the absence of any concrete news…'

'We feared at first that he might have been kidnapped,' said Gamil, offering Prim a cigarette, which she took gratefully, 'but we've received no ransom demand. It's been a while now, so I think we can rule out that possibility.'

'When did you last see my father?' Prim asked.

'We were last in his esteemed company on the penultimate Wednesday in March, the twenty-third, at the Ministry of the Interior,' Gamil told her with laborious formality. He peered at the rotary calendar on his desk, reaching out with an index finger to pin it to the spot, as if he feared it might attempt to confound his calculations. 'Today is the eighteenth of April. So, three weeks and five days ago. We had accompanied him to a meeting with a group of deputies there. Afterwards Mr el-Madani and I returned to the office.'

'Without him?'

'Indeed. Mr Nevendon told us he was taking the rest of the day off to visit the theatre he patronizes. I presume you know about that.'

'Yes, I do.'

'The following day Mr Nevendon did not appear at his usual time, nine a.m. We consulted his diary, in case he had an appointment elsewhere that we'd forgotten about. At eleven Mr el-Madani telephoned the Villa Narcisse.'

'Is that where he lived – before he disappeared?'

'It is the villa the company makes available for the pleasure of its Cairo director,' Gamil said. 'The housekeeper informed us that the boss had left at his usual time.'

El-Madani picked up smoothly, and Prim guessed they had told the story to the police more than once. 'His driver told us that Mr Nevendon had asked to be dropped off at the Ezbekia Gardens. It was a pleasant morning and he preferred to walk the rest of the way. He never arrived.'

'And my father didn't return to the villa?'

'I fear not, Miss Nevendon,' el-Madani said regretfully.

Gamil gave a discreet cough from behind a raised hand. 'I fear we must consider the possibility of some sort of breakdown. The boss had many responsibilities. Many pressures.'

'Are you suggesting my father has lost his mind?'

El-Madani wrung his hands together. Prim suspected she'd hit a nerve. 'Sometimes the signs are not always obvious,' he told her. 'Even the closest friend or family member may be ignorant of what a person is secretly going through within. I know this from personal experience – a cousin.'

'I'm sorry, Mr el-Madani, I didn't mean to be rude.'

El-Madani smiled solicitously. 'You're concerned, Miss Nevendon. We understand that. So are we. But we must explore all avenues, face all possibilities.'

Gamil nodded gravely. 'The boss has been absent for so long now that we must begin to consider the worst of outcomes, I'm afraid.'

'You can speak plainly, gentlemen. I'm not going to faint. You think my father might be dead.'

Gamil's bright smile dimmed a little. He drew on his cigarette and exhaled slowly. The drifting smoke made Prim think of a soul leaving a body. 'I fear we must take that possibility on board,' he agreed. 'Perhaps your father has fallen into the Nile by accident or – and forgive me for suggesting such a thing – he has taken his own life. To be blunt, it could be that his body is yet to be discovered.'

'I don't believe for a moment that my father would do that. He was never a man prone to melancholy.' Even as she said it, Prim was forced to accept that everything she thought she knew about her father had been formed in a mind of a child. 'It's not how I remember him at all.'

El-Madani rested his forearms on the table and leaned forward. Prim wasn't sure whether he was playing the compassionate psychiatrist or the counsel for the prosecution. 'Are you aware, Miss Nevendon, that there was a shooting at the theatre your father supports, shortly after his disappearance?'

'I've heard about that. The police in England informed me.'

'Then we must ask ourselves if that event was connected to Mr Nevendon's disappearance. Perhaps he is in hiding somewhere.'

'From what?' Prim asked innocently, though the same thought had occurred to her every day since that Humber motorcar had pulled into the drive at Bevern Lodge.

'Neither Mr el-Madani nor I can imagine,' Gamil assured her. 'The boss was a gentleman of unimpeachable probity. The Cairo police have investigated your father's private life and found nothing to alarm them – I'm relieved to say.'

'Where are you staying, Miss Nevendon?' asked el-Madani.

'At the National.'

He smiled the *nothing-is-impossible* smile of a Fortnum's counter clerk. 'Then we could perhaps be of help there, could we not, Mr Gamil?'

'I'm sure we can,' said the other.

'Really? In what way?' Prim enquired.

'We've had no instruction otherwise, and so as far as Mr el-Madani and I are concerned, the boss is still our director. I don't see why you shouldn't make use of the Villa Narcisse while you're in Cairo. You are his immediate kin, after all.'

'That's generous of you, Mr Gamil.'

'And if we were to announce in the newspapers that Mr Nevendon's daughter has arrived to assist the search, well, who knows – it might encourage him to come forward.'

'It might, if he has access to newspapers,' Prim replied, not wholly convinced.

'Indeed. But I can't think of anything else that might do the trick.'

'And you can make use of the motorcar, too,' chipped in el-Madani.

'A motorcar?'

'Don't worry – there's a driver,' el-Madani went on with an embarrassed smile. 'We wouldn't want to subject you to the ordeal of driving in Cairo, Miss Nevendon. It is not for the faint-hearted.'

'Will it be the driver who was the last person to see my father?'

'Yes,' said Gamil and then, catching the look on Prim's face, 'Please rest assured, he's an honest fellow. We have every reason to believe his account.' He rose from his chair, perhaps to remind her that oil men have many calls upon their time. 'Please contact us if you hear anything. We'll do likewise. Are you planning to stay in Cairo for long?'

'As long as I need to.'

El-Madani rose, too. 'May I make a suggestion, Miss Nevendon, purely in the spirit of friendship?'

'Of course. Feel free.'

'Please don't think of playing the private detective. It would not be wise.'

'I don't follow you.'

'Cairo may seem, to a European, a somewhat romantic place, Miss Nevendon. But there are some in this city whose scruples would make a Chicago mobster blush.'

'I'm a grown-up girl, Mr el-Madani. I deal with theatre directors all the time. Al Capones don't frighten me.'

'Of course not,' el-Madani said with his corporate smile. 'But you will find plenty of very persuasive fellows here only too eager to assist you, always at a very competitive price. The nicer they seem, the more crooked they are. They will fleece you, even as they insist there's no one more honest this side of the Second Cataract. And they're the good ones.'

'And the bad ones?'

The smile vanished and el-Madani became stony-faced. 'They'll leave you in an alleyway with your throat cut. Please take care, Miss Nevendon. We want your father back almost as much as I'm sure you do. But we don't want to lose *two* Nevendons, do we? That would not reflect well upon us at all.'

Prim waited in the lobby while Gamil telephoned the Villa Narcisse to warn the housekeeper and summon Archie's driver to pick her up. It was half an hour before a polished dark-green Citroën pulled up outside, forcing its way between the donkey carts and the milling pedestrians. It was the only vehicle Prim could see that didn't have a fine film of dust on it.

'Miss Archie, I am Tarek,' the driver said with a grin as he held the passenger door open for her. He was a wiry man in his fifties with a sunburnt runnelled face and fingertips yellowed from the Turkish cigarettes that Prim would later learn he smoked almost constantly. 'Is most great pleasure to drive for daughter of Mister Archie,' he assured her in a voice that seemed to come from somewhere down beneath the tarmac. He pointed to the sky before he closed the door for her. 'Tarek means "guiding star". I serve Mister Archie five years. No crash – never once. Very safe.'

'I'm relieved to hear that,' Prim replied, returning his smile.

'Mr Gamil says we go to the National to get your things. Then home. After that, wherever you want. Is okay?'

'That would be wonderful, Tarek. Perhaps later you could take me to the Nimrod Theatre. Do you know where that is?'

Tarek's dark face lit up. 'I take Mr Archie there many times. Very good theatre. One day I go inside, maybe see what all the fuss is about.'

Settling into the back seat, Prim said, 'That's my plan, too,' though it was spoken as much to herself as to Tarek. She noted the smart interior: the leather hand-strap on the door pillar, the polished chrome ashtrays, the spotless floor mats, the pale-grey chauffeur's cap that Tarek had just settled firmly on his head, like an admiral on the bridge of his flagship. Why would Archie run from a life like this? she wondered.

At the Hotel National, Tarek waited in the lobby while she packed her bag and paid her bill. He loaded her suitcase into the boot for her, and soon they were away from the main streets and pushing through narrow lanes where the sun seemed barely to penetrate. Here the houses looked as though they'd suffered from the effects of shellfire: crumbling plaster, balconies with no balustrades, wooden arabesque shutters hanging crookedly from window frames. In the shadows, Cairo's darker side was plain for Prim to see: the ribs of the horses and donkeys showing clearly beneath their underfed sides, the dark wheals on their backs where the lash wounds had healed; the mangy dogs scavenging around the fruit-sellers' stalls; the hungry eyes of little children as they brushed away the flies. There were more women here too, she noticed, dressed from head to toe in black. Recoiling from the raw poverty, she reminded herself that things were probably not much better in parts of Limehouse or Liverpool. She remembered the early conversations she'd had with some of her young friends in the theatre world – about how Joseph Stalin's Russia would soon make poverty and social injustice a distant memory.

She hadn't bought that for a moment. Both Celestina and Archie had always been vehemently anti-Bolshevik. She recalled how the only thing they ever agreed on was that Britain needed a strong, patriotic leader, someone who could bang heads together, put an end to the seemingly eternal squabbling of political parties. Someone who could get things *done*.

The Citroën slowed to a crawl. Prim wound the window down because of the heat. Looking out, she saw two little boys squatting in the gutter by the kerb, grubby waistcoats buttoned over their *galabeyas*. They were playing with a piece of wire. Prim smiled and waved at them. They stared at her as if she were a mirage and didn't wave back.

'Is better this way, believe me,' Tarek said, his eyes catching hers in the mirror as she turned back from the open window. 'Here they think anyone in a motorcar is King Farouk, so they move aside. On Queen Nazli Street everyone ride in automobile, so nobody moves.' He banged on the horn. It didn't appear to have much effect. 'We'll get there soon,' he assured her happily. 'If God wills it.'

'*Inshallah*,' Prim replied, using the term she'd already learned was de rigueur when making any expression of intent or hope.

In the mirror, Tarek grinned. 'Spoken like a true Egyptian, Miss Archie.'

'How well did you know my father, Tarek?'

'Very well,' he said proudly.

'Did he ever confide in you?'

'What is "confide", Miss Archie?'

'Talk… man-to-man.'

'Oh, without the doubt.'

'What did you talk about – man-to-man?'

In the mirror she could see Tarek's lips purse. 'Oh, many things: football... politics... The boss, he makes the jokes to me all the time.'

'Jokes?' Prim couldn't remember her father having a particularly vibrant sense of humour. 'What about?'

In the mirror, Tarek looked embarrassed.

'Don't be shy, Tarek. I work in the theatre; I've heard them all,' Prim replied, hoping she would catch at least a whisper of something her father might have kept hidden – a mistress perhaps.

'Jokes about your king and Mrs Wallis Simpson. Men's jokes, Miss Archie.'

'Oh, *that*. That was two years ago, Tarek. Nothing more recent?'

'Only men's talk, Miss Archie. Not talk for ladies.'

Prim returned to looking out of the window. 'You can call me Prim,' she said absent-mindedly. 'Everyone does.'

'Certainly, Miss Archie.'

'Do you have your own view on where my father might have gone?'

'I tell the police, I say to them: Mr Archie has gone to America, to tell President Roosevelt how to run Standard Oil.'

Prim laughed. 'I think he might have sent a postcard.'

They emerged from the narrow lane onto a boulevard lined with acacia trees and electric street lamps in iron pillars seemingly plucked from the Champs-Élysées.

'Not far now, Miss Archie.'

Just as Tarek had warned, the traffic here was heavy. Within a hundred yards they came to a near-halt behind a flatbed cart pulled by a horse. The four women in black robes sitting on the back paid them no attention. A truck was slowly overtaking the cart, bellowing from the effort, like a mortally wounded buffalo. Noxious black smoke belched from its exhaust. Prim put her hand over her nose in a futile bid to keep out the stench of burning oil. With the other, she began to wind the window up.

The growl of the motorbike barely registered above the noise from the accelerating truck. The first hint of its approach was a sudden shadow falling across the half-closed window glass. Then it drew alongside, blocking Prim's view. All she could see was the rider and the passenger, straddling the machine with their knees sticking out. They wore long brown cloth jackets and chequered scarves over the lower part of their faces. The passenger's head turned towards her, and for an instant she thought she ought to give him a friendly wave.

Then she saw the gun.

Six

You and I, Nim, we know how easily the desert can kill us. It can do so without even trying. And mountains in a desert mean all the bad and empty places of the world melded together. Which is why I've come prepared.

I've heard oil prospectors say the loneliness can kill you before the heat and the thirst ever do. But the loneliness is a friend to me now. It's my protector. It sharpens my senses. It gives me the prescience of the jackal and the hyena. Otherwise, that little group of Huwaytat Bedouin who came down the defile between the two nearest peaks would surely have surprised me in the open. But I heard their voices echoing off the rocks long before I saw them. Did they know about the spring? I doubt it. When I got here I almost failed to find it again, which set the terror going in me, I can tell you. No one can live here for more than a few hours without water.

But I found it in the end. It looked just the way you and I left it all those years ago: a small patch of moss, the dampness in the dust masked by a rocky overhang. If anyone else had discovered it in the intervening decades, this place would be marked as a safe stop on a trail across the wasteland, fixed in the Bedouin memory, if not on an actual map. But they didn't even break their stride. Their camels kept lolloping along, necks swaying like sickly swans. Bound for the far greater comfort at Wadi Feiran, I reckoned. From my hiding place, I watched them disappear into the heat haze, their voices dying away until the silence returned.

I've set up a routine, like we used to – remember, Nim? A daily ritual. First, turn the sleeping bag inside out. We don't want scorpions scuttling in while we're burying the meagre expulsion of our bowels to hide the stink of human presence. Then we roll the bag tight and tie the straps, placing it above ground in a convenient niche in a nearby rockface to keep it away from snakes. Next, we check the strips of dried camel meat for signs of decay. We make sure the bags containing the dates and the nuts are secure – remember how cheeky the polecats and genets can be? When the food's gone, I'll have to hunt for myself: snakes, lizards, maybe an ibex if I'm lucky.

The last part of the ritual, then, is to whet the blade of my knife against a stone and clean and oil the rifle. Just like we did in the Great War. Only here, there's a different enemy. And despite all the care I've taken, there's still a chance that one day soon there will be other visitors to this narrow slash in Satan's blistered skin. And I need to be ready for them.

But in the meantime it's good to be back in the field. And best of all, Nim, old fellow, I've got you for company.

Seven

Prim was nine again and cowering, desperate to block out the raging of her mother's voice. Each syllable cutting like glass. Each word a gunshot, as loud as Archie's twelve-bore when he took her shooting for rooks in the orchard – words that Prim couldn't understand, grown-up words like *adulterer… dirty whore… in flagrante…*

But Prim wasn't nine any longer. She wasn't in her parents' sitting room covering her ears while Celestina accused Archie of some new betrayal. She was twenty-four, trapped in the back of a Citroën in a Cairo slum while a man on a motorcycle with a scarf over his face aimed a gun at her. And she was about to die.

And then: three blasts – over before her heart had time to beat even once. Three blasts that she knew weren't the sound of Archie shouting back at her mother, but real live gunshots, choking the half-formed scream in her throat.

She had no time to throw herself back from the car window. No space to avoid the unerring aim of the gun pointed directly into her face. Only enough strength left in her body to close her eyes and wonder whether dying would hurt very much.

But dying seemed to be taking somewhat longer than she expected. Could bullets pass through you without you realizing? Was the shock of their impact a form of anaesthetic, like ether or chloroform? She heard the car door open and Tarek's angry guttural Arabic as he hurled a torrent of invective, then his muttering as he got back into the Citroën. She opened her eyes.

No gun! No gunman. No motorbike. Only the mad Cairo traffic, and the memory of her own terror, as if she'd just witnessed a clever conjuring trick.

Looking ahead over Tarek's shoulder, she glimpsed the pillion passenger wave his arms in youthful elation as the bike weaved around the donkey cart and vanished. And with its disappearance came the shame. She had panicked like an ill-prepared understudy on the night the big call comes. The gunshots had been nothing more than the backfiring of the motorbike's engine.

Following the shame came the anger. How *dare* these stupid boys play with her emotions, her inner fears, forcing those painful old memories out of her that she'd thought she'd forgotten.

'Stupid hotheads, Miss Archie,' Tarek said in a low grumble. 'Their fathers should give them a good beating. They bring shame upon my city.'

'I thought they were going to kill us,' Prim replied, noticing that her hands were shaking.

'If they were thieves, they would have stolen your wristwatch. And I would have told them to give it back and not dishonour their mothers.'

'Then who were they?'

'Who knows? Maybe they were from Young Egypt.' Tarek made a flicking, dismissive gesture with his fingers. 'These nationalists have become bolder since Farouk became king. They see a European and they think to make a game with them. Make the Westerner scared. Make themselves big heroes for five minutes.'

'Were we in danger?'

Tarek grinned as he shook his head. 'If a European is harmed in Cairo, Miss Archie, then Russell Pasha becomes very angry. No one get no peace for a whole month.'

'Who's Russell Pasha when he's at home?'

'He is English – big fellow in the Cairo police. We call him Pasha because he is a great man. Like I say, if a European comes to harm here, Russell Pasha will get very angry.'

'Does that include my father, Tarek?'

Tarek's grin vanished. His eyes narrowed beneath his wiry iron-grey eyebrows. 'You should not worry about this, Miss Archie. All will be well.'

'How do you know that?' Prim asked.

Tarek put the Citroën into gear. Before he released the brake, he thumped his chest with his fist. 'I feel it – *here*,' he said. 'The boss is alive. I know he is.'

In the conference room of the British embassy the stately turning of the ceiling fan was doing little to stir the torrid air. The ambassador had kept his jacket on, in deference – or so Harry Taverner assumed – to the ghosts of his diplomatic ancestors in far-flung stations across the Empire, men who would rather die of heatstroke than appear improperly dressed. Protocol demanded that he do likewise. The meeting had only just begun, and already he could feel the sweat breaking out on his upper lip. Discreetly he dabbed it off with his fist.

'I want no extracurricular adventures on my turf, young Mr Taverner,' Lampson was saying, a cautionary finger raised in warning. 'Let us all be clear about that from the start.'

'I've already made your views known to Mr Taverner, Ambassador,' said Geoffrey Courtney, the Service's Cairo head of station – a somewhat grandiose title, Harry reckoned, given that until his own arrival yesterday, Major G. W. Courtney had been the only officer in post.

'It's not going to be easy without assistance from the police,' Harry said. 'Major Courtney tells me there's little expectation of a surveillance team.'

Ambassador Lampson managed to convey deep disappointment without moving a muscle in his face, or anywhere else on his body that Harry could detect. 'Lack of resources – or so I'm informed by Thomas Russell,' he said, in the voice of a vicar announcing the next hymn number. 'He's the head of police here.'

'Major Courtney has briefed me, sir.'

'Then I'll assume you know that Russell Pasha has got his hands full chasing heroin smugglers, weeding out nationalist troublemakers and trying to ensure the extremists in Palestine don't export their anti-British violence across the border. That doesn't leave much left over for chasing missing oil executives.'

'I understand, sir,' replied Harry, trying not to sound despondent.

'I'm afraid,' continued Lampson, 'that whether one is dealing with the Foreign Office, the Colonial Office, the General Officer Commanding British Troops in Egypt, the Cairo police or the bloody maître d' of Shepheard's Grill Room, "lack of resources" seems to be the current mantra. I hope things are better back home.'

Harry wondered if replying 'not really' would make Lampson think he was disloyal. He made do with a sympathetic grimace and said, 'Without surveillance, Ambassador, there's always the possibility that Miss Nevendon will slip through our fingers. If she knows where her father is and has come here to join him—'

The ambassador cut him off with a charming smile. 'I'm sure they teach you fellows to rely on your initiative,' he said. 'And you have Major Courtney here, if you need help. He assures me you come highly recommended. Let me know how things progress.'

Outside, in the lush embassy gardens, Harry at last got to take off his jacket. It felt like shedding a skin, freeing his true self from a carapace he didn't recognize. He felt suddenly undefended, alone and at risk – not from any human threat, but from the possibility of professional ruin. Sure, he could mount a pretence at surveillance. But what did Lampson and Courtney expect him to do: follow Prim Nevendon around all day like a lovestruck puppy? Cairo wasn't even his city. He was a Vienna hand, comfortable with Viennese ways and fluent in German, tuned to receive the subtle signals of a European posting. Here, he was little more than a glorified tourist.

Highly recommended, my arse, he thought. Lampson was just being polite. But at least one thing was clear to him now: if Primrose Nevendon gave him the slip, Harry Taverner would be the fall-guy.

On the street side, the Villa Narcisse was a modern white stucco pillbox with narrow slits for windows, as if it was expecting a frontal assault. At the back a pleasant veranda gave onto a shady garden bordered by dense beds of flowering jasmine that were Tarek's pride. Inside, it was English colonial: gleaming teak floorboards and banisters, the air thick with the smell of beeswax polish. It looked to Prim as if Madame Sauvier, the Franco-Lebanese housekeeper, ran the place with the fearsome attention to detail of a Guards Brigade sergeant-major. Her cold eye appraised the new arrival and appeared to find her wanting in all respects.

During the guided tour, delivered with the curt efficiency of someone doing a stocktaking exercise, Prim could sense Archie in every room, every corridor. She could almost see him sitting at the little white wrought-iron table in the garden, sipping a pink gin – his favourite – while he read the daily newspaper at the end of a busy day of doing whatever it was that great oil men did when they weren't out taming gushers. She wondered where these images in her head were coming from. Were they updated versions of childhood memories? Were his letters speaking to her? Perhaps she was simply doing what she did in her professional life: dressing a set before opening night.

A pilgrimage to the master bedroom yielded little. Standing at the foot of Archie's bed, Prim could detect the scent of Bay Rum cologne that she remembered from her childhood. She opened the wardrobe to find his suits and shirts hanging there like sacred robes, and in the bathroom all his toiletries still in place on the glass shelf above the sink, priestly unguents ready for the next anointing. This is how I used to feel, she thought, when I made my solitary clandestine visits to his empty study at Bevern, after he'd walked out on me and Mother: Prim, the great archaeologist, taking the first human step in three millennia across the threshold of a lost temple to a powerful pharaoh.

Madame Sauvier's voice coming from the corridor broke into her reverie. 'Will you wish to avail yourself of this bedroom for your stay, Mademoiselle?'

'No, keep it the way it is – in case he turns up unannounced,' she replied over her shoulder. 'By the way, have you tidied in here since he left, Madame Sauvier?'

'No, Miss Nevendon,' came the answer from the doorway. 'I had no need, other than to dust each day. The boss was always a very orderly gentleman.'

No sign of a hurried departure then, Prim thought. Just a very orderly gentleman telling his driver to drop him off at the Ezbekia Gardens so that he could walk the rest of the way to his office – exactly as the corporate Mr el-Madani had told her. But did that mean Archie was taken unawares, or had he gone to some trouble to cover his tracks with the camouflage of normality?

Leaving her father's bedroom, Prim followed Madame Sauvier to a neat guest room with a view of the garden.

'I trust this will suffice,' the housekeeper said bluntly and went off to fetch fresh towels for the washstand.

Prim watched her go with unease. Madame Sauvier had maintained a cold reserve from the moment she'd arrived. Was it simply her nature, or did she consider the Villa Narcisse a shrine to be guarded jealously? She hoped it wasn't the latter; she'd need the help of everyone who knew Archie if she was going to make progress in finding him.

A few moments later Tarek arrived with her suitcase and left her to unpack. As she unlocked the case, Prim thought again of the gunman on the motorcycle. The fear came back to her like an electric shock. Had Tarek been right when he'd called those two men young hotheads? Or was the incident connected to the shooting at the Nimrod Theatre? If it was, then it confirmed her growing belief that Archie had probably vanished for his own safety.

But it meant something besides that. Though Prim couldn't imagine how, whoever Archie was hiding from knew that his daughter had arrived in Cairo. And if the gunman hadn't pulled the trigger, then it had to be a warning: *Come no further.* In her head, she heard el-Madani's smooth business-school voice: *Please don't think of playing the private detective… There are some in this city whose scruples would make a Chicago mobster blush.*

———

Prim spent the rest of the afternoon in her father's study. Again, it seemed almost a perfect replica of the one that called to her from her childhood memory, only with bright Egyptian sunshine streaming through the window. On the shelves, wedged amongst the books on the petroleum industry, were ones she could have sworn she'd leafed through as a child: *The Arts and Crafts of Ancient Egypt* by Flinders Petrie; *The Discovery of the Tomb of Tutankhamen* by Howard Carter; papers by Arthur Evans, who'd unearthed the Minoan palace at Knossos on Crete; works in French by the great Champollion... They had seemed to her then like faint echoes coming to her from far away and impossibly long ago. But here, with the hot sun outside and the scent of jasmine on the sultry air, they seemed instead like guidebooks to places she could step into simply by opening the door.

Attempting to fill the room with Archie's imagined presence, she again experienced the same churning competition between hope and fear that she'd felt in the *Celaeno*. And again he would not come to her.

She had hoped there would a typewriter on his desk – the one at which he'd composed his letters to her. But there was not. Just a letter stand, an Anglepoise lamp, a telephone and a small personal phone book. Wishing she'd brought the letters with her and not entrusted them to Granny G, Prim pulled back the chair and sat down.

He hadn't bothered to lock the desk drawers, so she rummaged through the contents, feeling like an intruder, praying she wouldn't stumble across embarrassingly intimate letters to a mistress. But she needn't have worried. There was nothing out of the unusual.

And no diary.

Had her father ever kept one? She couldn't recall. If he had, perhaps the police had taken it. She went in search of Madame Sauvier, who had no answer for her. Returning to the desk, Prim pulled from the bottom drawer a collection of printed programmes from plays that the Nimrod Theatre had staged. They stretched back over a decade. Beneath them she discovered a thin blue book no larger than her hand. Written on the faded cover was the legend *Officer's Record of Services*. When she picked it up and leafed through it, she saw that it was Uncle Nim's army paybook. Tucked inside were two small photos. The first was of the grinning brothers in uniform, with the Pyramids for a backdrop. A scrawled caption on the back read: *Pharaoh's generals on leave, Sept. 1917*. Prim judged it must have been taken shortly before Nimrod was killed in the advance on Jerusalem.

The other photo was a copy of the one on Grace's table back in London: the brothers at an unnamed archaeological site, the single word *TURQUOISE* and the year, *1913*, scrawled in the bottom right-hand corner. After gazing at the two pictures for several moments, a sad half-smile on her face, Prim returned the photos to the paybook, consigning them to the darkness of the desk drawer with the reverence of someone reinterring human remains.

Around four, the telephone rang. The call was from Harry Taverner – she'd left the number of the Villa Narcisse with the desk at the Hotel National when she'd checked out. She was surprised at how pleasing it was to hear that easy English drawl again, always seasoned with just the right hint of good humour.

'Wondering if your first day in Cairo has left you in need of a sundowner? I'm parched. I think I've discovered the eleventh plague of Egypt.'

'And what is that?' Prim asked, trying to sound nonchalant.

'Councillors of His Majesty's Foreign and Colonial Offices. They seem to think I'm some sort of travelling salesman.'

Try having a gun pointed in your face, she wanted to say, but didn't. 'As a matter of fact I could do with a drink, too. It's been that sort of day. Where do you suggest?'

'I'm told there's a houseboat-cum-bar on the Nile by the Semiramis Hotel. It's called the Cleopatra Club.'

'How very original.'

'It comes highly recommended. The band is supposed to be top-flight.'

'Well, that sounds wonderful. But I didn't pack a cocktail dress.'

'They say it's quite relaxed. Shall we meet there?'

'I've got to drop by my father's theatre first,' said Prim. 'I can pick you up afterwards, if you like.'

'Kind of you, but there's really no need to break the taxi journey. I'll find my own way to the Cleopatra.'

'That's not what I meant,' Prim went on. She adopted a Grosvenor Square society drawl. 'One has a driver now – don't y'know.'

'Good heavens,' Harry replied admiringly. 'Have you won the football pools?'

'It's a long story.'

'I'll wait outside the embassy then,' he said. 'We're on Shari Lazoghli, at the north end of the Garden City district. You can't miss us. Just look out for the flag.'

Prim affected the society whine again. 'Then I shall inform my chauffeur.'

'Does he have a uniform and a peaked cap?'

Prim laughed. 'You're confusing me with one of the Mitford girls.'

'Not Unity, I hope – the one who's got a thing for Adolf Hitler.'

The throwaway comment made her fingers tighten on the telephone receiver. Not a hint of foreknowledge in his voice. Just that same relaxed tone, the one she'd got so used to since she'd first met him at Southampton. He couldn't possibly know – could he? – about the cruel insults that got scrawled on the gate pillars at Bevern: *Nazi scum; Adolf's mates; fascist filth...* Or about Celestina's angry response to the policeman, Swinnell, when he and Sergeant Mullen had come calling: *What do you think we're going to do – raise a giant statue of Signor Mussolini on the lawn? Signal from the dovecote to submarines full of Nazi spies off Seaford?*

No, he couldn't possibly know about such things. Because if he did, then the charming Harry Taverner was lying through his teeth to her about working for the British Council.

Praying that her slight pause before answering hadn't been enough to betray the turmoil in her mind, Prim tried to match his own conviviality. 'Take it back at once, Mr Harry Taverner, or there'll be a twelfth plague of Egypt on its way to torment you. Haven't you seen *The Mummy* with Boris Karloff? My curse will last down the ages.'

'I stand suitably chastised,' he said with a laugh. 'But don't get your mummy wrappings caught in the back wheel of your limousine. Remember what happened to Isadora Duncan.'

They agreed a time. Then he rang off.

Not Unity, I hope – the one who's got a thing for Adolf Hitler...

Just a throwaway joke that meant nothing, Prim decided. Just a hothead on a motorcycle brandishing a gun.

Nothing at all to worry about.

———

As she stood on the pavement gazing at the swing door and the darkened lobby beyond, the Nimrod Theatre looked much smaller than it ever had in Prim's imagination. It was narrow with three storeys, the upper two fronted by matching pairs of rectangular bay windows covered with intricate arabesque wooden shutters. A poster in a glass-fronted display case on the wall advertised *A Midsummer Night's Dream*. The handwritten label pasted to the glass told her, in both English and Arabic: *Closed until further notice.*

Prim had been around theatre people long enough to know that every story, every anecdote, comes fully rehearsed, but not always true to the original text. Things get embellished for dramatic effect, or to get a laugh or the audience on your side. Sometimes they're simply looted from someone else's life, repurposed for the ensuing admiration. But she was pretty sure all the stories Archie had ever told her about the Nimrod Theatre were the gospel truth, even if they were Nim's truth rather than his own.

She could recite them from memory: how the two brothers, on leave from the front and tired of camel trips to the Pyramids and expeditions to the bazaars, had bemoaned the lack of cultural nourishment to be found in wartime Cairo. How they had discovered the Karnak, finding to their surprise that its performance of *Uncle Vanya* – with a cast of English-speaking local actors – was actually rather good. How the little auditorium became a means of temporary escape from their duties on the staff of General Allenby. The friends they had made amongst the cast and crew. The promise Uncle Nim had made to Archie that, when the war was over, he was going to stay in Cairo and dedicate himself to turning the Karnak into a venue that could hold its head high against anything in London's West End. They were the only tales Prim could remember her father ever telling her about the Great War.

She tried the middle door and found it was locked. So too were the doors on either side. Between the theatre and the next building lay a narrow passage, where she assumed the stage door must be. She looked back to the street. Tarek was watching her from the Citroën. Pointing, so that he'd know what she intended, Prim stepped tentatively into the shadows.

The heat of the day had pooled here in the semi-darkness. The narrow space stank of urine. But Prim wouldn't cover her nose and mouth because she needed all the air she could get. God, she thought, it's worse than the Woolwich Empire on a Saturday night after the show's closed.

Once she was inside the passageway, her eyes got the measure of the gloom. At the far end, where it ran slap into a brick wall set between the theatre and the adjacent building, she could make out a doorway, just as she'd expected. It even had a sign hanging from a bracket above the lintel: *Stage Door and Deliveries.* She had seen no signs of life in the foyer, so she reckoned the door was bound to be locked. But what was the point in coming here if she didn't at least try?

To her relief, when she tried the handle, the door opened.

Once inside, she found the little lobby as hot and sultry as the ladies' Turkish baths on Duke of York Street – a friend had taken her there after they'd had a little too much champagne at an opening night and she'd thought she was going to melt. She looked around, the only light coming from the open door. Usually in places like this there was a cheerful gatekeeper in cloth cap and braces, someone to keep the stage-door-Johnnies away from the actresses and to tell you of the time Leslie Howard or Fay Compton played the venue. But this one seemed abandoned.

Prim could think of few more mournful places than the backstage area of a theatre that had gone dark. Looking around, she saw a noticeboard with a handwritten warning in English against raised voices and running during performances, and a rehearsal schedule. Painted in yellow above the board was an arrow that pointed down a narrow corridor; it bore the legend: *Manager's Office. Mr M. Bannoudi.*

'Hello, is anybody there?' Prim called.

She didn't expect a reply, but even a caretaker would have been a welcome presence, because the place had the atmosphere of an unattended morgue. The fact that there had been a shooting here, though she didn't know precisely where, lent it a grimness she could sense in every nerve. She could even smell the aftermath, a fetid odour that she knew instinctively was the stench of death. Dear God, she thought, they can't have bothered to scrub the blood away properly.

The manager's office was barely more than a cupboard, the light from its one small window scarcely enough to show her anything other than its emptiness. She moved down the corridor past the cramped dressing rooms to a small flight of stairs leading up to the wings and the crossover behind the stage. Flicking on the lights, she was relieved to find the electricity was still connected.

The crossover – the place behind the stage – was the worst mess she'd ever seen, a stage manager's nightmare. Props discarded everywhere. A rack of costumes gathering dust. Upturned chairs and pieces of scenery. The stench was stronger here.

Oh no, there's a severed animal's head!

It was lying in the wings. Eye sockets empty. A swollen tongue lolling from the rotting mouth. Prim felt her stomach churn.

Then she remembered the poster outside: *A Midsummer Night's Dream*. Feeling like a fool, she laughed at the head's ludicrously exaggerated ears and the gaping eye holes for the actor playing Bottom to see through. "'Though she be but little, she is fierce,'" she recited to herself, which helped keep her courage up.

The safety curtain was down, cutting off her view of the house. Going over to the main lighting board, Prim threw the levers to bring up the lights and then pushed her way past the nearest edge of the curtain and stepped out onto the apron, coming to a halt centre-stage, just before the footlights. She looked out over the auditorium, as if she'd been given the task of telling the audience that, sadly, for reasons quite beyond the management's control, tonight's performance had been cancelled. Two hundred seats, she reckoned, all quite standard: faded scarlet velour. Above the rear stalls was a circle three rows deep, and an even narrower upper circle above that, the tiers supported by pillars brightly but somewhat childishly painted to resemble those of an ancient Egyptian temple.

She'd been in plenty of small theatres before. Indeed, she preferred them. The atmosphere was more intimate. Intimacy, she believed, required a leaner, more muscular set. You could get away with more in a larger theatre. But in a place like this, the audience would see at once your every misstep. Not that Prim was giving her attention to theatre design at that precise moment. She was staring at the audience of one – a man. He was sitting in an aisle seat three rows back from the stage. A man with his chin tucked in, as if he'd fallen asleep during the performance and stayed that way after everyone had left. A man whose contorted expression of agony was more authentic than anything an actor could manage. A man with half his forehead blown away.

89

Prim was too shocked, too appalled to scream. And anyway the stink was so strong here that it stopped up her throat. All she could do was stare at the dead man and the flies that were crawling in the blood-mat of his hair. Which was why, when she heard the boards of the stage creak behind her, it sounded as loud as anything a boy on a motorcycle could manage.

Eight

Harry Taverner glanced at his wristwatch again. Thirty minutes late. Time to start worrying.

'Been stood up, have we, sir?' asked the British sentry guarding the embassy gates. He was six foot two and suntanned, bored out of his mind watching the traffic, impervious to the occasional shout of something vaguely anti-British that he could do nothing about.

'Something like that.'

'Never mind, sir. Caters for all appetites, Cairo does,' the sentry said, very nearly winking. 'If you know where to look.'

'Thank you. I'll bear that in mind.'

Returning to the office, Harry telephoned the Villa Narcisse. In the earpiece he heard a woman's voice answer. 'El Nasriya seven-four-nine-two. The Nevendon residence.' It was the same voice that had answered his earlier call. Good English, but with the hint of a French accent overlaid on Arabian vocal cords. Syrian, or Lebanese, he guessed. A chauffeur *and* a housekeeper. Maybe he'd chosen the wrong profession.

'Is Miss Nevendon there?'

'Who's calling?'

'A friend, from the British Council.'

'I'm afraid Mademoiselle Nevendon left quite some time ago.'

The news took the wind out of Harry, leaving him breathless the way a rugby tackle at his old school used to do. Something had happened to her; he was sure of it. Ending the call, he paced the little office for a minute or two. Maybe she'd been held up, or her visit to the Nimrod Theatre had overrun. What if she'd had an accident? Or, like her father, had decided to vanish? Was Primrose Nevendon an innocent abroad? Or maybe – just maybe – was she an accomplice?

Major Courtney had gone home hours ago. So had his secretary, the redoubtable Mrs Fulready-Laycock, wife of the military attaché. In his own mind, that made Harry the Service's sole officer in Cairo. He was the man on the spot. Technically he could do what he wanted, within reason. He weighed his options. He was sure of one thing: he was likely to be blamed by London for anything that might have befallen Prim, regardless of his unsuccessful plea for police surveillance. *Bad luck, Taverner, old boy... No reflection on your conduct, of course, but there's a post we think you'd be exactly right for, in Timbuktu...*

Taking up the office keys, Harry unlocked the small armoury safe. The only weapon in it was a Webley revolver, too bulky to conceal under his jacket. And if Primrose Nevendon was still at the Nimrod Theatre and safe, he'd have a hard time explaining to her why the British Council required its administrative staff to go about armed to the teeth. Besides, if any harm had befallen her, it had likely happened some time ago; it was already far too late for him to intervene. He left the revolver where it was, closed the safe and spun the combination wheel. Then, locking the office door behind him, he went downstairs to the lobby and signed the keys over to the duty night-clerk.

Out on the street the desert air was warm and sultry. The moon was yet to rise above the skyline and the stars were hidden by a haze that ringed each street light with a dusty halo.

'Taking my advice then, sir?' said the sentry smugly as Harry waited for a taxi to pass. 'Try The Lotus House off al-Din Street. Officers only, so the bints are clean. Less chance of catching Nefertiti's revenge, if you get my drift, sir. The taxi wallah's bound to know it.'

Harry smiled. 'I don't think the ambassador would approve.'

'Don't invite him then, sir,' the sentry shot back.

'I'm on my way to the theatre actually. But thanks anyway.'

Though the sentry was looking firmly ahead at the street, Harry sensed the man's chin lift a little in an expression that said silently, *Ah, the 'theatre' – one of those sissy boys…*

A cab pulled over. Harry couldn't help noticing it had no lights on.

'Silly buggers,' the sentry growled. 'Street lights, see – so in their minds, there's no point in putting their own lights on. If they drive into a wall, it's God's will anyway.'

Harry could sense the underlying contempt in the sentry's voice. He'd already picked up a similar disdain for the population amongst more than a few of the embassy staff. It was almost as if independence had never happened. 'You're a fount of information, Private,' he said as he opened the cab door.

'Happy to be of service, sir. Enjoy the show.'

The taxi swung out into the traffic, apparently without the use of wing mirrors, judging by the accompanying screech of brakes. Harry settled nervously into the rear seat. *Maybe I'm overreacting*, he thought. *Maybe the sentry was right in his assumption: maybe Primrose Nevendon has simply stood me up.*

———

The taxi made it to the Ezbekia Gardens in one piece and without the assistance of its headlamps. But Harry's anxiety remained undiminished. Indeed, when he saw the police car parked in the lane outside the Nimrod Theatre, he struggled even to remain composed. On the pavement a plainclothes officer in a suit and tasselled tarboosh was conducting an animated conversation with the driver. On the far side of a parked dark-green Citroën was an ambulance with a red cross on its side and the legend *Kasr al-Ainy Hospital* in English and Arabic. His worst fears apparently confirmed, Harry Taverner paid off the taxi and approached the detective. As he did so, the ambulance pulled away from the kerb. The fact that it did so with no urgency filled him with dread – an ambulance has no need to hurry if the patient is already dead.

'Excuse me—'

'Go away, please, mister,' said the officer, turning towards him. 'This is crime scene. No reporters.'

'I'm not a journalist,' Harry replied. He glanced at the departing ambulance. 'I want to know what's happened to Miss Nevendon. We were supposed to meet—'

'How you know the Englishwoman is here?' the detective asked suspiciously. 'Who tell you this?'

'She did – Miss Nevendon. We had an appointment. She failed to show up.'

'You are husband?'

'No. We're just acquaintances. What's happened?'

'Is police matter, sir. Confidential.'

'Miss Nevendon is a British citizen, Officer. If some harm has befallen her, I really need to know.' A flash of inspiration struck him, in the shape of a recollection from his meeting with Ambassador Lampson. 'If you're too busy, perhaps I should call Major-General Russell at police headquarters.'

It seemed to do the trick.

'You know Russell Pasha?'

'We're acquainted,' Harry responded casually.

The officer's shoulders straightened a little and he adjusted the tarboosh on his head. It wasn't exactly snapping to attention, but it was all Harry needed.

'The English lady is safe,' the detective said, pointing to the theatre entrance. He withdrew a grubby notebook from his breast pocket. It had a stub of pencil attached by a length of string. 'What is your name, sir? For police record.'

Whatever had occurred inside the theatre, Harry didn't want his footprints recorded anywhere near it. 'Sam Spade,' he said.

The detective gave him a hard look. For a moment Harry feared his flippancy was going to get him into trouble. Just my luck, he thought: an Egyptian detective who's read *The Maltese Falcon*. Then the man licked the end of the pencil stub. 'How you spell this, Mr Sam?'

'S.P.A.D.E. Spade – as in shovel,' Harry replied, already on his way to the nearest swing door.

'Harry! Thank God for a friendly face!'

Primrose Nevendon was standing in the theatre's little foyer next to a stout Egyptian woman of about fifty. In Harry's eyes, the contrast couldn't have been greater: Prim in wide caramel linen culottes and a blue polka-dot sailor shirt, the older woman in a dark-brown worker's tunic that wouldn't have looked out of place in a Soviet poster of happy *kulaks* toiling on a collective farm.

'Thank God you're all right,' he said. 'When I saw that ambulance, I feared the worst.'

95

Prim dropped the bag that was slung over her shoulder and took a step towards him. Her face was cold and pale, as though she'd walked a long way on a wintry wind-blown beach. 'Harry, it's quite dreadful – absolutely awful,' she said. 'I can't get it out of my head.'

'What's happened? I asked the detective out there; he wouldn't tell me. Are you hurt?'

'A bit shaken, but otherwise I'm fine.'

'So who was that in the ambulance?'

'That was poor Mr Bannoudi.' Noting Harry's blank look, Prim added, 'He was my father's manager here. He's been murdered.'

Harry put just the right amount of surprise into his voice, for a man who wasn't supposed to know about the Nimrod's recent bloody history. 'How awful. I do hope you weren't in any danger.'

'Whoever did it had already gone by the time I arrived.'

'I realized something must have happened to you when you didn't show at the embassy. But *this* – it must have been the most dreadful shock,' Harry said consolingly, while he ran the competing theories around his head, each more unsettling than the last: Archie Nevendon mixed up in organized crime; Archie Nevendon part of a murderous Nazi espionage ring; Archie Nevendon the traitor to British interests in the Middle East covering his tracks…

'I keep seeing his face, Harry. It was simply terrible,' Prim went on, and for a moment he thought she was speaking of her father. She turned to the woman behind her. 'Mind you, the worst shock of all was when Madame Nasoul here came up behind me. I almost jumped right over the top lighting catwalk.' Prim gave the woman a friendly rub on the shoulder to show there was no hard feeling. 'Madame Nasoul, this is Mr Taverner from the British Council. Harry, meet Madame Aleyna Nasoul.'

They shook hands.

'Aleyna runs front-of-house and does all the admin,' Prim explained. 'You're poor Mr Moussa's right-hand woman really, aren't you?'

Embarrassed, Madame Nasoul bowed her head.

'Was it a robbery?' Harry asked, trying to sound suitably naïve.

'Aleyna says there was no money kept on the premises,' Prim answered, glancing at Madame Nasoul. 'They've been shut for a while, you see.'

She was playing nervously with her nails and Harry wondered if now might be the time to steer her towards the subject of the earlier shooting – the one he wasn't meant to know about. 'Yes, I saw the notice outside,' he said, gesturing vaguely towards the entrance to the stalls where they'd found the body. 'I assumed it was to do with all this.'

Her reply wasn't at all what he was expecting. Prim's eyes began to gleam with welling tears. 'It's been an awful day, Harry. And not just because of... because of finding poor Moussa Bannoudi like that. This morning a boy on a motorcycle pointed a gun at me. I thought I was going to die.'

Madame Nasoul laid a sympathetic hand on Prim's arm. It gave Harry enough time to stifle his alarm, strip his response of any telltale insight. 'Why, that's dreadful,' he said, playing the innocent. 'You must have been frightened out of your wits. I know I'd be.'

Prim Nevendon laughed and wiped away the tears with the back of her hand. 'Tarek says it was only a couple of nationalist hotheads having fun with a European. Even so, I'm beginning to wonder if coming here was such a good idea.'

'Maybe I can ask someone at the embassy for help,' Harry suggested solicitously. Then, as if the thought had only just occurred to him, 'Have you told your father about any of this?'

'My father?'

'Does he have a bodyguard or anything like that?' He saw the uncertainty in Prim's frightened eyes. She didn't know how to answer him. 'Only a thought,' he said in a blithe tone. 'All these kidnaps you hear about in the newspapers these days… Don't important executives sometimes employ chaps like that?'

For a moment she simply looked at him, and Harry wondered if he'd overplayed his hand. Then she said, 'Would you mind awfully if we postponed our drink at the Cleopatra Club? After what's happened, I don't think I'd be much company.'

'No, of course. I quite understand. I'd forgotten all about it.'

'Another time, perhaps – when I'm feeling a bit cheerier.'

'I look forward to it. Are you sure you'll be all right getting home? You should really have someone with you.'

'I've got Tarek. He's waiting outside in the Citroën.'

'Ah, the chauffeur.'

She gave him a weary smile. 'I'm truly not that grand. Very ordinary really. This has all been a bit of a shock. I feel as if I've stumbled into a gangster movie.'

'Well, you're bearing up like a trouper,' Harry replied admiringly. 'If I can be of any assistance, just call me at the embassy.'

She nodded her thanks and stooped to retrieve the bag from where she'd dropped it. 'I can take you back there – to the embassy, if you want,' she said, hoisting the bag over her left shoulder. 'You've come all this way for nothing; I feel a lift is the least I can do.'

'That's kind of you,' Harry said.

'We'll have to make a little detour on the way, to drop off Madame Nasoul.'

'That's fine. Lead the way.'

When they stepped into the street, the police car had gone. Harry settled into the front passenger seat of the Citroën, Prim and Madame Nasoul in the back. As they passed the Ezbekia Gardens and the Opera House, Prim asked, 'Harry, how did you know where I was?'

'You told me you were visiting your father's theatre.'

'Did I tell you the name or the address? I don't think I did.'

'No mystery,' he assured her. 'I asked at the embassy. They'd all heard of it – the Nimrod Theatre. Seems it's quite famous in Cairo.'

She lapsed into silence. But Harry could hear the thoughts in her head even above the honking of motor horns and the revving of engines. *Then they must have told you about the shooting… and about my missing father… and you haven't said a word.*

Harry looked fixedly ahead, even though the traffic reminded him of a Roman chariot race, and cursed himself in silence. He'd made the sort of basic error that would have earned him a rebuke from the training staff on his first day with the Service. It had been one of the earliest things they'd told him: you don't need to speak in order to betray yourself. You can do it just as easily by what you leave unsaid.

'Are you being serious, young Taverner?'

Major Courtney peered at Harry over the top of his horn-rimmed spectacles. He was balding, thin-faced, with the apologetic air of a provincial bank manager looking for a reason not to agree a loan. It was the next morning, and the office ceiling fan was fighting its usual rearguard action against the heat. In the corner Mrs Fulready-Laycock was typing up the latest security briefing for the ambassador.

'I don't see that we have a choice,' Harry said.

'But if you disclose your identity to our Miss Nevendon, what's to stop her doing a bolter?'

'Nothing, really,' Harry admitted. 'But I think we can safely say Primrose Nevendon could be in significant and immediate danger. And she's not going to be of any use to us dead.'

Courtney conceded the point by lifting his spectacles back up the blade of his nose. 'No, of course not. You're quite right. But you've heard what the ambassador said: no scandal. He won't stand for it. And I'm not sure that you revealing to Miss Nevendon that you're an officer of this Service is strictly in line with that injunction.'

Mrs Fulready-Laycock lent stern emphasis to her boss's statement by returning the carriage of her typewriter with a crash, as if she were loading a howitzer.

'I can't stay close to her, if I don't,' Harry said. 'It's as simple as that, sir.'

'What exactly are you proposing? Recruiting her – with *that* family's history?'

'No, sir. Just offering her our protection.'

'And what makes you think she'd take it?'

'I think she already knows how much she's in need of it.'

'I could suggest to the ambassador that he asks the Egyptians to declare her *persona non grata* – have her expelled, for her own safety,' Courtney said.

'If she knows where Archie Nevendon is, how does that help us?'

'How, then, are we to protect her?'

'Bring her into the embassy,' Harry suggested. 'That way we can keep an eye on her.'

'Good heavens, no,' replied Courtney, appalled. 'The ambassador would lose a wheel. What if her father's got himself embroiled in something unsavoury and she's in cahoots with him? Can you imagine the headlines: *Nazi agent offered sanctuary at British embassy?* There's more than just your career at stake here, young Taverner.'

'I don't think she's a Nazi agent, sir.'

'Do you have proof of that?'

'It's rather difficult to prove a negative. Isn't that what they say?'

Courtney pondered this proposition for a moment and then said grudgingly, 'I *suppose* I could ask the army to provide a couple of men to guard this villa that she's staying at.'

'That might work,' Harry agreed.

Courtney turned to his secretary. 'Do you think your husband might make the request, my dear? It would carry more weight coming from the military attaché.'

'I can certainly ask Bernard for you,' said Mrs Fulready-Laycock in the clipped tones of the diplomatic wife *en poste*. 'I'm sure General Weir could find a few stout fellows who'd prefer that, over guarding the Suez Canal and training the Egyptians out in the scorching desert.'

'There we are,' said Courtney. 'Problem solved. I might even get the ambassador to ask Anglo-Levantine if they'd care to chip in with the costs. It's their villa, after all.'

The telephone rang, struggling to make itself heard above Mrs Fulready-Laycock's renewed assault on her typewriter. When she lifted her fingers from the keys to answer it, the momentary silence was sepulchral. 'It's Major-General Russell, at police headquarters,' she said. 'He'd like a word.'

Courtney took the receiver. Harry sat cross-legged in his chair, pondering the futility of attempting to mind-read one end of a phone conversation.

'Interesting,' said Courtney when he'd returned the phone to Mrs Fulready-Laycock, 'and surprisingly quick for the Cairo police. The dead man at the Nimrod Theatre was definitely the manager, this Bannoudi fellow.'

'I know that already, sir,' Harry replied, wondering why the head of the Cairo police would come down off his mountain to pass on such low-level intelligence. 'His assistant, a woman named Nasoul, identified him at the scene.'

Courtney gave him a smug look, the sort that Harry guessed he kept specially for visiting London know-it-alls. 'Bet she didn't tell you the killers gave his kneecaps a shave with something sharp, right down to the bone.'

'Ouch!' said Harry, wincing. 'No, she didn't mention that.'

'They also removed both big toes. Very cleanly, according to the police surgeon – with a blade of some sort: a cleaver, or a chisel. And they did it before they had a sudden attack of compassion and shot him in the back of the head.'

'I think I can guess the question they were encouraging him to answer,' said Harry. '"Where's Archie?"'

Courtney wasn't inclined to disagree. 'The interesting thing is, judging by the distribution of the blood stains, they don't think he was tortured at the theatre,' he went on. 'But he was certainly killed there. So what's all that about?'

'Same as the earlier shooting at the Nimrod,' Harry suggested, 'to make a point – put the fear of God into Archie Nevendon, should he ever pluck up the courage to return.'

'I shall put *that* in the in-tray,' Courtney said after a moment's consideration.

'Kneecaps and toes,' said Harry, grimacing. 'Making a point about the dangers of running away?'

'Could be. Obviously not Europeans we're dealing with.'

'What makes you think that?' Harry asked.

'A European wouldn't descend to that level of barbarity.'

'You haven't had much to do with the Gestapo, have you, sir?' Harry said, trying not to sound too flippant. 'It looks to me like we're dealing here with some very hard people, whoever they are.'

Courtney conceded Harry's point with a shrug of defeat. 'There is one other thing Russell Pasha said to me. He asked me to pass it on personally.'

'What was that, sir?' Harry asked.

'I shall quote him exactly: "Tell Mr Spade to refrain in future from mocking my officers. And tell him he doesn't hold a candle to Sherlock Holmes." I assume he was referring to you.'

Nine

Reflect for a moment on just how lucky we are, Nim, old boy. Look up for a while: the crags cutting into the night sky like a saw-blade gouging out whole fistfuls of stars. What could be better than this? Why, it's even better than when we were in Cairo on leave, taking an interval beer in the little upstairs bar at the Karnak Theatre, halfway through The Importance of Being Earnest. *Remember what you said to me: 'We could be in Flanders, inhaling phosgene or getting our noddles blown to bits. Yet here we are: cold beer and a pretty decent performance, given that it's not the Theatre Royal, Drury Lane. Drink up, Archie, old fellow.'*

And what did I say to you? I recall the exact words. 'Here's an idea: when the war is over, we'll stay in Cairo. To hell with going home. We'll raise some money, buy this place and come here every night. And when we're not here, we'll be out in the Valley, picking up where old Howard Carter left off. We'll dig a tomb or two. Find another boy king. Make our names. What do you say to that, old sport?'

But the only tomb we dug was yours, Nim. And I laid you in it, didn't I? I didn't know Division was going to put you on that bloody raid. I swear I didn't. I'd never have suggested it to the planning conference otherwise.

Look at me now, Brother. I'm weeping like a girl. You didn't weep, not even when you were in the hospital, dying.

I swore to Mother I'd look after you, didn't I? I promised her. I gave her my word. You were always her little boy, Nim. I was too much like Father for her – she couldn't look at me without disgust. Said I had no soul. But what am I doing here talking to you, if I haven't got a soul?

I did everything I could, Nim. I swear I did. I kept the theatre going, didn't I? Just as you made me promise. If anything was to happen, keep the place going: that's what you said. I even named it after you. But now I've gone and done something really bad, Nim. Worse than anything we ever did in the war. Worse than not protecting you. And now they all want me to pay for it.

Can you hear that sound, Nim? That's the bell ringing for the second half. Let's take our seats. The curtain's about to go up again, and we don't want to miss the show, do we?

Ten

After leaving Harry Taverner at the embassy, Prim Nevendon returned to the Villa Narcisse and poured herself enough of Archie's gin to float a battleship. Moussa Bannoudi's murder had raised her fears for Archie to almost unbearable heights. It took all her courage to replay in her mind what had happened at the Nimrod Theatre just a few hours before. The sight of Bannoudi's corpse had been bad enough. But the jolt of terror that had gone through her body at the sound of Aleyna Nasoul's footsteps on the stage boards behind her was as real in her recollection as it had been in the moment.

When she'd stopped screaming (on reflection, she preferred to think it was only the one scream, and a short one at that) Aleyna had explained tremulously why she had come. 'Because the police tell me – at last! – that I am free to take the accounts from Mr Bannoudi's desk. Before, they do not let me do so. I worry so much; Mr Nevendon would be angry if they were stolen. And criminals, you know, they will take anything, even if they don't know what they are stealing.'

In truth, Prim had caught barely half of it, because her nerves were shot. But both women had managed to calm the other sufficiently to find their way back to the manager's cubbyhole of an office. From there, Aleyna had called the police – the line, thank

God, still connected to the exchange. Then they had waited, too appalled to return to the auditorium and Bannoudi's bloodied corpse, sharing the stunned companionship of two strangers on a life-raft after a sinking.

The accounts Aleyna Nasoul had come for were now in the bag that Prim had carried from the theatre. It lay against the side of Archie's desk. But Prim hadn't the calmness yet to take a further look. That would have to wait until tomorrow.

That night she slept barely an hour in one stretch, waking frequently from the same recurring dream of the manager's bloodied face mouthing a warning in a language she couldn't understand, but in a voice that was clearly her father's.

Her interview next morning at the Cairo police headquarters required little more from her than a retelling of the statement she'd made the previous evening, which was a blessing, because a stuffy office smelling of sweat was not a good place to be when your head was throbbing. It was noon when she returned to the Villa Narcisse. Even with her sunglasses on, the midday glare made her squint, so she chose indoors rather than the garden for what she planned to do.

In the shadowed privacy of her father's study Prim took the bag that Aleyna Nasoul had given her and laid it on Archie's desk. She did so almost reverently, as if it was appeasement that she was making to an easily angered deity.

In Bannoudi's office, while they'd waited for the police to arrive, Aleyna had explained that after the attack on the Nimrod and Archie's disappearance, the police had made only a cursory inspection of the theatre's books. Finding nothing obvious to suggest financial foul play, they had nevertheless refused her permission to remove them. In Aleyna's opinion, they had been too ignorant to understand what they were looking at, and too afraid of losing face by admitting it. 'I go to them every week to ask they let me take the books for safekeeping,' she had complained wearily to Prim. 'They say, "No, you must wait." So I wait. When I grow tired of waiting, I go to them again this morning and I say, "I wish to take the accounts, for the safety, you understand." And what do they say to me in return, after all this time?'

Prim had said she couldn't imagine.

'They say, "Nothing to do with us, lady. Take what you want." Can you imagine it?' Aleyna Nasoul had shaken her head, as if to imply the world was full of fools. 'Are the police in England like this too, Miss Nevendon?'

Prim had been forced to admit that, in her limited experience, they were. Which was why she had been disinclined to mention the books either to the officers who'd arrived in response to their distress call or to the nice captain who'd conducted this morning's interview. In Prim's experience, the more you stuck to telling policemen only what they needed to hear, the better it was for you. Now, picking up one of the books that Aleyna had entrusted to her – a slim volume, paisley-print cardboard cover – she began to leaf through the pages.

She quickly saw the police had been right to disregard the contents. They were prosaic, much as she had expected: payments for actors and tradesmen; wages for backstage crew; expenses… all written in Moussa Bannoudi's neat, educated hand. Nothing out of the ordinary.

In the book labelled 'Receipts' she could read for herself the tribulations of the Nimrod Theatre. Long before the bloodbath had closed it, the venue had been struggling. Prim couldn't find a single performance that had sold out. She dreaded to think what it had been costing her father to keep Uncle Nim's dream alive.

Concluding that he hadn't been stealing money from his own theatre company, Prim put the books back in the bag. She then turned her attention to the Villa Narcisse's visitors' book, which she had taken from beside the telephone in the hallway barely twenty minutes ago. 'The police have inspected it thoroughly, Mademoiselle,' Madame Sauvier had insisted, regarding the book very much as a document of state, and its secrets not to be revealed to all and sundry. But Prim had taken it anyway.

She began to leaf through the pages. The names meant little or nothing to her. Some had titles helpfully appended for the official record: ministers of the Egyptian government; senior officers from the British garrison; visiting luminaries from the oil industry. The women listed appeared to be wives, girlfriends or mistresses. She went back six months, imagining the dinner parties her father had hosted, hearing him regale his guests with those wittily trenchant views of his, always the lynchpin of the evening, standing to make a particular point, stocky, commanding, captivating, as compelling as Oswald Mosley, only without the uniform and the racial bigotry. *The old aristocratic orders of entrenched privilege are finished; the future lies in the hands of the technical men; look at Germany: if they can wean themselves off their irrational hatred of the Jews, then before my time is done they'll be sending rockets to the moon, you mark my words; they've already set up a German Society for Space Travel…* That, she remembered with a smile, had always been her father's contradiction: a man who loved nothing more than digging up the ancient past, yet who couldn't stop his imagination carrying him into the future.

The only reason the name *Hermione* jumped out at her from the visitors' book was because Prim had designed the set for a production of *The Winter's Tale* that had won her a few plaudits. Making the statue of a supposedly dead queen come to life had been a bit of a challenge, especially with a difficult director and a very tight budget. She stopped the page in mid-flick and smoothed it flat, keeping her eyes fixed on the entry:

23rd May 1937. Seven p.m.

A supper party then, judging by the time. Prim noted the guests: several Egyptian gentlemen and their wives invited, including Mr Gamil and Mr el-Madani from Anglo-Levantine Oil, a British colonel from the garrison at Abbassia and his lady wife…

And *Hermione.*

No surname. No partner recorded. Just Hermione. And entered not in her own hand, but in Archie's. Hermione – a dead statue suddenly come to life.

Prim set down the book, went to the door, opened it and called out, her voice echoing forlornly off the villa walls, 'Madame Sauvier, can you spare me a moment, please?'

At first there was no response, but after a minute or two the housekeeper appeared, her brogues clacking on the tiles.

'Does a "Hermione" ring any bells with you, Madame Sauvier?' Prim enquired pleasantly. 'A friend of my father perhaps?' Even as *friend* left her lips, she was already thinking: more likely a mistress, or a dancer from one of the cabarets.

'We have many guests at the Villa Narcisse,' Madame Sauvier said, in the sort of tone you'd receive at Fortnum's if you told the sales assistant you were after a jemmy for house-breaking.

'And can you recall a Hermione amongst them? It would have been last year, towards the end of May.'

'Without a surname, I regret I am unable to help, Mademoiselle Nevendon. I like to maintain a proper formality with the guests. It is appropriate, yes?'

'Do you keep the place settings?'

The temperature of Madame Sauvier's severity dropped a degree or two. 'We do not.'

'Did my father ever have female company to dinner, Madame Sauvier?'

'*Je suis désolée,*' said the housekeeper majestically, to indicate that the well of her cooperation had run dry.

'Me too,' Prim replied. 'Very *désolée* indeed. If you should happen to recall anyone—'

When Madame Sauvier had gone, Prim closed the door and returned to her father's desk. The entry in the visitors' book remained an irritant to her thoughts, like a midge that's flown into her ear. *Hermione – the statue that comes to life...* Why hadn't Archie added a surname? Why did Hermione have to be invisible, hidden amongst all the other perfectly ordinary names? Was it even a name? Maybe it was a cipher for something else entirely, or a prompt to aid her father's memory. Maybe someone had brought their pet with them. Maybe Hermione was a poodle.

There was no plan to what Prim did next. Or at least if there was – if her mind had made the connection – she was unaware of it. Her intent had been only to keep on searching for something in Archie's closed world that she might have missed. She opened the bottom drawer of his desk and withdrew the stack of theatre programmes she'd discovered the day before. Some of them bore the title of the Karnak Theatre and dated to the Great War: *Arms and the Man* by Shaw; a touring version of *Razzle Dazzle* that had played at the Theatre Royal in London... Then there were more contemporary productions, this time under the Nimrod banner: *Murder in the Cathedral* and Noël Coward's *Private Lives*.

And, of course, Shakespeare.

Somehow Prim already knew she would find a programme for *The Winter's Tale* amongst the collection. It was tucked under one for *The Merchant of Venice*. Pulling it out, she studied the image on the cover: a stylized statue of a Greek goddess, complete with flowing white gown and a diadem. In small print at the bottom was the play's run: 15th April until 28th May 1937.

The date in the visitors' book fitted.

Prim's heart began to pound. Flicking past the testament to Nimrod Nevendon on the inside cover, she went straight to the cast list. Running her finger down the column, she consigned to oblivion: *Leontes, King of Sicilia; Mamillius, a young prince; four lords of Sicilia; a mariner; a jailer...*

And there she was: *Hermione, Queen to Leontes.*

Prim looked across to the name of the actress playing the role. Ifaya Jabour.

Turning hurriedly to the cast's biographies, she came across a portrait photograph of the actress, done in chiaroscuro for dramatic effect. A striking young woman, perhaps a few years older than Prim herself. Clearly Middle Eastern, eyes large and deep-set, bone structure to die for, the sort of face to grab an audience by the scruff of its neck and demand of it three hours' rapt attention, with a twenty-minute interval that couldn't go by fast enough. But an amiable face nonetheless – not a trace of your Marlene Dietrich cut-crystal coldness in sight. Reading the brief text below, Prim learned that:

After studying the dramatic arts at the American University at Cairo and training with the Rameses Theatre Troupe under the guidance of Mr Youssef Wahbi, Miss Jabour has performed roles in both the Egyptian and Western traditions. This is her debut season with the Nimrod Theatre Company.

'Hermione-Ifaya, I've got you,' she murmured to herself. 'Welcome aboard. I'm Primrose – Prim to my friends. Did Archie speak kindly of me? Did he speak of me at all?'

What had she been hoping for? Prim wondered. A matriarch with a face and a body that screamed *happily married with forty grandchildren?* A bitter spinster who'd taken a lifetime vow of abstinence? How about *anyone* but a bewitching young woman guaranteed to attract the attention of a fifty-three-year-old theatre patron with the power to give her employment?

But then she thought of her affair with Harold Armitage back in England. He'd been twenty years her senior – about the same age gap – and she'd never once felt exploited. Indeed, she'd been able to wrap him around her little finger. 'Hypocrite,' she murmured.

Laying aside the programme, Prim returned to the accounts with renewed interest. Now she had something specific to look for. *Someone* specific.

Leafing through the book for 1937, she quickly found the listing for *The Winter's Tale.* To her relief, she saw that the actors had been paid directly; it seemed that Egypt had so far avoided the plague of theatrical agents. It took her only seconds to spot the weekly payments to Ifaya Jabour. Then, taking the other productions in chronological order, she followed the actress's employment with the Nimrod Theatre all the way to *A Midsummer Night's Dream.* And there the payments ceased – just a fortnight before the attack and the theatre's subsequent closure.

Had the young woman been taken ill? Had she been fired? Or was her absence due to something else entirely, something that might also explain Archie's disappearance? Out of nowhere Prim heard Celestina's voice in her head: *Your father is like bad clay. Too many impurities. Too many voids. Nothing good will ever be made of it.*

She returned the accounts books to the bag. She'd seen enough to understand that Ifaya Jabour would be her key to unlocking the mystery of Archie's disappearance. But merely taking these first tentative steps onto the path had exhausted her. Deciding that sunlight was a better aid to contemplation than the frowsty shadows of the study, she was about to drop the bag into the bottom drawer of the desk when she noticed something lying under Uncle Nim's army paybook. She hadn't registered its presence yesterday because she'd been too fascinated by this curio from her family's past. She placed the bag back on the desk, reached into the drawer and pulled out what she saw was another book, much like the ones she had only a moment ago finished inspecting: marble-effect cardboard cover, cloth spine, a slim volume. Too slim to be a diary. Maybe too slim to be anything other than a forgotten notebook half-full of meaningless jottings.

Opening the book, Prim read: *Nimrod – Monies to Bank.* Beneath was a telephone number prefixed with the word *Ezbekia,* denoting the local exchange. On the following pages were columns of figures, each line with a date attached.

Why wasn't this little book in with the others – the ones Aleyna Nasoul had taken from Moussa Bannoudi's office drawer? Was Archie keeping a second set of accounts?

Flicking through the pages, Prim saw that the entries stretched back about two years. The amounts were shown in Egyptian pounds: so much per week. Two years; one hundred and four entries, if they were all recorded. At first the figures meant little to her, but Prim prided herself on her mental arithmetic – and on her familiarity with theatres that were hard pressed to keep the lights on and the shows running. Somehow these figures just didn't look right.

Picking a single month at random, she ran a few mental calculations using the exchange rate that Cook's had quoted her when she'd bought her traveller's cheques in London. The results proved her suspicions. In order to make the amounts Archie was depositing each month, the little Nimrod Theatre would have had to be full every night, and every seat in the house priced at the going rate for the royal box.

'Oh, Archie,' she whispered, imagining him standing in front of the desk watching her, the way he sometimes did when she was young and sitting at her colouring book, 'what on earth have you been up to?'

Anglo-Levantine Oil had thoughtfully provided their Cairo director with a private line to his study. Beside the telephone lay Archie's personal phone book, its plump leather cover inscribed with his gilded initials. Prim felt like an intruder as she began to trawl through the entries.

Archie's business and social circles were extensive, but it didn't take her more than a few minutes to find the Ezbekia number she'd seen in the notebook. With a growing feeling of trepidation, she called the operator and asked to be connected to the Nabil-Magdy Bank. It took longer to be put through to the manager, but eventually she found herself in conversation with a softly spoken Egyptian who told her very politely but regretfully that there would be no point whatsoever in coming to discuss her father's account with him – the bank, sadly, had not been favoured by any such gentleman. They held no account for a Mr Archibald Nevendon. Or for the Nimrod Theatre.

Ending the call, Prim cupped her chin in her hands and stared around the room. She peered into the shadows cast on the walls from the shuttered windows, sensing they might hold an answer for her, though she knew now that it wouldn't be a good one. Then she sought out the intervening bright strips of sunlight, as if they were beams from a torch that would help her to see the path ahead and avoid whatever was lurking there. Whose money had Archie been paying into the bank? – because, by any measure, it couldn't all come from the Nimrod. And where was it going, if the bank manager had no record of any account linked to Archie or the theatre?

The ringing of the telephone in the hall jolted Prim out of her reverie. Hearing Madame Sauvier answer the call, she slipped the little accounts book back into the desk. Then she placed the theatre programmes on top and quickly closed the drawer. Her heart was thumping as if she herself were guilty of a crime, complicit in a robbery – or worse. A moment later she heard the click-clacking of Madame Sauvier's brogues in the corridor, followed by a rap on the study door. It made her think of a prison warder approaching a cell.

'Mademoiselle, it is Mr Taverner calling, from the embassy.'

'Tell him I'll be right out, Madame Sauvier. Thank you.'

When Prim reached the hall and raised the handset to her ear, Harry's voice, though tinny, was exactly what she needed to hear, calm and reassuring.

'Just calling to see how you are, after yesterday's little shock. Bearing up all right? Anything I can do?' His consideration alone raised her spirits. There was no one else in Cairo she knew with a shoulder to lean on, apart from Michael Luzzatto, and he was the sort of fellow who'd assume she was besotted, rather than in need of wise counsel. So yes, she decided, there was a lot that Harry Taverner could do. Smiling for what felt like the first time since she'd arrived, she said, 'You know that drink you suggested – at the Cleopatra Club? If the British Council allows you out, how does tonight suit you? I think it's time I let my hair down a little.'

Wedged incongruously between the native feluccas and barges, the Cleopatra Club was a large houseboat moored beside the Nile's eastern bank just below the Semiramis Hotel. Save for the name, it was as un-Egyptian as Prim could imagine. It looked more like a Mississippi paddle-steamer that had made a serious navigational error. The superstructure was painted a gleaming white and had promenades around each deck, festooned with lanterns as if ready for a fleet review.

It's quite relaxed, Harry Taverner had told her on the phone when he'd first suggested it, before that awful episode at the Nimrod. But as soon as Tarek dropped her off, and before she'd even set foot on the gangplank where a liveried flunky waited to welcome her aboard, Prim could see he'd been misled. Shimmering gowns and tailored lounge suits made their slow perambulations around the promenades in the warm night air. From somewhere inside came the sound of a dance band doing a fair tribute to Benny Goodman. This was Savoy level, she reckoned, or the Pierre in New York, only with palm trees on the street outside. And she'd come dressed for a summer garden party in Eastbourne.

Harry was waiting for her on the deck. 'I'm glad you could make it,' he said as they shook hands.

'I thought this was going to be casual.'

'So did I. Apparently this is what passes for casual in Cairo – if you're amongst the right set.'

'Are we the *right* set?' she asked, thinking of the squalor of the lanes that Tarek had driven her through yesterday.

'As long as Farouk and his government choose not to kick us out, I'm told we are. Better enjoy it while it lasts. The British Council is paying.'

'How very generous of them.'

He lifted one hand to shield the side of his mouth, as if to ensure only she could hear him. 'You can thank Mr Chamberlain's government. When it comes to what's important, the good-time budget is the bit that never gets slashed. Without a decent expenses budget at the Foreign Office, the Empire would collapse overnight.'

'Then we should make the best of it while it lasts,' Prim said, enjoying his invitation to conspiracy.

'What shall we celebrate?'

'My first day in Cairo without incident – if you discount an hour at the police headquarters giving my statement to a very nice Egyptian police captain.'

'Then here's to many more ordinary days.'

She looped her arm through his. 'That's a sentiment I can drink to. Lead on.'

A flight of carpeted stairs took them down into the club, a tourist's impression of the palace from *One Thousand and One Nights*, all plush drapes and lanterns, gilded armchairs, sofas to sink into and waiters done up as Sinbad the Sailor. In one corner was a bar where the lights turned the spirit bottles into jewels. There were fewer people down here, the dance floor all but empty, save for a few couples. But they were as smart as those up on the promenade decks. Prim guessed it was a little early for Cairo's nightlife to get going.

'I could murder a Sidecar,' she said when Harry asked her what she'd prefer, and bit her lip at her choice of the word *murder*.

The barman, in a sequined bolero jacket and tarboosh, mixed their cocktails with the rapt attention of Toscanini conducting a Mahler symphony. They drank and danced a little, then Harry asked if she was hungry. 'I could eat a crocodile,' Prim said.

'Hold my jacket,' he replied. 'I'll dive in and wrestle a couple for you to choose from.'

They climbed up to the top deck and the open-air restaurant, with starched linen and silver cutlery. Waiters in tunics stood at the corners like guardsmen at the funeral of George V, and just as expressionless. The restaurant was almost empty, only three other couples eating, so they got a table at the side where they could look out over the Nile. The night had a faint sheen of warm mist to it, and at any other time she'd have had no objection if the mood turned romantic. Harry was a good-looking boy in his very English way, but she knew there was a falsity between them right from the start, if only because they were trying so hard to skirt around the events of the previous day. Harry called over one of the uniformed waiters and they ordered *sayadiyah* fish for her, pigeon for him. And a bottle of Meursault – he was happy with the white if she was.

'I'm not sure I can take the tranquillity,' she said.

'Really?'

'My second full day in Cairo and I've not yet had a gun pointed at me, and no one I have a connection to has been killed,' she went on with a bright smile. 'Isn't that lovely?'

He raised a finger to his lips in warning. 'Shush! There might be a plague of frogs along in a minute.'

'Or the boat could sink,' she said in faux-alarm.

'Look, I've offered to wrestle crocodiles. I draw the line at being expected to tow this thing onto a sandbank with my teeth clamped on a rope. I'm not Popeye, you know.'

She laughed. 'Just Harry Taverner from the British Council, who turned up at my father's theatre yesterday like a knight in shining armour.'

He held her gaze, giving nothing away. Then he said, 'Would you object if I were to – how shall I put this – get a few things off my chest?'

'I suppose it would depend on what those things were.'

'I'm going to have to admit that I haven't been strictly candid with you.'

Strange, she thought, the way you can know something without ever having really formed its essence in your mind. Harry Taverner had always seemed to her more than simply the sum of his pleasing parts. 'It's funny you should say that, Harry,' she said, in a tone designed to tell him she'd known it all along, 'as I've had my suspicions.'

'Oh. For how long?'

'Since we boarded the *Celaeno* together. Let's call it a feeling. You – appearing out of nowhere. Simply happening to have a ticket for Cairo. The British Council's theatre man who doesn't know much about the theatre.' She held his gaze and found she was rather enjoying putting him on the spot. 'Are you one of those engaging international confidence-tricksters? You know: from the movies, the type who charm vulnerable women and steal their inheritances? If you are, I'm afraid you've picked the wrong gal. I'm almost broke. If it wasn't for my paternal grandmother, I'd probably still be at home.'

He laughed at that, and she found it oddly reassuring. 'Nothing so mysterious, I'm afraid.'

'Then I'm all ears.'

There was no bravado in the way he placed his elbows on the table and steepled his fingers, regarding her over the tips.

His confession, it seemed, required a penitent's humility. 'First of all, I need to make it clear that I'm not actually attached to the British Council.'

'What a surprise,' she said, favouring him with a tilt of her mouth that wasn't quite a smile. 'So who exactly *are* you "attached" to?'

'Well, here's the thing, you see. I'm not really at liberty to tell. Shall we simply say I work for the government and leave it at that?'

'You're a *spy*. How exciting.'

He laughed again, this time as if it were the most ridiculous of suggestions. 'As you yourself said yesterday, nothing so grand.'

'Then how did you know I was coming to Cairo? I told no one except Celestina and Granny Grace – Archie's mother.'

'Special Branch were watching you. They followed you to London, saw you going into the Imperial Airways office.'

Prim rolled her eyes. 'Mother said those two Keystone Cops who came to Bevern weren't local.' Then, making a play of studying Harry's face, she added, 'Mind you, you don't look like my idea of a spy. I've always imagined spies as being weasel-faced little men in raincoats and trilbies – like the sort of fellows who lurk outside hotel bedroom doors, ready to catch adulterers at their indiscretions.'

'You're thinking of private investigators and newspaper reporters.'

She studied him again in the light cast from the nearby lantern, where insects of alarming size thrashed ecstatically, but fatally, against the glass. She was enjoying how much her inspection was making Harry squirm. Then she relented and said, 'I'm guessing we're here because of my father, not because you thought a girl who'd had a shock or two needed a tonic.'

'I know that he's missing, yes.'

'And you've been sent to find out if I know where he is. Is that it?'

'The answer to that question would calm a lot of nerves in London,' he replied.

'Why?'

Again the penitent's smile, inviting her forgiveness. 'That's also something I'm not really at liberty to say.'

'Daddy's just an employee of Anglo-Levantine Oil. I can't imagine he knows any state secrets.'

'London seems to think he might know enough to be of help to our enemies,' Harry went on. 'A lot of people think a war is coming. And your family, if I may say so, has a history of what my superiors would consider misplaced loyalties.'

So there it was. The ghost at the feast, destined to haunt her for the rest of her days. Prim's jaw stiffened. 'Why don't you simply come out and say it?' she asked, staring at him over the top of her wine glass as if she was taking aim. 'You won't offend me; I'm quite used to it. Fascist sympathizers – isn't that what you mean? Fifth columnists. Friends of Adolf Hitler. That's the sort of thing we get scrawled on our gateposts at Bevern Lodge all the time. Just because Mummy's papa was a supporter of Mussolini, Archie once wrote a few articles in the *Daily Mail* in support of Germany and we take foreigners at the Fraternity.' She looked out over the blackness of the river, as if searching for the last scrap of reason in a world that was fast losing its judgement. 'What do they think we do there – send Morse-code messages to the Reich Chancellery in Berlin about the state of the defences of East Grinstead?'

He let her attempt at bitter humour die in silence. Then he said, almost casually, 'Tell me, Miss Nevendon, how long have you been a member of the British Union of Fascists?'

Eleven

There are some people, Prim Nevendon believed, who thirst for an apology the way an addict craves a hit. She'd met a few in her time: individuals for whom one *sorry* was never enough. There had been the boyfriend who couldn't forgive her for criticizing Stalin in front of his friends at a workshop run by the Workers' Theatre Movement, and who had insisted on contrition every time they met afterwards, until she finally decided his surly hero-of-the-proletariat good looks weren't worth debasing herself for. Long before him there had been the scriptures teacher, demanding that she apologize to God – not once, but every time she attended Sunday school – for her lack of faith. As she held Harry Taverner's gaze across the table at the Cleopatra Club and waited for the anger in her to subside, she earnestly hoped he wasn't one of them. Because, quite frankly, of all the wrong turns she'd taken in her life so far, she'd had enough of apologizing for that one. Taking a slow breath to steady herself, she replied, 'I can't tell you how many times I've told a policeman that I'm *not* a member any longer.'

'But you were, once,' he suggested gently, as if it might have slipped her mind.

'I was eighteen. It lasted a matter of months. I walked away.'

'Why did you join in the first place?'

She made a play of considering her motives. 'Oh, let's think now. How about wanting a better world? How about not believing that Bolshevism is the answer to all our ills? Maybe I just did what a lot of people in England have done, especially those in my parents' circle, though they won't admit it now: I fell for a line.'

'That's easily done,' Harry said lightly.

'I was young. The movement was all about sweeping away the old, replacing it with the new, being done with the inefficient and corrupt. It seemed to offer an exciting vision of the future,' she went on in well-rehearsed tones, because she'd made the same explanation to Special Branch on more than one occasion. 'No more society riven by class and privilege, but a system that works – one based on strength of character and body. A system that gets things done, that isn't afraid to change things. That's appealing to a young mind. We were still coming out of the Depression; we had politicians interested in nothing but their own positions and power. We looked across to Germany and saw a movement that wasn't content to let the old ways choke the nation into irrelevance. Most of my friends and colleagues looked to communism for the answer. A few looked elsewhere. More than a few in fact – though they've mostly scuttled under the nearest log by now.'

Harry leaned back in his seat, an ironic smile on his lips. 'I've worked in Berlin and Vienna, Prim,' he said. 'I've seen the Nazi Party at first hand. It's ugly. Very, very ugly.'

'Yes, well, we all know that now, don't we?' she answered, refusing to meet his gaze.

'I've seen the Jews being beaten up in the streets,' he went on, 'people arrested and imprisoned, the show trials. It's brutal, soulless and inhuman. If that's the future, it isn't one that any decent person with a conscience would want to have anything to do with. It's government by gangsters in smart uniforms.'

'Do you think I don't know that now?' Prim replied vehemently. 'Do you think I don't read the newspapers? That's why I left Mosley's party, for God's sake. That and all the silly salutes and the strutting.' She studied Harry Taverner's face to see if her salvoes were finding their target. But he gave her no hint, reclining in his seat with a face that was unreadable. 'Look,' she went on, 'at the Bevern Fraternity we even have a young Jewish girl called Gertrude Bernbaum. She's an artist, a bloody good one. She's a refugee from Stuttgart. We all love her. Do you think my mother would have taken her in if we were the sort of people you've just described? There – I've bared my soul. What else do you want me to say? I was young and impressionable. I made a mistake. That's it.'

Without speaking Harry let her climb down from whatever parapet she was teetering on. Then he said, 'I'm glad we cleared *that* up' and poured her more wine. 'Now, let's get down to practicalities.'

She had nothing left to give him. So, exhausted, Prim let him order her life for the foreseeable future.

Travelling without a bodyguard, he informed her, would from now on be out of the question. He couldn't provide her with armed police constables, because he'd been told that resources were overstretched. But three privates and a corporal from the Military Police at Abbassia barracks were already on their way to the Villa Narcisse. She was not to venture out without at least one of them in attendance, preferably two.

'Why do you think I need all this protection?' she asked when he'd finished. 'It sounds like house-arrest to me. And I don't care for it.'

Like a doctor telling his patient the tests had turned out worse than he'd hoped, Harry said in a regretful tone, 'I'm afraid the police say Moussa Bannoudi was tortured before he was shot. Somebody was trying to make him talk, presumably about your father's whereabouts. Which means—'

But Prim's mind had skipped ahead of him. 'Oh God! *Me?* Why would anyone think I could tell them where he is?'

'Because you're here in Cairo. It's as simple as that.' He refilled her wine glass. She half-expected him – still in his doctor-at-your-bedside guise – to lift it to her lips and tell her she'd feel much better if she were just to take a sip or two. 'Right now, my prime desire is to keep you safe,' he said.

'Do I have any say in all this?'

'You're a private citizen. We can't compel you to do anything,' he continued. He looked too solicitous for his profession, she thought, but perhaps they taught you that at spy school. 'But we can't let you remain at risk from the same people who went to work on the unfortunate Mr Bannoudi, can we? So we'd ask the Egyptians to expel you – for your own protection, of course.'

That left her speechless. She finished her wine. 'Looks as though you have me over a barrel, Harry Taverner,' she said, as much to the dregs at the bottom of the glass as to him.

'The question is, where do we start? In the search for your father, I mean. Any ideas?'

Prim at last felt as if she had a chance to take the initiative. She was about to tell him how she'd discovered the existence of Ifaya Jabour when she saw his gaze swing away to something behind her. She turned to follow it and found herself looking up at Michael Luzzatto.

'Well, what a pleasant surprise,' he said, giving her his trade-mark movie-star grin. 'Hope I'm not interrupting a romantic *tête-à-tête* or anything. Maybe you two would care to join me for a drink, down in the bar,' he went on, in that Middle Eastern American accent she had found disconcertingly melodic aboard the *Celaeno*. 'Forget His Majesty King Farouk and his ministers, I'll introduce you to one of the guys who really runs this place.'

'That would be lovely,' Prim replied, readily agreeing before Harry Taverner could continue rearranging her life. Saved by the bell, she thought.

The bar was busier now, Prim noted, the clientele a mix of prosperous-looking Egyptians and Anglos. Taking the last free bar stools, they made themselves comfortable and Luzzatto insisted on buying the first round. 'So how's British culture standing up to the heat?' he asked Harry with a grin, as the barman set the drinks down on the counter.

'With equanimity, as usual,' Harry replied. 'You know us British: we're forbidden by royal decree from perspiring in front of the natives.'

Luzzatto tilted his head. 'You're making fun of me, right, Harry?'

'Wouldn't dream of it, old boy.'

Prim raised her glass and gave them both a teacherly look. 'Now, now, boys. We're all friends here. Let's raise a toast: to Egypt. May we each find in her what we're looking for.'

They touched glasses. As if on cue, the quartet in the corner began playing 'Just Friends'.

But Mike Luzzatto wasn't ready to drop his theme. Looking at Harry over the rim of his tumbler, he said, 'You granted the Egyptians independence in 1922 and yet here you are, sixteen years later, and you still have troops garrisoned in Cairo and on the Canal. You sort of run the police. You tell the government what it can and can't do. To an American, that doesn't sound much like independence.'

Harry's laugh was designed to defuse. 'You're asking the wrong fellow, Mike,' he replied. 'I'm culture. You want the Foreign Office, or Colonial. I merely promote Gilbert and Sullivan and William Shakespeare.'

'You don't have an opinion?'

Refusing to be cornered, Harry said, 'As I see it, Egypt has its own king, its own government, political parties. We're not interfering, we're helping them find their feet.'

'Seems to be taking them an awfully long time to learn to walk,' Luzzatto responded wryly. 'What about Palestine?'

'What about it?'

'You've got the Arabs there in full revolt against you. The Jews don't care for you because you've slammed the door on immigration, and you're reneging on the Balfour Declaration. The Peel Commission that was supposed to offer a solution has been rejected by just about everybody—'

'Wouldn't it be nice if one of the gentlemen in this bar asked me to dance?' Prim interjected diplomatically.

Mike Luzzatto took the hint and was already sliding off his bar stool when the band suddenly broke off the tune they were playing. With a hurried count, they launched into Cole Porter's 'It's De-Lovely'. From the entrance to the bar came the sound of a hand clap, fractionally behind the beat. The bartender glanced that way and Prim's gaze followed.

The man who had just entered had his hands above his head, showing his appreciation for the band's choice by beating his palms together. The sound they made reminded Prim of a butcher slamming a joint down on a cutting block. She had never seen hands that big. How dangerous do your hands have to be, she wondered, for a band to stop mid-bar and start playing your favourite tune?

Surrounded by a cabal of smart young men and their languid consorts, the man made his stately way towards an empty table beside the dance floor. The men looked as though they'd given up smiling before they'd graduated out of shorts; the women – blank-eyed and draped in clinging cocktail dresses – looked as animated as stems in a vase of silk flowers.

As the group passed the bar, the man spotted Mike Luzzatto. His craggy face split into a grin. 'Mr Luzzatto, sir, what a pleasure it is to see you here,' he called out in a deep voice that almost drowned out the musicians. 'Let me buy you a drink. What say you and I talk a little more business?'

Luzzatto stepped away from his stool and allowed himself to be enveloped in a bear-hug. It was the sort of clinch, thought Prim, that would crush anyone not wearing a bulletproof vest.

'I guess I'm with friends,' Luzzatto replied, drawing breath as the bear released him.

'You have friends? This I must see!' said the man with a brief barrage of laughter. 'Bring them over. I insist.'

A snap of the huge fingers, a sudden scurrying from the bar staff, and before she knew it, Prim was sitting at the table while one of the smooth young men filled her flute from a vast ice bucket that contained enough champagne bottles to keep the Royal Enclosure content on Cup Day at Ascot.

Shakir Hamad was a bald bruiser of fifty in an imported Savile Row suit. He had the polished manners of an English aristocrat and a neck that looked to Prim as if it had been cut from a Dunlop tyre. He was one of Cairo's leading property entrepreneurs, or so Michael Luzzatto assured her as they all shook hands uncomfortably across the ice bucket. Prim didn't need to stretch her imagination far to believe he was a gangster.

'And what brings you to our ancient and beautiful city, Miss Nevendon?' Hamad asked in a voice that made Prim wonder if his larynx hadn't been sandblasted at some point in its development.

'My father owns a theatre here.'

'Oh, you are *that* Nevendon?'

'You know of him?' Prim asked, unsure whether that would be a benefit or a peril.

'Of course. I read in the newspaper that he has disappeared. Have you come to find him?'

Prim had never given thought to the possibility that Archie's vanishing might be news. On reflection, it seemed obvious. She glanced at Harry, but he was wearing his impenetrable sun-never-sets-on-the-Empire face, as if he were a bronze statue, a viceroy mounted on his charger staring fixedly out over his dominions.

'It seemed the right thing to do,' she said. 'Better that I'm here rather than in England.'

Hamad laid one huge hand on his breast, as if to make a pledge to the death. 'If you need help, young lady, then I stand ready. I have many contacts. I know a lot of people. You need some doors opened, Shakir Hamad can kick them in for you.'

'That's very kind of you,' Prim assured him, 'but hopefully there won't be any kicking required.'

Hamad seemed to find this uproariously funny. 'Ah, I admire much the English and their wit! I like very much your Max Miller – the Cheeky Chappie. That is Hamad, yes? – a very cheeky chappie!' When his mirth at his own unlikely description of himself had subsided and his vast shoulders had stopped shaking, he asked, 'And what do you think of our new Egypt, Miss Nevendon? Is much improved now we have shown the English who is the boss, yes?' He looked at Harry. 'No offence, Mr Taverner.'

'None taken,' Harry replied.

'I haven't had much of a chance to look around yet,' Prim said lamely.

'You need a guide, call me.' It sounded more like a command than an offer of assistance. Hamad took a business card from his breast pocket and handed it to her. She noticed the manicured fingernails and the gold rings the size of knuckledusters. 'I know the right people,' he went on. 'The others – all thieves. Steal your shirt off your back without you even noticing.'

'I'll bear that in mind, Mr Hamad.'

'Mr Hamad was born in a poor village and now he lives in the same neighbourhood as princes,' said Luzzatto, as proudly as if he'd achieved the rise himself.

'Not bad for a penniless Lebanese boy, eh?' Hamad crowed.

'Oh, I assumed you were Egyptian, Mr Hamad,' Harry said.

'No. I am from Beirut. Maronite Catholic. Only I don't make the confession,' Hamad explained mischievously, showing teeth almost as perfect as Michael Luzzatto's. 'No point in making the confession – too busy making money. Maybe you English should take a lesson from that, eh?'

'I'm sure we could benefit from the advice, Mr Hamad,' Harry said, employing charm to make up for a lack of conviction.

Hamad found this, too, immensely entertaining. He ordered one of his slick young men to refill Prim's champagne flute. Before she knew it, she was what Celestina always referred to as 'dancing a foxtrot with the fairies'. Not drunk exactly – the company was too unnerving for that. But fortified, reinforced by the determination that Harry Taverner, and whoever he represented, wasn't going to call all the shots tonight. She fell silent for a while, letting Hamad play to his audience, which was clearly what he liked doing. The young men around the table responded to his every word with the over-bright enthusiasm of the quietly terrified. Mike Luzzatto, she noticed, was the only one apart from Harry who maintained an inexpressive independence.

It was midnight when Prim rose from her seat. 'Please don't think I'm being rude, Mr Hamad, but I've had a long day and I think it's time I was going.'

At first, Hamad would have none of it. The Opera Casino was waiting. How would his luck at the *Chemin de fer* table hold up without her beside him? But when she insisted, he acquiesced with grace, which surprised her because he didn't seem the sort of man to take refusal well. 'I trust we will meet again, Miss Nevendon,' he said. Then he took her hand and kissed it. It felt to Prim as if he was testing the flesh to see if it would tear easily.

Out on the promenade deck the night was hazy with the light from the street lamps along the bank and the lighted windows of the Semiramis Hotel.

'I think I should come with you to the villa,' Harry said, 'just to be on the safe side – till the boys from Abbassia barracks turn up tomorrow morning.'

'I'm a big girl, Harry. I don't need a chaperone.'

'It would be best. I'll sleep on the sofa.'

'I don't think so. I've got Tarek to look after me,' she replied, pointing to where the green Citroën was parked fifty yards away beneath an acacia tree. She waved and the car's headlamps came on.

'You've seen what these people did to Moussa Bannoudi,' Harry said, his voice suddenly a little plaintive. 'Your driver won't be able to protect you.'

'Maybe I should ask our friend Shakir Hamad,' she said, only half-jokingly. 'Protection is probably right up his street.'

'Look, I'd really feel happier—'

But Prim had had enough. 'You've lied to me from the moment we met, Harry Taverner. And tonight you accused me of being a fascist. I can do without dates like that.'

'That's not strictly true and you know it. Besides, I never said it was a date.'

'Oh, so now I'm not even date material. Thanks for nothing.'

Harry shook his head in defeat. 'That's not what I meant at all.'

But Prim wasn't ready to let him off the hook. 'You can thank the Secret Service – or whoever it is employs you – for that meal,' she said. 'But right now I'm tired and I'm going to bed. Goodnight.' And with that, she set off down the gangplank doing her level best not to flounce.

'Prim, be reasonable,' Harry called after her. 'Cairo's not safe for you.'

Reaching the shore, Prim acknowledged the salute of the doorman in his little makeshift booth. The Citroën pulled away from beneath the trees. When it drew level with her, Tarek brought it to a halt, leaned across and opened the rear passenger door for her. Turning her head, she saw Harry illuminated by the Cleopatra's lanterns. 'I don't need your bloody protection,' she shouted, 'and you're not travelling in my car. I thought you were a friend, Harry Taverner. I'll take that as a lesson about how wrong a girl can be.' Then, settling back into the seat, she unstrapped her shoes and threw them angrily into the footwell. 'Home, please, Tarek,' she said. 'And don't spare the camels.'

The first two taxi drivers Harry Taverner approached spoke no English. By the time he found one who did, the green Citroën was almost out of sight. 'Follow that car,' he ordered, feeling like the hero from a bad Saturday matinée B-movie.

Pulling away from the Nile, they skirted the Garden City area and crossed the broad Shari Qasr el Aini boulevard. The traffic was still heavy, but the trams had long since stopped running, so the driver kept his foot down. In the short time he'd been in Cairo, Harry had got to know the streets immediately around the embassy, which was not far away. He had done this not solely out of curiosity, but for the purposes of counter-surveillance, a habit he could not shake after his time in Vienna and Berlin. But as they entered the El Insha district he began to lose his bearings. Leaning over the dashboard, he could just about manage to keep the Citroën in view through the dusty windscreen.

He glanced at the cab driver. The man looked like a sleep-walker, eyes fixed on a spot far ahead, but otherwise unrespon-sive. Soon the street lights began to thin out and they were in lanes where ramshackle buildings of the old Khedive Cairo replaced the modern ones, decaying stucco towers with balconies straight out of *One Thousand and One Nights* and lofty mina-rets that pierced the night like daggers. Harry's intention was simple: he'd follow the Citroën until he was sure Prim Nevendon had reached her destination safely. Then he'd head back to the embassy, get the office revolver from the armoury safe and return to the Villa Narcisse to keep guard on the place until the soldiers arrived at dawn. He wasn't concerned she might spot him fol-lowing her; she'd probably already guessed what he was doing.

But if he was honest with himself, he was rather enjoying being back in the field, and after Berlin and Vienna it was a pleasure not having to worry a damn about counter-surveillance.

Now the street lamps had ended. The only illumination came from the windows they passed, flicking on and off like light bulbs strung on a faulty circuit. They gave Harry fleeting glimpses of peeling plaster and latticed shutters, piles of rubbish, blackened doorways gaping like open tombs. It was becoming harder to keep the Citroën in view. He told the driver to close in. The motor revved, the buildings lurched towards the side-window and for a moment Harry though they were about to be dashed to a pulp.

Speeding through a pool of light at a crossroads, a car with no lights on came out of nowhere. Through the shriek of brakes, Harry heard the voice of the sentry outside the embassy from the day before: *Silly buggers. Street lights, see – so in their minds, there's no point in putting their own lights on. If they drive into a wall, it's God's will anyway...* He braced himself for the impact. But tonight it seemed that God's will was tending towards the merciful. The other car swung into the narrow space ahead of the taxi, the driver oblivious to the near-disaster he had almost caused. Harry had time to register the absence of brake lights as well as headlamps.

By now they were only two vehicles behind the Citroën. Harry caught glimpses of the housing for its spare wheel, and the sloping rear window, in the lights from the car immediately behind. He thought he saw Prim's head turn towards him above the rim of the rear passenger seat, but then they were into another unlit space and his taxi driver had to slam on the brakes as the blacked-out car ahead slowed suddenly. Harry put his hands out to stop himself from striking the glass. He swore under his breath, but beside him the cabby's sleepwalker expression never changed.

And then they were out into a brightly lit street, bumping over tramlines. Harry could see now that the blacked-out car ahead was a battered dark-blue Hillman. Beyond it was the car that been directly behind the green Citroën. He peered forward for another glimpse of Prim Nevendon. But the Citroën was nowhere to be seen. The taxi driver slowed almost to a halt, awaiting instructions. On either side the street was empty of traffic, save for the Hillman disappearing to Harry's left – and, on his right, one unladen donkey cart in the far distance, making its leisurely way to only God knew where beneath the skein of overhead electric-tram wires.

Twelve

Nim, old boy – meet Ifaya. Ifaya, alias Hermione.

Clever trick for a dull old fellow like me, don't you agree? – using a pseudonym to hide her away from prying eyes. Of course I only did that to protect her.

Beautiful, isn't she? She's the answer to all those friendly arguments we would have over what the Old Man used to say. You remember? – about Nevendon boys having no use for nonsense like love. Love was nothing but sentimentality. We never thought to ask him what Mother might have to say about that. Then we went off to war, scared stiff we'd die before we ever got the chance to prove him wrong. You tried to find it by writing soppy letters to that girl back in England. I searched for it in the knocking shops of Cairo. Neither of us found it. You never got the chance, and I was looking in the wrong place.

I can't blame Celestina. She tried her best. But when you died in that hospital bed from the wounds the Turks and my carelessness inflicted on you, all my capacity for that emotion died with you. Or so I thought.

Sitting here in the valley, counting down the days and the minutes, taking the time to look back at what went wrong, I've come to realize that Prim is the child I should have had with Ifaya. I know that now. But that's the catch to living a life: nothing ever happens in the right bloody order. What is it Shakespeare calls it? – you ought to know. 'This strange eventful history', isn't that it? Well, let me tell you this for free, Nim, old sport: Ifaya Jabour is the most strange and eventful thing that's happened to your big brother since the day we stepped into the lobby of the Karnak Theatre in search of a bit of shade from the sun and a morsel of cultural gratification. What she ever saw in your brother – well, I'll leave that for brighter brains than mine to fathom. But see it she did. And I wouldn't be lying here now, talking to my darling sibling, if she hadn't.

So don't be shy, Nim. Come and let me introduce you to her. You can blame me for the state's she's in.

Thirteen

If Harry Taverner had learned one thing at the chilly, monastical minor public school his parents had sent him to, it was how to ride a punch without flinching. He was grateful now for the lesson. After barely two hours' sleep he felt as if he'd gone twelve rounds with Jack Petersen at the White City.

The other skill that school had taught him – long before the Service had sent him on its 'Withstanding Forcible Interrogation' course – was how to face the spotlight when it was brutally illuminating your own worst failings. He was particularly glad of it now as he sat before Major Courtney, his eyes feeling as if they were full of glass powder, while he stirred the tea Mrs Fulready-Laycock had made before she'd discreetly withdrawn because she didn't like to see the spilling of blood.

'Dear God, Taverner,' Courtney said in a dispirited voice, 'this is quite, quite unacceptable.'

'I'm sorry, sir, but I didn't know the area. It was pitch-dark; I'm new in post; I had no backup. One minute she was there, the next – well, she *wasn't*.'

'I'm not referring to you losing the target, Taverner. I'm talking about dinner at the Cleopatra Club. Couldn't you have taken her somewhere a little less expensive?'

Harry heard himself telling Prim over dinner the night before, *Without a decent expenses budget at the Foreign Office, the Empire would collapse overnight...* 'With respect, sir, it was you who recommended the place,' he said tentatively.

'Did I?' Courtney seemed surprised. 'Oh well, in that case we'll put it down to "operational investment". That should cover it.'

Apparently exonerated from all charges, save the minor one of losing the subject he was supposed to be protecting, Harry now delivered his defence. He told Courtney how he'd instructed the taxi driver to take him to the Villa Narcisse, and how he'd waited there until it was clear Prim Nevendon wasn't planning to return any time soon. How he hadn't called Courtney at four in the morning because there was absolutely nothing anyone could do that might locate her, given the acknowledged *lack of resources*.

'The good news, sir, is that I was able to form the conviction that Miss Nevendon is not a threat to national security.'

'Well, that's a blessing.'

'According to the briefing London gave me before I came out here, her father was a friend of Oswald Mosley in the twenties. He also flirted with the Italian fascists – his ex-father-in-law was an early supporter of Mussolini. And he's made no secret of his admiration for Herr Hitler. But Primrose—' Harry quickly corrected himself, 'Miss Nevendon seems to me quite genuine in her repudiation of her father's politics. More to the point, I don't think she has any better idea of where he is than we do.'

Courtney spooned more sugar into his tea, peering down as he stirred, as if he were a mystic at his cauldron. 'The question is: did she intend to pull a neat sidestep on you or was it involuntary? Was she just along for the ride? What do we know of the driver, this Tarek Shalaby fellow?'

'I called Anglo-Levantine first thing for a full rundown,' Harry replied. 'Apparently, Mr Nevendon hired him personally about a year ago – wasn't happy with the previous chap. According to a Mr Gamil – he's Nevendon's assistant – Shalaby is unimpeachable. No police record, utterly loyal. His wages are still being paid by the company, on the presumption that Mr Nevendon will reappear at some point or a new director will be appointed in his place. I've also spoken to the housekeeper at the villa. Somewhat hard-going, but I don't think she's involved, either.'

'Then we may assume this sudden disappearing act is solely down to the artfulness of Miss Nevendon,' Courtney said, slurping his tea noisily.

'It would appear so, sir.'

'But why? What's made her bolt? You didn't make an indecent proposal to the poor gal, did you?'

Harry ignored the suggestion, putting it down to Courtney's provincial humour. 'That, sir, is a question only Miss Nevendon can answer.'

'That's not actually a denial, Taverner.'

'I was referring to her disappearance, sir. Not to my behaviour.'

Courtney set down his cup, took up a digestive biscuit, broke it in two and dunked one half in the tea. Just before it disappeared into his mouth, he continued languidly, 'I think another call to Russell Pasha is required, though I don't suppose he'll welcome it. But there again, Miss Nevendon is as new to Cairo as you are, Taverner. And a green Citroën and a young European woman can't be *that* difficult to find, even for a police force with limited resources.'

———

On her arrival they had treated her as gently as if she were a sick bird and they were the children who'd found it, making her as comfortable as they could, unsure of what they should do with her or how they should behave in her presence; almost a little frightened of her, yet wary of their own ability to cause her harm by their own carelessness. Then they had left her to sleep. But the muezzins' haunting pre-dawn calls to prayer were louder here than on her first morning in the city, and so Prim had lain curled up on the mattress they had made up for her, while Tarek's brother, whose name was Ashraf, took his family to the local mosque to observe the *fajr* prayers.

The only light came from a bare bulb in the main living area, spilling in through the bedroom door. When they'd arrived, Ashraf, roused from his sleep, had boasted to her that the apartment was the only one in the building with electricity – he'd run a cable off the pole at the corner of the street. Prim closed her eyes again, willing herself back to sleep. From the living room came the sound of Tarek snoring.

Why had she done it? What contrarian pixie had scrambled her brains in a moment of madness? How on earth was pulling a stunt like that going to help her in any way whatsoever?

Prim's sudden bouts of wilful caprice had always been legendary. Archie had praised them. Celestina had hated them. Granny Grace had called them the sign of a strong character. Because of them, teachers had labelled her 'inconsistent'. More than once they'd almost got her expelled from school. Maybe that was why the world of the theatre had attracted her so – surrounded as she was by people who, by temperament, found the stultifying consistency of ordinary life so impossible to bear. What was coming here to Cairo, or suddenly telling Tarek to switch off the car's lights and swing a hard left at the rapidly approaching crossroads, if not the living proof of it?

Or maybe it hadn't been a whim at all. Maybe she'd planned it from the moment Harry Taverner had asked her about her youthful and, thankfully, brief flirtation with the British Union of Fascists. That had been a bloody cheek. How *dare* he? Yes, maybe this had been her way of sticking up two fingers to the world that Harry Taverner represented. But what had really flipped her spring was thinking about what awaited her at the Villa Narcisse. Madame Sauvier she could just about tolerate. But four sweaty British soldiers from the Abbassia barracks on hand to lock her away like Rapunzel in her tower was more than a girl should be expected to bear.

Tarek had manoeuvred the Citroën with the skill of a Grand Prix driver, slamming on the brakes and swinging the steering wheel, turning into the darkness of the narrow lane with such force that Prim had slid into the door handle and bruised her shoulder. But the satisfaction of glancing back and seeing the taxi carrying Harry Taverner shoot past had been worth every second of terror.

She knew it was only a temporary escape. Although she had her traveller's cheques and passport in her bag, she had no illusions about the precarious position in which she'd placed herself. She knew she would eventually need Harry's help. When she'd learned a little more about Ifaya Jabour, and Archie's dubious financial dealings, she'd call him at the embassy and turn herself in, plead for assistance. Surely he'd forgive a bout of girlish rebellion.

Turn myself in.

Prim allowed herself a grin. It made her feel like the heroine of a pulp detective novel. She made pistols out of her fingers and muttered, in a Jimmy Cagney voice, *You dirty rat...*

When Ashraf and his family came back from prayers and Tarek was awake, they all sat around the kitchen table and breakfasted on a spicy stew of fava beans, tomatoes and spices, spooned into the mouth with hot fresh flatbread, all cooked on an iron stove that Prim reckoned had been forged when Victoria was a girl. She knew she was the object of much curiosity, but with a lot of smiling and Tarek's help, they managed a communication of sorts.

'What now, Miss Archie?' Tarek asked, when Prim had helped Ashraf's wife with the washing up. 'My brother says you stay all the time you want – his guest.'

'I don't want to impose, really I don't.'

'Is no problem.'

'And I don't want to get you into trouble, either – though I suppose it's a bit late for that,' she said, promising herself that she would write a letter to someone – Harry Taverner, Anglo-Levantine Oil, the police, Neville Chamberlain or the Archbishop of Canterbury, she wasn't sure who – taking full responsibility for Tarek's actions. But the simple logic in his answer lifted her spirits.

'You are Mr Archie's daughter,' he said. 'What you order me to do is order from Mr Archie himself, no?'

'No. I mean yes – if you want to put it that way. I'm certainly not going to argue.' And when she thought about it, what law had either of them broken anyway?

Even though the sun was now up, the apartment seemed in perpetual gloom. Beyond the kitchen window, almost close enough to touch, was a wall of dirty concrete. 'Where exactly are we, Tarek?'

'In Bulaq district,' he replied. 'Very easy to hide here. No one speak to police in Bulaq.'

She laughed. 'Hide? I'll stick out like a sore thumb the moment I walk out of the door.'

'We find you clothes. Make you look like Egyptian woman,' he grinned. 'Ashraf will ask his daughters.'

She shook her head, smiling at his impervious conviction that everything would be all right. 'What about the car? Isn't it a bit obvious?'

'Is not problem, Miss Archie. My brother has a workshop very near here. I will hide motorcar there.'

'Actually I was hoping you would drive me somewhere. There's someone I need to speak to – about my father.'

'Where you want to go, Miss Archie?'

Prim looked out of the window again, at the grim, grey wall beyond, and wondered if she'd simply swapped one prison for another. 'Do you remember where we dropped off Madame Nasoul, when we left the Nimrod Theatre?' she said, her back to Tarek. 'Do you think you can find it again?'

The apartment lay below the avenue de la Reine Nazli, in the shadow of the Jesuit College. While Tarek waited in the car, Prim climbed the narrow stairs to the top floor and knocked. Aleyna Nasoul greeted her warmly, but with the shared reserve of those who have seen great violence at close quarters. 'Come in, my dear, you look exhausted,' she said, stepping aside to let Prim enter. A pair of women's shoes lay close to the door and a glance told Prim that Aleyna, still clad in her plain worker's tunic, was barefoot. She stooped to remove her own shoes. 'You are finding it hard to sleep, yes?' Aleyna suggested. She patted herself on the head. 'Too many thoughts in here, that is the problem.'

'Something like that.'

'I see poor Moussa's face, even in the daytime when I am not dreaming,' Aleyna said. 'And then I begin to cry.'

Prim took her hand and squeezed it. 'In his letters, my father always spoke very highly of Mr Bannoudi. He sounded like a very decent man.' It wasn't strictly true; Archie's letters had been infrequent and not exactly exhaustive in their detail. But it seemed the right thing to say. 'Have you thought more about why anyone would want to harm him?'

Aleyna Nasoul lifted her shoulders in a shrug of bewilderment. 'I think about it often. But I cannot find the answer.'

'Do you mind if we talk? There are some things I need to ask you.'

Aleyna didn't mind at all. It would be good to talk, she said, woman-to-woman. Her husband, an assistant superintendent at the Lord Kitchener Hospital, had never really approved of her working at a theatre, although he'd had no objection to her boosting his modest government pay. This would be the first time she could really open up about what had happened at the Nimrod. Besides, welcoming Mr Nevendon's daughter into her home was a great honour, she said, regardless of the circumstances.

The little living room was a cosy haberdashery of red, yellow and gold. A bench ran along three sides, covered in bright throws and cushions to serve as a sofa. There was a Turkish carpet on the floor and mirrors in intricate frames on the walls. It reminded Prim of an unusually opulent waiting room at a railway station. Aleyna invited her to sit while she prepared coffee. It arrived rich and dark, served in little brass cups. They spoke about Moussa – Aleyna struggling to maintain her composure – about the earlier attack on the Nimrod and Archie's disappearance. Then, keeping her eyes firmly on the other woman's face but her expression impassive, as she wanted neither to lead nor to dissuade, Prim said, 'Aleyna, does the name Ifaya Jabour mean anything to you?'

Her greatest fear was that it would mean nothing at all. In that event, she would have to locate and question other members of the cast listed in the programme she'd found in Archie's desk. Now that the Nimrod was dark, they could be scattered throughout Cairo or even beyond. Some might have left Egypt altogether. It could take weeks to get the answers she wanted.

To her relief, Aleyna Nasoul replied without hesitation. 'Of course. Ifaya was a darling.'

Prim reined herself in by sipping at her sweet coffee. 'Can you tell me about her?'

'What do you want to know? She was the flower of our company. Everyone loved Ifaya.'

'Including my father?' Prim asked, laying her coffee cup down on the low octagonal table that Aleyna had set between them.

If she understood the implication contained in Prim's question, Aleyna offered Prim no clue, other than, 'But of course. Mr Nevendon was a father to all of us. Even to me – at my age!'

'Was there a *special* relationship between them: between Ifaya and my father?'

Now Aleyna understood. 'Ah, you want to know if he was her lover?'

'To be blunt, yes.'

'If he was, they kept it very secret, which in Cairo is not an easy thing to do, I may tell you.'

'You saw no evidence of it?'

'None at all. He was very respectful to her, as he was to us all.'

'Could they have maintained a relationship without the company, and the management, being aware of it?' Prim asked, knowing that at home that level of secrecy would be impossible, given that the typical English backstage atmosphere was made up mostly of nitrogen, oxygen and gossip.

'I suppose they could have,' Aleyna agreed doubtfully. 'But if so, they were very discreet.'

Discretion didn't sound like Archie's style, so Prim asked, 'Why did Ifaya leave the company? Was she dismissed? Did she find a better role elsewhere? What was the reason?'

'Her father was unwell. She went home to be with him. We were all very sad – everyone apart from her understudy, of course.'

It sounded plausible enough, Prim thought. She recalled how the accounts had shown that Miss Jabour's wages had stopped shortly before Archie went missing. But it didn't mean it was the truth. 'Is she still there: at home, I mean?' she asked.

'I think so. She did not return.' Aleyna's face clouded. 'And that is a blessing, given what occurred later – the shooting, Mr Nevendon's disappearance… And now poor Moussa—'

'Yes, a blessing indeed,' Prim agreed, though the only blessing she was counting at that moment was discovering the existence of Ifaya Jabour. 'Do you happen to know where her home is, by any chance?'

'She spoke of it often; a village called al-Sarhan. "The most beautiful place in the whole world," I remember her telling me. "A simple village, but honest."' Aleyna's smile was warm and motherly. It made Prim want to hug her again. 'It is a good thing to come from honest roots, don't you agree, Miss Primrose? A tree cannot bloom for long without them.'

What does that make me? Prim wondered. Archie's concept of honesty had always been somewhat malleable. 'Is al-Sarhan far from Cairo?' she asked.

Aleyna laughed, though not unkindly. 'It is not in Egypt at all. It is on the Lake of Galilee, near Tiberias.'

'In *Palestine?*'

'Of course. Ifaya Jabour is a Palestinian.'

Damn, Prim thought. She couldn't ask Tarek to drive her all the way to Palestine. Besides, she wasn't even sure she'd be allowed in. She'd read the newspapers, heard the reports on the BBC: Palestine was turning into a battlefield. First there'd been a general strike called by the Grand Mufti of Jerusalem, followed by attacks on British troops. There had been Arab protests against the increasing numbers of Jewish immigrants fleeing persecution in Europe. There'd been frequent bombings and murders: the Palestinian Arabs against the British; the Palestinian Arabs against the Palestinian Jews; the Jews against the Arabs; even the Arabs against the Arabs… And the British taking draconian reprisals against everyone who took up arms. How could she possibly reach Ifaya Jabour in such circumstances? Would she even be permitted to cross the border?

There was only one person she could think of who might help her. And last night she had – metaphorically – slammed the door in his face.

'We didn't really want her to go, not with all the fighting going on there,' Aleyna was saying, 'but when a father is on his sickbed, a daughter's duty is clear. We know this, yes?'

'Yes, yes, of course we do,' Prim replied, pushing aside for a moment her conflicted thoughts about finding Ifaya Jabour. 'There is one other thing I need to ask you, Aleyna, if it's not too much trouble. Can you tell me, please, who maintained the Nimrod Theatre accounts?'

'That would have been Mr Bannoudi's responsibility, Miss Primrose,' Aleyna said. Her body took on a more formal posture, her tongue sweeping across her bottom lip as if to remove something that tasted unpleasant. Prim couldn't tell whether it was a hint of guilt that she knew about the exaggerated takings, or merely a recognition that talk of finance required a more businesslike demeanour.

'Did you ever see them?'

'It was not my place.'

'Could you explain to me the procedure with the takings?'

Aleyna frowned. 'I do not follow you, Miss Primrose.'

'How was the money banked?'

'It was taken from the safe in Mr Bannoudi's office every Monday morning and placed in a bag. This would be ready for me promptly at ten o'clock. Mr Moussa was very particular about the time. He liked things to be regular.'

'It was *you* who took it to the bank?'

'A duty I have carried out every Monday for the past two years,' Aleyna Nasoul said solemnly, as if she were describing a religious obligation.

'And you never once thought to take a peek inside the bag?'

Aleyna looked horrified. 'It was not my place to look,' she insisted. 'Mr Moussa trusted me. Mr Nevendon trusted me. I would sooner die than break this trust.'

Prim smiled in appreciation. 'I'm sure you would. But there seems to have been quite a lot of money being paid in. Surely someone drove you from the theatre to the bank on these occasions. Was it Tarek Shalaby perhaps – my father's driver?'

Aleyna Nasoul laughed at this, her strong, dependable features creasing into girlish amusement. 'Gracious, no. What an extravagance that would have been.'

'You mean you *walked*?'

'Is not very far, maybe twenty minutes. I would leave just after ten and I am there well before half-past. They say at the bank they have no need of a clock with Madame Nasoul to tell them the time.'

'Wasn't that a little risky?'

Aleyna seemed confused by the suggestion. 'Why should it be risky, Miss Primrose?'

'A bag full of money? You, a woman, in the middle of the city? I'm not sure I'd care to carry the takings from the Adelphi to Barclays Bank on the Strand on a predictable schedule every week for two years. And that's only five minutes' walk. Didn't Mr Bannoudi insist on having someone accompany you?'

Aleyna seemed to think the suggestion fanciful. 'There was no need. I was never in any danger.'

I was never in any danger.

The words sent a chill of premonition through Prim's body. Aleyna Nasoul couldn't possibly know that Moussa Bannoudi had been tortured – neither she nor Prim had had the stomach to approach his body, and Prim had only learned of it last night, from Harry Taverner. Should she reveal it now? Should she warn Aleyna to be on her guard? What good would it do? She couldn't protect the woman. And it must surely have occurred to Aleyna that, with Archie missing and Moussa Bannoudi dead, she too might be at risk. For a moment she just stared at the other woman, wondering what to do.

'Is there something wrong, Miss Primrose?' Aleyna asked.

'What was the name of the account the money was paid into?'

'I was not informed, Miss Primrose.'

'And you never got a receipt?'

'Everything was arranged with the bank by Mr Nevendon and Mr Bannoudi. I was merely the courier.'

Prim smiled. 'I've taken up too much of your time already, Aleyna,' she said. 'I'm sorry to have troubled you. You've been more than helpful.'

As Aleyna escorted Prim to the door, she said, 'Miss Primrose, you haven't told me why you are so interested in Miss Jabour.'

'Oh, I'm simply trying to make sense of it all,' Prim replied, putting on her shoes. 'But it would be nice if we could get the theatre back on its feet, once we've found my father. I understand it wasn't doing awfully well.'

'Too much competition,' said Aleyna ruefully.

Prim waited for the contradiction between empty theatre seats and bags filled with money to sink in. But it didn't. Aleyna Nasoul simply gave Prim a little wave of goodbye, keeping her hand close to her body as if trying to prevent the wish escaping into an unfriendly world. 'If you are like your father, I'm sure you will make that happen.'

'Take care, Aleyna,' Prim said. 'I don't know where my father has gone, but after what happened to Mr Bannoudi, I'm pretty sure I'm not the only one searching for him.'

Tarek was dozing in the car when Prim returned. He'd wound down the driver's window because it was already hot even though it was barely nine. As she climbed into the passenger seat beside him, she noticed one of his Turkish cigarettes smouldering in the ashtray. He woke with a start and reached out one leathery tanned hand to stub it out. 'Where do we go to now, Miss Archie?'

'Well, if I'm not going back to the Villa Narcisse for a while, I'll need some things – girl's things. I've only got what's in my bag.'

Tarek suggested Cicurel's, a department store on Fouad Street. Very fashionable, he said. Sensible prices. All the smart ladies in Cairo go there. Then, as if he'd made the choice for her, he drew deeply on his cigarette, exhaled through the open window and started the car.

There was a policeman in a white tunic directing traffic at the junction by the railway station. They passed close enough to see the gleam of the sun reflected in his polished belt buckle, but he showed no interest in the green Citroën, nor in the woman within it, so Prim guessed Harry Taverner had been right when he'd lamented the parlous state of police resources. Besides, what crime had she committed, apart from causing professional embarrassment to a member of the British Secret Service?

Les Grands Magasins Cicurel was a modern slab of glowing white concrete set on one of Cairo's most fashionable streets, as swish as any department store in London, Paris or New York. It had three tiers of display floors around a vast central atrium that rose to a gilded ceiling. The sales staff were mostly men, all dressed in dark suits, all with the stiff, consoling attentiveness of undertakers. Prim sought out the women's section, where a stylishly dressed Egyptian matron served her in faultless English. She chose carefully; her money wouldn't last for ever. She was halfway through her shopping when an elderly woman dripping in jewellery caught the attendant's eye. Politely, but with just enough condescension to make clear her place in the pecking order, Prim was directed to a much younger assistant. By the time she'd made her own choices, the other customer – eschewing anything so vulgar as cash – was signing for a diamond bracelet at the jewellery counter. As Prim fished in her bag for her purse, a flash of inspiration came to her.

'I think my father may have an account here,' she said sweetly. 'Would you be kind enough to check? It's Nevendon. Mr Archibald Nevendon.'

The young woman assistant reached under the counter and produced a leather-bound book with the Cicurel name embossed in gilt on the cover. Flipping through the pages, she confirmed with a bright smile that, yes, the emporium was indeed privileged to extend such a facility to a Mr A. Nevendon.

'I'm his daughter,' Prim said. 'Is it possible to charge these to the account?'

The assistant looked embarrassed. 'I'm so sorry. I didn't recognize you, Miss Nevendon. It's only my second day here, you see.'

'Oh, that's quite all right,' Prim assured her, trying to sound as though credit accounts in fashionable stores were her birthright.

Still the assistant hesitated, glancing towards the supervisor for help, but she was ten feet away, fawning over the bejewelled customer. The assistant took a deep breath and drew up the courage to say, 'May I be so impertinent as to ask you to confirm the address? If that's not too much trouble. You see, it's only—'

'Your second day,' Prim said helpfully. 'I quite understand. I wouldn't simply take my word for it, either. It's the Villa Narcisse.'

Prim heard the breath leave the poor girl's body like the release of a pressure valve.

'And while I'm here,' she continued, deciding that if you're on a winning streak, you might as well keep playing, 'and now that you know that I am indeed who I say I am, do you think I might have a quick peep at the state of the account? Only Daddy's memory these days isn't what it used to be. He has a habit of forgetting things he's purchased.'

The assistant nodded in sympathy. 'I have a mother like that,' she replied, handing Prim the book.

Scanning the record of purchases took Prim mere seconds. A blouse by Schiaparelli; a silk chiffon scarf by Chanel. Against each was recorded the initials *I. J.* written in a rather flowery – and clearly feminine – hand. The last purchase, a crocodile-skin evening bag, had been made a little over two months ago. 'That all looks fine to me,' announced Prim, struggling to keep her voice even. 'Would you like me to sign?'

'I'm so very sorry – I almost forgot to ask you,' the girl replied, holding out her pencil and smiling gratefully, as if Prim's honesty had saved her from instant dismissal and an inevitable life of crime.

As Prim stepped out into the glare of the sun, the Cicurel bag under her arm, she felt as if she'd committed the perfect crime. The loot stolen and no one hurt.

When she reached the car, Tarek asked, 'Where we go now, Miss Archie?'

Placing her purchases on the back seat and climbing in after them, Prim said, 'Seeing as the Cairo police don't appear to consider me public enemy number one, I'd like to go to Shepheard's Hotel, if you don't mind.' It wasn't purely for pleasure; she had something else in mind. As they pulled out into the traffic, narrowly missing a vendor's bicycle with a shelf over the front wheel piled almost to the rider's eye-level with wooden trays of salted fish, Prim went on, 'Tell me, Tarek, did you ever drive a young actress named Ifaya Jabour to the Villa Narcisse?'

'Maybe a few times,' Tarek said, shrugging. 'She worked at the theatre, for Mr Archie. Why do you ask me this?'

'She was having an affair with my father. Did you know that?'

Tarek let out a bellow of laughter. 'Mr Archie, he tells me many things, but he does not tell me that.'

'You didn't know?'

Tarek drew on his cigarette. The pungent smoke added to the stifling fug in the car, even with the windows open. 'This he did not reveal to me.'

Prim could detect disappointment in his voice, as if a close friend had been less than honest with him. 'Think back to the time before he went missing – where did you drive him? Anywhere out of the ordinary? Did he have any unscheduled meetings?'

Tarek thought about this for a moment as he artfully avoided a horse-drawn waggon piled high with sugarcane and then a crowded tram coming in the opposite direction. 'Just business. Sometimes to his theatre. Also to Heliopolis to fly in his aeroplane.'

'His *aeroplane*?' Prim said, startled. She remembered what she'd said to Harry Taverner when they boarded the *Celaeno* at Southampton. *This is the first time I will have been aloft in an aeroplane since my father took me up at Shoreham... I was nine and frightened stiff...*

'Anglo-Levantine – they have their own machine,' Tarek said in wonder. 'No taking train for rich men, eh? Rich men can fly like the birds.'

'Well, he's certainly managed to do *that*. Do you know where he went on those occasions?'

'Sometimes to Alexandria. Sometimes to Geneifa. Sometimes to Haifa.'

Haifa, Prim thought – in British Mandated Palestine. Then she heard Aleyna Nasoul's voice in her head, so clear that the woman could have been sitting in the Citroën's back seat with her: *Ifaya Jabour is a Palestinian.*

'Did he tell you why he wanted to go to Haifa, Tarek?'

'The company, they have very big terminal there. Is usual for him to go to Haifa.'

'When was the last time he went there, can you remember?'

'Oh, six weeks ago. Maybe seven.'

'Did you ever go with him?'

'No, Miss Archie. I take him to Heliopolis aerodrome, and I pick him up when he returns.' He let out a nervous laugh. 'No way Tarek Shalaby go up in aeroplane. Is crazy idea.'

Prim settled back into the warm leather seat. She longed to close her eyes and sleep, though the day had barely begun. Was it the sun, or a lethargy brought on by having too many thoughts fighting each other in her brain? Snap out of it, girl, she told herself. She needed a clear head. Because there was someone else she wanted to see, and questions still to be asked. Questions like: how was it that Aleyna Nasoul had set off on a journey by foot every week for two years, at the same time and presumably along the same route, carrying an ordinary bag stuffed with more money than Uncle Nim could ever have expected his beloved little theatre to make, and had never once attracted the attention of a single opportunistic street thief? All in a city where boys on motorcycles felt such disdain for the police that they waved pistols in the faces of impressionable young Englishwomen.

Fourteen

Michael Luzzatto had slept late. It was almost noon when he threw open the tall windows of room twenty-two at Shepheard's Hotel and leaned against the iron railings of the French balcony. He drew deeply on the expensive cheroot he'd purchased from the *tabac* on Emad al-Din Street and let the babble of downtown Cairo rise with the heat and spill into the room. The honking of motor-taxi horns, the clatter of horse-drawn carriages with their sunshades raised, the shouts of bellboys and street vendors, all these pricked his ears like wrong notes played by a poor orchestra. The only place of calm seemed to be down on the terrace, where the waiters were preparing the tables for lunch.

Letting his gaze wander to the building across the street, Luzzatto read the signs above the shop fronts: *Sinclair's Pharmacy*; *The Anglo-American Bookshop*; even the jeweller's at the end of the row, though owned by an Indian family, displayed the British royal crest and the legend *By Appointment to Queen Mary*. He shook his head disconsolately. The pharaohs had come and gone; the Greeks had gone; Napoleon had gone; the Ottomans had gone. But when were the British going to settle *their* bill and check out? It was sixteen years since Egypt had gained her independence, yet they were still here and showed no sign of leaving. If that was to be a benchmark, the British wouldn't give up their League of Nations mandate to govern Palestine for a century. He would never get to raise his children on the shores of Galilee. They would never know *Eretz Israel*.

Although Michael Luzzatto was Italian-American by birth and carried a passport with the American bald eagle engraved in the cover, by lineage he was an Ashkenazi Jew. He could trace iterations of the family name back two hundred years, to the Luzzkins – serfs in imperial Russia. Persecution had driven the Luzzkins first to Vienna and then to Dubrovnik; Michael himself had prayed in the very synagogue they would have attended there, climbing the narrow flight of stone steps to the little temple on the third floor and sensing family ghosts around him as he recited the *Amidah*.

From Dubrovnik his great-grandfather had taken the family to Naples, which was where the family name became Italianized. And in 1886 his grandfather was amongst the first immigrants to crane their necks and gaze in wonder as they passed beneath the Statue of Liberty on their way to a new life in America. The Luzzatti had prospered in their adopted home. Dealing in real estate had made Michael's father a fortune. And while the son might have appeared superficially a handsome, carefree playboy with a trust fund and not a worry in the world, in truth Michael Luzzatto was a thoughtful, intellectual man with a fondness for modern art and the works of Beethoven. He was also an agent for the Jewish National Fund, set up to purchase land in British Mandated Palestine for the re-establishment of a Jewish homeland. Which was where his animus towards the British came into the picture.

As individuals, Michael thought the British just splendid, if a little sniffy. Take the couple he'd met on the flying boat, for example. They'd been delightful. Taverner had been a pleasant and engaging travel companion, and Primrose Nevendon a joy, even if she did have that British way of making you feel an unsophisticated bum every time you opened your mouth. But when it came to those in power, that was a different matter altogether. Put a Limey in a uniform and, in Michael's humble opinion, he could make Machine Gun Kelly or Al Capone look like elementary-school teachers.

Until his last mission to Palestine, Michael Luzzatto's job had been straightforward. A potential plot of land would be identified, the owner located, a deal struck, the legal papers signed. Often the vendors were absentee Arab landlords, wealthy men living in Cairo, Damascus, Beirut or Amman. The Fund was by no means the only Jewish organization buying up land; around one-and-a-quarter million plots had been purchased since the beginning of the project some fifty years before – almost one-third of a million acres.

The Palestinian farmers, the *fellaheen*, had had little influence on this transfer of the land that they tilled. Battling low prices in reward for their hard labour, many had sold their own plots to the very landlords who had then sold it on to the Jews. Michael had seen a little of the plight of American agricultural workers during the time of the great Dust Bowl and he sympathized with the *fellaheen*. But if the landlords didn't want the land, there were those who did. Onto these newly purchased acres came settlers fleeing persecution in Germany, Poland and Russia, men and women eager to join their brothers and sisters, some of whose families had been there since the time of the Second Temple in Jerusalem. And look what a triumph they had made from all these acres of malaria marsh, scrubland and sand! One had only to use one's eyes. Tel Aviv hadn't built itself, had it?

And now the perfidious British were trying to slam the door in their faces. After first supporting the project of a homeland for the Jews on their ancestral land, they were now appeasing the supporters of the Grand Mufti of Jerusalem and enforcing a drastic reduction in Jewish immigration. And that meant reducing the sale of land. On his last trip they had made it clear to Michael that he was no longer welcome in Palestine. Indeed, they had all but frogmarched him to the quayside and forced him aboard the next departing steamer – for Athens, it so happened.

But Mike Luzzatto wasn't a man to crumble in the face of John Bull. Hadn't the Limeys learned the measure of American determination at Concord and Lexington, Bunker Hill and Yorktown? It would take more than a few tea drinkers in shorts and sola topees to get the better of a Luzzatto!

Thus determined, he had purchased a ticket with Imperial Airways and had snuck in through the back door, via Alexandria – which was just perfect for the meetings he had scheduled with some absentee landlords in Cairo. The British were bound to discover what he was up to eventually, but his Italian name and American passport meant his entry into Egypt had gone unnoticed, so far.

This morning's meeting with Shakir Hamad – who had a collection of *dunums* in the Jordan valley for sale, quarter-acre plots that one man with a donkey or camel could comfortably plough – had gone well. Hamad had wanted top dollar, of course, as the Arab insurrection in Palestine had pushed up prices alarmingly. But Mike was confident a deal could be done. His next appointment wasn't until two that afternoon. Which was why Luzzatto was allowing himself this present moment of relaxation and reflection, and the reward of an extremely decent cheroot.

The phone extension on the desk rang, breaking rudely into his thoughts. He took another puff of his cigar, rose from the chair and went to answer the call. It was one of those old-fashioned receivers, the sort that hung on a pillar, and he was forced into a momentary juggling act to get the earpiece to his ear.

'Mr Luzzatto, please forgive the intrusion,' said the voice of Ahmed, the concierge, 'there's a young lady here in reception asking if she might have a moment of your time.'

One of the girls from the Cleopatra Club, Michael assumed. Maybe his success in so far avoiding the British could be consummated with something a little more exciting than a cheroot, excellent though it was. True, he didn't have too much time to spare, but it was good of old Shakir Hamad to think of his comforts. 'Does she have a name?' he asked.

'She does, sir,' replied the concierge. 'Miss Primrose Nevendon.'

From her seat in the lobby, Prim had a good view past the over-blown pharaonic columns with their palm-leaf capitals, through the huge Moorish arch to the stairs. Not that she expected any difficulty spotting him amongst the other guests: Michael Luzzatto was a man who stood out from the crowd. Even so, when she saw him striding down the narrow strip of plush carpet like a movie star at a premiere – not the leading man, his lean features looked a little too amoral for that – she sensed the purpose in him as strongly as if it were a hot wind blowing in from the street. He was dressed in a pale summer suit perfectly tailored to match his athletic frame, his curly dark hair oiled and parted down the middle. He grinned when he saw her and waved. It was the sort of grin, the sort of wave, you delivered when you hadn't seen an old friend for years. You're playing a role, she concluded. You'd make a good Iago. Let's hope to God I'm not reading for Desdemona, because right now I need you, and I'm in no position to be choosy.

'Say, I'm beginning to think fate is trying to throw us together,' Luzzatto enthused as he shook her hand vigorously. 'Care for a cocktail? How's Harry T?'

Prim assured him Harry was just fine.

'Is that so? The doorman at the Cleopatra told me you two had some kind of disagreement – went home in separate taxis.'

'You asked, did you?' Prim said, blushing as she felt the anger rise. She considered telling him to keep that perfect nose of his out of her business, but she couldn't afford to make an enemy of him – not yet.

'I was merely curious. Hope I wasn't the cause of the spat.'

'I can assure you, Mr Luzzatto, there was no spat. Mr Taverner and I arrived separately, and we each had the intention to leave separately. I'm afraid the doorman must have misread the situation.'

'I stand corrected,' he replied, indicating with an outstretched arm the way to the Long Bar. 'And you may call me Mike – that's if you can find it in your heart to forgive me for being nosy. After all, by now shouldn't we consider ourselves buddies?'

'I can if you can… Mike. Buddies it is.'

Finding a secluded table in the Long Bar, Luzzatto ordered an Old-Fashioned for her and bourbon on the rocks for himself. 'To what do I owe the pleasure?' he asked.

Prim raised the glass to her lips and waited until the wash of citrus, whisky and bitters had eased the dryness in her mouth before replying. She felt the way she had at school when she'd been summoned before the headmistress: wondering which secrets she could afford to give up and which to keep hidden. 'That gentleman you introduced us to at the Cleopatra – the Lebanese gentleman—'

'Shakir Hamad, you mean?'

'Yes… Mr Hamad. How well do you know him?'

'You might say we're business colleagues.'

'Do you work for him?'

Luzzatto gave her a sideways glance. 'That's a mighty strange question to ask.'

'*Do* you?'

'As a matter of fact, no, I don't.'

'Then how do you know each other?'

'He owns land. I'm in real estate. I guess you could say that we have a mutual interest.'

'Is he a gangster?'

Luzzatto's laugh spilled a droplet of bourbon over his chin. He dabbed at it with the back of his hand. 'And I always thought you English were renowned for your circumlocution – isn't that what they say?'

'Not this one, Mike. I say what I think. What's your answer?'

He thought for a moment, choosing his words carefully. 'His lawyers would deny the accusation, of course.'

'But is it true?'

'Let's just say he knows a lot of people.'

'Is he dangerous?'

'Not to his friends.'

'Can you arrange a meeting? I need to talk to him.'

Luzzatto tilted his head and squinted at her. 'Is this about your missing father?'

'You overheard Mr Hamad and me speaking about that?'

'Couldn't help it. You were sitting right across the table from me, remember? Is that what the spat was about – with Harry T? He wouldn't help you, so you think Hamad might.'

'That's none of your business, Michael. Harry T – as you call him – has his own agenda.' Prim fluttered her eyelashes at him theatrically. '*I*, on the other hand, am simply a poor little English waif alone in a strange city. Are you going to come to my rescue, Michael Luzzatto, or must I find my knight in shining armour elsewhere?'

Luzzatto turned his glass, making the ice tumble and the bourbon swirl. He took another sip, this time a long one. 'Give me a day or so,' he said. 'Let me see what I can do.'

Prim walked back into the Shepheard's lobby alone. Luzzatto had asked where he could reach her once he'd spoken to Shakir Hamad. That had caused her momentary panic. But she had nimbly sidestepped the problem by insisting that *she* would be the one to make contact. Then she'd noticed the look in his eyes: intrigued, admiring. That simple solution to her predicament – taking the initiative – had given her a surprising sense of power. The pleasing sensation still lingered when she spotted the telephone booth by reception.

Prim knew she would have to tackle the issue of Harry Taverner eventually. Even with Shakir Hamad's assistance, there would be problems ahead that only someone with Harry's connections could solve. And there was still the Cairo police to consider. This wasn't London. She was pretty sure the Egyptians wouldn't require proof of a crime to take her into custody and hand her over to Harry's people. They might be waiting for her right now, ready to arrest her the moment she left the hotel.

Slipping inside the booth and closing the lattice door behind her, Prim took Harry's business card from her bag and lifted the handset. She put her index finger into the dial – and stopped. What if there was a wiretap on the line? She'd been to the movies; she'd seen the way the FBI listened in to hoodlums discussing their crimes. Did they do that sort of thing in Egypt? How long did they need to work out where the call was coming from?

But what was the alternative? She rang the number anyway.

The man who picked up the phone after the second ring spoke in the clipped, cold tones of a duke, so she knew she'd probably reached the embassy. And when she asked to be put through to Mr Taverner of the British Council she detected just enough of a pause in his response to know that Harry hadn't been lying when he'd opened up to her over supper at the Cleopatra Club.

'May I know who is calling, please?'

A moment to think: if she gave her real name, would they start tracing the call? Would they be on their way before she'd even got through to Harry? She couldn't quite picture who *they* were, but she was imagining the stern-looking men in fedoras chasing Robert Donat in the film *The 39 Steps*. Then she saw the numbers listed on a poster on the wall, the local Imperial Airways office amongst them. 'Tell him it's Miss Celaeno,' she said in a flash of inspiration, using the name of the flying boat that had brought them both to Egypt. The male receptionist, if that was what he was, asked her to spell it, to be sure he had it right, and then to wait. After a few moments hanging on the line she heard Harry's familiar voice.

'Hello. Who is this, please?'

'Hello, Harry. It's me. How are you?'

The sigh reached her clearly, even down the wires of the Cairo telephone system. 'Ah, I guessed right. *Celaeno* – very inventive. With that sort of initiative, you should be working this side of the counter. Are you all right?'

'I've been better.'

'I mean, are you safe?'

Prim found herself surprisingly touched by his concern. 'Yes, I think so.'

'Where are you?'

'Don't ask silly questions, Harry.'

'You've rather set the cat amongst the pigeons. My cheeks are still scarlet.'

'I'm sorry. I didn't mean to cause you embarrassment at work.'

'I feared for one awful moment that you'd been abducted.'

He sounded genuinely concerned, but she worried he might be trying to drag out the conversation so they could trace the call. 'I just wanted to let you know that I'm making some progress – concerning Archie. For a start, there's a woman involved.'

'Does she have a name?'

Prim laughed into the mouthpiece. 'Come on, Harry. I've read detective novels. I've seen the movies. I'm not going to hand you everything in a basket tied up with a bow, am I?'

His voice on the line suddenly became very serious. 'Look, Prim, this isn't a game. After what they did to Bannoudi, you need to be very careful. Whoever your father has got himself involved with, they're not comedians. It's not the Crazy Gang we're dealing with here.'

'Listen carefully, Harry,' she said bluntly, ignoring his warning. 'You need to gain access to an account at the Nabil-Magdy Bank of Cairo. My father was paying money into it each week, regular as clockwork. Quite a lot of money actually; more than the theatre was making in receipts. I don't know into whose account, but I don't think it was his.'

'We'd have to go through the Egyptian Ministry of Finance and that could take some time,' Harry replied. 'They might not want to play ball.'

'Well, at least try. If we can find out who Archie was paying money to, we might discover where he's gone.'

Harry promised he'd do his best. Then he urged her to return to the Villa Narcisse. 'I can't even begin to pretend you're safe until we can get you some protection.'

Prim dismissed his concern with a shallow laugh. 'Are you telling me you haven't got the Cairo police on my trail yet?'

He chuckled at that. 'Have you the slightest notion of what sort of shoestring we're working on here? If you were a member of the Sabini gang you'd be less likely to be arrested. Besides, from what I understand, we stopped hanging people for storming off in a huff back in the eighteen-fifties.'

Prim ended the call with an unembellished 'Bye, Harry. I'll be in touch.' She knew he'd been trying to reassure her, but as she settled the handset into its cradle she felt more scared than she could ever remember, as if she were hanging onto the only rope preventing her from plunging from a very high summit. Where the fall would end was lost to her, though she feared it lay in depths she could not dare to imagine. What was certain was that her strength was running out. Before she knew it, it would fail her completely. Then she would lose her grip.

Then she would fall.

Fifteen

Home to the nascent Egyptian air force, the aerodrome at Heliopolis was a desolate patch of ground with no discernible runway, a cluster of permanent wooden buildings roasting in the sun, a line of parked British-supplied biplanes and a sprawl of tents, but otherwise no apparent sign of life. Beyond the perimeter, which was marked with occasional posts rather than a proper fence, lay a small village of mud-brick single-storey houses. The highest feature in the landscape was the minaret rising from the village mosque. Anglo-Levantine's hangar sat in the civilian zone, a dusty, sand-blown corner given over to commercial enterprise. In truth, observed Prim, there wasn't much about the place that wasn't dusty and sand-blown.

The journey from Shepheard's Hotel had taken just under half an hour and Prim was finding the heat a trial. They had stopped en route so that Tarek's sister-in-law could give her a linen scarf to cover her head and neck. The gift, Tarek had explained, was not to soothe cultural sensitivities; it was to keep the grit out of her mouth, and her scalp from boiling. So far it had managed only limited success in either, but she appreciated the concern.

Seeking out the only area of temporary relief from the blazing sun, Tarek parked the Citroën in the shade cast by the hangar wall. The huge doors were open, but again Prim could see no one around. When she stepped inside, it took a moment for her vision to adjust to the change of light, and she could smell the interior before she saw it in any detail. It had a warm, oily scent cut with the sharper tang of petroleum.

'Hello, is anyone there?' she called out, her voice echoing from the shadows. Receiving no reply, she searched for signs of the office that Mr Gamil had spoken of when she'd phoned to arrange the visit.

Obscuring most of her view was a twin-motor biplane with an enclosed cabin. The taut silver-painted fabric beneath the windows bore the company name: *Anglo-Levantine Oil Exploration Company*. Tilted pertly on its tail wheel, the machine looked sleek and modern. It reminded Prim of why she had been so taken with the blandishments of fascism: the promise of a future where speed, technology and power would shape the world afresh, sweeping away the old, the corrupt and the inefficient – the revolution of the new. To a young woman on the cusp of adulthood and eager to forge her own path, it had all sounded so enticing. It had only been when she started attending meetings and found herself in the company not of eager ambassadors of a brave new world, but of angry, bitter, resentful bigots and fake patriots that the flirtation had suffered a fatal collision with reality. Though she had swiftly rejected fascism's tenets, that brief phase of her life still held power over her: the power of embarrassment.

Prim ducked under the nose of the aeroplane. Now she could see a door and an interior window in the far wall, suggesting a storeroom rather than anything so grand as an office. Making her way around that side of the machine, past the engine with its cowling latched open, a metal tray set on the floor beneath, which she assumed was there to catch an oil leak, she called out again, 'Hello... Mr Allaway, are you there? It's Prim Nevendon.'

The engineer appeared at the office door. Clad in grease-stained overalls, he was sandy-haired, in his forties and had the inquisitive, freckled face of a man who had first learned how to tinker with machinery at his father's knee, and who would go on doing so until they put him in a coffin. And even then he'd have firm opinions on the handiwork of the coffin-maker.

'Miss Nevendon, I've been expecting you,' he said in a gentle Scottish burr, giving her a smile that revealed a missing front tooth. 'Mr Gamil phoned to say you were on your way. It's a pleasure to meet the Big Man's daughter.' He held up one blackened palm. 'If you'll forgive me, I won't shake your hand. I'm changing an oil filter. They last about two flights in this place, what with all the sand.'

'I quite understand, Mr Allaway. It's very good of you to spare me your time,' Prim said.

The engineer nodded a greeting to Tarek and asked, 'So how can I be of help, Missy?'

'If it's not too much trouble, I'd like to look at a list of my father's recent flights. Is that possible? I assume you keep some sort of record for the company.'

Allaway nodded. 'Of course. They're all in the machine's technical log. But I'm not sure that will tell you very much. The police came to take a wee look, after the boss went missing. But there was nothing out of the ordinary.'

'I'm trying to build up a picture of my father's recent past,' Prim said. 'Just to get a sense of him, you understand.'

Allaway's reply sounded uncomfortably like a reminiscence at a graveside. 'Aye, he was a good man. Never on his high horse. Always had time for a wee chat. Let's see what we can find.'

The office was long and narrow. Down one side ran a workbench with a vice and a drill, and various other pieces of equipment Prim couldn't name. On the other side were shelves with cardboard boxes of spare parts resting on them, and a library of what Prim assumed were maintenance manuals. Withdrawing a book about the size of a sketchpad, bound with protective metal pages, Allaway laid it on the workbench for her to inspect. On the front were the words *de Havilland DH89 Dragon Rapide*, along with the manufacturer's serial number and the registration letters she'd seen painted on the side of the aeroplane. Allaway helped her to make sense of the entries, showing her how the flights were recorded, their length and destination. He pointed out Archie's signature and where he'd recorded any faults that he'd found while he'd been aloft. Seeing her father's handwriting again, as she had in his study, brought Prim closer to him. Glancing back through the office window at the Rapide, she could visualize him sitting in the single-seat cockpit, completing the record of a flight, eager to join the waiting Tarek in the Citroën, before heading back to the Villa Narcisse to prepare for a discreet rendezvous with Ifaya Jabour.

'If you have any questions, just give me a wee shout,' Allaway told her, leaving her to study the log while he went back to his work on the machine's engine.

The first thing Prim discovered as she inspected the book was that Archie's signature appeared infrequently. Most of the flights had been performed by the company's pilots. She could count on one hand the number of times her father had been aloft since the start of the year. Two recent flights stood out immediately: both, as Tarek had told her, from Heliopolis to Haifa and back.

Haifa – where the oil pipeline from Iraq terminated. Haifa – in Palestine. Prim wondered how far it was from Haifa to al-Sarhan. Not far, she guessed.

The most beautiful place in the whole world – or so Ifaya Jabour had told Aleyna Nasoul. *A simple village, but honest...*

We could do with some honesty around here, said Prim to herself, glancing back to the imaginary Archie seated in the Rapide's cockpit.

Checking the times and dates, she found that on both occasions the machine had stayed on the ground at Haifa for a few days before Archie had flown it back to Cairo. The rest of his entries meant little to her. There was a trip to and from Alexandria in February, and two in late March to a place called Geneifa. The name rang a bell.

'Tarek, when I asked you about driving my father here, you mentioned that he'd flown to somewhere called Geneifa. Where is that?'

'I don't know, Miss Archie. Sometimes the boss tells me where he goes, sometimes he doesn't. I think it is here in Egypt.'

Prim returned to the entries in the log. Looking at the two trips to Geneifa, she spotted something that made no sense to her. Each of the two return flights had a separate entry between the outbound and inbound legs: *Geneifa local.* She didn't understand what that meant, so she called Allaway back.

'A local flight,' he explained, as if it was blindingly obvious to anyone but a fool. 'Alight and land at the same place.'

'Why would he do that?'

'The engineer at Geneifa might have wanted him to make a test flight. Let me look.' He wiped his hands on his overalls and ran a finger over the page. Then he shook his head. 'That's not it. He's recorded no faults that might have required an air test.'

173

'Then why else would Archie fly around for,' Prim checked the departure and arrival times for both local flights, 'two hours and thirty-six minutes in the first instance, and two hours and forty-five in the second?'

Allaway shrugged. 'Numerous reasons, I suppose. He might have wanted to spot company tankers making their way up or down the Gulf of Suez. Maybe he was scouting out useful sights for the company to set up an exploration base. Or it could be that he was just up there looking at the scenery. They do that sometimes – pilots. When they're not paying for the petrol.'

Or searching for a place to hide, thought Prim. The realization struck her like a punch to the heart. 'Where exactly *is* Geneifa, Mr Allaway?'

'On the Suez Canal,' the engineer told her. 'As the crow flies, it's about fifteen miles from the head of the Gulf. We have a base there.'

'And how far could he have travelled during those periods?' she asked. 'I don't see any mileage recorded anywhere.'

'That, Missy, is because we don't log miles; we log time aloft. Time counts against the useful life of engine and air frame. Whether the machine flies from here all the way to Athens or just goes around in circles overhead is of no concern to an engineer. It's keeping it up there that's important.'

Prim stared at the logbook as if it were a prop at a séance. She strained her imagination to hear Archie's voice whispering to her from beyond the veil. Sensing she was keeping Allaway from his work, she asked, 'Where could my father have gone in the time that he was airborne from Geneifa?'

'That would depend on the winds he encountered.'

'Surely you can make an estimate.'

'Aye. If he didn't want to arrive home with no fuel in the tanks, which he wouldn't, then a good two hundred miles before he'd have had to turn back. And that would reduce by a couple of miles for every minute he spent loitering over whatever it was he was looking at. Obviously we can't know how long he spent doing that.'

'Might it be possible to search an area that size?' Prim asked. 'From the air, I mean.'

Allaway looked at her as if, on a whim, she'd suddenly broken into Swahili instead of English. 'Are ye suggesting the boss might be hiding somewhere around Geneifa?'

'It's a thought, Mr Allaway.'

'Well, good luck if you're thinking of looking for him. You're talking about an area of, what...' he frowned as he calculated the figure in his head, 'something in the region of one hundred thousand square miles.'

'*Oh*,' Prim replied, chiding herself for asking what the engineer must think was the lamest question he'd ever heard.

'Area of a circle: *pi* times radius squared.'

'Yes, of course,' said Prim, remembering her maths lessons at school, which had bored her almost into insensibility.

'It's a pretty big place, Egypt,' Allaway went on sympathetically.

'In a straight line then, where could he have reached in that time?'

Allaway pursed his lips. 'To the north, as far as Port Said. To the south, perhaps halfway down the Gulf of Suez. But once out of sight of this aerodrome, he could have turned in any direction.'

'What about east and west?'

'One way Sinai, the other the desert. Nothing much in either, to be frank, unless you like looking at sand and mountains.'

'Could he have flown into Palestine?'

'In the time he was aloft, barely. He might have reached the border between Sinai and the Mandate, but not much further.'

Prim asked if she could make a copy of Archie's flights. The engineer provided a pencil and paper for her to copy out the details from the logbook. 'You've been really very helpful, Mr Allaway,' she said when she had finished. 'I'm sorry to have taken so much of your valuable time.'

Allaway smiled. The missing front tooth made him look fifteen again. 'I'm only sorry I couldn't have been of more assistance, Miss Nevendon. We all want the boss back safely. He was very well thought of around here.'

Prim slipped the sheet of paper into her bag and went back out into the hangar. Pausing by the sleek glass nose of the Rapide, she looked up again to the empty cockpit. When she'd looked in this direction from the office, she had felt much closer to Archie. Now her sense of loss only deepened.

Walking around to the rear of the fuselage, she saw the passenger door was latched open. Peering inside, she gazed into the steeply slanting cabin. There were four rows of single seats on each side of a narrow aisle. The interior smelled of oil and leather polish. At the far end she could see past a half-bulkhead to the small triangular instrument panel set at the glass apex of the cockpit. She imagined she could see her father's broad shoulders as he sat at the controls – a man so at home in the ancient past, yet so happy to be in the vanguard of humanity's march towards the future. What had been in his mind, she wondered, looking down from that high vantage point as he left the fertile green banks of the Nile and headed out over the scorched red earth of the desert? Had it been fear – was he searching for somewhere to hide? Or had it been love – for a woman named Ifaya Jabour? Was Archie Nevendon the hunter or the hunted?

As Prim re-emerged into the blazing sunshine, she felt certain that she must follow the trail to Haifa and then on to the village of al-Sarhan. And to do that, she would need Harry Taverner's help. If anyone could get her into Palestine, it would be him.

Sixteen

I never resented lending you money when you found yourself on your uppers, Nim, old fellow. Not once. 'Performing the duty of the paterfamilias I was destined to become': that's what Father said to me whenever I accomplished some minor act of benevolence, like letting you borrow my spinning top or wading into the duck pond to save you from accidentally drowning yourself. Protecting the family is what he meant, of course. But that's a Member of Parliament with a divinity degree from Cambridge for you. The Old Man couldn't say, 'Good morning, boys' without dropping into Latin or quoting from St Augustine; that's if he noticed us at all and remembered who we were.

I often wonder if he had the slightest inkling how much it cost me to keep you safe from the tyrant we knew as Nurse Brandt. From the day she arrived, it was always 'Nurse', remember? Never 'Nanny', not even 'Miss Brandt'. Only to each other did we ever call her 'The Brute'.

I'm sure Mother knew what was going on, but she hadn't the guts to speak up. She was as frightened of the Old Man as we were of bloody Nurse Brandt. After that first time, when she thrashed you raw, I swore I would take the beatings for you. Didn't you ever wonder where I disappeared to, all those times she made you wait in the nursery in childish terror before the punishment was delivered?

Don't you recall how I'd return with the good news: Nurse Brandt has forgiven your sins. Cleared the slate. All transgressions forgotten. Just one whack, that's all you have to suffer. Then you can pull up your shorts and get on with your stamp-collecting.

What I never told you, Nim, was this: as we got older it wasn't only the thrashings that I was taking for you. I knew it was dirty from the start, but it hurt less than the strap, at least on the outside. I couldn't tell the Old Man, could I? He'd have called me a milksop. He thought chastisement was character-building – and sporting with the domestics was simply part of finding one's manhood. I guessed only later that they were complicit.

That's why women have always been a problem for me, Nim. If I didn't fear them, I expected them to throw me to the wolves. Poor old Celestina never really stood a chance.

I was like that right up until Ifaya came into my life. When I met her, I thought I could change, make myself anew. Start again. Forget. But falling in love made me take my eye off the ball, Nim. And now I've put your dream at risk. For me, that's the greatest betrayal of all.

Old Bannoudi and I tried our best, we truly did. But the competition is fiercer now than it ever was when you and I were in Cairo together. There's the Rameses; the Majestic; the Kursaal; more theatres on Emad al-Din Street than there are on Broadway, I swear it. And the masses don't want the cultural stuff so much these days. All they want now is risqué cabaret and variety acts. If I could have found a camel that juggles and a female camel trainer who could belly-dance, maybe I'd never have had to do that deal to keep our little place afloat.

I tried, Nim. God help me, I tried. I went to the European banks. They turned me down flat; wouldn't take the risk. I tried the Arab financiers. They smiled and said they'd get back to me. Never did. I tried the Jews, but they're investing in cinema these days. No one wants to subsidize quality any more. If David Garrick came back from the grave and said he had an unknown work by William Shakespeare, or a forgotten play by Molière, they wouldn't touch it unless it had a part for a comedienne with a cleavage and a voice like Nellie Melba. These days, it's nothing but tits, tassels and trumpets.

What else was I supposed to do, Nim? I had to get down in the gutter. And as you and I both know, the gutter in Cairo isn't a place for those with weak stomachs.

In the end I did find someone to lend me the money. A slippery devil and no mistake. Maronite Lebanese, name of Shakir Hamad. Fat fingers in just about every unsavoury pie you can cook. And he's friends with some very bad people indeed, Nim – chaps who are worse than the Turks, the Syrians and the bookies at Royal Ascot all put together.

At the time it seemed like the perfect answer. Hamad spun me some nonsense about 'usury' – how it was against his people's ethics to charge interest on a loan. I'll admit it: I fell for it. I was desperate, wasn't I? Without it, we'd have gone dark inside the month. It appeared the obvious solution: enough cash to keep going until things improved, and no extortionate charges on the loan. Why, we even managed to keep some over to repaint the lobby and put up your picture in pride of place, Nim, my darling young boy – right next to mine. I'd stand there in the lobby with Bannoudi and Madame Nasoul and think, proudly: Look at us – Nim and Archie Nevendon, impresarios to the discerning theatregoer.

Christ in His Heaven, Nimrod, old pal – if only I'd known what Shakir Hamad really wanted in return…

Seventeen

It was the day following Prim's secretive phone call, and Major Courtney had taken Harry to the Gezira Sporting Club for an early lunch on the pavilion veranda. Harry chose the lamb cutlets; Courtney raised a fuss because he'd wanted devilled kidneys and they'd stopped serving breakfast an hour ago.

'Do as you're bloody told,' Courtney instructed the apologetic waiter. 'Chop-chop! We haven't got all day.'

The waiter took Courtney's rudeness without flinching. 'Yes, Bimbashi. As you command.'

Harry looked the other way, out of embarrassment. He had learned in the few days he'd been in Cairo that *bimbashi* was the English bastardization of the Turkish word for a major, a throwback to the Ottoman days. He had also noted how Courtney appeared to like the appellation. That was something else he'd learned since arriving in the city: sixteen years after granting Egypt independence, his own people still thought of themselves as imperial rulers. He'd seen in Vienna and Berlin how Herr Hitler's thuggish followers considered themselves superior beings. It was too easy, he thought, to fall into the trap that hubris could set for the self-regarding.

The food arrived and they began to eat.

'I had a call from Russell Pasha this morning,' Courtney

said, to the accompaniment of thundering hooves a little way off as two jockeys exercised their horses on the gallops. 'He's come through on the names you wanted investigated. Hamad and Luzzatto – sounds like a dodgy variety act at the Hackney Empire to me.' Courtney licked his lips and leaned back in his chair, pleased with his own wit. 'What's their routine: a song, a dance, and a knife in the ribs?'

'With Hamad, that wouldn't surprise me, sir,' Harry replied. The heat was making the lamb cutlets something of a trial. 'Not sure about Luzzatto.'

He had taken the precaution of asking for traces on both men after the American had interrupted the supper he was having with Prim Nevendon at the Cleopatra Club. It wasn't that his suspicions had been unduly aroused – other than by Hamad's air of suppressed power and his coterie of slack-eyed, obedient young men – but in the Service's dictionary the word 'coincidence' had a very brief definition: *coincidence – see 'unlikely'.*

'The American came back clean,' Courtney said. 'He cleared customs at Alexandria, papers all in order.'

'I know; I was with him. He joined the Imperial Airways flight at Athens.'

'Then you'll be pleased to learn that the Egyptians have nothing recorded against him. Nor do we.'

The news did not fill Harry with as much confidence as Courtney might have expected. He knew how notorious the Service could be for not passing information between one station and another. Sometimes it seemed to him as if the different desks were in jealous competition rather than working for the same side: the German desk considered themselves far superior to the Italian desk; the Soviet desk despised the French desk… And then there was the work ethic. When Friday lunchtime arrives, do we plan a meeting to assess the results of our recent toil in the nation's defence? Do we plan for the new week ahead and the threats to come? Not on your nelly. We down tools and set off upcountry for a spot of decent shooting; back in on Monday, but late, just in time for lunch at that great little place around the corner from Broadway Buildings.

Merely thinking about it made Harry want to be back in Vienna, in the field, feeling the breath of consequence on his neck, knowing that what he was doing was important. Anything would be better than sitting here in Cairo, playing private detective in the search for Archie Nevendon and nursemaid to his daughter – a task at which he had so far failed miserably.

'What about Hamad?' he asked.

Courtney stabbed a piece of devilled kidney and raised the fork. His thin lips parted with great ceremony and Harry could have sworn he heard him mutter, 'Open wide' as if he were a dentist about to make an oral examination of his own mouth. 'Ah,' he said. 'Now that's a different story altogether.'

'I'm not surprised. He looked like a thug. Rich, manners, smart suit… but a thug all the same.'

Courtney munched. Then he pulled a face, as if he'd found a piece of kidney that was undercooked. 'If ever there was an untouchable criminal, young Taverner, your Mr Hamad would appear to be that man.'

'What a surprise,' Harry said.

'Prostitution, heroin, loan-sharking, gun-running – you name it. Arms to the Syrians, land to the Jews, cash for the Central Committee for National Jihad in Palestine… He's even got shares in Anglo-Levantine Oil. Absolute rotter in all respects. If he was in London, they'd probably offer him free membership of the Athenaeum.'

'Then why isn't he in prison? Or dead?'

'Because Hamad is always the bridesmaid, never the bride. Everything suspected, nothing ever proved. He knows the right people – powerful people who can protect him.' Courtney waved his fork as if it were a conductor's baton and he suspected Harry might be a fraction behind the beat. 'He has more than a few of King Farouk's friends in his pocket, and members of the Wafd nationalist party. He's also been highly successful in maintaining an impenetrable wall between himself and his acolytes. They do the dirty work; Hamad sits back and takes the profit. You could squeeze him and ten other people into a cupboard, throw in a bucket of camel shit and, when you opened the door, Mr Shakir Hamad would be the only one still wearing a pristine shirt. No one's been able to lay a glove on him.'

'Could he have anything to do with Archie Nevendon's disappearance?'

A quick twist of the fork to bring the overture to a close. 'Always possible, I suppose. But I have the feeling that soon we're going to be far too busy to care.'

Now we're getting to the nub of Major Courtney's sudden desire for a private, intimate lunch, thought Harry. He doesn't want Mrs Fulready-Laycock passing on to her husband, the military attaché, or even worse the ambassador what he's going to say.

'One doesn't have to be a member of this Service to know that the Peel Commission's report last year didn't exactly result in a solution to the Palestine problem. One has only to read the newspapers,' Courtney announced, having first glanced round to ensure he wasn't about to be overheard. 'Sir Harold MacMichael, the high commissioner in Jerusalem, has sent me a secure cable. Things are getting hotter there by the day. There are places where our troops hardly dare go. It's close to getting out of hand.'

Harry forced his face into a suitable mask of concern. In Vienna, reading the German newspapers had been a small but important part of his job. He'd warned London more than once that the Nazis viewed with relish the attacks in Palestine against the British authorities and the Jews. *Yes, we know*, had been the reply on each occasion. Harry suspected that the notes of his reports were annotated with the line: *Has drawn conclusions beyond the officer's competency.*

Courtney was wielding his fork again. 'To be totally frank with you, in my opinion we've made an absolute hash of it. We promised a Greater Arabia to the Arabs because we needed their help against the Turks in the Great War, and we promised the Jews they can have a national home in the land of their ancestors. Now you may well ask if we had any right to make those promises, but we were the ones holding the parcel when the music stopped, and it doesn't take a Bertrand Russell or a Wittgenstein to see there's a contradiction there.'

Harry agreed that, for anyone with half a modicum of reason, it didn't.

'Neither side will get what it wants, and the violence will only get worse,' Courtney continued. 'We've already had a couple of our senior people murdered there. No matter how many perpetrators' houses we demolish, no matter how many terrorists we string up, nothing improves. Neither the Arabs nor the Jews seem to understand the bloody rules. If it were up to me, I'd let the League of Nations give the mandate to someone else – let some other poor buggers try to make a go of it. Let the Belgians or the Portuguese sort it out. Let them deal with the bombs hidden on the roadside that go off when our army lorries pass. Let them clean up the mess when an Arab murders a Jew, or when a Jew lobs a bomb into an Arab market in retaliation.'

He didn't elucidate why, in particular, the Belgians or the Portuguese should be chosen for these onerous duties, but Harry nodded in diplomatic sympathy. 'Why don't we just let the Palestinians run the place themselves?' he asked.

Courtney looked at him as if he'd taken leave of his senses. 'Good God! You can't simply let minor territories that happen, by geographical fortune, to have strategic importance act on their own whims. Imagine the chaos. Besides, if we handed out self-government to all and sundry, what would the chaps in the Colonial Office do all day?'

Harry couldn't be sure if Courtney was joking. 'From what I've witnessed in Vienna and Berlin,' he said, 'Jewish immigration into Palestine is only going to increase. Where else are they supposed to go? Britain doesn't want them; America doesn't want them—'

Courtney cut him off. 'Whatever happens, two things are certain. First, we're going to stay here in Egypt and guard the Suez Canal – it's of vital interest to the Empire. Second, there's going to be a great deal more bloodshed in Palestine before it's over.'

Having concluded his peroration, Courtney laid down his knife and fork, dabbed his little mouth with a corner of his napkin and beckoned the waiter to remove his plate. Harry wondered if he was expecting a round of applause. 'That sounds like a fair assessment to me, sir,' he said, wondering how this was of any consequence to him. He was supposedly on leave, filling a very temporary post as a favour. London had promised him he'd soon be back in Vienna, where there were more pressing matters to tackle than questionable imperial policy and whether there were devilled kidneys available on the menu.

But Courtney hadn't finished. 'If we end up in a shooting war with the Germans,' he said, leaning towards Harry as if to impart a confidence he didn't want anyone overhearing, 'protecting the Canal and keeping Egypt on our side will demand far more resources than the government realizes. As far as I'm concerned, the fate of Archibald Nevendon is going to feature very far down our list of priorities – probably just below the state of the embassy flowerbeds. And that goes for his daughter, too. I've decided to overlook your little wobble there, my boy. Frankly, it will be all hands to the pumps. Therefore I'm going to recommend to London that they make your post here permanent.'

'He'll meet you on the Qasr el Nil Bridge,' Mike Luzzatto had told Prim when she'd called him from Cicurel's, using Archie's customer account to gain access to the courtesy phone. 'This evening at six.'

And here she was, at the appointed time, standing beside the great stone obelisk with its guardian bronze lion, gazing out through the ironwork at the white sails of the feluccas lying like chips of bone against the blood-red river at sunset. It ought to be romantic, she thought, but I'm worried sick about where I'm going – too sick to care that passers-by will take me for a tart. In her mind she transported herself from the Nile to the Thames, placing herself on Lambeth Bridge. Would I agree to get into a car with a man I've met only briefly in a nightclub and who looks like a casting director's dream for an underworld gangster? Probably not. But then Cairo isn't London. Maybe it's the history, maybe it's the desert air. Maybe I'm being seduced, falling for a fantasy, the way everyone went crazy over Rudolph Valentino when *The Sheik* came out.

'Miss Nevendon, if you please—'

She turned back to face the road, and there was a shiny black Lancia saloon with wire-spoke wheels. But it wasn't

Hamad leaning out of the passenger window and inviting her to climb into the back seat, it was one of his handsome young men, wearing sunglasses despite the sinking sun, his oiled hair brushed slick against his skull and a moustache as sharp as a switchblade.

'Come, please... the boss is waiting.'

They drove on across the bridge and into lush gardens on the southern tip of Gazira Island, then over a smaller bridge into an area of palm trees and smart houses. The sun had almost dipped below the horizon when they stopped before a set of high metal gates set into a whitewashed wall with coils of razor wire on the parapet. More like a military base, or a prison, than a home in a smart area of Cairo, thought Prim as her nerves threatened to get the better of her.

A flunky the size of a prizefighter hauled the gates aside, the hinges shrieking like a torture victim. Then, without a word being exchanged between the driver and the gate-guard, they were rolling slowly up a gravel drive lined with acacia bushes towards a low, flat-topped building that looked like a beleaguered desert fort out of a Beau Geste novel.

Another of Hamad's smart young men escorted her through the house, saying not a word to her. Was everyone here sworn to a vow of silence? Were they afraid they'd incriminate themselves the moment they opened their mouths? Prim caught glimpses of simple, rustic furniture and traditional woven hangings on the walls. *Mr Hamad was born in a poor village and now he lives in the same neighbourhood as princes*, she recalled Mike Luzzatto saying at the Cleopatra Club.

At the back of the house was a set of wide doors, latched open and giving her a view of a purple sunset, the near-horizon lacerated by the branches of tamarisk trees, the scent of their blooms heavy in the evening air. Prim passed through and onto a wide terrace. At each corner was a burning flambeau set on a pole, to ward off the encroaching chill of night – no electricity here, for the boy from the poor village. In the centre was a wrought-iron table surrounded by enough chairs for a large family, but Prim had seen no sign of women or children in her journey through the house.

The only person at the table was Shakir Hamad. He was wearing pressed Oxford bags and an open-necked cream shirt with a blue cardigan draped over his enormous shoulders, looking for all the world as if he was taking his ease after a hard day on the water at Cowes. 'This is indeed an honour, Miss Nevendon,' he said, rising from his seat and kissing her hand. He invited her to sit, dispatching the nearest of his smart boys, who returned with an ice bucket containing a bottle of Perrier Jouet and two champagne flutes faster than anything a waiter at Shepheard's or the Semiramis would achieve, even with the added incentive of an electric cattle-prod. 'How might I be of assistance?' Hamad asked, filling her glass. Prim noted that he hadn't asked her whether she cared for any.

'When we met at the Cleopatra Club, you very kindly suggested I should contact you if I found myself in need of help.'

'And it was no empty promise, madam, I assure you.'

'You said you were aware that my father had gone missing.'

'It was in the newspapers. Your father was an influential man. It is a man's duty to make himself influential.' Hamad raised his glass. 'We have a toast in Lebanese – *Sahtain*. It translates as wishing someone two healths. That seems appropriate in the circumstances, does it not? *Sahtain* – to your health, and to your father's.'

Prim, too, raised her champagne flute. '*Sahtain*, Mr Hamad.'

They drank and Hamad went on, 'So, how may I be of assistance?'

'I assume you know my father supported a small theatre near the Ezbekia Gardens.'

Hamad nodded. 'I have had the pleasure of attending a performance there more than once. I may look like a rough Lebanese peasant boy, but great art makes no judgement upon the class of those who appreciate it. I have a penchant for English Jacobean drama – your William Shakespeare, for example. I enjoy the themes of revenge and justice. They echo very much the Arab tradition.'

'You'll know of course that there was a shooting at the theatre, a little while after my father disappeared.'

'I read about it, yes.'

'I should also tell you that the manager of the theatre was murdered there a couple of days ago. I was the one who found him.'

'I heard about that too,' Hamad replied, in the sort of tone he'd use if she'd told him about finding a forgotten umbrella in the theatre's cloakroom. 'But I didn't know it was you who came across the poor fellow. You must be asking yourself whether you have arrived in a city of assassins.'

'A friend of mine thinks I might be at risk because of it.'

'Would that friend be the English gentleman in whose company you were dining at the Cleopatra? I regret to say I have forgotten his name.'

'Harry – Harry Taverner. Yes, it was him.'

'Is Mr Taverner a policeman?'

'No, of course not.'

'Just a concerned friend?'

'Harry is as new to Cairo as I am. Naturally he's rather worried for me.'

Only now did Hamad adopt an expression of concern. On such a heavy, battered face it looked like merely another version of menace. But his gravelly voice was sympathetic. 'Is it protection you seek, Miss Nevendon? I could arrange that, if you're concerned for your safety.'

'It's not that, thank you,' Prim said. 'It's something else.'

'And what is that?'

Prim drew a deep breath. 'I've discovered my father was banking far more money than the theatre was making.'

Hamad's little deep-set eyes fixed on hers as if he were taking aim through the sights of a rifle. 'Have you really. That's very enterprising of you. Go on.'

Having committed herself, retreat was no longer an option. Prim set down her champagne flute and folded her hands together in what she hoped was a businesslike stance. 'I've seen the accounts. There is no way the theatre was taking in that level of receipts. I need to know where the cash was coming from.'

'That is natural. But I still don't see how I can help you.'

'My father entrusted the money to a member of the staff. That person carried it to the bank each week. I'd rather keep their name out of this because I believe the person concerned was not involved, simply an innocent courier. But what I want to know is this: who was giving my father the money, and how could anyone make the same journey each week with so much cash on their person – for five whole years – and never once fall prey to a thief? And all in a city that I am reliably informed has a thriving criminal underworld?'

Hamad said nothing. Prim felt the discomfort of an actor whose cue has been missed. To fill the gap, she continued rather too quickly, 'I think that whoever was providing the money was confident that no one would dare interfere with its transfer to the bank. That's the sort of protection I'm interested in...'

She had nothing left to say. In her mind she waited for the prompter in the wings to deliver the required lines and save her. She could hear the cicadas chirruping in Hamad's darkened garden like the murmuring of an embarrassed audience. Hamad's expression stayed frozen for a moment, which Prim found alarmingly disconcerting. Then a grin shattered it like a hammer taken to porcelain. A great gust of laughter came out of him.

'Hah! Are you implying I mix in such circles, Miss Nevendon?' The grin turned into mock-distress. 'I must confess I am hurt.' He laid one great palm against his chest to staunch the mortal wound she had inflicted upon him. 'You come into my house, you take one look at a poor fellow from an even poorer village, you see his rough exterior – and, in your European fashion, you decide I am the sort of fellow who spends his days consorting with criminals. If I were not such a good-hearted fellow, why, I would be inclined to take offence.'

Was he teasing her? Was he joking at her expense? Prim had the awful feeling that in a moment the grin would vanish and a terrible violence would be unleashed in Shakir Hamad. 'I meant no disrespect,' she said hurriedly. 'It's just that when we met at the Cleopatra Club, you did say you knew a lot of people. You even spoke of kicking in some doors on my behalf, should I need it. Well, I need it now. So I was wondering if you might point me in the direction of the right doors to kick.'

Hamad's grin did indeed fade. It was replaced by the slyness of the once-poor village boy who had learned how to live amongst princes. 'Are you sure you want to do that, Miss Nevendon?' he asked, reaching out to pour more champagne.

'Sometimes it is wiser to let doors remain shut, don't you think? Unless we are certain that what we will find on the other side will not harm us.'

'I'm sure,' Prim said, with more certainty than she felt.

Shakir Hamad raised his glass in another salute. 'In that case, I shall be honoured to assist you in any humble way I can. *Sahtain*, Miss Nevendon.'

Prim echoed the toast.

Hamad raised a cautionary finger, the flames from the nearest flambeau glinting on the gold rings. 'But I think it would be only proper of me to warn you: if it should happen that what you discover on the other side displeases you, please don't say that Shakir Hamad didn't warn you.'

The line was as scratchy as hell. It had taken most of the day for the operator to put the call through to Jerusalem. But at ten o'clock that night, while across the city Prim Nevendon was taking her leave of Shakir Hamad, the concierge at Shepheard's Hotel dispatched a bellboy to Mike Luzzatto's room to inform him that, by the miracle of modern technology, a connection had been made. Hurrying down the carpeted stairs to the lobby, Mike Luzzatto reached the public telephone booth, entered and closed the door behind him.

Mike was more confident than Prim had been when she, too, had stood in this same booth, that the British wouldn't have the line tapped. He knew they weren't that efficient. Nevertheless, he was careful in the extreme. What passed between him and the male voice at the other end over the following minute was sufficiently obtuse not to prick the ears of the operators in either the Cairo or Jerusalem exchanges, or anyone waiting outside for the booth to become vacant.

'*Shalom*, old friend,' Mike said when he heard a familiar voice on the line. 'How are things going where you are?'

'*Aleichem shalom*, Michael,' replied the voice. 'Things are so-so. We have good days. We have bad days. Yesterday was a good day. For tomorrow – only the Lord can answer that. How did your meeting with the vendor go?'

'Well enough,' Mike said. 'I think he'll sell. But I have something else that might be of interest.'

'Go ahead,' urged the voice on the line.

'Rockefeller's daughter is in town.'

For a moment the line only fizzed and crackled. Then came the response: insouciant, almost bored. 'Okay. We weren't expecting that. If you're certain, I'll pass it on to the friends of Hazan.'

'Oh, I'm certain. She was on the British flight that stopped at Alexandria. She's in Cairo as we speak. I wondered at first if the name was just a coincidence. But I heard her in conversation talking about Rockefeller. It's her all right.'

'Do you think she knows where her father is?'

'I'm not sure; it's too early to say. But here's the thing – the guy she was talking to is a friend of Amalek.'

Again the empty echoing hiss, like the needle on a gramophone when the song has ended, while the caller in Jerusalem digested what Mike had told him.

'Are you still there?' Mike asked, afraid the operator had cut him off.

'I'm still here,' the voice replied. 'Thanks for the information. I'll pass it on. If she heads our way, do what you can to let us know. It's the first real break we've had since al-Sarhan.'

Mike ended the call, stepped out of the booth and made his way to the hotel terrace. Beneath a spreading palm tree a local quartet was making a fair fist of 'Stompin' at the Savoy'. He found a seat, hailed a waiter and ordered a beer. It had been a good day, he thought, settling back and opening the copy of *Fortune* magazine that the concierge had procured for him. The lead article concerned the rising attacks on Jewish businesses in Germany, and Hitler's increasingly hysterical rhetoric against Jews in general. Mike fought to keep the anger from showing on his face; this was not the place to get noticed. It was only a matter of time before the British learned he was in Cairo, and he still had work to do.

When the beer arrived, he laid aside the magazine. He studied the chilled glass for a moment, delaying his reward while he replayed in his mind the brief conversation he had had with his friend in Jerusalem, mostly to ensure that he had maintained proper operational security.

The man with whom he had spoken – in the personal code they had agreed upon before Mike was thrown out of Palestine – worked for the Jewish Agency in Jerusalem, an organization set up to facilitate the immigration of Jews from Europe. 'Rockefeller' was Archibald Nevendon, the name chosen because of both men's connection with the oil industry. The 'friends of Hazan' was their code for the Irgun, the Jewish paramilitary defence force in Palestine; they had chosen it in memory of one Israel Hazan, a seventy-year-old poultry dealer and the first Jew to be murdered in the Arab attacks on Jaffa two years earlier. And 'Amalek' – the biblical enemy of the Israelites – was their term for Haj Amin al-Husseini, Grand Mufti of Jerusalem and leader of the Palestinian Arabs. Mike was confident that if the British had managed to wiretap the line from Jerusalem, they would be none the wiser, unaware that he had just passed on a warning to the Irgun that Archie Nevendon's daughter had turned up in Cairo – and had sought a meeting with a gangster suspected to have channelled money and arms to the Palestinian Arab cause.

Lifting the glass to his lips, Michael Luzzatto accepted his reward. Yes, he thought, all in all it had been a very good day.

Eighteen

Harry Taverner arrived at the offices of the Nabil-Magdy Bank promptly at ten o'clock, two days after Prim's phone call. He had arranged the appointment in the guise of assistant attaché (commercial) at the British consulate. He came without confidence, going through the motions rather than with any real hope that his enquiry on her behalf would yield results. He was a patient, optimistic man. If asked, he would probably tell you he'd learned his serenity in the eternal calmness of the Dart Valley in Devon where he'd grown up, spending solitary hours alone on the riverbank in the school holidays waiting for the fish to bite, watching the kingfishers hunt and the otters roll and twist in the water. He needed every ounce of it now.

'You see, Mr Khaled, we're concerned that Mr Nevendon might have been the victim of extortion before he went missing,' he explained to the charming but unreadable young executive into whose office he had been escorted by a male assistant. 'He's a British citizen. It's beholden upon us at the embassy to do all we can on his behalf. I'm sure you understand.'

But Mr Khaled had gifted him a sad smile and little else, regretting enormously that he must inform the honoured sir that he was unable to confirm whether a Mr Archibald Nevendon had ever maintained an account with the bank. Or if he had, where the money from the Nimrod Theatre had gone when it arrived. But if the esteemed gentleman would care to return with a court order, or better still an official instruction from the Minister of Finance, the bank would be honoured to reconsider his request. And as it was a Friday and the bank maintained a European schedule, perhaps the assistant attaché (commercial) would forgive him, but there were other matters demanding his time…

Thus rebuffed, Harry was forced to spend several depressing hours going over the police reports on the shooting at the Nimrod, the murder of Moussa Bannoudi and the original investigation into Nevendon's disappearance. He sought further information on Tarek Shalaby, in case Prim had been under duress when she'd called, but after consulting both the police and Anglo-Levantine, he concluded that the driver was acting under Prim's instructions. He even went to Shalaby's house in the company of the single Egyptian police constable that Russell Pasha had allowed him to borrow for an hour. The way in which the policeman dealt with Shalaby's relations appalled him, and he was unsurprised when the visit produced no practical information whatsoever. In the end Harry was forced to admit that he could see no obvious wide-open doors that had been missed.

Over the next three days he played the tourist. He visited the Pyramids, fending off all manner of hawkers and beggars, young and old, with the embarrassed diffidence of the Englishman abroad. He took a felucca ride on the Nile, fixing his eyes on the timelessness of the riverbank where farmers still took their water buffaloes to drink in the shallows, rather than on the dead cats and other detritus that flowed past the boat. He visited the museum and feasted his eyes on splendours great and small. And it was during this foray into the past that he finally accepted the inevitable. It came to him as he studied a collection of dusty artefacts from the Middle Kingdom lying forlornly in a glass case. He saw in his mind Mrs Fulready-Laycock sitting at her typewriter on a hill of faded debris from ages past, banging out a letter for London that would consign him to the same fate: to become just another exhibit from a long-forgotten time, no longer relevant, no longer functioning. That sealed it for him. His only escape route was to help Prim Nevendon find her father before Major Courtney set the Service's creaking wheels in motion to make his posting permanent. And right now she was making that a good deal harder than it needed to be. All he could do was bide his time and wait for her to call again.

Shakir Hamad's message reached Prim around the same time that Harry was staring into the dusty museum display case and contemplating his equally dusty future. It was her eighth day in Cairo and some thirty-three days since her father had gone missing, and the mechanism by which it reached her was a mystery. It didn't come via Mike Luzzatto, and Prim could only marvel at it. She concluded that Hamad must maintain some sort of nefarious nervous system that ran deep through the cramped lanes and alleyways of Cairo. A friend of Tarek's brother arrived at the house with the simple instruction that she should go at once to a vegetable shop at the end of the lane. There she was handed a terse, unsigned note in English: wait at a certain crossroads in the old city at the appointed time later that day. And to the minute – according to the Helvetia wristwatch that Granny Grace had bought her for her twenty-first – the same smooth young blade who'd driven her across the river last time turned up at the wheel of Hamad's shiny Lancia, though only God knew how he'd managed *that*, given the traffic.

'Well, my dear young lady, the news I have for you is somewhat complicated,' said Hamad when she was led into his company. The sleeves of his cream silk shirt were rolled to the elbow and the brown flesh on his powerful forearms was pocked and gnarled like cane sugar left too long in the sack.

'I had a feeling it might be,' Prim replied.

'Firstly, I have to confess I have not been entirely frank with you.'

Oh God, not another one, thought Prim, remembering how Harry had said almost the same thing to her at the Cleopatra Club.

'Your father and I had a business arrangement,' Hamad went on, running one meaty hand over the crown of his bald head. 'And I am waiting for his return so that it may continue to flourish.'

'Are you telling me the money he was banking each week was yours? Was my father washing dirty money for you, Mr Hamad?' The directness of her question surprised even Prim. She could sense the sudden trepidation amongst his smooth young men, as if they expected an imminent eruption of volcanic anger. She wondered where the courage to ask it had come from; she'd never have taken a risk like this in England. But Shakir Hamad merely offered her the hurt face of a child unfairly chastised.

'That is a most discourteous slander, Miss Nevendon,' he said, feigning betrayal as he spread his great arms to present his chest to her, defenceless: Caesar inviting Brutus to stab him again. 'Here am I, a simple fellow who seeks only to be of assistance to the daughter of a friend. In Egypt a friend does not accuse another friend of such a thing. And I thought we had learned our manners from you English.'

'But is it true?' Prim asked, refusing to fall for the theatrics.

Hamad's smile was dazzling, almost as blinding as a smoke-screen, which Prim assumed was its purpose. 'A simple loan, Miss Primrose,' he said. 'Nothing more sinister than that.' He shrugged. 'As I told you before, I have a great attachment to the Nimrod Theatre and all its endeavours. What little help I can give pleases me greatly.'

'Am I then to believe that the reason the person carrying the money went unmolested all that time was because they were under your protection?'

'Call it the benefit of having a reputation,' Hamad said, as if he was speaking of an expense account. 'I can offer the same courtesy to the daughter of my old friend Archie, if she would not consider it presumptuous.'

It was an intriguing offer, Prim thought, but she doubted it would extend to the British authorities in Palestine. Only Harry could help her get there. 'Do you know where my father *is*, Mr Hamad?' she asked bluntly.

'If I did, I would tell you at once, Miss Primrose.'

'And do you know anything about the shooting at the Nimrod, and the murder of Mr Bannoudi? Does your reputation help you there at all?'

'That is a rather more complex issue,' Hamad replied regretfully. 'In that regard, I must sadly be somewhat circumspect.'

'You mean, you're not going to tell me.'

'Let me put it this way: when my very good friend Archie accepted my generous offer of financial help, it attracted the attention of certain third parties.'

'Third parties? That sounds ominous.'

Hamad gave a regretful smile. 'These third parties then also wished to enter into certain unspecified agreements with him.'

'You're being very vague, Mr Hamad. I assume that's deliberate.'

Hamad nodded. 'Sadly, I am not at liberty to disclose – let alone discuss – either these third parties or the nature of their arrangements with your father.'

'Would these third parties be located in Palestine, by any chance?'

Looking into Shakir Hamad's eyes was like watching the safety curtain come down at the end of the first act. You knew there was much activity going on behind, but you wouldn't see the results until the stage manager signalled for the curtain to go up again.

'Would you like me to have young Ahmed over there drive you back to where you're staying, Miss Primrose?' Hamad said, rising from his seat to show her out. 'At Mr Ashraf Shalaby's residence, I believe – the brother of your father's driver.'

Prim smiled and said that would be very generous of him. But she knew he hadn't made the offer solely out of concern for her safety. Or even to save her the walk to a tram stop. It was to remind her that he could reach her any time he chose.

Mike Luzzatto looked up from his copy of *Fortune* at the woman who had just that moment called his name. If she hadn't been wearing the same familiar dress, he might not have recognized her. In the few days since he'd last seen her, Prim Nevendon seemed to have grown a new persona: more confident, more assured, her stride brisker and her jawline more determined than before. He laid aside the magazine and rose to shake her hand.

'I owe you my thanks, Mike,' Prim said as she slipped into the empty seat across the little ottoman table from him.

'Really?' he replied, waving for a waiter. 'Why is that?'

'Shakir Hamad.'

'Ah, yes. Did you get what you wanted?'

'Well, yes and no. But thanks for arranging it.'

The waiter arrived and Luzzatto asked her what she wanted – a Daiquiri. For himself, he ordered another Tom Collins. 'Any closer to finding your father?' he asked when they were alone again.

She tipped her head from side to side. 'Again, yes and no.'

'Well, in this world sometimes that's as good as it gets,' he said with a consolatory smile. 'Made it up with Harry T yet?'

'I'm going to sound like a stuck record, aren't I?'

When the drinks arrived, Luzzatto raised a toast to her health. As they touched glasses, he said, 'So you've gone into business with Hamad.'

'I wouldn't go that far.'

'Hamad's not the only one with friends in this region, Prim. I know a few people, too. Maybe I could help.'

Her smile gave nothing away. 'But I'm not buying or selling – what do you Americans call it? – real estate.'

'I get it: you're trying to find your pop. I thought maybe I could help.'

Prim laughed. 'I've never thought of Archie as a "pop".'

'Well, like I said, if there's anything I can do—'

Sipping her Daiquiri, Prim kept her eyes on his for longer than mere politeness required. Beneath his veneer of handsome insouciance, she thought she detected a hint of perspicacity. As if Luzzatto knew more about her than he was letting on. Maybe it was a trick he used to convince a woman he was *simpatico* – nothing but a seduction technique. It had to be that; he couldn't possibly have even the slightest connection to Archie, no matter how well travelled he might be or how many people he might claim to know. 'That's kind of you, Mike,' she responded. 'But I'm pretty sure I'll be leaving Cairo soon, and I can't say when I'll be back.'

His eyes widened. 'Well then, there's only one thing for it. We must throw you a farewell party, right now.'

'But there's only the two of us. It won't be much of a party.'

'Good enough for me,' he said, raising his glass again. 'I've already had the concierge book a table at Santi's tonight. I'm told the food is excellent. It'll be good not to dine alone.'

'But I can't change.'

'I wouldn't want you to.'

'I mean *clothes*.'

'You look great as you are.'

If Prim was being honest with herself, it was only now that she'd made the decision about Palestine, committing herself irrevocably to a new course and the challenges it would bring, that the real loneliness of being adrift in a strange city was finally hitting home. So she said yes.

'Wait here a moment, Mike, while I tell my friend Tarek to spend the evening with his family and pick me up later.'

'Sure thing,' he said, and she could see in Luzzatto's eyes he was already running scenes in his imagination that might require her to keep a steady head.

In the Citroën she sat in the front passenger seat and pur-loined the rear-view mirror while she fixed her make-up.

'Are you sure he is a good man, Miss Archie?' Tarek asked.

'He's a young, handsome, rich Italian-American on his own in a big city,' she replied as she pouted at her lipstick. 'Any more respectable and he'd be Amish.' But it went over Tarek's head.

At Santi's the food was as good as Mike had promised. He was grand company, full of interesting and humorous anecdotes.

After the meal they danced, and his dancing was everything Prim had expected it to be – as smooth as his sharkskin suit. She knew from the start that he would ask her back to his room at the hotel. But she wasn't going to fall for that. While it was an appealing thought, she had learned long ago that flattering an already-sizeable male ego only ever really benefited one of the parties. Besides, if she was serious about reaching al-Sarhan, she would need to court a different man altogether. Deftly she fended him off while leaving his pride intact.

When Tarek picked her up after a nightcap at Shepheard's, Prim was feeling mellow for the first time since she'd arrived in Cairo. She dozed in the back of the Citroën as they made their way to Ashraf's house, for what Prim planned would be her last night there. She slept soundly, and when the call of the muezzin woke her briefly very early the next morning, she was able to recall dreamily just before she fell back to sleep a pleasant night spent in good company, though for the life of her, she couldn't remember if she'd mentioned Palestine when Mike Luzzatto had asked her where she was going next.

At noon, to Harry's immense relief, Primrose Nevendon walked into the British embassy in Cairo's Garden District as if nothing had happened. She sat calmly but a little stiffly in the lobby, hands clasped neatly in her lap, while Harry was summoned – like someone waiting for an appointment with the dentist, he decided, after he'd taken the red-carpeted stairs at a pace utterly in contravention of the dignity expected by the Foreign Office of its officers abroad.

'Thank God you're all right. I've been worried sick about you.'

'I'm not giving myself up – I haven't done anything,' she insisted. 'I want to make that quite clear.' Harry assured her it was as clear as daylight, noting a steeliness about her that he hadn't observed before. And when she said, 'Still no news of my father, I'm afraid,' it was delivered as if her absence had been merely a matter of popping down to the shops.

'Well, that's a shame,' he said. 'My enquiries have so far proved fruitless, too.'

'But I know much more than I did when I arrived,' she asserted brightly. 'He's been having an affair with a young actress.'

'That would be wonderful,' Harry said.

'What do you mean – wonderful?'

'Affairs, London can tolerate. If we were worried about people having affairs, we'd have to maintain files on half the Cabinet.'

Prim shook her head. 'That's not all there is to it. He's also been washing dirty money for a gangster – the chap we met at the Cleopatra Club.'

'Shakir Hamad?'

'That's him. I'm surprised you remember, seeing as how you were more interested in my youthful political indiscretions.'

'I remember the night well – the night *you* did the midnight flit, and *I* landed the opprobrium of my boss.'

Prim winced. 'Sorry about that. Just got a bit hemmed in, that's all. And I'm not very good when I get hemmed in. Anyway I don't think the dodgy money is the end of it. Hamad spoke about "third parties" getting involved—'

Harry looked appalled. 'Hamad? You've been with him?'

'If by "been with him" you mean two innocent meetings, then yes. If you mean it in the *Sunday Chronicle* sense, consider your face slapped.'

Harry said sternly, 'This isn't Tunbridge Wells, Prim. God alone knows what could have happened to you.'

She could hear the genuine concern in his rebuke, so she let it pass. 'I think it could have been one of those third parties who staged the shooting at my father's theatre. I think they're the ones who then murdered poor Mr Bannoudi to try to make him tell them where Archie has gone.'

'Did Hamad give you any clue as to who *they* might be?'

'No. He wouldn't say. I got the feeling that even he was wary of them.'

'Well, there's little point in asking the Egyptians to sweat him and make him talk. Your Mr Hamad has friends in very high places.'

'He's not my friend, Harry,' Prim said hastily. 'But I am sure everything points towards Palestine. I need you to help me go there.'

Harry looked at her, astonished. 'You want to go to *Palestine*?'

'That's where the actress is. Her name is Ifaya Jabour. She might know where I can find Archie. He might even be with her.'

'We'll need permission,' Harry replied doubtfully. 'But I suppose I could try to swing it. Anywhere in particular?'

'A village called al-Sarhan,' Prim said. 'Apparently it's the most beautiful place in the whole world. I doubt that's true; I used to think East Grinstead was wonderful. But I'm sure that's where we'll start to find some answers.'

Nineteen

A thousand feet below them the sandbar of the Bardawil lagoon cut like scar tissue through the glittering blue-green face of the Mediterranean. Now that they were out over water, the ride was smoother. Passing Port Said off to their left, the Rapide had bucked alarmingly in the thermals rising from the desert, lifting her from her seat before slamming her back down again and bringing her uncomfortably close to retching – a poor reward for all Harry's hard work over the preceding five days, she considered.

He had worked miracles. First he'd had to get his boss – whose name he declined to reveal to her – to give him permission to make the journey. Then he'd had to clear their entry into the Mandate territory with the British authorities in Jerusalem. But his greatest triumph had been persuading Anglo-Levantine to fly them there in the company aeroplane – the very same one she'd seen on her first visit to Heliopolis aerodrome. It would save them the torture of an eighty-mile drive from Cairo to Ismailia, a ferry across the Suez Canal and a train journey from Kantara over the top of the Sinai Peninsula to the border crossing at Raffa, and then onwards up the coast to Haifa. The Rapide could do the entire journey in well under three hours.

The pilot was one of Anglo-Levantine's people, though Prim had to stop herself seeing Archie at the controls whenever she looked past the bulkhead to the little cockpit. Through the window to her left, the sunlight gleamed on the silver fabric of the lower wing and danced on the struts and bracing wires. To her right, across the narrow aisle, Harry dozed in his seat. He'd been that way since they left Heliopolis, imperturbable even when the machine bucked and lurched. Here *she* was, dress clinging to her like damp medical gauze, yet his shirt appeared barely creased and he seemed in the folds of a pleasant slumber. She remembered a recent hot summer day at Bevern Lodge when everyone had got a little too exuberant on rum punch, and Angus, the playwright who was sweet over her, had up-ended an ice bucket over Gianni, the Italian boy, whom he saw as a threat. Gianni had carried on talking to her as if it had never happened, refusing to give Angus his victory. In a crisis, she reckoned, Harry Taverner would have the same level of sangfroid. It gave her a measure of confidence for what lay ahead.

Soon the seascape below lulled even Prim into drowsiness and, when she woke, a glance at her wristwatch told her they'd been aloft for two and a half hours. She felt the Rapide sink and knew they were preparing to land. Harry was already peering out of his window, his attention fixed on something off the right wingtip. Prim undid her seatbelt and slipped in behind him. Now she could see the slopes of Mount Carmel rising from the coast, green with oak and scrub, flecked with white where the stone and boulders caught the sunlight breaking through the leafy canopy.

They swept in towards Haifa, and Prim could see a British cruiser at anchor in the bay, a brooding grey shark amidst the passenger steamers and the sailing dhows. She saw a green lamp flash beside the aerodrome control building and then they were down and taxiing across the dirt apron towards a hangar, where a military open-topped truck awaited them. Beside it was parked an Austin saloon painted a drab desert beige. Leaning nonchalantly against the bonnet was an army officer. Mid-thirties, Prim reckoned, with a pugnacious jaw that suggested he was no regimental dandy. In her limited experience of British officers, she had found them smart and punctilious. This one, with scuffed boots, no tie and an open shirt, looked as though he'd come hotfoot from digging in his allotment.

'Welcome to Mandated Palestine,' he said as they stepped out of the Rapide. 'My name's Wingate – Orde Wingate – Military Intelligence, Jerusalem.'

'Pleased to meet you, Captain Wingate,' Harry replied, noting the three pips on each of the man's shoulders. 'Harry Taverner, from the embassy in Cairo.'

'And this must be Miss Nevendon,' Wingate said, extending a hand for Prim to shake. 'Still no news about your father, I'm afraid.'

'You know about him?' Prim asked, surprised by Wingate's directness.

'Only what my brigadier has told me: influential British oil man with inside knowledge of the pipeline that may be of help to the Germans or the Italians, now missing.'

On the aeroplane, Harry had told Prim to leave the serious talking to him. She'd bridled at that, but he'd explained that the authorities in Palestine would be more inclined to assist if they thought Archie's disappearance was a security threat. Any hint that it might be connected to a romantic liaison and they'd almost certainly withdraw their help. Lack of resources, he'd explained, was as much a tribulation to the mandated territory as it was to Cairo.

'Have you heard anything that might help us, Captain Wingate?' she asked.

Wingate shook his head. 'Not a squeak, I'm afraid. I do keep my ear to the ground – lot of good contacts amongst the Palestinian Jews. But so far, nothing.'

'What about the Arabs?' Harry asked, picking up the two small suitcases they'd brought with them.

'That's not so easy, I'm afraid. The tame ones, like the Nashashibi tribe, will talk to us, but most of what they tell us is designed to hurt the untamed ones.'

'Untamed ones?' Harry echoed, frowning at Wingate's off-hand description.

'I'm speaking of the followers of Amin al-Husseini, the Grand Mufti. Their only connection with your father is that they keep trying to blow up his oil pipeline – that's when they're not shooting at us from behind rocks or planting mines for our trucks to run over. Funny old world, isn't it? We free this place from the rule of the Ottoman sultans, and the only thanks we get come in the form of dynamite. There's no pleasing some people.'

'Does the family name Jabour ring any bells, Captain Wingate?' Prim asked, attracting a quick glance of concern from Harry.

'Jabour?' Frowning, Wingate searched his memory and found it wanting. 'Not one that springs to mind, but then my job is to focus on the troublemakers, you see. Why do you ask?'

'I believe my father may have had a connection to the family,' Prim replied.

'And they're from the Galilee area – is that what I'm to understand, from Mr Taverner's phone call?'

'Miss Nevendon thinks he may possibly have spent time there in the recent past,' Harry interjected.

'It's just an idea,' Prim said. 'We're clutching at straws really.'

'When we get to Tiberias, have a word with the district commissioner,' Wingate suggested. 'Perhaps he'll be able to point you in the right direction.' He glanced at his wristwatch. 'We'd best be on our way. The special train leaves in half an hour.'

'We're going by *train*?' Harry said, surprised.

'There's a platoon of Manchesters going to Galilee – reinforcements. We're going with them. It's better than risking a long road journey.' Wingate opened the Austin's rear door and gestured to Prim to climb in. 'Unless, of course, you're eager to run over a mine, or have something with a fizzing fuse thrown through the window by a chap in a *dishdasha* who'll swear on his mother's grave that he was nowhere near when we arrest him later.' He grinned. 'Can't promise you the *Flying Scotsman*, but I can guarantee they won't attempt to blow us up.'

As Wingate started the car and pulled away from the Rapide, Prim wondered how he could be so sure of their safety. But there was a restless audacity in his eyes that reassured her. We're in competent hands, she thought. And as if to prove it, he was soon deep in conversation with Harry, declaiming how much he preferred soldiering in Palestine over Sudan, and what splendid men and women the *kibbutzniks* were. Archie, she decided with a smile, would have loved him.

No! Archie *would* love him.

Dr Yousef Jabour's morning surgery had been a busy one. He preferred it that way. He was a young man, barely thirty, and his devotion to the health of his scattered flock in and around the lakeside town of Tiberias on the shore of Lake Galilee was, as yet, undiminished by routine. His patients, for the most part, were poor: agricultural workers from the orange groves, or shepherds and goat herders – hardy people who toiled in the surrounding hills. But financial reward was not Dr Jabour's motivation. As he had often told his father, if he'd wanted wealth he would have stayed in Damascus, where he had studied.

When the last patient, a child of eight suffering from bacterial blepharitis, an eye infection, had been treated and rewarded with a sugary *zalabiyeh*, Dr Jabour shuttered his house and waited for the expected knock on the door. He didn't have to wait long.

The man who tapped the agreed signal was dressed in the simple brown cloth robe of a *fellahin* and looked as though he had arrived straight from tilling his meagre plot. In fact he was not a local man. Known to Dr Jabour only as 'the Syrian', he had crossed over from Transjordan with a group of Bedouin, slipping into Tiberias unobserved. Like Yousef himself, he was a member of the Black Hand, a disparate and fluid group that had vowed vengeance for the death of Izz al-Din al-Qassam, one of the revolt's torchbearers, slain in a shootout with the British more than two years before.

Jabour checked the lane to ensure they were not observed and hurried the man inside. When the Syrian pulled back the hood of his *galabeya*, the doctor found himself looking into the eyes of a bearded man about his own age. But where the physician's eyes were brown and good-natured, the newcomer's had the hardness of a man for whom killing a fellow human being would count for no more than the slaughter of a goat at the feast of Eid al-Fitr. The two men wished peace upon each other and shook hands.

'What news of your uncle?' the Syrian asked.

'Preparing himself for heaven,' said Yousef. His uncle was in hospital in Jerusalem, his cancer being treated by Jewish physicians. The irony was not lost on him.

'You should remove him. The Zionists will surely kill him.'

'They have better facilities.'

The Syrian waved a cautionary finger. 'But your skill is given to you by Allah, Lord of the Worlds – may His blessings and peace be upon our Prophet Muhammad and upon all his Family and Companions. There can be no better skill than that.'

Yousef Jabour echoed the pious declaration, lest the Syrian question his fidelity, then said, 'Surely it is not forbidden to want the best care for one's relatives.'

The laugh the Syrian gave had a hard edge to it. 'Have you been taking advice from the Englishman, Brother? We would not like to think you had.'

'He hasn't been here since before al-Sarhan,' Dr Jabour said hurriedly. 'I would have told you if he had.'

'I hope so. Our brothers in Cairo tell us his daughter arrived there. She may already be here in Palestine. Perhaps she knows where he is.'

'The last person you thought might know *that* died before he could unburden himself,' Dr Jabour said.

'The apostate Bannoudi? Yes, we were unsubtle in that regard, I fear.'

'Almost as unsubtle as sending a team of Damascus gunmen to shoot up the Englishman's theatre, wasn't it?'

'Sometimes a point must be made,' the Syrian said. 'We hoped it might cause him to break cover.'

'But instead it only drove him deeper into the thicket.'

'What are you suggesting, Yousef?'

Yousef Jabour swallowed hard. The Syrian's barely hidden ruthlessness scared him. Always had. 'If she comes here, it would be best to befriend her,' Yousef suggested. 'After all, if she knows of al-Sarhan, then she knows about my cousin Ifaya. And if she knows where the Englishman is hiding, perhaps we should let her guide us to him.'

A dark cunning infused the Syrian's lean face. 'A lamb to attract the wolf?' he said, almost smiling. 'A daughter to ensnare a father. I approve.'

Yousef Jabour lowered his eyes. He didn't want the Syrian to see what was in them, in case he was found wanting. 'We are all engaged in a great struggle,' he said softly, as much to his own conscience as to the Syrian. 'Others have made far greater sacrifices than I.'

The Syrian took Yousef by the shoulder and his grip felt like talons sinking into his skin. 'You were not made for battle, Physician. We know that,' he replied, close enough now for Yousef to catch the animal smell of a long and arid journey across the desert. 'But you are trusted. And this business with your cousin will surely be but a small and fleeting pain.'

'Then I am ready to do anything you ask,' Yousef said.

The Syrian's smile was like a poorly stitched wound opening. 'You were never doubted, Brother,' he answered. And with that, he went outside to retrieve the packages of small-arms ammunition he had carried across the River Jordan hidden in a sack of walnuts.

They drove along the Haifa waterfront where the steamers were moored, past boxy whitewashed houses, past the flour mill that towered above the tiled rooftops like a crusader fortress, until they came to a building that looked to Prim as if it had sprung from the pages of *The Prisoner of Zenda*. Were it not for the platform extending on each side, she might have taken it for an ornate Ruritanian town hall magically transported to the Levant.

Wingate brought the Austin to a halt. They spilled out and he led the way through the station to the platform, where a detachment of British soldiery was drawn up in loose order. Clad in knee-length khaki shorts, Wolseley pith helmets on their heads, they looked bored and listless, their muscular bronzed limbs suggesting these were seasoned troops who'd seen all that Palestine had to offer and found it only marginally more appealing than Aldershot or Catterick. Their officer was a fresh-faced boy who Prim reckoned hadn't seen much of anything. He couldn't be older than nineteen.

Spotting Wingate, the soldiers suddenly discovered smartness, coming to attention even before their officer had issued the command or raised his open palm to his temple in salute. Captain Wingate, Prim reckoned, must have a reputation.

A dirty black locomotive was raising steam. Behind the coal tender were coupled two carriages painted a fading green. Prim saw the words *Southern Railways* painted on the coachwork. The train looked so out of place she had to stifle a laugh.

Then she noticed an odd contraption being attached to the cow-catcher at the front of the locomotive. It looked like a low-slung cart with a small wheel at each corner, flanged to fit the railway track. As she watched, four policemen emerged from the station waiting room. They were escorting two Arab men, both handcuffed, who stared ahead with the sullen acceptance of the condemned. With the cart now attached to the front of the engine, the two men were unceremoniously bundled aboard, made to sit and their manacles were attached by chains to eye-bolts set into the chassis.

'Now we're ready to go,' said Wingate contentedly. 'Didn't I promise you we'd be safe from sabotage?'

Prim stared at the two Arabs as the purpose of their presence dawned on her.

'Hostages?' asked Harry dubiously, putting her thoughts into words.

Wingate's mask of good-fellowship slipped a little, and Prim caught sight of a cold ruthlessness beneath. 'Think of them as our insurance policy,' he said. 'They get a pleasant ride to Tiberias. We avoid getting blown up and derailed. Good outcomes all round.'

Wingate instructed the young lieutenant to get his men aboard. Then he led Prim and Harry to a compartment in the first carriage. It smelt oddly familiar, a woollen scent of commuters' well-worn suits, the olfactory memory of pipe smoke, the waxy hint of varnished veneer. There was a faded poster in a frame on one wall, advertising day-trips to Ilfracombe that no one had bothered to remove when they'd craned the carriage aboard whatever cargo ship had carried it from England. Wingate settled himself down opposite Prim, making a cushion for his head with his hands. He seemed eager to be away, as if it were all a great adventure. A whistle blew, a gust of smoke billowed past the window, the compartment lurched and, with a metallic screech, they began their journey. We're off to the seaside, thought Prim. I'm going up to London to ask Granny G to fund my madcap scheme. It's a ghost train, Archie's spectre is waiting for me in the tunnel and I'll never get out alive.

They were rolling across a wide plain of fields and orchards, with the slopes of Mount Carmel off to their right. Prim could see, high up on a crest, the pale face of a little monastery set amongst the cedars and olive groves. She had looked down on it from the air, and now she was looking up at it from a train.

'That's the Carmelite monastery at al-Mukhraqa,' Wingate told her. 'Supposedly it marks the spot where God accepted the prophet Elijah's sacrifice over that of the Canaanites. On that same mountain, a few years back, they dug up human bones they think are more than half a million years old. In this land it doesn't matter where you look or where you tread – you can't escape history. It's in the soil beneath your feet. It's in the air you breathe. All told, it's a bloody nuisance.'

A gust of coal smoke flew past the half-open window, making Prim cough. 'I agree,' she said. 'Sometimes it's possible to have a little too much history.'

'There again, how can you tell who you are if you don't know your history?' Wingate asked.

'It depends on who's writing the history,' Harry said casually. 'I've spent the last couple of years in Vienna and Berlin. They're writing a history there that serves only one purpose: exclusion and hatred. Herr Hitler has just about managed to convince the Germans that he's Frederick the Great and Bismarck rolled into one. He's made it pretty clear that if there's war in Europe, the Jews will be forced out.'

'All the more reason for them to find shelter here in their ancestral homeland,' Wingate said. 'It's not as if they don't have a historical claim to it. Beneath the al-Aqsa Mosque in Jerusalem lie the ruins of the Israelites' Second Temple. How's that for staking a claim?'

'Will the Arabs ever accept that?' Prim asked.

'I believe it will be in their interest to do so,' Wingate said. 'The influx of European Jews into this land has led to tremendous progress. They'll want to share in it.'

'And what if they don't?'

'Look at America. The Sioux and the Cheyenne didn't build the Empire State Building or the railways, did they? In England the Anglo-Saxons didn't build the Tower of London. Peoples get subsumed. One group supplants another. It's part of what makes us what we are. We were doing it when those bones up on Mount Carmel were running around with spears. I dare say we'll be doing it when there are cities on the moon.'

'You mean the survival of the fittest?' Harry said doubtfully. 'I've heard a lot of that sort of thing in Germany.'

'What I mean is: you can't stop the tide from going out and coming in. If you think you can, you're fooling yourself. Swimming against it only makes it harder to reach dry land, that's all.'

Beneath a dazzling sky the little train chugged purposefully onwards past olive groves and stands of cedar. Now the breeze was carrying the engine smoke away from the window and Prim could breathe again.

Despite Wingate's earlier impatience to be away, he now seemed untroubled by their leisurely progress. Without preamble, he suddenly began speaking in a foreign language. It took Prim by surprise, and more than a moment to realize it was Hebrew. Seeing the questioning look on her face, he smiled and said, 'Matthew, chapter seventeen, verse twenty-two. "Now while they were staying in Galilee, Jesus said to them, 'The Son of Man is about to be betrayed into the hands of men, and they will kill Him, and the third day He will be raised up.' And they were exceedingly sorrowful."'

'Oh yes, right,' said Prim, somewhat unnerved by his intensity.

'I mean only that I hope you find what you're looking for at Tiberias on the shores of Galilee, Miss Nevendon, and not betrayal and sorrow.'

'I'm not too sure *what* I expect to find, to be honest. I'll be content if it's not just a dead end.'

'I wish you luck.'

'Will we be safe?'

'Safe enough,' Wingate replied. 'Most of the violence happens at night – foreign fighters slip over the Jordan and incite the local hotheads to fire off a few rounds at our patrols, or plant dynamite under the railway tracks. They did it a few nights back, near Samakh. That's where young Lieutenant Strachan and his Manchesters are heading – to have a friendly word with the locals to encourage their continued good manners.' He gave a shark's smile. 'Then we'll motor up the shoreline to Tiberias and deliver you to the district commissioner.'

Since they'd left Haifa, Harry had been quietly watching the landscape roll by as if he was on a pleasant but unchallenging sightseeing trip. Prim knew it was a front. She was sure he'd been making a careful assessment of their unusual escort. His silences were the most productive of any man she'd ever met. Now he stretched his legs as if waking from a pleasant nap and said, 'My head of station in Cairo painted a picture of almost continual internecine conflict. But you're telling us the area around Tiberias is peaceful.'

'For the most part, it is,' Wingate agreed, 'otherwise you wouldn't be here. We've only had a couple of outbreaks recently: one last December, when some Arabs murdered a Jew at Kfar Hittin. The other was just a few weeks ago – a spot of bother in an Arab village in the hills to the west—'

Wingate's pause was barely long enough for him to draw breath. But it was wide enough for Prim to sense the icy inevitability of what would come next. And even before he found his voice again, she was praying for her intuition to fail her.

'A little place barely worth fighting over,' Wingate continued. 'The locals call it al-Sarhan.'

Twenty

Samakh was a dusty nondescript little place of square, flat-roofed houses on the flat southern shore of Galilee. The railway halt boasted not even a single platform to alight upon. The town seemed deserted, save for the three army trucks waiting beside the line. Parked nearby was an open-topped motorcar, the driver dozing behind the wheel. Apart from him, the only other sign of a welcoming committee was a single Bedouin and his donkey, both of whom watched the train pull in with a profound and timeless apathy. But had Samakh matched Venice for splendour, Prim would scarcely have noticed. All she could think of was al-Sarhan and what she would find there.

A spot of bother… A little place barely worth fighting over, Wingate had said. Prim knew his kind. Archie had frequently indulged in the same sort of infuriating English understatement. 'A spot of bother' could mean anything from a raised voice all the way to bloody murder. And she wouldn't know which until Captain Orde Wingate, Lieutenant Strachan and their panoply of British might in Palestine – two score suntanned men of the Manchester regiment – had, in Wingate's own words, *a friendly word with the locals to encourage their continued good manners.*

Harry had been a rock. He'd said nothing, shown no reaction when Wingate had uttered his awful pronouncement. She supposed that's how spies were trained – to give nothing away, to remain unreadable even when the world was ending. But as they had left the compartment he had gently, and without display, squeezed her hand.

The troops climbed aboard the trucks. Wingate greeted the driver of the car in Arabic, explaining to Prim and Harry that he was a Palestinian Arab police constable – one of the few not yet intimidated by the rebels into leaving the force – sent by the district commissioner. Prim and Harry climbed into the rear seats, and Wingate, slipping in beside the driver, ordered them forward as if they were the vanguard of an invading army. Once out of Samakh, they followed the western shore, climbing through a fringe of palms and on into groves of small, hardy oaks where fallen flags of red anemones and banners of blue lupins streamed amongst the rocks. Prim could see out across the lake towards the misty cliffs of the southern Golan. Close inshore, fishermen cast their nets into the flat water, the spray glinting in the lowering sun of late afternoon. It would take no effort at all, she thought, to picture a baptism in the transparent shallows. She wouldn't even have to close her eyes to see it. She wondered if Archie had come this way, and what visions his love of history would have conjured up for him. She tried to imagine her father and Uncle Nim trowelling biblical treasures from the rocky soil. But to her surprise, she found the picture too fragile. It wouldn't hold. It wouldn't fix. It burst like a soap bubble, leaving only fleeting fragments of temporary beauty.

That troubled Prim. If she could imagine a baptism from the time of Jesus so intensely that it felt real, why couldn't she sense Archie and Nim in the very landscape they'd been born to inhabit? For a moment she felt betrayed by her own memory. She thought again of the time the police had come to Bevern

S. W. PERRY

Lodge, when she'd sought comfort in remembering how Archie had helped her play at being archaeologists on the lawn, digging up the fake plaster artefacts that Celestina had made specifically to be rediscovered by their eight-year-old daughter. But again the childhood picture in her head seemed unusually flimsy. It was almost, she thought, as if she'd made it up. As if it had never happened.

She wished again that she'd brought Archie's letters with her and not left them with Granny G in London. Reading them now might make his outline sharper, turn him from a ghost – a living one, because she wouldn't countenance the alternative – into something more substantial.

There again, his messages had never been what she might call *unrestrained*. So maybe it was the landscape that was overwhelming her, permitting Prim only its own memories. Perhaps she was simply tired from the long journey. But at least, for a short while, the uncertainty made her forget about al-Sarhan.

A deep-throated command woke Prim from her torpor. Drawn by the rough male voice, she saw Lieutenant Strachan's sergeant standing by the door of one of the trucks, bellowing at the Manchesters to get out. She glanced at her watch. They'd been on the road for almost an hour.

Looking around, she saw they had stopped on a track beside an orchard of acacia trees. No more than fifty yards away lay a small cluster of tumbledown stone houses, box-square, with tiny slit windows that looked as if they'd been designed for archers to shoot arrows at crusaders, rather than to let in light. Some of the Manchesters were advancing on the little hamlet, and although their riffles were slung over their shoulders, Prim was horrified to see that they had fixed bayonets.

Outside the houses a group of villagers had gathered. They stood as if frozen, so bewildered and confused by what they were witnessing that not one of them had thought of running away. The women had their children gathered around their embroidered loose-fitting robes, clutching their little hands tightly as if they feared the troops were slave-traders of old. No one seemed to know quite what to do.

The Arab policeman who'd driven them up from Samakh had already left the car. Now he was addressing an old man who stood at the door of the one house that seemed marginally less dilapidated than the rest. His thin, almost toothless face was as weathered as the ancient oaks Prim had noticed on the way up. By the dignified way he answered the policeman's questions, she guessed he was the village headsman. Then his expression turned to one of distress, and although Prim couldn't understand the words, his animated protests needed no translation.

The Manchesters entered the houses in pairs. Within moments, the village menfolk were being led out at bayonet point and placed under guard, away from the women and children. They stood in a line, sullen-faced, resentful, humiliated at being unable to protect their families. Then more soldiers went into the houses and began throwing out their meagre contents: bed sheets, pots and pans, children's toys, little wooden stools, family heirlooms... In a grotesque dance they began to trample them underfoot, smashing with rifle butts what they could not crush with their boots. The women and children looked on with terror in their eyes, the menfolk with impotent fury. Prim watched all this open-mouthed, save for when she cast a glance at Harry and saw the grim, silent set of his jaw.

Wingate and Strachan went over to the menfolk and began to speak with them, Wingate leading the questioning in Arabic.

The villagers' responses seemed mostly ones of embittered denial. There was a lot of frantic hand-waving. Wingate called over a burly sergeant, who listened intently to what the captain told him – Prim was too far away to hear clearly. Wingate then pointed to one of the houses. The sergeant doubled off to one of the trucks.

Lieutenant Strachan came over to where Prim and Harry were standing. 'Move back, please, Mr Taverner, Miss Nevendon,' he said, pointing to a small, twisted oak standing beside the road, its bark bleached by the sun. 'About *there* would be sensible, if you wouldn't mind.'

The villagers were ordered at bayonet point into the orchard, away from the houses. As Prim and Harry looked on from their new vantage point by the oak, two soldiers each carried a wooden box from one of the trucks. They followed the sergeant into one of the houses. A short while later they emerged at the run, joining the other soldiers by the trucks.

The explosion, when it came, felt to Prim like being dropped face-down onto a firm mattress from a height. Without having a hard edge to it, it encompassed her, tore the breath from her body in a single thump and moved on. A thick pale-grey cloud now bloomed where before the house had stood. As it drifted away on the wind, it revealed a large pile of debris from which broken rafters poked like the fingers of a buried hand clawing to break free, and a single remaining mud-brick wall. A brief shower of dusty detritus rained and then all was silent, save for the wailing of the family whose home it had once been.

Wingate, with a faint smile of satisfaction on his face, now decided the required chastisement for whatever crime the hamlet had committed had been sufficiently administered. He produced a whistle from his breast pocket and blew it, the note echoing forlornly from the surrounding hills. Like a pack of fox hounds, the Manchesters reassembled. Wingate got back in the car. Strachan ordered his men to re-board the trucks and the entire column moved off up the road, leaving the little hamlet looking as though a hurricane had just passed over it.

'That's supposed to get them on our side, is it?' Harry asked, looking straight ahead rather than at the back of Wingate's head.

Wingate turned to look over his shoulder. 'They got off lightly, Mr Taverner. You can't treat these people with kid gloves. They'd merely laugh at us.'

'Surely all you've done is to make enemies of them,' Prim said.

Wingate sighed. 'Your sympathy is wrongly directed, Miss Nevendon. Last September the rebels shot dead the district commissioner in Nazareth. They assassinate their own people if they catch them serving with the police. They shoot at our soldiers in ambushes. What are we supposed to do – ask them if they wouldn't mind being a bit more civil? If I had my way, I could end this revolt inside a month. All it needs is the right weight of lead fired in the proper direction.'

After that, the journey onwards to Tiberias was conducted mostly in silence. Prim was too busy wondering about Wingate's throwaway mention on the train of an incident at al-Sarhan. If it was anything like the violence that had been visited upon the little village, his words did not bode well.

The sun was sinking over the hills behind them when they arrived, casting a golden blush on Lake Galilee and making the cliffs on the distant eastern shore glow as if they'd been lit by a good set designer. Harry had cabled ahead before they'd left Cairo, reserving two rooms at the Hotel Tiberias. Basic accommodation only; not the bloody bridal suite, Major Courtney had ordered. And all subsistence to be met in cash, and by Harry personally, at the time. No bills arriving in the post later to startle the purse-keepers at His Majesty's Colonial Office.

But the Tiberias turned out to be a comfortable establishment with a quaint, rustic feel about it. And it overlooked the lake.

Wingate wished them good luck and took himself off to the district commissioner's office in town, promising to tell the official of their arrival. He planned to return to British headquarters in Jerusalem at first light.

Prim was glad. What she had witnessed in the little village, along with the block of ice he'd left in her stomach after his throwaway comment on the train about al-Sarhan – which was even now refusing to melt – had made him uncomfortably malignant for her, even if she wasn't entirely sure he deserved it.

The air was cool, with a soft breeze drifting down towards the shore. They dined on the terrace: fish from the lake and a rather good local wine. Harry made a silly joke about ordering three more portions and getting a few loaves and then they'd be able to feed the five thousand. Prim said she was pretty sure every single tourist who'd ever eaten there probably said the same thing.

'I was trying to take your mind off al-Sarhan,' he said with a defensive smile.

'It'll take more than a silly joke, I'm afraid.'

'Sometimes a silly joke is exactly what's called for.'

She smiled. 'And I thank you for it, Harry. Honestly.'

'Besides, what Wingate said on the train – it's probably nothing.'

'But it might be everything.'

Harry propped his chin in one palm, trying to appear royally unconcerned. 'Look, there's no reason to assume whatever happened there involved Archie or Ifaya Jabour. No reason at all. And remember, at Haifa aerodrome when you asked him, Wingate didn't even recognize her name. He's in Intelligence, for God's sake. If it had been anything bad, he'd have known about it.'

Prim accepted his reassurance, as much to please Harry as to quell her own fears. They sat in silence a while, watching the purple of evening spreading across the surface of the water. Then, out of nowhere, she said, 'It troubled you, didn't it – what we saw in that village? Admit it.'

Harry held up his wine glass to catch the changing colours of the lake through its curved bowl. Prim could see he was conflicted.

'I'll admit it didn't please me,' he replied at length, after taking a sip of wine. 'But honestly, if this was Germany instead of Palestine, they'd have beaten up the men and the women and sent them to a camp.'

'Is that supposed to excuse it?'

'They have a place named Dachau, you know,' he went on, evading her question. 'It's where they send their political prisoners. Some of them don't even make it that far. They just get a bullet in their heads.'

'That doesn't make what we saw right, though, does it?'

Harry shrugged. 'If you have any bright ideas about how to put down a revolt, I'm sure Mr Chamberlain and Lord Halifax will be only too happy to give you a fair hearing.'

'You must have seen the fear in the eyes of those women and children.'

'Of course I did.'

'Didn't it mean anything to you?'

'What do you take me for, one of the brownshirts?'

'Why didn't you say something?'

'Like what?'

'I don't know – what about ordering Wingate and Strachan to stop.'

'I have no authority over them. This is their patch. They would have ignored me. Or put me under guard.'

'So we simply go along with it. What does that make us, Harry?'

He shrugged. 'Look, most governments these days do beastly things. I suppose we should be grateful ours is a little less beastly than most. Call it progress.' He held her gaze, waiting for her counter-attack. It didn't come.

'Well, I'm going to write to my MP when I get home. I don't suppose anyone in England has the faintest idea that we do things like that.'

Harry said, 'I can see now why you didn't find common cause with the British Union of Fascists.'

'Is that meant to provoke me?'

'Of course not. We're just having an interesting conversation over a pleasant supper in a beautiful setting.'

She looked away. 'I still don't know whether to take it as a compliment or throw this wine in your face, Harry Taverner.'

'It's too nice an evening to argue about things we can't change,' Harry said. 'Care for a stroll?'

They walked down to the shoreline where the fishing boats were tied up. To their left, the ancient houses tumbled down to the water's edge, some with domes rising from their flat roofs, others looking so ancient they might have been standing here since Herod Antipas ruled Galilee. Gazing out across the lake, Prim said, 'Don't you think maybe it would be better if we weren't here at all?'

'But I thought you wanted to find Archie.'

'Don't be so obtuse, Harry,' Prim replied, tossing her head. 'I didn't mean *us*, I meant Britain.'

'We're here because the League of Nations has given us a mandate to be here.'

'We're here because our government thinks the region is important to our interests,' Prim said. 'Otherwise we wouldn't have come all the way out here to defeat the Ottoman Turks.'

'They were allied with the Germans. We were fighting a war,' Harry responded, to the accompaniment of creaking timber as two fishing boats rubbed together in a sybaritic embrace.

'And we made all sorts of crazy promises to the Arabs to convince them it was in their interests to assist us,' Prim countered. 'So here we are – stuck with it.'

Harry gave her an admiring glance. 'Have you been attending those workers' educational classes they put on at night-schools in places like Highgate and Islington, by any chance?'

'That's very patronizing of you, Harry Taverner.'

'It wasn't meant that way.'

'I have a lot of theatre friends. They're mostly socialists. And, like everyone else, I have ears and I can read. But my opinions, I hope, are my own.'

'I didn't mean to be rude. Can we both agree on the proposition that it's a lovely evening and the scenery is to die for.'

He was definitely right about *that*, Prim thought. Suddenly she felt an intense loneliness, a desperate need for human comfort.

'You can kiss me if you want to, Harry.'

The words seemed to fly out of nowhere. Prim wasn't even sure they were hers. They certainly hadn't asked her permission to escape.

Harry turned his face towards her. Prim didn't know whether to blush or weep.

'That's a very generous offer,' he said gently. 'But I think the setting, and the fact that you're probably feeling a little out of your depth and anxious, are clouding your judgement.'

'You mean you don't *want* to kiss me?'

'I didn't say that.'

Prim rolled her eyes to the darkening sky. She sighed, though she couldn't tell whether it was a sigh of disappointment or relief. 'Don't tell me you're not interested in girls, Harry.'

That seemed to take him aback. 'What? No. I mean yes. Girls – splendid. Every one of them.'

'I won't think any the less of you, I promise,' Prim replied quickly, as if by giving her words a push, they might somehow overtake the others and nullify them. 'Most of my male friends in the theatre aren't interested in girls. It won't matter.' She drew breath, but realized there was yet more to do to set things right. '*Although…*' she stretched the word to breaking point, 'I have to say it is a *teeny-weeny* bit disappointing.'

Harry's laugh was reassuringly deep. To Prim's ears, it was the best antidote to embarrassment that he could have offered. 'I have to say I am hugely honoured, but it wouldn't work. It wouldn't be right.'

'Can't I decide that for myself?'

'By all means. But *I* have a duty to remain professional.'

'Oh yes – *professional*,' Prim said laboriously. 'I suppose there must be a handbook for English spies. In bed by ten p.m. No reading by torchlight. And definitely no impropriety after lights out.'

'Mock all you like – I deserve it.'

'It's just that I never took you for a cold fish, Harry Taverner.'

He gave her a regretful smile. 'There's someone in Germany, you see. I'm rather fond of her. If things were different—'

'Oh, I see. Sorry.'

'Nothing to be sorry about, I promise you.'

Prim fanned her cheeks. She stared out across the lake. 'How very embarrassing.'

'And nothing to be embarrassed about either, honestly.'

'Oh well, your loss, Harry Taverner,' she said with what she hoped was a teasing smile and not just a floozy's leer.

'Which I shall bear nobly and with regret.'

After that, each buried whatever discomfort remained by playing the tourist. They wandered in the cooling air, pointing out with exaggerated delight all the strange and novel things to be seen in a place where history oozed from the earth whenever you trod upon it. And Prim discovered she was able to push the loneliness down into the same vault in which she was holding her other troubles at bay – like her fear for what had really happened at al-Sarhan, and whether Ifaya Jabour had been caught up in it. She managed to laugh at Harry's awful jokes, even gift him her trust, which had been an on–off affair ever since they'd met. But as they said goodnight and went to their separate rooms, she resolved that the next time she went somewhere romantic she'd invite Mike Luzzatto along instead. He would never let scruples get in the way of a pleasant fling.

The district commissioner's house was guarded by two armed sentries. One of them, rifle slung across his back, was patting down an Arab who had arrived with a petition or a letter of protest, it was impossible to tell which. Arms raised above his head, he was waving the sheet of paper aloft like a flag of defiance. Harry and Prim were allowed entry with no more than a cursory request to state their business.

The Tiberias district commissioner was a scholarly-looking Welshman named Hughes, bespectacled and diffident. He seemed to Prim a strangely unmartial fellow to be running a district in Palestine during a revolt. She could better visualize him administering an antiquarian archive deep in the bowels of a provincial university. He sat behind an ornate Ottoman desk, a photo portrait of King George VI on the wall behind him and a view from the open window of the ancient town walls. The scent of roses wafted from the garden – planted, Prim assumed, to remind Mr Hughes of home.

'Forgive me, Mr Taverner,' Hughes said, being the sort of official who assumed the male must be the instigator of the visit, 'but I'm not entirely sure what it is you desire of me. I received a message via Jerusalem, but it was somewhat vague. Which government department do you work for again? The cable wasn't clear.'

'The Colonial Office,' Harry said. 'General Assistance.'

'General Assistance? I'm not familiar with that.'

'We assist British citizens in need. Generally. We're quite small.'

Hughes raised his chin and delivered a relieved smile, as if *small* explained everything. 'That would account for it. We don't get to hear much about what goes on at home, and they're always reorganizing. How can I be of help?'

'Miss Nevendon here is trying to locate her father. He's in oil.'

Hughes, being a very literal-minded man, let out a bray of delight. 'How very uncomfortable for him, poor fellow.'

'He's *missing*,' Prim said.

Hughes looked at Prim for the first time since he'd shaken her hand. 'Oh, I *do* apologize, dear lady. Please do forgive my flippancy.'

'I believe my father has connections with someone who comes from a village not far from here,' Prim said. 'The family name is Jabour. I'm trying to reach a Miss Ifaya Jabour. Does that ring any bells?'

'Jabour... *Jabour*...' Hughes made a meal of searching his memory. 'They're not one of the area's notable families, like the Tabari – they're the prominent Arab tribe around here.' The Welsh metre kept pushing through his Colonial Office English and Prim wondered if he ever looked out of the window hoping for a nostalgic glimpse of Llangorse Lake.

'They come from al-Sarhan,' she said. 'We understand that's not far from here.'

The district commissioner's eyes widened, as though divine revelation could easily be plucked from the Galilean air. 'Ah yes, where they had a bit of trouble a few weeks back.'

Prim felt the old fear come flooding back, stealing away her equilibrium and rocking the floor beneath her feet. Harry came to her rescue. 'Captain Wingate told us the same thing,' he said calmly. 'But he could give us no details. Perhaps you could tell us what happened, Mr Hughes.'

Prim wanted to hug him for the reassuring calmness in his voice, for the way he delivered the words her own mind could only jumble in petrified gibberish.

'It was nothing out of the ordinary,' Hughes replied. 'There's a kibbutz close by and, when you get that combination, trouble will usually follow.'

'But it wasn't serious trouble?' Harry asked, as if to think otherwise would suggest a feverish mind.

'In the scheme of things, not really. Just a handful of casualties.'

'*Casualties?*' Prim managed. 'Do you mean deaths?'

'Only a handful, Miss Nevendon. And we don't really know if the Arabs attacked the Jews or if it was Jewish violence perpetrated against the Arabs. It's even possible it was a factional Arab dispute. The rebels don't take kindly to their own people trying to live harmoniously with the Jews. Or us, at the moment.'

'You'd know if an Englishman had been killed, though,' suggested Harry, helping steer Prim back onto the rails.

'Oh yes. Of course.'

'Is it safe to travel there?'

'There's been no subsequent tit-for-tat, so things are quiet at present. If you think that going there is important enough—'

'It is,' Prim said. 'I really need to find this young woman. Are you sure you haven't heard the name Jabour?'

'It does ring a bell, but I can't place it,' Hughes replied, frowning. 'I'll tell you what, why don't I ask my secretary. His people are Bedouin. They've been in Tiberias for a century – settled here when the Egyptians briefly annexed Palestine from the Ottomans. If the Jabour tribe is of any consequence, he's bound to know.'

'That would be most kind of you,' Prim said.

Hughes loped into the next room and began speaking to someone in Arabic. Seeing the fear lingering in Prim's eyes, Harry whispered, 'It's all right. He said he'd know if Archie had been at al-Sarhan when the trouble broke out – if he'd been hurt there.'

Hughes returned a short while later, beaming with satisfaction. 'I *knew* I'd heard the name somewhere. ' he said. 'There's a Dr Yousef Jabour right here in Tiberias. He runs a surgery near the al-Amari mosque. I can draw you a map, if it would help.'

'Could you spare your secretary for a short while?' Harry enquired. 'I'm afraid neither of us speaks Arabic.'

'I'm ahead of you there, Mr Taverner,' Hughes said in a tone that made Harry think the district commissioner was enjoying getting one up on a visitor from London. 'I suspected you wouldn't have the language. I'm pleased to be able to tell you that Dr Jabour speaks passable English. He learned it in Damascus, studying medicine, or so my secretary informs me. He even has a telephone.' Hughes indicated the set on his desk, making a sweeping gesture as if he was inviting Prim and Harry to avail themselves of the riches of King Herod's treasury. 'Perhaps you would like to call him – warn him you're on your way.'

Dr Jabour replaced the telephone handset in its cradle. He stood motionless for a long time, staring around the empty surgery. I wish the Syrian was still there, he thought; he would know what to do. The Syrian was a man of action, a fighter, decisive under extreme pressure, whereas *I* – the quiet, unremarkable Dr Jabour with a medical degree from Damascus – I prefer the role of counsellor. Whenever we men of the Black Hand gather in the shade of some unobserved olive grove, or in a nondescript house, and speak of resistance against the Jews and the English, whom we hate in equal measure, I will be the one advising caution.

Dr Jabour was often given to wondering if the others thought less of him for it. Perhaps that was why they kept him in the dark about many of the things they planned. His pride told him it was because he was more valuable to them if he didn't know the details. That way, should the English arrest him and seek to beat information out of him – which the others assured him was a constant risk, because perfidy ran in the English blood – he could tell them nothing. His insecurity, however, whispered to him that it was because they thought him weak.

If only the Syrian were here now to tell him what to do.

The doctor thought of their last meeting. *A lamb to attract the wolf.* That's what the Syrian had said when, again playing the role of counsellor, Jabour had suggested subterfuge rather than brute force. *A daughter to ensnare a father.*

And now the lamb had presented itself for tethering. The lamb was already on her way.

It was a shame there was no time to contact the brothers, but what further assurance did a hesitant man need than a sign like that? The time to set aside cautious counsel had come. It was time for him to place his trust solely in himself. It was time for him to *act* – and act alone.

Twenty-One

Your old pal Archie is worried, Nim. I don't know how long I can keep going. It's not like back before the war, when you and I were young bucks and fit as fiddles. The desert didn't seem to trouble us so much in those days. Yes, it was tough going; but we thought little of sleeping on hard ground, of the sun hammering down like a demented blacksmith at his anvil. We'd happily dig away amongst the ruins, caring not a jot if we unearthed bugger-all, doing it for the thrill. If we had enough food, if the well didn't run dry, we didn't care about hardship. But that's all changed. You're lucky, you're immune to pain now; and as for me — well, nothing lives to my age in this place, Nim. Not even the scorpions.

I feel bad about bringing Ifaya to this place. You can see she's not made for it. But I wanted so much for you to see how beautiful she is, what a spirit she has about her. I treasure that quality. You'll believe me when I tell you that most of her family is not so hot on cultivating spirit amongst their women. They're traditional, you see. Old-school. Been in al-Sarhan for generations. They'd have preferred Ifaya to sit around with the women and do little but cook, sing, sew and breed. But Ifaya wasn't having any of that.

And, to be fair, her father was surprisingly far-sighted. He's an educated man, you see — a lawyer. Without his support, she'd never have been allowed to travel to Egypt to study and become an actress.

I'm damned sure I wouldn't have let our Prim go swanning off like that; I worry about her even now, surrounded by all those nancy boys and communists in the theatre. But Ifaya's papa is a stubborn old bird. 'If that's what my beautiful girl wants,' he told the family – and when I say 'family', Nim, I'm talking about a whole caravan of uncles, cousins, nieces and nephews – 'that's what she's going to have.' And when push came to shove, he even welcomed yours truly into the fold. That put the cat amongst the pigeons, I can tell you.

If the boot had been on the other foot, randy old reprobate that I am, I'd have told me to take a running jump. Marry an infidel with almost twenty years on my little girl? I would have said: never! But Papa Jabour saw the way things were going. He reckoned that if anyone could give his daughter the wealth and security she would never otherwise find in a Palestine rapidly heading for chaos, then who better than a fully paid-up son of the greatest empire on earth?

Of course I hadn't told Ifaya about those friends of Shakir Hamad's, had I? How they'd got their fangs into me. What I'd had to promise them. Well, it's natural, isn't it? I wasn't going to spoil everything.

I really believed I had it all under control, Nim. The whole shebang running as sweetly as Tarek Shalaby's green Citroën. And then dear old Papa Jabour went and got himself laid low by cancer.

I found him the best medical care in Haifa. Paid for everything. But it was clear he didn't have long left. Overnight the power in the family fell to Ifaya's brute of a brother, Kazem. And he wasn't the broad-minded fellow his father was. Big brother Kazem was a leading member of the Black Hand gang, and the nastiest piece of work to trouble Galilee since King Herod.

But that didn't mean he couldn't spot an opportunity when one presented itself.

Twenty-Two

At first the way to al-Sarhan ran between fields of wheat. Then, as it rose and twisted, dipped and snaked, there were lemon groves that gave shade from the sun and lonely cedars rising like dark guardians. It wasn't a road as such, more a dusty, rutted farm track. But Dr Jabour's ancient Ford motorcar seemed to know the way as well as any donkey, for the steering wheel never moved more than an inch or two. It was the morning after Prim and Harry had gone to the physician's surgery in Tiberias and it felt at last to Prim, if not to Harry, that they were inching closer to their quarry. When she had asked if it would be wiser to telephone ahead, Dr Jabour had laughed. There was no electricity in al-Sarhan, let alone a telephone.

'Let me get this right, Dr Jabour,' Prim was saying now, her elbow bouncing on the rim of the open window while Harry slouched in the rear seat, 'Ifaya is the daughter of your father's brother. You're her cousin, right?'

'That is correct,' Dr Jabour confirmed. 'I have known her all my life.'

It hadn't taken Prim long to form an opinion of Dr Jabour. His neatly cropped black hair was receding, though he was still young. A hollowed jaw pitted by a childhood affliction. Large brown irises peeping out over the prominent ridges of his cheekbones. If she hadn't already known he was a physician, she'd have put him down as a junior schoolmaster who hadn't quite learned how to quell an unruly class. She suspected that his polite, reserved exterior hid a deeply traditional man. During their brief conversation he had spent a lot of time kneading his fingers together as if he feared being caught in her company and rather wished she'd go away. And yet when she'd asked if he was willing to take her and Harry to al-Sarhan, he had agreed without hesitation.

'I don't wish to pry,' she said now, watching him drive along the track as they bumped and rattled over the hard ground, his eyes staring fixedly ahead as if he feared they might be rushing headlong towards a hidden precipice, 'but yesterday, when we came to you, I rather sensed you were reluctant to speak of her.'

'There was a disagreement amongst the family,' Dr Jabour replied. Prim noticed his hands tighten on the wheel. 'She was always headstrong. She chose a path many of us disapproved of.'

'You mean becoming an actress?'

'A woman displaying herself in public for men to look at is not proper,' Dr Jabour announced solemnly. 'Her brother, Kazem, remonstrated with his father many times over the iniquity of it – the disgrace it brought upon the family. But my uncle is a stubborn man and prone to error.'

That's just tickety-boo, thought Prim. I'm in the hands of a man whose views of women on the stage are positively Jacobean. Does he know about Ifaya's affair with Archie? If he doesn't, probably best to keep it to yourself for the time being, girl. We don't want him having a heart attack and driving off the road, do we?

'If we find she is not at al-Sarhan, do you think anyone in the village might know where she is?'

'You must wait until we reach al-Sarhan,' Dr Jabour said inscrutably. He made a play of concentrating on the road for a while. Then he continued, 'May I ask you something, Miss Nevendon?'

'Of course. Ask away.'

'Miss Nevendon,' began Dr Jabour with a trace of uncertainty in his voice, 'would you please tell me: do you wish to go to al-Sarhan to find my cousin? Or to find your father?'

In the rear-view mirror, she saw Harry's somnolent form suddenly tense and his eyes snap open. You don't miss a trick, do you, Harry Taverner? she thought. Turning her face to the doctor, Prim said, 'You know about him? You know about Archie?'

'Of course. He is the other reason for the dispute amongst our family.'

Not only Jacobean in matters of entertainment, thought Prim. We're talking Montagues and Capulets here, too. 'Because of his friendship with Ifaya?' she probed cautiously.

'A relationship that is highly improper,' Dr Jabour replied, his voice suddenly resolute. 'And not merely because he is a European and a Christian.'

'What do you mean?'

Keeping his eyes firmly on the track ahead, perhaps to avoid looking at her as much as to stay within the ditches on either side, Dr Jabour went on, 'Miss Nevendon, please explain to me how we are supposed to welcome your father into our house when the English come here to rule over us and beat us when we protest?'

'Oh,' said Prim, taken aback. It took her a moment to judge how to respond. 'I'm sorry to have to tell you this, but my father is just an oil man who lives in Cairo, Dr Jabour. Neither our king nor Mr Chamberlain, the prime minister, seeks his approval in matters of foreign policy. Or if they do, he's kept it very quiet.'

They swung around a sudden bend. Prim grabbed the dashboard.

'I think you are mocking me, Miss Nevendon,' Dr Jabour said as he changed gear.

'You're right. I'm sorry. It was ungracious of me.'

'Where is your father now? Does he not worry that you are travelling with a man who is not your husband?'

A glance in the mirror told Prim that Harry was smiling. 'I'm from the government, Dr Jabour,' he said. 'It doesn't count. We're all neutered at birth. Stops us pecking each other's feathers out.'

Dr Jabour's brow furrowed. 'I don't understand,' he replied, looking at Prim. 'Why does your government send a eunuch to protect you?'

'Harry's only joking, Dr Jabour. It's his English sense of humour. It doesn't travel well.'

But humour was not a medicine Dr Jabour seemed to hold much stock by. 'You make a joke because you think I will not understand?' he said indignantly. 'Do you think we Arabs are children?'

'No, of course not. Harry didn't mean to offend you – did you, Harry?'

'Last thing on my mind, honestly.'

That's just great, thought Prim. We've caused offence and now Jabour's going to stop the car and order us out. Thanks a bunch, Harry. You've a great career ahead of you in the Diplomatic Corps.

'When your General Allenby came here in 1917, we hailed him as our liberator from the Turks,' Dr Jabour suddenly declared, as if Harry's joke had been a signal to begin a sermon.

'I was in the crowd when he entered Jerusalem at the head of his army. I was fifteen. My father told me that our future was assured. That the British would give us liberty. But now you treat us worse than dogs. You tell us we are of no account. You do not ask us what we want, or how we feel when you make your plans to give away our land to the Jews. When we protest, you hang us, shoot us, blow up our houses, insult our women. Is *this* the future your General Allenby intended for us? Well, let me tell you, Miss Nevendon, this land was never yours to give away. One day you English will be gone, and this land will become part of a new *Bilad al Sham*.'

The car hit a rut and bounced, forcing Dr Jabour to halt his broadside while he fought the steering wheel. After that there was a brief period of embarrassed silence, broken only by the growling of the engine. Prim said nothing. It was a trick she'd acquired at parties, listening to her drunk Bolshie theatre friends blaming Wall Street and the Jews for all mankind's ills, and had honed during her brief flirtation with the British Union of Fascists, listening to inadequates blaming the Bolsheviks and, yes, the Jews, for all England's woes. It gave Dr Jabour's polemic nowhere to go.

And then Harry said, as casually as if he'd woken at the end of a conversation, '*Bilad al Sham* – I'm afraid you've lost me there, Doctor.'

'It is the Greater Syria of ancient times,' Dr Jabour announced proudly. 'When we are allowed to go our own way, to make our own choices, *Bilad al Sham* will be returned to us.'

'Well, that's absolutely splendid,' Harry replied, and Prim marvelled as he lifted a hand to his mouth and yawned. She'd watched actors do that – misdirect the audience. '*What* exactly will be returned?' he asked. 'And returned to *whom*?'

244

'All of it,' proclaimed Dr Jabour. 'Palestine, Lebanon, Transjordan, Syria itself, all united in one great caliphate. We will have our place in the League of Nations. We will have respect.'

'I don't recall *that* being in the proposals of the Peel Commission last year,' Harry said amiably.

Dr Jabour let out a bitter laugh. 'Partition, Mr Taverner? Why should we agree to this land being partitioned in favour of the Jews?'

Harry shrugged. 'So that each side gets *something* of what they want, rather than no one getting anything?' he answered. 'It's just a suggestion.'

Prim clapped her hands together. 'That's enough politics for now, boys,' she said. 'And Harry, if Dr Jabour is being kind enough to drive us to al-Sarhan, we really should allow him to concentrate on the driving.' She held Harry's gaze in the mirror and watched as he gave a diplomatic smile. But the eyes did not match the mouth. He's taking notes, she thought. They'll end up in an official report somewhere. It's what spies do, isn't it? A brief conversation in a motorcar on a Palestinian dirt track and, before you know it, it's in a policy document under the heading *Local opinion on the ground*, being read by the people who make the decisions. Jesus Christ, he's worse than a theatre critic. Is *anything* I've ever said to him taken in confidence?

'You do know that Mr Nevendon is not in al-Sarhan, yes?' Dr Jabour said, coming down from his lectern as swiftly as he had stepped onto it.

'Well, I wasn't sure,' Prim answered, her mouth creasing in disappointment. 'But I'm hoping someone there might tell me where to look next. It's the only lead I have.'

'If I wished to send a message to your father, how would I do so?'

'I couldn't begin to tell you, I'm afraid.'

'But surely you must know where he is.'

'Believe me, Doctor, I wouldn't have come all this way if I did.'

'But how can you *not* know?'

The vehemence in Dr Jabour's voice surprised her. Fearing it might signal another diatribe, she said hurriedly, 'I was living in England. He was in Cairo. By the time I got there, he'd gone. He didn't leave a forwarding address.'

'But here you are, nevertheless.' It sounded like an accusation.

'I found out about his relationship with your cousin. A friend of Ifaya's mentioned that al-Sarhan was her home. So here I am, hoping that Ifaya – or, failing her, someone close to her – might point me in the right direction.' She glanced back at Harry. 'Or perhaps I should say, here *we* are.'

She hoped Harry might indicate his support with at least a smile. But he still had his note-taking face on. And when she looked back at Dr Jabour, she was just in time to catch a terrible apprehension cloud his face. It was involuntary, she was sure of that. And fleeting. But she saw it nevertheless. She saw it as clearly as the sunlit track ahead, and the collection of little houses coming into view amongst the orange groves.

The most beautiful place in the whole world.

While Prim had always maintained a healthy scepticism about Ifaya's claim as recited to her by Aleyna Nasoul, as they approached the village she had to admit the setting was indeed bewitching. Al-Sarhan lay in a soft cleft between two hills, surrounded by orange groves and fields, watered by a spring that had probably flowed over the rocks when Solomon ruled. The square, flat-roofed houses were of pale stone quarried from the Galilee hills, their courtyards linked by walls of mud-brick bleached by the sun. Who had built them, and when, was anyone's guess: Israelites, Persians, Romans, the early followers of Muhammad, Crusaders, Ottomans, Egyptians, Ottomans again... Prim wouldn't have put money on the newest being less than a century old.

At first sight the village seemed inhabited mostly by goats. They wandered imperiously around the earthen central square, grubbing at the dirt or sleeping in the shadows cast by the little mosque. Then Prim spotted women and children sitting in the doorways, with bowls of what she took to be seeds or fruits laid out around them as they worked, while their menfolk toiled in the groves and the wheat fields. They looked up at the car's approach, their faces expressionless, as if they'd seen everything they cared to see, wishing now only to be left in peace.

Then Prim began to see beyond the surface.

The flakes chipped by bullet strikes from the stone, ugly as ulcers. The black scorch marks around some of the window frames.

And at the far end of the village, like an altar awaiting a sacrifice, sat a motorcar much like Dr Jabour's. Only this one was rust-red where it wasn't soot-black. The wheel hubs sat on hardened beds of melted rubber, the doors riddled with shot, the roof peeled back like foil where the blast had ripped it from the coachwork.

Dr Jabour killed the engine and pulled on the handbrake. Expressionless, he climbed out. Prim and Harry followed.

Even at a distance Prim could smell it. Like an oven that's been too long uncleaned. And the stink of gasoline still lingering. And something else: the smell of burnt fat.

A little place barely worth fighting over, Wingate had said.

Prim sensed the eyes of the villagers on her back as she followed Dr Jabour towards the wreck. She couldn't speak. She had designed sets for plays containing thousands of words, plays that described every human experience, yet now she couldn't utter a single one of them.

Dr Jabour did it for her.

'I have tried not to speak of Ifaya since it happened,' he said. 'Not because of the lechery she committed with your father, though that is cause enough for her name to be stricken from my memory—'

He paused, staring at the burnt-out wreck. And although al-Sarhan stayed exactly where it had been for centuries, Prim felt a tremor churn the ground beneath her feet, so that nothing in the world seemed safe and permanent.

'I agreed to bring you here, Miss Nevendon, so that you could see the consequences of your father's many sins,' Dr Jabour continued, his voice seeming to reach Prim's ears only after it had made a long and plaintive journey around the surrounding hills. 'I wanted you to see it for yourself. This is where my cousin Ifaya died.'

Twenty-Three

I swear to God, Nim, I didn't even know she was there. If I'd had even an inkling she was planning to go back to al-Sarhan to speak to her brother, I'd have talked her out of it. Truly, I thought she was in Alexandria, taking care of a sick friend. That's what Ifaya told me, and she'd never lied to me before, not once. She even had Tarek drive her to the station, clever girl.

But the train she boarded wasn't going to Alexandria. She was going back home.

Stupid idea. Stupid, stupid bloody idea! Kazem was never going to change his mind about me and his sister, was he? I could have offered him everything I had, and more, and he'd still have turned his back on us.

It was all going swimmingly before her father fell sick. He'd given us his blessing, despite what the rest of the family thought. He'd only ever wanted what would make his daughter happy, and to hell with custom and religion. He didn't even care that I was English, and there were some amongst the Jabouri who thought that was enough to kill him for. They might have done it too, if they hadn't been frightened of Kazem — and there was a lot about the son to be frightened of, I can tell you that for nothing.

When Papa Jabour fell sick, I flew up to Haifa to see him in hospital. 'Look out for my boy, Kazem,' he warned me. 'He's the one you've got to watch. When I'm gone, the power will fall to him.'

I'd never cared much for Kazem Jabour. He was a thug. Shakir Hamad told me what he was up to. How sharp his talons were. How hard they clung onto you once you were in their grip. He was the muscle in Palestine for a gang based in Damascus. They were using the revolt in Palestine to further their goal of a region-wide Muslim caliphate, attacking British troops, murdering Jews, assassinating Arabs who disagreed with them... Kazem had set up a neat little sideline, too: smuggling explosives.

Well, it didn't take the Jews long to learn what he was up to. And they weren't going to stand about twiddling their thumbs while Kazem Jabour went about his murderous business. The fact that Ifaya had gone to see him, to beg him to respect Papa Jabour's approval of our marrying, didn't matter to them one jot – not that they even knew. It was just the devil's ill luck that Kazem's car was the same make and colour as the taxi that brought her up from Tiberias.

So there it is, Nim. That's why my darling Ifaya is here with us tonight. And believe me when I say I'll take eternity in hell if I must, simply for her assurance that it was quick, and that she didn't suffer.

Twenty-Four

How real is the grief we feel for the death of someone we never knew? wondered Prim Nevendon as she stood beside Dr Jabour's rickety Ford, her hand braced against the warm metal of the door pillar because her legs no longer seemed willing to support her. In that moment the pain she felt for Ifaya's death seemed real enough. There was no denying the choking feeling in her breast, or the frantic, futile searching in her memory for someone who was no longer there. In the days since discovering Ifaya's existence, Prim, in her own mind, had made Archie's lover as familiar to her as anyone she had ever known. The photo in the theatre programme had given her a face. Aleyna Nasoul's memories had given her substance. There were the signatures on Archie's account at Cicurel's in Cairo, written in Ifaya's flowery, generous hand, to give her passion and a personality. All told, Prim thought, enough fragments to make her *real*.

Having contrived the climax of his own little drama, Dr Jabour seemed unsure what to do next. If he expected some sort of penance from her, an admission of guilt or regret, Prim wasn't about to indulge him. She stayed silent.

'Stay here, please,' he said brusquely. Leaving her and Harry by the car, he strode towards one of the houses. A change had come over him, Prim noticed as she watched him. A weary confidence – as if he'd won a victory against a tough enemy.

'Well, that's a setback,' Harry said under his breath. 'Not what we were hoping for at all. Bad luck.'

And Prim had no answer for Harry, either. All she could see in her mind was Ifaya's bloodied corpse slumped in the passenger seat of the mangled, rusting car.

As Jabour ducked into one of the houses, Harry asked casually, 'How's your memory, Prim?'

'What?' Prim said distractedly.

'I said, "How's your memory?"' He could have been enquiring about the weather.

'What do you mean, *my memory*?'

Only now did he turn his face to hers. 'When you telephoned our good doctor yesterday from the district commissioner's office, how did he sound to you?'

'How did he *sound*?'

Harry's hand closed around her left bicep, as if he feared she was about to stumble. 'I know all this has come as a shock. But concentrate – it's important. What was Jabour's response?'

'Pleasant enough, why?'

'What did he say to you, when you introduced yourself?'

Why was Harry being so bloody practical? Why wasn't he taking her in his arms and letting her cry out her confusion and frustration on his shoulder? 'Nothing much,' she managed. 'Nothing particularly forthcoming. What do you want me to say?'

'There wasn't any "Goodness gracious, Miss Nevendon, what an extraordinary coincidence! I was thinking of you only this very minute, seeing as how my cousin got shot to pieces on account of your dear old papa and now – all of a sudden – here you are. Isn't serendipity wonderful?" Nothing of *that* sort?'

'No, Harry,' Prim said firmly, resenting his flippant line. 'Nothing of *that* sort.'

'So what exactly *did* Dr Jabour say when he answered the telephone? To the letter, if you can remember.'

'I don't know. "Hello", I suppose.'

'*Try.*'

So, while the goats ambled and bleated, while the women and the children in the doorways watched her and Harry with unreadable faces and in silence, Prim tried. 'It was something like, "Hello, Miss Nevendon. I'm pleased to hear from you." That was it, pretty much.'

'No surprise?'

'Not that I could tell.'

'No incredulity that you, of all people, should suddenly turn up in Tiberias and seek him out?'

'What are you saying, Harry?'

Harry dropped his voice, his lips barely moving. 'Dr Jabour *knew* you were here in Palestine. He had warning that you were coming.'

'That's ridiculous! How could he have known *that*?'

'On the assumption that he's not a doctor of clairvoyancy, someone told him.'

It took Prim no time at all to imagine who. 'It was Hamad, wasn't it?' she said. 'Bloody Shakir Hamad.'

'Keep your voice down. Try to look like we're admiring al-Sarhan in all its glory.'

'I remember Hamad telling me that when Archie had taken that loan from him, to keep Uncle Nim's theatre afloat, it had opened the door to what Hamad called "third parties". I asked him who he meant, but he wouldn't tell me.'

Harry drew his cigarette case and lighter from inside his

jacket, handed Prim a cigarette and lit it for her. While he was close to her with the lighter, he whispered, 'When we were in the car, Jabour asked if you knew how he might send your father a message. He's been told to find out if you know where Archie is.'

Prim's gaze flickered wildly around the village. Every face it alighted on now seemed to be staring at her malevolently. 'Told by whom?' she asked as she exhaled a cloud of cigarette smoke that drifted slowly in the sultry air. 'The bad people Hamad let into Archie's life?'

Lighting his own cigarette, Harry said from between half-closed lips, 'Keep your eyes on me. We don't know who might watching.'

'What do we *do*?' whispered Prim.

'Plan for the worst,' Harry said. He turned away from her, opened the Ford's door, dropped to his knees and felt under the front seats.

'What are you doing?' Prim asked, looking down at him.

'Looking for a gun.'

'Oh dear God.'

Harry stood up. 'It's all right. Nothing there. But if Jabour pulls any tricks on the way back, I'll deal with him from the rear seat.'

'What do you mean, *deal with him*?'

But Harry wasn't of a mind to elaborate. Instead he said, 'Listen closely. Stationary or moving, if at any time I tell you to get out, then open the door, stay low, wrap your arms around your chest, tuck your head into them and roll out.'

'*What*?'

'We won't be going fast enough to hurt yourself too much. Do you think you can do that?'

Prim tried to stop her mouth gaping. 'What do I do then?'

'Find whatever cover you can, until I can catch up with you.'

'Bloody hell, Harry! I wasn't expecting this.'

At that moment Jabour emerged from the house he'd entered and began to head back towards the car. Harry put his arm around Prim's shoulder and turned her towards one of the foraging goats. It had a kid in tow, and Harry pointed at the pair as if he and Prim were at London Zoo. With a childish grin on his face, he said out of the corner of his mouth, 'If it starts to look as if he's not taking us back the way we came or he suddenly tells us there's a better route, that's when I'll make my move. If you can grab the wheel and steer us into a ditch or off the road, that would be helpful.'

Prim opened her mouth to answer, but no words came out.

'I fear you've had a wasted journey, Miss Nevendon,' Dr Jabour said as he reached them. 'I have asked, but the last time your father was here was many months ago. No one I spoke to has seen him since.'

Prim could only stare at the doctor. He had turned from a harmless, diffident physician into a thing of menace. 'Why did you bring us here, like this?' she asked, catching a sudden anxious glance from Harry.

'You asked me to, Miss Nevendon,' Jabour replied evenly.

'But why didn't you tell us about Ifaya at the start?'

'I told you when we arrived. I wanted you to see the results of your father's actions. I wanted you to see how we must live when the English interfere in our lives.'

It was said without hostility, and Prim had no response. She stared at the burnt-out car.

'We really should be getting back to Tiberias,' Harry said. 'The district commissioner is expecting us. He wasn't all that happy about us coming to al-Sarhan on our own. He said he'd have a patrol on standby in case we ran into any trouble. We wouldn't want you getting into any difficulties with the authorities on our account.' As a shot across the bows, it was the best he could manage in the circumstances.

Jabour took his place at the wheel of the Ford. Harry made himself as comfortable as he could on the hard springs of the rear seat. Sliding in beside Jabour, Prim said, 'You haven't told us who launched the attack on the village, Dr Jabour. You haven't told us who killed Ifaya.'

The doctor waited until the motor was running before answering. 'Who do you think it was, Miss Nevendon?' he asked, his face a picture of aggrieved innocence that even Prim, who by nature was trusting, couldn't take seriously. 'Who else would attack a peaceful village of law-abiding Arabs? It was the Zionists, of course.'

As al-Sarhan receded in the Ford's rear-view mirror, soon to become lost amongst the orange groves and hills as if it had never existed, Prim's hopes of finding Archie faded with it. Thinking about it now, she realized they had died weeks ago, killed in the same unmarked moment as Ifaya Jabour. The trail had gone cold. She had nowhere else to turn. And now, according to Harry, she might have walked headlong into the same sort of trap that had cost Moussa Bannoudi his life. Glancing at Dr Jabour as he leaned forward in concentration over the steering wheel, she tried to rehearse the instructions Harry had given her, but the bouncing of the car jumbled them up in her head. If she had to get out while they were moving, was she to put her hands over her head or around her body? Should she step out or roll? Even though the track was uneven, they were travelling at some speed. She glanced at Harry in the mirror, hoping for guidance. But if he had detected any perfidy in Dr Jabour and was planning to strike, he was disguising it well. He looked half-asleep.

When it became clear to her that they were indeed retracing the route towards Tiberias, and that Dr Jabour was probably innocent of the intended crime of kidnap, Prim allowed herself to relax a little. There were still questions that needed to be answered, but she was almost too frightened to open her mouth in case she bit her tongue as the Ford juddered over the bumps.

'Dr Jabour,' she began, steadying herself by gripping the edges of the passenger seat, 'you told us on the way up that the relationship between my father and your cousin had caused ill feeling amongst the family. You said Ifaya's father – your uncle – had quarrelled with his son—'

'With Kazem, yes.'

'Would it be possible to meet them?'

'No,' said Dr Jabour bluntly.

'Why not?'

He let out a grunt of contemptuous laughter. It coincided with a thump as they ran over a rut. Prim felt her teeth rattle.

'Kazem Jabour does not choose to make himself available to the English,' Dr Jabour said loftily. 'They are beneath his contempt.'

'What about your uncle?' Prim asked. 'Do you think it would be possible for us to talk to him? Or doesn't he like us, either?'

'My uncle is in hospital in Haifa. He suffers from cancer of the lungs. If Allah, the most merciful and benevolent, forgives him the sin of allowing his daughter to commit that which is *haram*, soon he will be in paradise.'

'Oh,' replied Prim. 'That's a shame.' She had had enough of the bumps, and she had had enough of Dr Jabour's evasions. Turning her head towards him, she said bluntly, 'Have you heard of someone named Shakir Hamad? He's a Lebanese gentleman who lives in Cairo.'

Behind her, she sensed Harry suddenly sit up and lean forward. She felt his hand on her shoulder. 'I don't think we need trouble Dr Jabour with any of that,' he said as they swung into a bend in the track between a clump of low jujube trees.

'Oh, I think that's exactly what we need to do,' she said, watching Jabour's profile to see if she'd landed a hit. 'In fact, given that Dr Jabour seems to think my father is a sinner, which on balance I can't really deny, I would like to ask him—'

Dr Jabour's foot slammed down on the brake pedal. Prim raised her arms to protect her face as the windscreen seemed to fly towards her. Through her spread fingers she caught a glimpse of something blocking the track ahead. Then her nose was squished against her hands and Harry's head was almost on her shoulder. The Ford came to an abrupt halt and stalled.

Dr Jabour let fly a stream of Arabic, which Prim reckoned was a curse, in anyone's language. At first she thought it was directed at her. But as she fell back into her seat she saw, through the glass, a motorcycle and sidecar blocking the road. Hidden as it was by the bend in the track and the surrounding jujube trees, they had almost run straight into it.

A young woman was standing over the motorcycle, an oily wrench in one hand, her face turned towards the Ford, which had stopped barely an arm's length from her. She seemed oddly unperturbed for someone who had narrowly escaped being mown down. Dr Jabour leaned out of the driver's window. His voice softened and Prim understood he was asking if the woman needed help.

She was barely twenty, Prim reckoned. She had a thick mane of black curls and a round, cheerful face smeared with grease.

She was dressed for a hike, in shorts and a military khaki shirt with button-down pockets and lapels. Replying to Dr Jabour in Arabic, she pointed at the motorcycle's engine and pulled a face.

'Get out,' hissed Harry into Prim's ear. 'Now!'

For a moment she thought he was telling her to get out and lend a hand. But what did he expect her to *do*? She was a set designer, not an Automobile Association patrolman. Did he expect her to salute and ask the girl how she and Harry might be of help? She barely knew a spark plug from a sardine.

But Prim was nothing if not obliging, so she turned to open the passenger door. And as she did so, she noticed out of the corner of her eye that Harry was already out of the back seat, crouched low and furtive, like a spiv caught on the Mile End Road by the constabulary. He was slipping through the gap between the half-open rear door and the pillar, as if to make his escape.

All his instructions came flooding back to her in a jumbled mess, inducing not action, but inertia. When she turned her head to look to her front, it felt as if she was wearing a deep-sea diver's helmet made of heavy brass. Her neck muscles seemed to have turned to jelly. Just moving her head seemed to require a huge effort. But somehow she managed it. And now she was peering out of the windscreen.

But the picture had changed. The girl was pointing at her, not at the motorcycle's engine. It was still the same wholesome out-doorsy young woman. It was still the same broken motorcycle. It was even the same track, the same jujube trees. But by some clever illusionist's trick, some whisking away of the conjurer's cloak, some flourish of misdirection, the oily wrench in the girl's hand had transformed itself into a dull metallic-grey pistol. And it was now levelled directly at Prim's forehead.

Twenty-Five

It was the sweetest little ambush imaginable. The Service's directing staff on his rudimentary and somewhat improvised training course in the Scottish Highlands would have given it top marks. They would have admired its elegant simplicity. They would have praised the unthreatening choice of bait: a solitary female in distress. Who could resist? It was perfect, even down to the anticipation of an attempted breakout: exiting the Ford, Harry had rolled no more than once before two young men, dressed in much the same wholesome outdoorsy manner as the woman with the Mauser pistol, had emerged from behind the nearest jujube tree and encouraged him to get to his feet with a firm but measured kick to the ribs. While one trained a revolver on him, the other dusted him down, laughing happily as if it was all a prank.

Harry could see that Prim was already out of the car. She was only a few feet away from him, hugging herself like someone who has just emerged from a cold sea after a bracing swim. He could see the fear on her face as she stared at the pistol the young woman had trained on her.

In the time it had taken Harry to get to his feet, a second pair of boys – their faces, like those of the two who were guarding him, browned by the sun – had appeared from out of nowhere to drag Dr Jabour from the driver's seat and pin him face-down over the hot bonnet of the car.

The woman was the commander, it appeared. The boys kept glancing at her, waiting for further orders. She directed a series of barked questions at Jabour, again in Arabic. The doctor's replies were hindered somewhat because his jaw was compressed against the curve of the bonnet, his head pinned there by the splayed hand of one of the boys. But when his eyes turned towards Prim and the name Nevendon rang out from his grunted Arabic as clearly as a warning bell, Harry knew there would be no future in pretending that he and Prim were a brace of innocent hitch-hikers.

As if to prove it, the woman turned her face to one of the boys standing beside Harry. She fired off another whipcrack instruction, though to Harry's ear it was in a language other than Arabic. Hebrew, he reckoned. The boy nodded. He was wiry and muscular, with a mop of dark hair piled up on one side of a high forehead, as if he spent his life permanently in the teeth of a side-on gale. 'Who are you? What are you doing riding in a terrorist's motorcar?' he asked, with an accent that Harry, fluent in German, placed easily: *Bayerisch*, the accent of southern Germany.

There seemed little point in subterfuge, so Harry said amiably, 'I'm Harry Taverner and that', a nod towards Prim, 'is Miss Primrose Nevendon. I think she might take it as a personal favour if your friend put that gun away.'

The boy translated this into Hebrew. The woman laughed. Lowering the pistol, she called out to Harry, 'My English, she is no good. You speak to Itzak. He tell to me what you say.'

This time the accent was from Eastern Europe, possibly even from Russia. The woman reverted to Hebrew, delivered with only a little less steeliness than before. But at least, Harry noted, the pistol remained pointed downwards. The boy named Itzak translated her words in a detached voice, as if he was reading a riddle from a Christmas cracker.

'What is your relationship with this man?' A nod towards the prone torso of Dr Jabour.

'We don't have a relationship with Dr Jabour. He's helping us out, that's all.'

A pause while this was sent down the telegraph wires and a reply received.

'Why do you seek assistance from the cousin of the terrorist Kazem Jabour?'

Harry was careful to deliver his answer in terms that couldn't be misunderstood. 'We know nothing of Kazem Jabour. We've never met him.'

'In what way is the cousin of the terrorist Kazem Jabour assisting you?'

'Dr Jabour offered, very kindly, to take us to al-Sarhan. That is all. I repeat, we know nothing about his cousin, Kazem.'

'Why do you visit the Arab village of al-Sarhan, if you are English?'

'Because Miss Nevendon is searching for her father. He is missing. He was the friend of someone who came from the village. We thought they might know where to find him.'

'Why does this man Nevendon have a friend in a terrorist village?'

'They were in love.'

A longer pause while the dots and dashes were keyed down the line into the crackling ether. The young woman with the gun laughed, but the laugh had a hard, dismissive edge to it. Then the reply came back fast. 'Name this person.'

And because Harry, too, had smelled the roasted wreck of the bullet-riddled car at al-Sarhan, his reply was delivered in a tone that was almost reverent. 'Her name was Ifaya Jabour. Her death pains Miss Nevendon greatly. She believes her missing father has lost someone he cared for deeply.'

Now there was confusion at the telegraph exchange. The young woman with the pistol engaged in a five-way conversation with her boys, to which Harry, Prim and Dr Jabour were not party.

When the next signal came, it was delivered seemingly by proxy from some higher authority, and relayed to Harry by the boy Itzak. 'The death of this person was a tragic mistake. It was not intended. The target was the terrorist, Kazem Jabour. These things happen in war. It is to be expected.'

At the front of the car, the young woman's expression suggested this explanation should now be accepted by all reasonable people. It was time to move on to more important things. She spoke to one of the boys holding Dr Jabour, who stepped away and began to search the car. He opened all four doors and poked about under the seats. Harry was about to reveal that he had already done so and there was nothing incriminating to find, but decided it would raise as many questions as it would answer.

At the back of the Ford was the spare tyre, strapped vertically against the bodywork below the rear window. Beneath it, protruding from above the bumper, was a small luggage rack, on which was strapped a box. Harry had noticed Dr Jabour stow his medical satchel there before they'd set out from the surgery in Tiberias. As he watched, the boy undid the straps and opened the lid. He took out the battered leather case, opened it, peered inside, then returned the satchel to its resting place. He called to the woman and, by his tone, Harry knew he was giving it the all-clear.

Then, as if it was part of his act – merely another trick in his carefully choreographed routine – he pulled out a canvas sack slightly larger than the satchel. He held it up, turning it for his audience to see. It bulged, as though whoever had filled it had been extravagantly generous. Its fabric strained at the seams, stretched tight over the copious contents. Harry half-expected it to tear asunder as he watched.

The boy looked at his audience. Though silent, his face said: *Notice, please, that this sack is just an ordinary sack. No hidden zips or pockets. No wires attached. No artifice. I place one hand inside: thus. And* – pausing for his audience to follow – *I pluck out... a walnut!*

Harry waited for the applause. But it did not come.

The boy turned the nut in his fingers. The sunlight shafting through the jujube branches played on its wrinkles as if it were a finely cut diamond.

Do you see? Just a common-or-garden walnut. Available at any market from here to Jerusalem. But now watch...

With great ceremony, the boy let the walnut fall from his hand. Gripping the base of the sack, he swung it upside-down. The walnuts spilled out in a dusty downpour.

And... magic! Before our very eyes, the cascading contents are transmogrified into pure gold, glinting in the sunlight. They clatter to the ground, lying atop the walnuts like jewels scattered in the dirt by a generous potentate. They have become not walnuts, but shining .303-calibre brass rifle cartridges.

After that, things happened – at least to Prim's memory – in a weird, entwined dance that was at the same time frantic and yet deathly slow. The young woman with the gun held a brief discussion with her boys. Her jaw had tightened with a resolution that Prim found frankly terrifying. Her barked Hebrew sounded fierce and guttural. Each response came back delivered in a staccato burst, as if a decision had already been made and they were simply giving their approval to some already-discussed course of action. Then she saw Harry being pushed past her and into the front passenger seat of the Ford. The woman with the gun gestured for her to climb into the back. It never occurred to Prim to resist and, before she knew it, she was sitting behind Harry, one of the boys to her right, the other in the driver's seat. The boy beside her had the barrel of his revolver pressed against the back of Harry's seat. He had a grim smile on his face that Prim didn't much care for.

Looking ahead, she saw the remaining two boys pull Dr Jabour from the bonnet. The woman handed one of them her pistol and, without further command, they began to lead the doctor towards the dense jujube trees beside the track.

The woman shouted a final order to the driver of the Ford, who pressed the starter button and set the little engine thumping. Then she began hauling the motorcycle aside. When the way ahead was clear, she swung effortlessly onto the saddle and began to kick-start the bike. And in the moment before the engine caught, Prim heard a single pistol shot echo from behind the jujube trees, followed by the panicked clatter of flapping wings.

The car ride was brief, though that was only the start. The Ford travelled barely a few hundred yards before it came to a halt beside a dusty brown Chevrolet flatbed truck. A swarthy man in a grubby vest sat in the boxy cab, staring straight ahead. Three younger men with scythes stood around a mound of barley sheaves, sharing a drink from a clay jug. They reminded Prim of the itinerant agricultural workers who laboured in the fields around Bevern Lodge each summer. They showed no interest in the Ford until it stopped. Then they moved. Fast.

Before either of them had time to utter a word, Prim and Harry were bundled out of their seats and up into the back of the truck. Sensing the power in the hands that pushed her down onto the boards, the strength of muscles honed by hard toil, Prim wasn't of a mind to protest. She heard the Ford rev as it pulled away, and then everything went dark as a tarpaulin was thrown on top of her and she felt a covering of barley sheaves weighing her down. It felt like being buried alive. After all that had happened – the end of her hopes of finding Archie; learning of Ifaya's death; and now the murder of Dr Jabour – this deep, dark pit she was in seemed a fitting end. Perhaps even a fair punishment.

She began to whimper. 'They killed him. Just like that. Like a sick dog. He was a *doctor*.'

'Ssshhh,' whispered Harry in the darkness. 'They won't hurt us. It's not our fight.'

The closeness of his body gave her a little comfort. She reached out and found his hand. His fingers squeezed hers. It felt reassuring. Then somebody stood on her ankle as they climbed up. Prim bit her tongue. She didn't want to give them the satisfaction of knowing they'd hurt her. For a moment she thought she was shaking with misery, but it was only the boards beneath her beginning to tremble as the truck's engine started up.

The next part of the journey had begun.

Twenty-Six

They had been on the move for what felt like hours. To Prim, pinned beneath the stifling tarp and the barley sheaves, they could have driven all the way around Galilee and into Transjordan. Or north, into Lebanon. Or south, back into Egypt. But wherever they were going, every yard of it was torture. Her mouth was parched by the dust that rose from the flatbed's boards every time they hit a bump, her body ached as if she was being trampled by a herd of stampeding horses. Harry's take on it was equally depressing. During their brief shared whispers he gave her an alternative: he reckoned their kidnappers were simply driving around to rob them of any coherent sense of time spent and distance travelled. When at last the Chevrolet stopped and the motor died, Prim didn't care who was right or where they were, only that the whole miserable experience was over.

At first, nothing much happened. She felt movement around her, and once again a foot landed intrusively on her body, this time on her right wrist. She yelped, but received only a sharp command to stay still and be quiet, delivered in heavily accented English. Then she heard male voices speaking urgently in a language that sounded much like the one she'd heard the young woman with the pistol use.

After a few moments she sensed the bales of barley being lifted and then the tarpaulin. A blaze of sunlight blinded her. Then she was back in darkness, struggling to breathe through the coarse weave of what she assumed was a sack of some sort that had been thrown over her head. Strong male hands took hold of her limbs and manoeuvred her to the edge of the tailgate. I'm on my way to the gallows, she thought. They're going to hang me. Do I get a last request?

When she called out for Harry and heard him reply, 'It's all right. Don't be afraid,' it sounded like the reassuring hail from a lifeboat at the very moment she could no longer tread water. She felt her legs swing free. A hand between her shoulder blades eased her forward.

The fall, when it came, felt the way she imagined jumping off a skyscraper would feel, her stomach taking a nauseating upwards flight path. But that must have been her mind playing tricks, because almost immediately her feet were on firm ground. She stumbled forward like a parachutist after a misjudged landing.

This time the hands that grasped her, and steadied her, were female. Prim heard women's laughter. She let herself be steered forward, one tentative step at a time. A hand tapped below her right knee. Like a well-schooled horse at the farrier's, she lifted her step and then she was walking on a timber floor. She knew she was inside because the air was hot and stuffy. She could smell freshly sawn timber and the scent of creosote. For an instant, friendly memories rushed in on her – of the beach hut the family used to rent at Eastbourne for the summer holidays. Then she was back in the nightmare.

They set her down on a bed with a rickety metal frame, as if she were a patient in a sanatorium that had run out of money.

It still had the faint smell of disinfectant about it, and she heard its discordant protest as they tied her wrists to the tubular bars on each side, though they left her legs free. Dear God, what were they going to do – torture her, the way poor Moussa Bannoudi had been tortured?

There was no pillow and so she was forced to lie prone, the sack over her head rising and falling against her face like bellows as she breathed. Prim tried to steady herself, because the bellows were going too fast and she didn't want these people to know how scared she was.

She heard a loud hammering coming from outside and wondered if a mob was trying to get inside to lynch her. But the blows had a pattern to them: three strikes, then a pause, then three more strikes, another pause, another three blows... Prim was beginning to wonder if it was some sort of code, or maybe it was designed to confuse and intimidate, when the noise stopped as suddenly as it had begun.

In the silence that followed, she believed she was alone. She turned, so that one side of her face was against the mattress. Then she tried to slide her head out of the sack. But it was tied loosely around her neck and the knot ended up under her jaw.

She heard a chair scrape on the floor, which sent such a shock through her body that for an instant she thought she'd been electrocuted.

'Lie still and let me help you,' said a woman's voice. Young, Prim guessed. Good English, but with an accent that she could place no more precisely than Mediterranean. Then she felt hands against her throat, twisting as they untied the knot keeping the sack in place. 'Raise your head a little, dear.'

Prim did as she was told and a moment later the sack was gone, her surroundings revealed to her.

In the grounds of Bevern Lodge there had been a shepherd's hut that she had played in as a child, and that Celestina had commandeered for her pottery supplies. The interior of this place looked much the same: planks over an internal timber frame, but far newer. There was a window, but it let in very little light because someone had fixed a cover over it on the outside. Now Prim understood the source of the hammering.

'There,' said a female voice. 'Is that more comfortable?'

Prim tried to turn her head to see who the voice belonged to. But tied to the bedframe as she was, her movements were limited. To her immediate left was the wooden wall. To her right, a collection of agricultural implements propped against the far side. She tried to look up and back but couldn't tilt her head enough to see behind the bed, which was where the voice was coming from.

'Best you don't see my face, dear,' the voice said. 'Best for both of us.'

'Where am I?'

'Somewhere safe, I would like to think.'

'Well, I don't feel safe,' Prim replied. 'I feel as though I've been kidnapped.'

A bright laugh, as if this was all nothing but a dormitory prank. 'Come now. A short while spent in a little discomfort – that hardly counts as kidnapping.'

'Then I'm free to go?'

'That rather depends on you, dear,' the voice said. 'Please, tell me your full name.'

'Not before you tell me yours.'

'You can call me Rachel, if you like.'

Although she couldn't see it, Prim knew the answer was delivered with an evasive smile, a smile that annoyed her intensely.

She didn't like evasion; it wasn't in her nature. 'All right, *Rachel-if-you-like*,' she said with a sigh. 'My name is Primrose Nevendon. But you already know that. Harry told your friend with the motorcycle.'

'But I wasn't there, Primrose,' said the woman who called herself Rachel. 'So I need you to speak plainly with me. No evasion when I ask a question. Then we get on together just fine.'

'Look, the only question I feel like answering right now is this: what manner of monsters are you people?'

'Monsters, dear? There are no monsters here.'

'I meant back there, outside al-Sarhan. Dr Jabour – shot out of hand. Are you going to shoot us too: me and Harry?'

'If I may say so, Primrose – may I call you Primrose?'

'Do I have a choice in the matter?'

'If I may say so, I think you are being a little over-theatrical,' Rachel continued.

'That poor man wasn't even allowed a hearing.'

But as far as Prim could tell, the voice called Rachel had no interest in Dr Jabour's fate. 'Tell us, please, who is Harry?'

'You know perfectly well who he is. He was in your truck, with me.'

The chair squeaked again and the voice said, 'But does Harry have a surname?'

The question had the same weary, superior tone that Prim recalled the two detectives using when they came to Bevern to tell her and Celestina that Archie was missing. Simple questions – each one designed to trap.

'He told the motorcycle girl that, too. Why don't you ask her?'

'His full name, please, Primrose. We don't want to be here until Hanukkah comes round, do we?'

'It's Taverner,' Prim said. 'Harry Taverner. Why are you asking me questions you already know the answer to?'

'And does Mr Taverner work for the British Mandate government in Jerusalem? We haven't seen him around here before.'

Around *here* before. Not in Lebanon, or Transjordan, or Syria, but *here*. Harry had been right when he'd whispered to her that they were being driven around solely to confuse. 'He's just a friend,' she said, trying to hide her tiny victory beneath a cloak of nonchalance. 'He works for the British Council, in Cairo.'

'Are you sure he's not a smuggler of weapons to the Arabs – like the doctor was?'

'No! Of course not.'

'And you, Primrose? Tell me about yourself. I'm all ears.'

'What do you want to know?'

There was a pause and Prim guessed the speaker was considering her performance so far, not with unalloyed pleasure. But when Rachel spoke again, it was in a breezy, matter-of-fact tone, as if they'd just that moment encountered each other on the street. 'I would like very much to know what you are doing here in Palestine. And in al-Sarhan, of all places. It is an unlikely destination for a tourist, don't you think?'

'I'm not a tourist,' Prim responded. 'I'm searching for my father. He's missing. Look, Harry explained everything to the girl with the motorcycle.'

'Why don't you tell me instead? Then we can all be sure of what was said and what wasn't. In the heat of the moment, things can get misunderstood. Let's start with why you were riding in a motorcar with a terrorist who was carrying enough bullets to kill a hundred Jews. Or if that doesn't trouble you, a hundred Englishmen?'

The question was asked in a friendly voice, but Prim understood the implication behind it clearly, and it frightened her. Was she on trial? Had the hanging merely been postponed?

'He was simply giving us a lift,' she replied, hoping Rachel could hear in her voice a willingness to help, to sort everything out before it got out of hand. 'Like a taxi driver.'

'To al-Sarhan, of all places?'

'You don't understand,' Prim said hurriedly. 'My father was in a relationship with Dr Jabour's cousin, Ifaya. I learned about that in Cairo, where he disappeared. I also discovered that Ifaya Jabour comes from – she *came* from – al-Sarhan. We were directed to Dr Jabour by the district commissioner in Tiberias. He wouldn't have done that if he'd known the doctor was smuggling arms, would he? It stands to reason.'

'So you knew nothing of the ammunition?'

'Of course not. We were only there because Dr Jabour offered to take us to the village and ask, on my behalf, if anyone had news of Ifaya and my father.'

'And had they?'

'No, other than the news that you people had killed Ifaya.'

'You people? What do you mean by that?'

Prim's response was a bitter laugh. 'Dr Jabour said it was the Zionists who killed her. I'm assuming that's you.'

For the first time since the woman named Rachel began speaking, Prim detected a note of irresolution in her voice. 'That was not intended. We misidentified the car. It was her brother, Kazem Jabour, who was the target.'

'I'm sure that was a great comfort to her.'

The note of irresolution vanished. 'Did you know that Kazem Jabour controls the smuggling of terrorist explosives here in

Galilee? Explosives that are used to blow up British soldiers as well as Jews?' Rachel asked tersely.

'I can't believe Ifaya would have had anything to do with that,' Prim said defensively. 'From what I've learned about her, she wasn't the type.'

'She was his sister. Sisters often admire their older brothers enough to follow them.'

Her gaze fixed on the ceiling, Prim shook her head. 'There was a family disagreement, over her relationship with my father. Ifaya had a career in Cairo, acting in his theatre. She was in love with him, I presume. I don't know why she went back to Palestine. Maybe it was to win Kazem over.'

'Tell me, Primrose, do you have any reason to believe your father might be in Palestine? If he had been in that car with Ifaya Jabour, we would know about it.'

Prim's inability to face Rachel – to see the person behind the voice, to be able to confront her inquisitor – was becoming a torment to her. There was no escape from it. She couldn't cover her ears. She couldn't drown out the relentless, oh-so-reasonable line of examination. It was like being trapped in detention with a teacher who really liked you, but just couldn't stop trying to reason the rebelliousness out of you. She wondered where Harry was. Were these people treating him kindly? Somehow she doubted it. He was only here because of her. She had led him into jeopardy – a jeopardy with a voice called *Rachel-if-you-like*.

'What's your plan, Rachel?' she snapped as the anger overwhelmed her. 'Are Harry and I going to end up as a headline in the London *Daily Herald*: *Englishwoman in search of her father disappears in Palestine?* I mean, thank God my surname isn't Jabour. You kill one Jabour without a trial, and another for being in the wrong place at the wrong time. Is that how you Palestinians – whatever your religion – solve *all* your arguments?'

It seemed like minutes before Rachel replied and, when she did, her tone was infuriatingly pleasant. 'Maybe we should let you get some rest, dear. You've been through a difficult time, that's clear. Maybe you'll feel better after a nice nap. How does that suit you, Primrose?'

For Prim, it was the infuriating reasonableness that was the fuse. It was simply too much for her. 'It's Prim!' she shouted, which was normally something she tried to avoid, having an aversion to theatrical outbursts. 'P.R.I.M. *Prim*. Like a Victorian prude – get it? Do you understand, *Rachel* or whatever your name is? Fucking *Prim*! No one calls me "Primrose" unless it's my mother lecturing me about how I'm wasting my life!'

But her attack petered out before it had truly got under way. The voice named Rachel was too incorporeal to take a hit. Prim's angry words died in the no-man's-land between them. She heard a sigh of disappointment and then the chair scrape on the floorboards. Then footsteps, slow and deliberate. Not retreating but punishing. Withdrawing favour. Withdrawing company. A door opened and then closed. For Prim, in the silence that followed, the only victor in the fight was loneliness.

Harry's interrogation, on the other hand, was more direct. It was conducted with surprising cheeriness by a rotund, ageing man with white hair and a scattershot of dark freckles on his fleshy face. He had deep, wise eyes, and introduced himself as Bachmann. Someone of gravitas in the community, Harry reckoned. Not a professional interrogator, but a man valued for his experience and wisdom. A leader. Perhaps even a rabbi.

Bachmann didn't bother to hide his face, covering his head with nothing more clandestine than a battered straw sunhat.

Harry was sitting on a bale of hay. They hadn't tied him to anything, presumably because they were sure he was unlikely to make any sudden moves that might provoke the muscular youth with the bandanna across the lower part of his face and the shotgun cradled in his lap, who sat only a few feet away from him in what Harry assumed was a shelter for farm animals, because it stank of ammonia and manure.

'So, young man, let's see what we can make of all this *meshugaas*,' Bachmann said, pulling up a milking stool that looked barely sturdy enough to support his considerable bulk.

Harry looked at him blankly, but he could hear the German accent in the man's speech, marking his interrogator as a recent immigrant.

'*Meshugaas* – craziness,' expounded Bachmann with a broad grin that turned the freckles into bands, like the veins in polished marble.

Having heard the accent, Harry replied in his fluent German. 'What's crazy, Herr Bachmann, is that neither Miss Nevendon nor I have the faintest idea what we are doing here. Perhaps you'd be good enough to explain why we are being held against our will.'

Surprised by Harry's German, Bachmann widened his rheumy eyes. But he replied steadfastly in English, as if German might burn his tongue. 'Well, that's a surprise, I would say. Have we caught ourselves a true-blooded Aryan of the master race? Are you going to demand all my worldly possessions before you stamp my papers and allow me to leave, like the last time I heard someone speaking *Hochdeutsch* to me?'

Harry gave a conciliatory smile. Inside, he was enjoying a modicum of professional satisfaction: he had taken the initiative at the start of the very first round. He decided they had sent not a skilled interrogator, but someone whose judgement and wisdom they trusted. And that, Harry thought, was good news because it meant an open mind. 'I am English, Herr Bachmann,' he said, reverting to his native language. 'But if I were not here in Palestine, I would be at my desk in the British embassy in Vienna; where, I am pleased to say, we have managed to provide papers for numerous Jews to leave that country. I'm guessing you understand what I'm talking about.'

Bachmann's face lit up. 'That is indeed a relief to hear, Herr… Herr…'

'It's Taverner. Harry Taverner. I'm surprised the instigator of that very neat little roadblock we encountered back there hasn't told you already.'

Bachmann looked unconvincingly crestfallen. 'I am a simple man. My memory is not what it was. I may have misheard what they told me. Best to be sure, yes?'

So, thought Harry, not a professional, but astute enough to pass himself off as bumbling. He revised his sense of advantage. Bachmann wasn't bumbling, he was a wily old fox, and therefore to be treated as dangerous.

Harry had already decided on his strategy. He had known, from the moment that Prim and he were separated, that their interrogators would be searching for little discrepancies in their stories – evasions or downright lies that could be stored away and brought out later, to devastating effect. It was the oldest technique in the book. He had therefore resolved to tell as much of the truth as he could. Better that than inadvertently contradict something Prim might say.

As to who these people were, Harry had had time enough to narrow the choices. Based on the briefing Major Courtney had given him in Cairo, and Captain Wingate's words on the train from Haifa, he was certain they were in the clutches of either the Haganah or the more militant Irgun, paramilitary groups raised to defend Palestinian Jews from attacks launched by their Arab neighbours. So far as he knew, both groups were still notionally pro-British. Or if not pro, then at least not yet anti. How long that might last, Harry did not know.

'Let me take a guess, Herr Bachmann,' he said. 'You're troubled by the fact that Miss Nevendon and I were travelling in the same vehicle as Dr Jabour.'

Bachmann smiled, displaying large and very yellow teeth. 'While I have great admiration for your fine country and its empire, Mr Taverner, there are some of your countrymen in Palestine who are not beyond smuggling arms to anyone who will pay well for them. I may say that we ourselves have benefited from such a trade. But we would be fooling ourselves if we thought that indicated unwavering faithfulness. Do you see our dilemma?'

Harry assured Bachmann that he saw it as clear as daylight. As briefly as he could, he recounted how he had been ordered to Cairo to assist Miss Primrose Nevendon in the search for her missing father, and that the search had brought them to al-Sarhan. Their presence in Dr Jabour's car could in no way be taken to imply any nefarious connection with a man who, until only hours before, they had assumed to be nothing but an innocent relation of the late Miss Ifaya Jabour.

'So, Mr Harry, when you tell me you work for the British government, am I to assume you mean British Intelligence?'

'I'm sure you understand, Mr Bachmann, that even if that was what I meant, I couldn't tell you. You'll have to take my word that everything I've told you is true.'

A look of deep regret came over Bachmann's face. 'Sadly, Mr Harry, I must tell you that the British word has proved itself to be rather less than dependable of late. I am speaking of the permitted numbers of Jews allowed to settle here in Palestine. Once the famous British word was all for it. Now, not so much.'

Harry remembered what Wingate had told him when he'd met them at Haifa aerodrome: *I do keep my ear to the ground – lot of good contacts amongst the Palestinian Jews...* He looked Bachmann in the eye and said, 'Then if my word is not good enough, perhaps some of your people might have heard of a Captain Wingate?'

Bachmann met his gaze but showed no acknowledgement.

'He's at British headquarters in Jerusalem,' Harry continued. 'He was ordered to bring us from Haifa to Tiberias. If anyone should care to ask him, I'm sure he'd be happy to reassure them of our bona fides.'

Bachmann smiled. 'We have a saying, Mr Harry: "A faithful friend is the medicine of life".'

'I wouldn't say Wingate was a friend. But he'll vouch for us.'

'A tonic then, if not entirely a medicine.'

'Something like that.'

Rising to his feet, Bachmann laid a hand on Harry's shoulder. 'Hopefully this can all be resolved amicably,' he said.

'That would be really great,' Harry replied.

As Bachmann turned to leave, he paused. 'I have to tell you, some of the younger spirits here were all for shooting both of you,' he said, as if he'd only just remembered. 'They were inclined to believe you were in league with the terrorists. It is a good thing that the young still listen to their elders, don't you think?'

The boy with the shotgun across his knees ran one hand over the barrel as if he was stroking a pet dog. The scarf across his nose and mouth creased as he smiled. Harry felt a cold shudder course through his body.

Before he stepped outside, Bachmann went on, 'Personally, I think you're both clean. But then I am, by nature, a trusting sort of fellow. As for your lady friend's missing father – that's another matter altogether.'

In the long hours that followed, Prim remained tied to the uncomfortable iron bedstead. She dozed fitfully, waking in a sweat from a recurring dream in which a man was led to his death in a dark wood. Sometimes it was Dr Jabour; sometimes it was Harry; sometimes it was her father. But whoever the victim was, she would wake with a jolt in the instant before the killing shot rang out.

She knew evening was coming on because there was less light penetrating the covering over the window. At one point a tractor grumbled past. She knew it was a tractor because old Elwyn, the handyman-gardener at Bevern, drove an ancient Saunderson that had been around since the Great War, and which sounded just like it. The breathy phutting sound made her unbearably homesick. A short while later she heard the pealing laughter of children. Outside, she suspected, was a normality she would instantly recognize. Yet here she was: tied to a bed like one deranged, subjected to an interrogation, a prisoner in the hands of people who could shoot someone without compunction. It made no sense.

It was almost dark when she heard the door open. A voice she recognized as Rachel's said, 'How are you doing? Not too uncomfortable, I hope. You must be hungry. I've brought you a bowl of *hamin* and a glass of Slivovitz to put the fire back in your belly. Do you think you might be up for that?'

Prim heard the clatter of a tray being placed on the chair behind the bed. Then a shape loomed over her, a brightly patterned scarf drawn across the lower part of the face. Rachel untied the cords binding Prim's wrists to the bedframe and set the chair next to the bed. The scent of meat and cumin rising from the tray made Prim remember how hungry she was. She sat up.

'Bachmann reckons you're probably innocent,' Rachel said through the scarf. All Prim could see of her face was a pair of huge brown irises with jet-black pupils at the centre and a smooth, tanned forehead, because Rachel wore a second scarf, just as colourful as the first, over her head.

'Well, that's a relief. Who's Bachmann when he's at home?'

Rachel's laughter was bright and childlike, the laughter of a little girl playing with a beloved grandparent. 'He's our guiding star, our lodestone. Bachmann has sacrificed much for our struggle.'

'Bachmann… Rachel… Why am I allowed to hear names spoken, when I'm not allowed to see any of you?' Prim asked, rubbing her wrists.

'It's for Rabbi Bachmann's protection, as much as ours. If the English come and ask him, he can tell them that he did not see our faces, that he mediated on your behalf with faceless terrorists, because that's what they think we are. We wouldn't want to place lies on Rabbi Bachmann's tongue, would we?' She handed Prim the cup of Slivovitz. '*L'chaim*,' she said. 'It means "to life".'

Prim drank and the plummy spirit was like a lifesaving transfusion. 'That's a strange toast for people who shoot doctors without a trial,' she countered.

'A little gratitude would not go amiss, I think,' Rachel replied with a sigh of disappointment. 'Here, try the *hamin*.'

'You sound like my mother used to, at the dinner table when I was little,' Prim said. But she took the spoon Rachel was offering and discovered the goulash was indeed tasty.

'And was supper good at your mother's table?' Rachel asked conversationally, watching her eat.

'It was until my father left. Then it all got a little difficult. I didn't dare mention his name.'

'But you have come all the way from England to find him.'

'Isn't that what a dutiful child ought to do? He might need my help.'

'But you haven't found him yet?'

'I told you before: no.'

Rachel kept watching her in silence until Prim had emptied the bowl. Her eyes were kind. If it hadn't been for the voice, Prim might have thought this was a different woman from the one who had questioned her. She handed the bowl back to Rachel, who set it down on the tray and then said, 'I guess this must all be very strange for you.'

'You could say that,' Prim replied, looking around her odd little cell.

'We had no real choice back there,' Rachel went on. 'That was live ammunition your doctor friend was smuggling. It would have been fired at Jews. It would have been fired at you English. Had it been your roadblock instead of ours, it would have made no difference. Your people might now be planning to hang him. Either way, tonight Galilee is safer for us both.'

'I can't believe Ifaya Jabour had anything to do with that sort of thing,' Prim said urgently. 'I *won't* believe it.'

Rachel took the tray and went to the door. 'Well, that's all academic now, I think.'

'Am I free to go?'

'Maybe soon. I hope so. *Im yirtzeh Hashem.*'

'What does that mean?'

'"If God wills it to be",' Rachel said. At the door, she stopped and looked back. 'I hope you find your father, Primrose. I truly do.'

'Thank you. But it's not looking promising. I've run out of options.'

Rachel nodded. 'I know what it is like to lose a parent. My family lived in Hebron. The Arabs were our neighbours, our friends. There were more than twenty thousand of them, a few hundred of us. We were mostly Sephardim, Jews from Spain, and many of our families had lived there for generations. Nine years ago – I can tell you the very day: 15th August 1929 – suddenly our neighbours came looking for us. They wanted to kill us, because of lies they'd been told. One in ten of the Jews in Hebron died, including my mother and father. If the British hadn't intervened, there wouldn't be any of us left alive there. I only survived because not all the Arabs in Hebron were murderers.'

Prim stared at the young woman by the door. She had no reply for her. She wasn't even sure that's what Rachel wanted.

'An Arab teacher at my school sheltered me.' Rachel's eyes lowered and Prim knew she was finding it difficult to continue. When she looked up again, the tears were clearly visible, even in the dying light. 'Understand me clearly, Prim. I don't hate them all, by any means – just the ones who wish us harm. And those I will resist with my life. This land is *Eretz Israel*, our home. It has been our home since before what you call the Old Testament was first written down. The Romans threw us out in the first and second centuries. They renamed it Syria Palaestina, to eradicate all memory of it. But we are a resilient people. We found new homes. But you English threw us out of your country in the thirteenth century, the Spanish in the fifteenth, the Russians in the nineteenth. The Poles and the Germans are throwing us out even as I speak. Where do you wish us all to go, if not *home*?'

Prim had no answer for her. It seemed too heavy a question for her ears to carry to her brain.

'So don't waste your tears over a man who swore an oath to heal, but carries bullets to our enemies so they may kill us,' Rachel said as she opened the door and stepped out into the dusk. 'Save them. Turn them into tears of joy, for when you find your father.'

It was almost midnight when a bellboy, his brown face almost geriatric with weariness from his day's labours and a round tarboosh a size too large for his head, found Mike Luzzatto in the terrace bar at Shepheard's Hotel. Luzzatto put down the nightcap he was drinking and the copy of Agatha Christie's *Murder in Mesopotamia*, which he was enjoying immensely, because although he'd never been to Mesopotamia it surely couldn't be very different from Egypt, and he liked atmosphere in his reading.

'Mr Mike, there is telephone call,' the boy said proudly, as if he'd laid the cable and built the exchange himself. 'Long-distance. So, very important. Is probably the president of the United States.'

Luzzatto followed the boy to the public telephone booth in the lobby and gave him a generous tip. By the time he closed the door to the booth and lifted the receiver, he had replayed in his mind any number of possible disasters, because he knew that no one would call him at this hour unless there was a crisis either brewing or in full flood.

'Luzzatto here,' he murmured into the handpiece. 'Who is this?' The noise on the line told him at once that this was indeed a long-distance call.

'Shalom,' said a familiar voice from far away. 'How are things in the land of the pharaohs?'

'I was about to head for my sarcophagus,' Luzzatto replied. 'You got problems there in the Promised Land?'

The laughter mingled with the crackling on the line. 'Thought you might like to know that Rockefeller's daughter turned up here.'

'Didn't I tell you she was on her way?'

'You'll never guess where we found her.'

'I'm guessing it wasn't on the Temple Mount.'

'She was pulled out of a car that belonged to a friend of Amalek. There were contraband cigarettes in the car.'

Luzzatto decoded the message as easily as if it had been his second language. Rockefeller's daughter: Prim Nevendon, daughter of the oil man Archibald Nevendon. A friend of Amalek: a terrorist. Contraband cigarettes: ammunition – explosives were cigars.

'Where is she now?'

'Here. Our wolf cubs brought her in.'

'Treat her kindly. She's an okay girl.'

'There was an Englishman with her,' said the voice that didn't belong to the president of the United States. 'It's not her father.'

Luzzatto saw an image in his mind, that of an Englishman. 'Let me guess. Tall guy, blond hair, handsome in that superior English way. Dimple on the chin. Talks a bit like Bertie Wooster, if Bertie Wooster knew how to look after himself in a fist-fight?'

'They weren't that specific.'

'Does he have a name?'

'Taverner.'

'That's the guy,' said Luzzatto with a grin. 'What's the issue?'

'Well, given the company the two of them were keeping, the youngsters here are a little concerned they're running with the wrong pack, and you know how impulsive the young can sometimes be. They don't listen to their elders. What's your take, Mike?'

Luzzatto thought back to the evening he'd spent at Santi's with Prim, trying to recall the conversation. 'I know she's looking for her old man, she told me so. She said he'd got something going with an actress from some village in your neck of the woods. Prim's a game girl, so I'm not surprised to hear she's turned up. But mixed up in that sort of malarkey? I don't buy it, not with Taverner carrying her bags. He works for the British government. Says he's something to do with culture, but I reckon it's more likely to be their version of the Feds.'

A throaty chuckle rumbled down the line. 'Then my call has not been wasted, Mike. I thank you. You can return to your sarcophagus, my friend.'

The line died and Luzzatto went back to his table on the terrace. He took a sip of Jack Daniel's and turned to his page in *Murder in Mesopotamia*. He thought of Prim Nevendon and hoped she was being treated all right; the Irgun could play rough sometimes. But the man whose call he had just taken had a big heart and would see fair play. So Luzzatto lifted the glass again and raised a silent *L'chaim* to his old friend Rabbi Bachmann.

The sky was bright with stars when Harry was led outside. The luminous tips of the hands on his watch told him it was ten past three in the morning. Insects trilled sweetly in the darkness, but the birds had yet to stir. There was no horizon, only the neat black ranks of unlit huts, like a military camp asleep. He wondered if Bachmann's reasonableness had failed and they were going to shoot him after all. But the masked boys around him seemed too jovial for a firing squad. He saw the dark shape of the Chevrolet flatbed loom out of the night. Three women stood close by. It was only when he came closer that he saw that one of them was Prim.

'They're letting us go,' she said. 'Rachel has just this moment told me. They're going to drive us somewhere and set us free.'

Harry said that was marvellous news, though he was wondering who in their right mind would drive a truck around in pitch-darkness. The boys helped them up onto the back of the Chevrolet. This time, as they began to move, there was no tarpaulin, no sheaves of barley, and they sat on the boards beside their guards. The headlamps sent out spears of light, though not enough to strike much more than the twisted trunks of trees and then a wooden signboard set high on posts, which made Harry think of a Wild West cattle ranch. He looked back as they went under it, hoping to catch some indication of where they'd been held. But all he saw, and then only briefly before it was lost to the night, were a few characters of Hebrew that meant nothing to him.

They drove until the blackness of the sky began to soften. Trees and hills emerged, outlined against a spreading lip of powdery pale blue on the eastern horizon. The birds were awake and full-throated now. So too were the boys and girls in the truck with them, who sang folk songs that held a haunting echo of distant places: the Ural Mountains… the Russian steppes… the lowlands of Silesia and the Polish Plain.

Eventually it was light enough to see the track ahead. The truck stopped; the tailgate came down. Prim and Harry were helped to the ground. 'Walk towards the dawn,' Rachel said, as if she were giving them a philosophical exhortation to lead a better life. 'Don't look back.'

Prim and Harry did as they were told. They walked until the sound of the truck's engine disappeared. Then they carried on walking. Only when they had crested a small hill, set on either side with low olive trees, did they stop. Ahead of them, maybe a couple of miles distant, were the still, silver-purple waters of the Galilee. And far below, clinging to the shoreline like the fires of a friendly camp, the first lights were coming on in Tiberias.

Twenty-Seven

Let me tell you straight from my heart, Nim, old fellow, not a word of a lie: I rue the day I first heard the name Kazem Jabour. If I hadn't taken that loan from Hamad, I could have kept him out of my life altogether. Maybe Ifaya would have stayed in Cairo, instead of sneaking back to al-Sarhan when I wasn't looking, hoping her brother would see reason, hoping he'd let her love whoever she wanted. But while Papa Jabour was reasonable enough, he hadn't passed that quality on to his son.

There was another family trait missing in Kazem Jabour, too. While – to me at least – Ifaya was beautiful beyond description, her brother had the face of Beelzebub after he'd gorged himself on the Carlton Club's plum duff pudding. Six foot four, eyes like drill holes. I use the term as I understand it, as an oil man. Those drill holes were deep and black, and you have no idea what sort of brutality was likely to gush out of them.

While Papa Jabour was a kindly fellow who took you at face value, wherever you came from, his son reckoned himself a modern-day Saladin, only without the tolerance. He hated us Europeans with a vengeance. There wasn't one of us he didn't want under the blade of his scimitar – me included. Held me personally responsible for stealing the oil he thought was his by right, even though it came from Mesopotamia and not Palestine. Told me to my face that I was in the pay of the Jews. Said that I, Archibald Nevendon, was plotting to hand Palestine to them, gift-wrapped. I told him it was nonsense. I told him the Peel Commission, the government – everyone involved – wanted a peaceful settlement of the issue, space and rights for both parties in a self-governing Palestine. But Kazem Hamad didn't want that. He wanted what his friends in the Black Hand desired: an independent Arab state stretching across the whole Middle East, without a single Jew, or a European, in it.

Not that he wasn't happy enough for me to foot the bill for his women and his whisky, when he turned up in Cairo. I thought it was to have a face-to-face chat, like two grown-up men of the world. But the only thing Kazem Jabour knew about the world was that he wanted to blow it up and rule over the rubble. The truth is, he was a thug and a bully. I can tell you this: my darling Ifaya didn't head for Cairo just because she wanted to be the next Joan Crawford. She wanted to escape her god-awful brother. It was the bravest thing she ever did, going back to al-Sarhan to plead with Kazem to accept me as her husband. And it cost her life.

The worst thing of all, Nim, is that she didn't have to go. What she never knew was that brother Kazem, God rot his eyes, had come to Cairo to see yours truly, several weeks before.

When he marched into my office, all decked out like Valentino in The Sheik, but without the looks, you could have knocked me down with a feather. I almost called Gamil and el-Madani, my executive assistants, to throw him out. Wish to God I had, to be honest.

But I didn't.

Then brother Kazem plants himself in the leather chair that I set aside for important visitors, looks me in the eye and – I'm paraphrasing here – says as bold as you like, 'Now then, Nevendon, I hear you people use a lot of explosives in your line of work.'

Twenty-Eight

The desk clerk on duty that morning at the Hotel Tiberias was a master at maintaining the impenetrable serenity of the professional hotelier. He had served his apprenticeship at the smart Bayerischer Hof in Munich, until the Nazis had fired him for the unpardonable sin of being Jewish. When two dishevelled guests walked in as the waiting staff were laying the tables for breakfast, he greeted their return with consummate tact, handing them their room keys with no more than a courteous, 'Welcome back, Mr Taverner... Miss Nevendon.' His gaze did not follow them as they climbed the stairs. He allowed himself not a hint of a knowing smirk. Nor did he comment when they returned a while later, looking considerably less unkempt, and took a table on the terrace, although throughout he did rather wonder why they hadn't discreetly shared a room in preference to the discomfort of the beach for their night-long romantic tryst.

'What do we do now?' Prim asked under her breath as she sipped at a cup of coffee and looked out at the fishing boats on the lake. 'Who do we tell?'

'For a start, I need to tell Wingate and the district commissioner about Kazem Jabour. It's obvious the Mandate government has no idea he's a terrorist.'

'What about Dr Jabour? Whatever he was up to, he deserved a fair trial at the very least.'

'I get the feeling the Mandate government would probably rather not be troubled.'

'And what about the people who killed him – the people who held us?'

'I think they were most likely Irgun,' Harry said. 'But we have no idea where we were held. And they didn't harm us.'

'But we know about Bachmann,' said Prim. 'Rachel said he was their guiding star, their lodestone. Those were her very words.'

Harry shrugged. 'I don't think he was their leader. He's a rabbi – I think they simply looked up to him for advice. Besides, I suspect it was his intervention that got us freed. Otherwise we might both be lying dead in a ditch somewhere. Let's take that as a win.'

Prim stared into her coffee cup. 'So what do we do now?'

'To be brutally honest, I think you've run out of options.'

'Do you think I haven't worked that out for myself, Harry?'

'There's one thing that troubles me, though,' he said pensively. 'At al-Sarhan we agreed that we both felt Dr Jabour knew you were coming.'

'Yes.'

'And so did the people who killed him. It was something Bachmann said to me.'

Prim looked at him. Her eyes felt as though someone had poured sand into them and her body ached. She longed for sleep. But what Harry had just said had brought her wide awake.

'I think Archie got himself mixed up in something that made him an enemy to both sides in this conflict,' Harry explained. He was recalling what Bachmann had told him: *Personally, I think you're both clean... As for your lady friend's missing father – that's another matter altogether*. But he wasn't about to add to Prim's burden by saying it out loud. 'I don't know what it was that Archie did, but given that we've run out of leads and still have no idea of where he is, or even if he's alive, I think you must face reality: the search has to end. Indeed I think it would be highly dangerous to even think of continuing. If Kazem Jabour had been at al-Sarhan when we were there, I'm not sure we'd be sitting here now.'

It was a while before Prim answered. As she sat staring out at the lake, a lone cormorant sailed silently overhead and down towards the shoreline. Prim watched it land before she spoke, and Harry could see the fight draining out of her. 'You're right, of course,' she said. 'You always are. Damn you!'

He got up from his seat and laid one hand gently on her shoulder. 'Wait here,' he said.

'Where are you going?'

'To see the district commissioner. And then I have some telephone calls to make.'

The colour drained out of the district commissioner's face as Harry briefly outlined what had happened since they'd set off for al-Sarhan with Dr Jabour. Harry gained no satisfaction from it. Indeed, he felt almost sorry for Hughes. A major figure in the Arab revolt had been operating with impunity within his area of jurisdiction and, like most bureaucrats, he was having trouble squaring that with any dereliction on his part.

'Do I take it, Mr Taverner, that while you told me earlier you were employed by what you called the General Assistance department of the Colonial Office, you are in fact a member of British Intelligence?' he said, as if trying to show he wasn't entirely inexpert.

'That would be mere speculation,' Harry replied with a friendly smile. 'But might I have use of your telephone? And in private, if that's all right with you.'

He then made three phone calls, using the district commissioner's private line and thereby avoiding the operators at several telephone exchanges. The first was to the Haifa offices of Anglo-Levantine Oil, where a helpful executive informed him that the next Rapide flight to Cairo would depart in four days' time. And that, yes, there were standing instructions to make space for Mr Nevendon's daughter and her official companion on the service, whenever they required it.

His next call was made to the British military headquarters at the King David Hotel in Jerusalem.

'Well, that's a turn-up for the books,' said Captain Orde Wingate after Harry had told him about Kazem Jabour's role in smuggling explosives, and the illicit ammunition found in his cousin's car. 'Can't thank you enough, old boy. I remember you asking me about the Jabour name when I picked you up at Haifa. Same family?'

'Yes.'

'Then I have news for you on that front. I took a peep at the files when I got back here, after I'd dropped you off in Tiberias. The only thing I could find on a Jabour of any stripe was in reference to that trouble at al-Sarhan that I spoke about on the train – a young woman of that name died in the fight there.'

'Yes, Ifaya. She was Kazem's sister.'

'We took statements, of course. But they're all very brief; the locals never tell us anything. You'd almost think they don't trust us.' A throaty laugh reached Harry down the line. 'The only other fatality was a Jew, a young fellow named Bachmann – the son of a rabbi from a kibbutz not far away.'

———

Harry's final call, made after a brief conversation with the district commissioner's secretary, was to the Hadassa Municipal Hospital in Haifa. It was his last throw of the dice.

'I'm very sorry, but you're too late,' a stern-sounding ward matron told him. 'Mr Jabour died two days ago. Are you a family friend?'

'Just an acquaintance,' Harry told her, with exactly the right amount of sadness in his voice. 'It was lung cancer, or so I was led to believe.'

'Yes, it was,' said the matron. 'He'd been in a coma for some time, I'm afraid. I understand he had a son and a daughter, but they haven't been to see him for some time.' Then, with the faintest softening of tone, she added, 'He was a charming gentleman... for an Arab.'

Days later Harry Taverner and Prim Nevendon climbed aboard the silver Rapide at Haifa aerodrome. They were the only passengers, although the company pilot told them they would not be flying directly back to Cairo. The plan, he explained, was to stop briefly at the Royal Air Force station at Ramla, a few miles south-east of Tel Aviv, there to pick up a sack of mail that had arrived from England. The letters were destined for the troops in Cairo, but by that mysterious and all-too-frequent artifice of the military postal service, they had found their way to the wrong place.

The diversion meant the journey would take perhaps forty minutes longer, including the stop at Ramla. And instead of being mostly over the Eastern Mediterranean, it would take them inland, bringing them closer to the Anglo-Levantine base at Geneifa at the head of the Gulf of Suez. It would also bring them closer to the mountains of the Sinai Peninsula.

'Geneifa,' said Prim as they taxied out, bumping over the uneven ground, the dust billowing beneath the biplane's wings. 'That's where Archie did his flying-around-for-no-reason thing. The engineer at Heliopolis showed me the log.' The Rapide's engines began to bellow. Prim's jaw took on a determined set. 'It's all I have left,' she shouted over the din. 'Maybe we should drive out there when we get back.'

Harry replied with something non-committal. He'd already resolved to call London when he got back to the embassy and tell them to post Archie Nevendon as missing presumed dead, before Major Courtney sent his letter asking for Harry to be placed permanently on the muster. He was eager to get back to Vienna.

They spoke little on the flight to Ramla. The errant mailbag was loaded and the Rapide airborne again inside ten minutes. The final leg to Cairo took them out across the sea for a while. Prim, sitting on the left just behind the little archway beyond which the pilot sat, could watch the waves breaking on the sand in the middle distance. The sun gleamed on the silver fabric of the lower wing. She stared into the reflected glare until it hurt her eyes. But she couldn't see Archie there, either. He was lost to her. And now she accepted it. She thought she ought to weep, but somehow the tears wouldn't come. It made her feel a traitor to his memory.

An hour out from Heliopolis and she was in a near-trance of loss and regret. She barely heard the pilot as he shouted above the clattering of the Rapide's motors. But the movement of his shoulder caught her eye.

He was gesturing towards the left, his arm bent like a mantis in the narrow space between the seat and the cockpit glass.

Prim looked out of the window. Below was nothing but flat, featureless rocky desert. But off the left wingtip, pushing above a layer of haze, she saw a ragged sawtooth line of mountains, red raw and desolate.

The pilot turned his head towards her and mouthed something. Prim couldn't hear, so she left her seat and went forward until she was standing against the bulkhead, leaning through the arch until her face was close to his.

'It's the Sinai,' he shouted. 'Impressive, what? Pretty bleak, though. No place to get lost in. God knows how the Bedouin find their way across it.'

Prim nodded. The mountains did indeed possess a menacing beauty. But looking at them seemed only to make her own desolation starker.

The pilot, who liked to give his passengers the benefit of his local knowledge, tapped Prim on the arm to get her attention again. 'It's where the ancient Egyptians did their mining,' he shouted helpfully. 'For turquoise. In fact they named the whole bloody peninsula the Ladders of Turquoise.'

Twenty-Nine

'It's in here,' Prim said, opening the bottom drawer of Archie's desk. 'It's the proof. I know where he is.'

The study at the Villa Narcisse was in shadow, the shutters drawn against the low, glaring sunlight of late afternoon. Alerted by a call from Anglo-Levantine, Tarek had picked them up at Heliopolis aerodrome. He stood now in the study doorway, watching intently while Prim rummaged in the drawer, as if he'd been called from an audience to watch a conjuring trick and was determined not to miss the sleight of hand.

Prim pulled out Uncle Nim's *Officer's Record of Services* book, opened the small, slim volume and withdrew the photograph of him and Archie at their dig. She handed it to Harry. Despite the gloom, he could easily make out the two men. They were dressed in voluminous shorts, pith helmets on their head, their sun-browned faces a darker shade of sepia than the backdrop of ancient stones tumbled amongst the rubble.

'Do you see – there?' Prim said, pointing to the lower right-hand corner of the photo. 'It says *TURQUOISE, 1913*. Archie is in the Sinai – at those ruins. That's where he's hiding. He's been in Egypt all the time.'

Harry studied the picture without answering. His lack of reaction was more than Prim could bear.

'It all fits,' she insisted. 'Those flights he took from Geneifa... He was searching for the site that he and Uncle Nim had dug back before the war.'

Harry laid the photo on the desk. To Prim, his lack of excitement felt worse than if he'd laughed at her. 'I agree it's plausible,' he said cautiously. 'But the Sinai is a big place. It's a wilderness of mountains and dried-up riverbeds. These ruins could be anywhere.'

Struggling to contain her frustration, Prim went on, 'But, Harry, someone at the museum here in Cairo must know where that is. All we need to do is ask them.'

Scratching his head, he replied, 'I agree, it's the best lead we've had so far. If you're right, Archie's picked himself a damned clever hiding place.' He turned to Tarek. 'Mr Shalaby, do you recall Mr Nevendon ever speaking of the Sinai?'

'Never, sir,' Tarek replied.

'Are there roads there?'

'There is a coast road. But inland, mostly is only camel tracks. Maybe is possible to drive along the wadis, but you must have a motorcar with good suspension and desert tyres.'

'Did Mr Nevendon possess such a motorcar?' Harry asked.

Tarek shrugged. 'Not to my knowledge, mister.'

Prim said, 'Then either he kept it hidden from everyone around him or he had help.'

'Well, it's a start,' said Harry, nodding towards the desk. 'But we need to identify where that photograph was taken. And I think I know the best person to show it to.'

It was almost dusk before they were ushered into Russell Pasha's office. Dressed in a well-tailored business suit, his grey hair cropped close to his lean and hawkish face, the head of the

Cairo police looked as fresh and as eager to be at work as if it was breakfast time. It was in stark contrast to the portrait photo on the wall behind him, thought Harry – of the sybaritic young King Farouk resplendent in the uniform of what looked like a nineteenth-century field marshal.

Russell got up from behind his desk and stepped forward to welcome them. 'Mr Taverner, Miss Nevendon – glad to see you both safely returned. How was Palestine? Did you have luck in your endeavours?'

'I think I know where my father is,' Prim said, coming straight to the point.

'How splendid,' Thomas Russell replied. 'Is he safe?'

'That, I'm afraid, we're not so sure about.'

Harry said, 'We need your help in locating the exact location, sir.' He looked at Prim, who fished the photo out of her bag and handed it to Russell. 'We believe Miss Nevendon's father has taken refuge at that archaeological site. It's somewhere in the Sinai Peninsula. We need an expert to tell us exactly where that is.'

Russell Pasha studied the picture for a moment before shaking his head. 'Archaeology's not my forte, I'm afraid. I'm a hunting man myself. But I know who might be able to help. I could show this to Monsieur Drioton. He's the director-general of antiquities at the Egyptian Museum here in Cairo. If anyone could tell you, it would be him. May I keep this and get back to you?'

Though reluctant to give up the photo, Prim knew she had no choice.

'Don't worry, it will be in good hands,' Russell said, seeing the concern on her face. 'I'll log it as evidence; that way it'll be official.'

He promised to get back to her at the Villa Narcisse as soon as Monsieur Drioton had an answer for her and then escorted Prim and Harry to the door.

'We think Mr Nevendon has got himself mixed up in some sort of trouble in Palestine, between the Arabs and the Jews,' Harry said. 'We believe he's in hiding.'

'Well, he's chosen a damned uninviting fastness in which to do it,' Russell said. 'I know the Sinai a little. It's where the Israelites spent two years when the pharaoh chased them out of Egypt. And so far those archaeologist fellows haven't managed to find a single trace of them. I hope he knows what he's doing, Miss Nevendon. It's not a place I'd care to linger in.'

By the time they reached the Villa Narcisse again, dusk had fallen. The day's heat lingered in the air and the crickets sang their hypnotic rhythms from the garden. Harry said he was returning to his room at the embassy and that, if she needed him, all Prim had to do was call. When she kissed him on the cheek, his smile had a hint of *maybe-if-things-were-different* about it.

'If we can locate Turquoise, will you come with me?' she asked.

'Of course. That's what I was sent here for.'

Prim spent the next two hours in Archie's study. Going by what Mr Gamil had told her on the day she'd arrived in Cairo, Archie had now been missing for almost six weeks. She sat at his desk, peering into the pool of light cast by his Anglepoise lamp on the polished leather, letting her thoughts play out as though it were a magical window through which she hoped she might see him. She sensed she was closer to him than at any time in the seventeen days since she'd arrived in Cairo. But he would not materialize for her. He was as absent as he had been at al-Sarhan, almost as if he were hiding from his own daughter. Staring into the electric gleam, she searched for him amongst the ruins of the place that he and Nim called Turquoise. The thought of him alone, in hiding, grieving for Ifaya, brought her close to weeping. She called out his name. But no reply emerged from the light. She hoped the memory of Uncle Nim might still haunt the place, bringing Archie some small measure of comfort and companionship.

Eventually, when the light showed her nothing but the scratches in the leather desktop, she turned the lamp off and went out of the study and called for Tarek. 'I'm going to my room to fix my face and change into something fresh,' she told him when he came padding up like a faithful retainer. 'After that, I want you to drop me off at Shepheard's Hotel.'

The office at the embassy was empty, Major Courtney and Mrs Fulready-Laycock having long since left. Alone, Harry composed a brief signal to London:

> Subject Nevendon: If still alive believed in hiding Sinai + Will attempt to locate + Possibly involved with rebel elements in Palestine + Irgun aware.

He waited until the signal was acknowledged and then phoned the night porter for a sandwich and a bottle of milk stout. While he waited for the feast to arrive, he thought of Prim and how well she'd conducted herself in Palestine. When he'd first set eyes on her at Southampton, Harry had never imagined a theatrical set designer from East Sussex would turn out to possess such determination, such strength in adversity. He'd been wrong, and he wasn't ashamed to admit it. Even so, a small part of him cursed the Rapide's pilot for opening his mouth. If the man hadn't been so bloody keen to point out the sights to his passengers, the signal he had just sent would have announced his mission a failure. He'd be making plans to return to England and then back to Vienna – and Anna, his star agent, the woman he knew he really shouldn't be falling in love with. But he couldn't abandon Prim now, not after all she'd been through.

When the night porter arrived, the bread in the sandwich turned out to be stale and the milk stout unpleasantly warm. Still, he thought, Primrose Nevendon was no doubt having just as tedious a night.

'Well, look who it ain't,' Mike Luzzatto said with a grin when he found Prim waiting for him in the terrace bar. 'The prettiest girl in Cairo's back in town.' He looked at her approvingly. 'And don't she look swell.'

'Don't be silly, Mike,' said Prim, rolling her eyes. 'American girls might fall for that sort of nonsense, but I'm from the English countryside. Chaps there rate you on how quickly you can castrate a baby lamb or tie a hay bale.'

'I always knew you Limeys were crazy,' he observed with a laugh. 'But I really don't see you as the cowgirl type.' He summoned a waiter with a wave of his hand.

Prim looked crestfallen. 'You've found me out, Mr Luzzatto. I admit it: I'm a fraud.'

'I doubt that very much,' he said. 'But if you are stringing me along, I hope it's the castrating-baby-lambs bit.'

'You'll have to get to know me better to find out, won't you?' she said with a sly smile.

Mike ordered champagne. He suggested they take a table in the Grill Room. Prim was only too happy to agree. She was starving, and not only for food. Inside, she felt an intense hunger for company. A need for the warmth of a caress. An ear to whisper in – be it a whisper of desire or a whisper of confession. And with Harry committed elsewhere, damn him, Mike Luzzatto was a pleasant enough alternative.

'So tell me again,' he said as they settled into their seats and the waiter poured the champagne, 'where have you been and what have you been up to?'

'It's a long story, Mike,' Prim said, taking her powder compact from her bag and checking her lipstick. 'Are you sure you want to hear it?'

'I'm all ears,' Luzzatto replied, leaning forward to narrow the space between them.

If Tarek hadn't made the journey before, Harry reckoned they would have missed Geneifa entirely. The dusty enclave of low tents and makeshift wooden huts set on the western edge of the Canal, only a few miles north of where it spilled into the Gulf of Suez, was almost invisible behind a screen of palm trees. They reached it after a two-hour journey east along a mercifully straight highway, the only traffic being ambling Bedouin camels and the occasional truck belching oily black smoke. Tarek, being a company driver, had polished the Citroën to a shine before collecting Harry at the British embassy, but by the time they stopped at the red-and-white painted pole that barred the entrance to the depot, the car was covered in a layer of dust that turned its dark-green paintwork into a dull olive hue. If there was an airfield, neither Harry nor Prim could see it. 'I suppose they just use an area of swept ground,' Harry said, when Prim voiced concern that they'd come to the wrong spot.

From the moment he'd joined her that morning, he'd noticed she was in an almost euphoric mood. Unusually garrulous, he thought. He'd put it down to her conviction that they were getting closer to her father. But Geneifa was business. So he had asked her to let him do the talking. It wasn't that he feared what she might ask – he'd learned by now there was no standing in the way when Primrose Nevendon had her mind set on a course of action – but he was, after all, supposed to be the British government's representative in the search and, in the back of his mind, he could still hear Bachmann's gravelly voice: *I think you're both clean... As for your lady friend's missing father – that's another matter altogether...*

The Egyptian guard recognized Tarek at once and raised the barrier. They drove on past stacks of rusting ironmongery that Harry assumed were something to do with oil exploration, past a bare patch of ground where a dozen young men, Arab and European, were playing football despite the heat, upturned oil drums standing in for goalposts, towards the drab, unprepossessing building that served as Anglo-Levantine's headquarters in the Canal Zone. The car's tyres crunched on the stony ground and a plume of dust rose in their wake.

During their phone conversation Gamil had informed Harry that he himself was due to visit the site and would be happy to escort them around. Harry had wondered about the executive's motivation. Was he simply being helpful? Or was his motive more attuned to protecting the company's reputation?

Gamil met them at the entrance to the headquarters building. Sporting a suit and tie, he looked uncomfortably hot. 'Forgive me, please,' he said as they shook hands. 'I would have preferred to have offered you the aeroplane again, but sadly it is needed elsewhere today.'

Harry assured him that Anglo-Levantine had done more to help them than anyone had a right to expect.

'I was sorry to hear that your visit to Haifa was not as productive as you had hoped,' Gamil said.

'Well, at least we know where Mr Nevendon *isn't*.'

Prim flashed Harry a sharp look, but said nothing.

'I understand you wish to speak to the superintendent here about Mr Nevendon's recent visits.'

'If that would be possible.'

'I have alerted the superintendent, Mr Mabruk. He awaits us inside. Please...' Gamil gestured for them to go ahead of him. 'First we will hear what he has to say, then we will have lunch. I regret that the senior officers' dining room here cannot compare to Cairo, but they do their best. The cooks do wonders with fish from the Gulf.'

Superintendent Mabruk turned out to be a softly spoken Egyptian with a fine, wiry khedive's moustache and twinkling eyes. He wore a brown boiler suit that gave him the look of a helpful garage mechanic and he spoke good English, slow and cautious, as if words were nuts and bolts that had to be properly tightened.

'The last time I saw Mr Nevendon in person?' he said, echoing Harry's question and glancing at Gamil for permission to speak on what was clearly, by his expression, an awkward subject. 'That would have been shortly before he went missing. I would have to consult my diary.'

'Was that when he flew the Rapide in here?'

'No. A few days before. I was away when he flew in.'

'And when you saw him, did he come by road?'

'Yes. With his driver, Mr Shalaby.'

Prim said, 'Tarek confirmed that to me some time ago.'

Harry nodded. 'Was there anything unusual about the visit?'

'Only that it was unexpected.'

'What do you mean: unexpected?'

'Usually the boss's visits are arranged in advance – from Mr Gamil's office,' Mabruk said. 'But this time he called me personally.'

'Did he say what he wanted to speak to you about?'

'Not at first,' replied Mabruk. 'But I believed I knew the reason, though I did not say so on the telephone.'

Out of the corner of his eyes, Harry caught Gamil's frown of warning. Mabruk's affable manner cooled suddenly.

'You believed what exactly?' Harry persisted.

Mabruk looked to Gamil for help. The executive straightened his tie and sighed. 'You may tell him, Mabruk,' he said reluctantly. 'Mr Nevendon is from the British government. We may consider him to be a gentleman of authority.'

Harry waited. He was aware Prim was watching intently.

The superintendent swallowed hard. He seemed reluctant to speak. When he overcame his reticence, it was in a voice so soft that for a moment Harry thought he'd imagined the answer.

'I assumed he wanted to come here to see what measures I had put in place after the issue with the explosives.'

Twenty cans of best-quality DuPont Nitramon, 92 per cent ammonium-nitrate gauge, along with a similar number of primer charges; used for seismic exploration and blasting. That was as far as the superintendent got before Gamil hurriedly took over the story, presumably because he thought it needed an executive assistant's careful handling. 'Of course we carried out our own investigation the moment we discovered it was missing,' he insisted.

'Stolen?' prompted Harry.

'Not stolen, Mr Taverner. We pride ourselves on our security here.'

Harry thought of the single guard at the gate and the single coil of barbed wire that served the Geneifa depot for a fence. 'If not stolen, then what?'

This was a little more difficult for Gamil to handle as smoothly as he clearly wished. 'It was… er… er… not there.'

'What do you mean: not there?'

'The boxes were there, but the explosives were not. A most regretful situation.'

'I'm sure it was,' replied Harry with a raised eyebrow.

'It was during a routine stock-check. Mr Mabruk is a most diligent employee. He opened the boxes, but the explosives were not inside. Only cans of lubricating oil.'

'Was this reported to the police?'

Gamil rallied a little. 'As I told you, an investigation was launched very promptly. We have our own internal security people.'

'And what did they conclude, Mr Gamil?'

'That there had been a mix-up somewhere.'

'A mix-up?'

'An error. Someone had mistakenly put the wrong supplies into the boxes.'

'And who carried out this very thorough investigation, if I may be so bold as to ask?'

Gamil said proudly, 'Why, it was under the direction of Mr Nevendon, of course. As director, he took the matter most seriously.'

'And that's what *he* concluded?'

'Mr Nevendon discovered it must have happened in Kirkuk. He was able to trace the dockets from the supply department.

The orders bore similar serial numbers. Someone must have got them confused. We here in Egypt would never have been so derelict in our duties.'

Harry asked, 'Did anyone in Kirkuk admit to the error?'

Gamil smiled regretfully. 'Mr Nevendon was unable to establish the culprit.'

'Didn't it occur to anyone that it might have been a deliberate act – that the explosives might have been swapped for the lubricating oil?'

It was Bachmann's voice that Harry heard replying, not Gamil's: *I think you're both clean... As for your lady friend's missing father – that's another matter altogether.*

'Why would anyone do *that*, Mr Taverner?' Gamil asked, perplexed.

'Oh, I don't know,' said Harry sardonically. 'Maybe they were indebted to someone who liked blowing things up.'

Thirty

I always thought I was good at spotting a dodgy contract, Nim, old fellow. God knows, in the oil business you'd be hard pressed to find one that wasn't. In my time I've written a few of them myself. But I thought I could handle Kazem Jabour. After all, I'd struck what I believed was a decent deal with Shakir Hamad. I even thought Kazem might honour Papa Jabour's acceptance of my love for Ifaya. And at first he did. But it didn't take long for him to go from surly tolerance to full-blown puritanical outrage. And that's where the small print came in.

He'd got himself mixed up with the Syrians, hadn't he? It was the Syrians who turned him from a thug into a monster. They gave Kazem a cause. And there's nothing a bully with a cause won't countenance if it gets them what they want. So that day when he walked into my office and said he knew I had access to a store of Nitramon, I knew then that I should have read the contract with Shakir Hamad a little more carefully.

Kazem gave me a choice: give him the explosives or it was off to Damascus for his little sister, swiftly followed by a forced marriage to a vile old ancient who had four wives already, and who liked to demonstrate his husbandly affection by beating them black and blue whenever it took his fancy.

And that wasn't all.

Wouldn't it be a shame, he said, if our theatre suddenly took it upon itself to spontaneously combust and burn to the ground? And for the cherry on the cake – in order that I shouldn't be overly troubled by any of these events – he'd have one of his gunmen shoot me in the back one day when I wasn't looking.

What was I supposed to do, Nim? I could hardly tap on Russell Pasha's door and ask for help, could I? Once that wily old stoat started poking around in my business, he'd have soon found out I was laundering money for Shakir Hamad. I'd have been finished.

So I did what any sensible chap would do when he finds himself with his privates caught in a bear-trap: I grabbed the fastest way to release the jaws.

Did I believe Kazem when he said the Nitramon would only be used against Jews and not against British soldiers? I told myself that I did. It's easy to lie to yourself when your back is against the wall. To be honest, as far as I was concerned, he could have used it to blow up King George VI, Franklin Delano Roosevelt, George Formby and the Aga Khan, so long as he let me be with Ifaya. That's how we think when the most important thing in the whole wide world is about to be taken from us. I would have done the same for you, Nim, if it had been on offer. Well, I might have spared George Formby.

But you know me, Nim. You know me better than anyone. Old Archie Nevendon is a fighter and he wasn't going take it lying down, was he?

So what did I do?

Well, I came up with a plan, didn't I? The simplest plan in the world.

See how you like this *contract, Kazem bloody Jabour…*

Thirty-One

Lunch in the senior officers' dining room was a tense affair, though Gamil was right about the quality of the fish. His former affability had been replaced by a wary reserve. Over a dessert of soggy bread pudding – the Anglo influence rather than the Levantine, and all the more incongruous in this hot, dusty place – he took on the manner of a bank manager having a quiet word with a client about the parlous state of their finances. And the client was Prim.

'I fear I have some disquieting news from our head office, Miss Nevendon,' he said, laying down his spoon and adjusting his tie. 'The board has reached the conclusion that, sadly, Mr Nevendon will not be found.'

Prim's spoon froze on its way to her mouth. It was a moment before she could reply. 'Then I'm afraid your board is mistaken,' she said coldly, though Harry noticed her lower lip had started to tremble.

'I should add,' Gamil continued swiftly, 'that if he were to appear at some later date, it would not now be appropriate for him to return to the position of director of the Cairo office. In consequence the company is now interviewing for his replacement. I'm so sorry.'

'Oh,' said Prim. The spoon continued on its way, though swallowing its contents almost made her gag.

'Dear lady, please do not be overly alarmed,' Gamil urged, apparently reluctant to play the heartless bearer of bad news. 'Until someone is appointed, I am instructed to continue to offer you all the facilities you have so far enjoyed. The board is not heartless.'

'No, it's very kind of them,' Prim responded, though it sounded to her unconvincing, almost discourteous.

'We will give you plenty of notice to vacate the Villa Narcisse,' he went on. 'I regret it has come to this, but I am sure you understand our difficulties.'

'Yes. Yes, of course I do. You've already been more than generous.'

Gamil gave her an uncertain smile. 'And should Mr Nevendon's disappearance turn out to have been caused by circumstances beyond his control, then the company will, naturally, review its position. So all is not lost.'

'No. Quite. Thank you for letting me know.'

After that, the dessert course was finished in silence. Gamil and Mabruk escorted them to the car, where Tarek was waiting, smoking one of his noisome Turkish cigarettes. He crushed it underfoot before opening the passenger door for Prim to climb in.

'A safe journey back to Cairo, Miss Nevendon, Mr Taverner,' Gamil said with a laboured smile. '*Inshallah.*'

Just before he took his place beside Prim, Harry said, 'May I ask Mr Mabruk one last question before we go?' The superintendent looked to Gamil for approval, but Harry went on almost without drawing breath. 'In the last few months, whenever Mr Nevendon came here, did he ever take anything away with him?'

'What are you implying, Mr Taverner?' Gamil asked sharply.

Harry put one foot on the doorsill, but didn't attempt to get into the car. 'I'm not implying anything, Mr Gamil,' he said. 'I'm simply asking a reasonable question.'

Gamil shrugged, as though eager to have the visitors out of his hair. Tentatively Mabruk stepped forward. 'Sometimes Mr Nevendon offered to carry small items with him back to Cairo, rather than waste time waiting for the next truck to make the journey,' he said defensively, like a man under cross-examination. 'The boss was not a man to stand on ceremony. We here at Geneifa admired him for it.'

From inside the car, Prim said, 'Harry, you're not suggesting Archie was responsible for the missing—'

'I'm just asking, that's all,' Harry continued, keeping his gaze on the superintendent.

'Well, I'm not sure you *should* be asking,' Prim said. 'Not like that, anyway.'

'Mr Mabruk, did you actually see the things he took with him?'

'Of course.'

'What were they?'

Mabruk looked to Gamil for help.

'Mr Taverner,' the executive said, 'are these questions really necessary? You cannot seriously be suggesting that it was Mr Nevendon who took away the Nitramon.'

Harry went on as if Gamil wasn't there. 'The things he took away with him, Mr Mabruk – if you wouldn't mind.'

The superintendent opened his palms as if to prove his own innocence. 'Just everyday things concerned with our work: tools… paperwork…'

'Did he carry a business case when he came?'

'I think so.'

'Could he have taken the explosives out in that?'

Gamil looked appalled. 'That, sir, is an outrageous suggestion.' By the look on Prim's face, she seemed to agree.

Harry persisted. 'Anything else he might have taken, Mr
Mabruk?'

'He took a set of tyres with him,' the supervisor said defensively. 'That was the last time he was here.'

'*Tyres?*' echoed Harry, taking his foot off the doorsill.

'Yes,' said Mabruk. 'He said they were needed out at Matruh,
for a survey into the Qattara sands.'

'Special tyres then?'

'Indeed,' said Superintendent Mabruk, pleased at the chance
to display his knowledge and steer the questioning to a place
that Gamil would find more acceptable. 'A set of low-pressure
ones with a wider tread. The sort we use for driving where there
are no roads.'

On the drive back to Cairo, Prim was silent for almost half an
hour. Harry could do little but look out of the open window
at the arid, empty landscape, the warm breeze ruffling his fair
hair. He knew there was a storm brewing, and it wasn't coming
from the desert. But it was the waiting for it to break that
was hardest. And when it did, it came suddenly and without
warning.

'You think Archie stole those explosives, don't you?' Prim
said icily out of nowhere, staring at the back of Tarek's head.
'You think he gave them to Kazem Jabour. You think he's a
criminal.'

Harry turned back from the window. He replied, 'I'm sorry,
Prim. It all fits together. I wish to God it didn't. But it does.'

'I thought you were my friend, Harry Taverner.'

'I am, Prim. Truly.'

'A friend wouldn't make an accusation like that.'

'A friend wouldn't deny the facts.'

There was a pause while she considered this. Then, shaking her head as if she could not accept his contention, she continued, 'It's just crazy speculation. That's all it is.'

'Put it all together and it's damning.'

'I *won't* believe it,' she said, as if to a third, invisible passenger he could not see.

'Archie got himself indebted to Shakir Hamad,' Harry began in a careful voice, giving her the answer he'd been silently rehearsing since they left Geneifa. 'And then Hamad offered him up on a plate to some very bad people. We know that from Hamad himself – he told you to your face, in Cairo.'

Still staring straight ahead, she nodded.

'Kazem Jabour was one of them,' Harry continued. 'That woman who interrogated you – Rachel – she said Kazem was a kingpin in the smuggling of explosives, yes?'

Another nod, short and reluctant.

'I don't know what threat Ifaya's brother used to coerce Archie, but it worked. Maybe he threatened to banish Ifaya to a convent for the rest of her life—'

Prim turned to him. 'The Arabs don't have convents, Harry,' she said, almost contemptuously.

'I'm speaking metaphorically. Maybe he threatened to harm her; he sounds like the type. Maybe he threatened to get Shakir Hamad to burn down the Nimrod Theatre. I don't know. But poor Archie was under Kazem's thumb, and if he loved Ifaya as much as you think he did, he'd have done anything to keep her safe. Even if it meant giving him stolen explosives with which to attack Archie's own countrymen. But somehow the Irgun found

out about those explosives and attacked al-Sarhan, probably
trying to put an end to Kazem. I don't know what Ifaya was
doing there when she got killed, but now both sides are after
Archie: Kazem because he blames Archie for his sister's death; the
Irgun because, somehow, they found out about him supplying
the explosives. Right now Archie thinks the one place they won't
find him is at Turquoise.'

Prim buried her face in her hands.

'And I hope, for both your sakes, he's right,' Harry said,
unable to tell if she was weeping or trying to block out his words.
It might have been both.

They drove on, Prim lost in her misery, Tarek's attention
fixed on the road ahead, Harry feeling like a brute. After a
while Prim lowered her hands. Harry could see she was exerting
a brittle control over her emotions. 'What makes you think
the Jews are after him, too?' she asked, her voice sounding
unnaturally calm.

'Something Bachmann said, when he was questioning me.'

'Tell me.'

'It won't change anything,' he replied reluctantly.

'*Tell* me.'

Taking a deep breath, Harry said, 'Bachmann told me he
thought you and I were innocent of involvement with Dr Jabour.
But he wasn't so sure about your father. And there's something
else. Bachmann's son was one of your pal Rachel's people – a
member of the Irgun. He died in the attack at al-Sarhan, when
Ifaya Jabour was killed.'

'How do you know this?' Prim asked, frowning.

'Wingate told me when I called him from Tiberias, after they
released us. It seems to me that Archie's got himself involved in
a blood-feud of his own making.'

For a while there was just the grumbling of the Citroën's engine. Then Prim said, 'Why didn't you tell me that before, Harry?'

'Because I thought you'd had enough shocks for one day.'

'I don't need protecting. I'm not made of porcelain.'

'I never thought you were,' he said, turning once more to look out at the scoured and barren rise of hills on the horizon. 'But even solid rock breaks eventually.'

'What are you going to do if we find my father – arrest him?'

'I don't have powers of arrest, Prim.'

'I won't judge him, Harry, not until I know the truth.' She tilted her head back. Her jaw hardened. 'He's my father,' she said, as if she were preparing herself for a battle. 'You saw that photograph of him with Nim at that dig. He's at his best when he's free like that. That's why he couldn't thrive at Bevern. He'll never survive long in prison.'

'Face reality, Prim,' Harry responded, wanting to hold her, comfort her, but knowing it would be the worst thing he could do at that moment. The only alternative he could think of was to go on telling her the truth. 'We have to find him, and fast. Then I'll work something out. But if either Kazem Jabour or the Irgun get to him before we do, then, for Archie Nevendon, prison will be a cakewalk.'

While a frosty silence returned to the interior of Tarek Shalaby's green Citroën, sixty miles away, in Cairo, a black taxi was pulling off the swish avenue de la Reine Nazli and into a shady side-street. It stopped in front of an incongruous belle-époque porch, the entrance to the Egyptian offices of the Pantellas-Athena Shipping Line of Piraeus, Athens. Or so said the gleaming brass plaque attached to one of the pillars. The taxi's single passenger was a Dutchman, an executive of the company. With his fair hair and pale complexion, he was easy to identify as European. He was fishing in his wallet for a tip when a motorcycle pulled up alongside.

Had Prim Nevendon been there to witness it, she might have recognized both the bike and the young man riding pillion. The pistol he now levelled at the unfortunate Dutchman would undoubtedly have been familiar to her, if only because she too saw it up close and from roughly the same angle – on her first full day in Cairo, when Tarek had been driving her to the Villa Narcisse. And it had scared the wits out of her no less than it did now to the shipping executive.

In fear for his life, the Dutchman proffered the open wallet in exchange. But it seemed that the gunman, his features masked, was not to be bought. His eyes, the only features visible to the terrified executive, were implacable, full of an almost joyful hate. Exactly as Prim had done seventeen days earlier, the Dutchman closed his own eyes tightly and waited for the awful smashing impact of the bullet.

It did not come. Instead he heard a peal of laughter and then the roar of the motorbike as it accelerated away.

This time there was no Tarek Shalaby to step out and remonstrate. But there *was* an anonymous black saloon belonging to the Cairo police department, parked a few yards away beneath a tree. And its driver was calm enough not to draw his own weapon and fire at the two men on the motorbike as it turned out into the Cairo traffic. Instead he set off in cautious pursuit. His aim was to track the gunman and his driver, rather than immediately engage what he assumed were two armed militants of either the Muslim Brotherhood or the Young Egypt movement.

So it was that an hour later, while Prim and Harry were still only entering the eastern suburbs of the city, the police were taking up positions in the Bulaq slums, outside a rundown repair shop into which the motorcycle had just coasted.

Thirty-Two

Mike Luzzatto threw open the shutters and let the noise and the smell of the Cairo street rise to greet him. From the depths of the room he heard the slither of expensive quilt as Prim Nevendon stirred, turning her head on the silk pillow of the bed.

'Close the window, Mike,' she called out, 'it's too loud and too hot. I think there's still some Meursault left in my bloodstream, and I hate wine when it's warm.'

He smiled at the memory of last night. He'd never expected it to happen; he'd thought she considered him a slimeball. How wrong he'd been.

It was an odd feeling. A mix of excitement, physical contentment and – yes – apprehension. Apprehension that it was a dream; that in the next moment he would wake up and be alone in his bed, with nothing to hold on to but a fantasy. Luzzatto looked back at the bed and the woman-shaped mound in the counterpane and the wave of fair hair that broke over the pillow. Wasn't a man supposed to feel like a conqueror at a time like this? Yet here he was, feeling as if the referee had announced him the loser on points, knocked down more often than he'd expected by an opponent who was faster on their feet and whose punch he'd found surprisingly devastating. It was a conclusion he'd come to the previous evening when, without the slightest hint of seductiveness, Prim had announced that she was going to spend the night with him.

She'd walked into the Long Bar as the sun was going down and he was on his first Jack-and-Coke. Apologizing for looking a bit wrecked – in fact she looked a million dollars – Prim had explained how she'd only just returned from some dusty hellhole on the Canal called Geneifa. Then she'd done two things in quick succession. The first was to order a Martini. The second was to instruct him to call housekeeping, because she was damned if she was going to share his bedroom if it was his habit to dwell amongst the usual disarray of *some* men she'd slept with. There was no getting away from it: Primrose Nevendon was unlike any woman he'd ever met. And he felt as guilty as sin for not telling her the whole truth.

But how could he? It would end their relationship before it had even got going. After all she'd told him, if she learned about his phone calls with Bachmann she would probably slap his face and he'd never see her again. And right now that really didn't seem something he wanted to risk.

You're losing your touch, Luzzatto, he told himself as he closed the curtains and headed back to the bed. Either that or, for the first time in your life, you're going soft on a dame.

At the British Residency on the east bank of the Nile, just a short drive south of the Qasr el Nil Bridge, Major Courtney set down the cup of coffee that Mrs Fulready-Laycock had made for him and called the morning meeting of the intelligence committee to order. It seemed to Harry a grandiose description for the gathering, given that the committee comprised solely the three of them.

'Well, young Taverner,' Courtney began, sounding to Harry unpleasantly like the ghost of one of his schoolmasters, 'I have read and digested your report on your perambulations through Palestine. Though I wouldn't go quite so far as to say I was impressed, I will admit you have made more progress than I thought you might. Well done.'

Mrs Fulready-Laycock beamed a matron's approval, as if he'd taken his cod-liver oil without complaint. 'Yes, well done. Well done indeed.'

'The question now,' Courtney continued, 'is this: in the event that Archie Nevendon is located in this desert fastness he's scuttled away to, like a latter-day Hereward the Wake, what do we intend to do with him?'

'My orders from London, sir, were only to find out if he'd gone over to the Germans with his inside knowledge of our oil interests in the Middle East,' said Harry, pouring his own coffee because Mrs Fulready-Laycock had strict ideas about rank.

Courtney scowled with displeasure. 'Providing explosives to terrorists isn't the sort of crime we can overlook, is it?'

'No, sir,' agreed Harry. 'But punishment isn't the remit of the Intelligence Service, either. That's up to the police and the courts.'

'It was so much easier when *we* ran this place,' Courtney complained, stirring his coffee vigorously. 'Back then we could try Englishmen under English law. Now we'll have to ask the Egyptians to put him in the dock.'

'But on what charge?' asked Harry doubtfully. 'If it's money-laundering for Shakir Hamad, then you yourself said Hamad had contacts in the government high enough to make him untouchable. And as for the explosives, Anglo-Levantine might well decide it's better for their reputation to let the whole thing drop.'

Courtney looked at him with a quizzical smile. 'When we find Nevendon, couldn't we just shoot him? Claim he was resisting arrest? My friends in khaki tell me we're not averse to that sort of thing in Palestine.'

'I think that would be exceeding the Service's legal powers, to be honest, sir.'

The nod Courtney gave in response was heavy and despondent. 'It's not like the old days any more, young Taverner. More's the pity.'

Harry wasn't sure if Courtney was joking, so he stayed silent.

'I suppose we could hand Nevendon over to the Mandate government in Tel Aviv – let them deal with him,' suggested Mrs Fulready-Laycock.

'Good idea, Hilda. Spot on,' said Courtney happily.

'That would be the sensible course of action,' Harry agreed, surprised to discover Mrs Fulready-Laycock even had a first name. In all the time he'd been in Cairo, he'd never heard it uttered, and she had never offered it.

'Well, Taverner, who's going to do it?' enquired Major Courtney.

'What do you mean, sir?'

'Who's going to winkle Nevendon out of the mountains?'

'The police, I suppose.'

'I can't see Russell Pasha taking kindly to the idea. He's got his hands full trying to catch heroin smugglers. I suppose he *might* give us a couple of Egyptian policemen.' Courtney sipped his coffee with all the tentativeness of a man stepping into a very hot bath. 'Seeing as how you've done all the work,' he went on, peering at Harry over the rim of his cup, 'I suppose you ought to lead them. Game for that, are we?'

'I suppose so, sir. If he's still alive.'

'God, wouldn't *that* be the preferable outcome. Solve a lot of headaches.'

'Not for Miss Nevendon, sir.'

'I presume you'll take her with you. If he is alive, maybe she can persuade her father to give himself up without a fuss.'

'I would hope so, sir.'

'That's settled then,' Courtney said, putting down his cup with a rattle of porcelain. 'Once we know exactly where he's hiding, we'll make the arrangements. I'll give you the station gun, just in case Nevendon decides to cause trouble.' He adjusted his braces like a man who's finished a particularly satisfying meal. 'And for God's sake remember what the ambassador said when you arrived: no extracurricular adventures. Nothing that might cause embarrassment to His Majesty's diplomatic mission to the court of King Farouk.'

'I'll bear that in mind, sir.'

'Oh, one thing I forgot to mention…'

'What's that, sir?'

'Happened while you were swanning around in Palestine. One of my sources has been keeping an eye on the Syrians here in Cairo. There's a suspicion that militants in Damascus have been giving succour to the nationalist faction here in Egypt – groups like the Young Egypt mob and the Muslim Brotherhood. He's been watching one of their diplomats for a while now. A few days ago he observed said Syrian diplomat having a cosy lunch at the Casino de Paris with an unidentified woman. Off his own bat, he decided to follow her when they went their separate ways. Thought it would be useful to put a bit of spin on the ball, so to speak, just to make sure it flew straight. Guess who she turned to be.'

'I can't imagine, sir.'

'That Sauvier woman – the housekeeper at the Villa Narcisse.'

When Major Courtney had concluded the meeting of the Service's Cairo intelligence committee, Harry immediately put a call through to Prim at the villa. Hearing Madame Sauvier answer gave him an oddly childish thrill of conspiracy. When Prim came on the line he said, 'Does this phone have an extension?'

'No. The one in Archie's office is a separate line. What is it? Have they located Turquoise?'

'I'm afraid not. Not yet.'

'Damn! The wait's driving me crazy, Harry.'

'I wanted a word in private. Are you alone?'

'What's this about, Harry? I've only this moment got in, and I'm on my way out again in a minute. Mike and I are going for a felucca ride on the Nile.'

'Mike?'

'Luzzatto.'

'Oh, the American fellow.'

Prim said breezily, 'He's taking me sightseeing. I needed something to take my mind off Archie and Turquoise. As I said, the waiting is driving me crazy.'

'That's jolly decent of him.'

For a moment there was silence on the line. Then Prim's voice again, sounding amused. 'Is that the sound of a nose being put out of joint that I hear in your voice, Harry?'

'Of course not,' he replied gruffly. 'You're free to see who you want.'

A peal of laughter. 'How very gracious of you, Harry. Any other gifts you feel like bestowing upon me?'

Harry felt the heat spread across his face. 'What I meant was it's no business of mine who you go boating with.'

More laughter on the line, as gently mocking as the first.

'It's the Nile, Harry, not Henley-on-Thames. We're not hiring a rowing boat for the afternoon.'

'I'm sure you'll have a wonderful time,' he said, recovering his equilibrium. 'I just wanted to remind you about security.'

At that, the flippancy in Prim's voice vanished. 'What do you mean, *security*? Am I supposed to be worried about something?'

'After what happened in Palestine, it would be wise to ensure you don't talk out of turn – to anyone.'

'If you're trying to warn me about something, why not simply say so?'

'It's only a spot of professional advice, Prim, that's all.'

This time the laughter had a cruel edge to it. 'Professional advice? My, I *am* a lucky girl, aren't I?'

'Look, I can't tell you the details, but that housekeeper of yours might have some friends in the wrong places. Nothing to worry yourself about really. But take it from an expert: loose talk can have unintended consequences. For your sake – for Archie's sake – think of that before you open your mouth in her presence. And be careful what you say to your American friend, too. I think he's clean, but we can't be too cautious.'

'Thank you, Harry,' Prim replied in a now-frosty voice, the laughter gone. 'I shall bear that in mind. If it's all right with you, I've got to see if I remembered to pack my sailor's outfit. You wouldn't want me to have to go boating stark naked, would you? Specially not if a handsome American's doing the rowing.'

Then the line went dead.

It was like staring at a painting one couldn't quite believe wasn't a fake, thought Prim as she sat close to Mike Luzzatto in the bow of the felucca. There were palm trees along the riverbank and oxen drinking in the shallows, men in white robes with dark faces tilling red soil, and ancient wooden waterwheels turning in the sunlight. If the boat touched the shore and she stepped out, she would find herself not in 1938, but in the time of the pharaohs. Surely it was nothing but a dream – rather like the night she'd spent with the man beside her.

Prim had no illusions. Mike Luzzatto had been a distraction, that was all. A way of freeing her mind, at least temporarily, from the turmoil. A means of shutting out Turquoise and what she might find there when, finally, she reached it. She wasn't expecting anything from Mike. She wasn't a fool. He could have any woman he wanted, and she had absolutely no intention of being an adornment, no matter how much he looked like a matinée idol. A tonic to pep her up, that's all.

And yet…

There was no denying she'd found him considerably less shallow than she'd thought. She'd discovered a self-deprecating side to him, and an inner self-doubt that only added to the exterior charm. She'd found him more knowledgeable, too. He was no pretty fool. It was only when he'd told her he was a Jew that her sense of being in control of the situation faltered. The Jews had killed Ifaya and her cousin, Dr Jabour. But then she'd recalled Rachel's tale of her childhood in Hebron and the murder of her parents. At that moment Prim had decided against making sweeping judgements about things you only vaguely understood. Blaming one man for the actions of total strangers seemed not only pointless, but also callous. Besides, it was far too early to worry about things that might later cause them to re-evaluate each other: like her brief and foolish flirtation with the British Union of Fascists. Mike wouldn't think much of her if he knew about *that*, given the way the Nazis in Germany were treating his people right now.

She felt his arm slide across her shoulders and leaned into him.

'A penny for your thoughts,' he said.

'Oh, nothing much. Just admiring the view; imagining myself as an Egyptian princess.'

'Say, why don't I snap my fingers and summon a slave to peel you a grape?' he replied with a deep laugh.

Yes, she thought as she listened to the murmur of the river and the thrumming of the breeze in the curved sail, you're the best medicine I could wish for – for the time being.

The call from Thomas Russell came at noon the next day, as Harry was putting the finishing touches to his report. Major Courtney had ordered what he liked to term 'tropical dress' – a removal of jackets, but not ties – because the office fan had so far achieved little more than turning the air into what felt like a bath of hot soup. They took an embassy car, marginally cooler because it had been sitting in the garage.

'I thought, gentlemen, that you might care to know there have been developments in our investigation into the shooting at Mr Nevendon's theatre,' the police chief said as they took their seats in front of his expansive desk.

Hoping for news of Turquoise, Harry took the cigarette Russell offered from a tortoiseshell case, almost as a consolation. But he had to admire Russell Pasha. Seemingly inured to the heat, his brow had yet to glisten, the armpits of his shirt yet to darken. As the smoke rose, Russell recounted how one of his officers had followed the gunman on the motorcycle, who had led them to the repair shop in the Buraq slums.

'We now have a trove of useful evidence,' Russell announced triumphantly when he'd finished. 'It includes a firearm – the terrorists did not surrender without a fight. I can tell you that it was used in the attack on the Nimrod Theatre.'

'How do you know, sir?' Harry asked, surprised by the certainty in Russell's voice.

'At my suggestion, our department has invested in a comparison microscope.'

'A what, sir?' said Courtney.

'It's a device that allows you to compare two separate images,' Russell explained. 'In this instance, cartridge cases. The ones we recovered from the repair shop had the same striations as those taken from the foyer of the theatre.'

'How novel,' said Courtney, as if Russell was describing a new way of growing cucumbers.

'They used it in the St Valentine's Day massacre enquiry in America. That was nine years ago. We've only recently caught up.'

Harry exhaled a ring of cigarette smoke at the ceiling and asked, 'What's the connection between a motor repair shop and a theatre?'

'I'm about to come to that, Mr Taverner,' Russell replied. 'We also found blood stains on the floor. Old ones, not from the shootout. And a chair that also had old blood stains on the seat and one of the legs. But the real clincher was the fingerprints. We dusted the chair, and the prints we took from it matched some we found in the manager's office at the theatre. They were Mr Bannoudi's. It seems clear that the repair shop was where they tortured him before they killed him in the theatre.'

'Then we're making progress,' said Courtney, and Harry thought he heard a distinct trace of professional jealousy in the station head's voice.

Russell raised a cautionary finger. 'What we can't yet resolve is this: the lads on the motorcycle were Young Egypt militants.

The owner of the repair shop has no known connection with the nationalist movement. But he was a petty criminal, an associate of Shakir Hamad's. It would be highly advantageous for us to link Hamad to the militants.'

'I think I might be able to help there,' said Harry, casting a diplomatic glance at Courtney, as if he was seeking permission to speak. 'We know that Archie Nevendon was laundering money for Hamad, presumably under duress, because the theatre was failing. But his association with Hamad opened the door to some even more unsavoury characters operating in Palestine, including a man named Kazem Jabour. He's a big player in the revolt there. I suspect Nevendon was being forced to steal explosives for Jabour. But something went wrong; Jabour's sister died. I don't know why, but Jabour holds Archie Nevendon responsible.'

'You think this Jabour character instructed Hamad's people to attack the Nimrod Theatre?' Russell asked.

'I'm sure of it,' said Harry. 'I also believe the Jews are after Nevendon, too. I guess they must have found out what he was up to – they were as likely to be targets for those explosives as we were. I've compiled a report for London. I'll let you have a copy as soon as it's complete.' He glanced at Courtney again. 'I assume Major-General Russell is on the distribution list.'

Courtney nodded. 'For this case, I'm sure that can be arranged.'

'There's one final thing before I move on to the main course,' said Russell. 'We recovered a notebook, some sort of work schedule. The entries were in Arabic, mostly run-of-the-mill stuff. But one of them pricked our interest: all it said was, *Vauxhall Light Six motorcar – tyres*. And the letters *MB*. I wonder if that stood for Moussa Bannoudi. Any ideas?'

Harry laid his cigarette in the ashtray on Russell's desk. 'One rather large one, sir,' he said. 'I've been wondering how

Nevendon managed to drive all the way to the Sinai without attracting attention, because his driver, Tarek Shalaby, certainly didn't take him. We know Nevendon himself took a set of low-pressure desert tyres away from the Anglo-Levantine depot at Geneifa. So he must have got hold of a Vauxhall Light Six from somewhere and asked Bannoudi to have it modified, so that it couldn't be traced back to him. I'd guess it was pure bad luck that Bannoudi chose a mechanic with links to Shakir Hamad.'

Russell reached for his in-tray and pulled out an innocuous buff folder. 'Right,' he continued. 'We're done with the mock-turtle soup, now it's onto the roast beef with all the trimmings.'

Harry leaned forward. He could see the folder had nothing written on the cover. What is it with policemen? he wondered. Are they all frustrated conjurers at heart?

Adopting a magisterial set of the shoulders, Russell announced, 'Our friend from the museum, Monsieur Drioton, has come up with the goods a lot quicker than I'd expect from an academic, and a French one at that.' He opened the folder and drew out the photo of the Nevendon brothers that Prim had entrusted to him. It was attached by a paperclip to a slim publication with a faded plain blue cover. Russell detached the document and slid it across the desk so that Harry could read the title: *Journal of Egyptian Archaeology*. And, below it, *Volume 1, 1913*. Then, opening the thin magazine to a page bookmarked by a turned-down corner, he offered it for Harry to inspect.

Major Courtney shifted his chair closer to the desk, determined not to be left out of an enquiry he'd had very little part in. Harry leaned forward, captivated by the photograph he could see printed on the fading yellow page. It was a reproduction of Prim's photo, although the caption *TURQUOISE, 1913* had been trimmed out. As he began to read the accompanying article, he caught the cloister smell of paper that's spent a quarter of a century in a half-forgotten archive:

Field reports: Two gentleman amateurs from England have been excavating in Sinai at a site once believed to have been occupied during the Ptolemaic period. Messrs Archibald and Nimrod Nevendon have concluded that the site in fact dates from the Coptic Christian era...

Harry's eyes skipped the rest, until they alighted on the last paragraph:

The site, named Bir Hathour, lies in high ground to the north-west of Mount Serbal, thought by some to be the Mount Sinai referred to in the Bible. It has gone largely untouched by professional archaeologists because of its remoteness and the paucity of its ruins...

To Harry's joy, the anonymous author had thoughtfully provided a hand-drawn map of the Sinai Peninsula. About halfway down its western edge and – judging by the accompanying distance scale – some fifteen miles inland from the Gulf of Suez, was a large cross, surrounded by stylized mountain peaks.

'Bir Hathour,' mouthed Harry. In his mind, he was speaking not to Russell Pasha but to Prim Nevendon.

'If I may use a modern American idiom, Mr Taverner, that is where your man is holed up,' Russell was saying, although Harry wasn't really listening. 'Given how long Nevendon's been missing, and knowing a little of the Sinai as I do, I take my hat off to him. A latter-day St Onuphrius, if you ask me.'

Harry looked up, a blank expression on his face.

'One of those desert hermits,' Russell expounded. 'Lived off dates for sixty years, which is more than enough for sainthood, if you ask me. Mind you, old Onuphrius didn't have the Arabs and the Jews after his blood, did he?'

Harry held the telephone handset against his ear while Madame Sauvier went in search of Prim. 'Did you have a good day out on the river with your American?' he asked when she came on the line.

'Yes, thank you, Harry. How's your day been?'

'We have an answer,' he said bluntly. 'The fellow from the museum has come back with the goods.'

A pause while Prim drew a loud breath that came down the wire like a squall coming in from the sea. '*And?*'

In reply, Harry couldn't be sure if he was delivering solace or a death sentence.

'It looks like we've found Turquoise.'

Thirty-Three

I don't know which is the hardest, Nim – the days or the nights. By day it gets so hot my mind goes off on journeys to places I don't want to be, even though being here is almost beyond endurance. By night I freeze. But at least at night I've got you and Ifaya for company – you two, the stars and the howling jackals.

If it wasn't for the spring, they'd have had my carcass to feast on weeks ago. Even back in 1913 it was barely a trickle – remember? It's not much better now. As for food, most of the dates and the nuts have gone. The dried meat, too. An ibex wandered into the ruins a few days ago. I got it with my first shot, but the meat went off in hours and I can't risk taking potshots; I'm not that good an aim and I don't want to run out of ammunition. If the worst comes to the worst, I need to keep a bullet for myself.

I was beginning to think I might be safe. No one knows where I am, I'm sure of that. The car Bannoudi got me was a gem. Lovely Vauxhall Light Six it was, pale blue. Bought it from a German steel salesman going home to Essen. I drove it as far up the wadi as I could, left it with the sheikh of a fly-blown little place with a well and three palm trees – settled Bedouin, they were. Splendid chaps. When he saw me coming, he must have thought Farouk was dropping by for a cup of char; can't imagine he'd seen more than three cars in his entire life.

Told him I was a Christian pilgrim, hell-bent on walking through the mountains to the monastery at St Catherine's. Gave him more cash than he'd made in a decade of herding goats and promised him twice the amount if the car was still there when I got back. Well, he wasn't going to take it to Monaco for the Grand Prix, was he? He grabbed the money and told me he reckoned all Christians were crazy, but that I was the craziest he'd ever met.

Did the job, though. I'll guarantee it's still there. If I ever get out of here alive, I'll pick it up and maybe head for Persia. That's if he hasn't siphoned off the petrol or lost the keys.

Yes, Persia would be good. The Shah wants it called Iran now, so a new future sounds about right. I'll change my name, too; get myself a job as a roughneck. They've got plenty of oil there and they need men who know what they're about. God knows, I'm too old for the French Foreign Legion, unless they can find me a job with a desk and an expense account.

But to be honest, Nim – and you and I were always that with each other – I think I'm fooling myself. It's time to face up to it: escape is just a dream. Always was. Maybe it would be best if they came for me now and put an end to it. I think I'm ready, Nim. The bell tolls and all that. It's tolling for your old pal, Archie. Who did something very bad indeed. And maybe it's about time he was honest with himself and called for the bill.

Thirty-Four

By the time they reached the chain ferry at Coubri, six miles north of where the Suez Canal spilled out into the waters of the Gulf, there was already a heat shimmer on the road. Tarek slowed the Citroën to a crawl as they approached a sandy embankment and a jetty thrusting into the sparkling water. The tyres rumbled on the wooden planks and then the car settled on the pontoon that would carry them to the east bank. The ferry reminded Harry of a quirky Thames houseboat. It had a pitched wooden roof to provide shade and wooden balustrades on either side. He half-expected to find it occupied by people in Oxford bags and summer dresses lounging and drinking Pimm's. But the only person he could see was the bored Egyptian engineer in oil-stained overalls beckoning them slowly forward towards the only other traffic on the barge: a milling herd of goats in the charge of a wizened Arab chewing a wad of *khat*.

They had left Cairo before dawn, after Tarek had returned from filling the Citroën's tank to the brim with free Anglo-Levantine petrol. There were two cans of it in the boot, and the smell had only increased with the rising temperature. Now, a little over two hours later, he was just about ready to tell Tarek to strap the cans to the rear luggage rack.

Tarek reckoned he could have done the journey in an hour and a half, but Harry had made him keep to a steady forty. They had many more long hours to go and there was no earthly reason to risk overheating the Citroën's engine this early.

The driver wasn't the only one in a hurry. As he cut the engine, in the near-silence Harry could hear Prim's feet tapping impatiently at the frame of his seat.

When Harry had called her with the news that Monsieur Drioton from the museum had come up with the goods, she'd been all for setting off at once. But that was Prim all over, Harry knew. 'It's not that simple,' he'd warned. 'Sinai is a bad place. We need to prepare.'

It had been like trying to coax a thoroughbred back into the starting gate after the race had begun. In the end he'd managed to make her see things his way, though her restlessness grew by the hour until she seemed almost permanently on the verge of a force-twelve hurricane. She'd cursed just about everyone for the scarcity and incompleteness of the maps Harry had purloined: the Egyptian police force, the British army garrison, the Egyptian Ministry of the Interior, the British embassy – even Harry himself.

'Why don't they show anything?' she'd demanded to know when he'd unfurled the best of the maps in the tiny makeshift office that Major Courtney had provided as headquarters for the operation to locate, recover or lay to rest Archibald Nevendon.

'Because there's sod-all there,' Harry had replied wearily. 'Apart from some settlements on the coast and St Catherine's Monastery further inland, there's little else but mountains and wadis – dried-up riverbeds that can become raging torrents if it rains, which apparently it does about once every hundred years.'

Only when Mr Gamil at Anglo-Levantine had provided a map of potential exploration sites along the western edge of the Sinai Peninsula had Prim mastered her frustration enough to watch without interruption, while Harry plotted the likely location of Bir Hathour.

While the site wasn't actually marked on the map, the survey team that had produced it had made a good fist of recording the contours of the area: the flat, narrow plain of the coast to the west, the expanse of desert area to the north that stretched all the way to the Mediterranean coast, and then the winding wadis, defiles and valleys squirming like snakes into the rising peaks that culminated in the wasteland where Moses supposedly received the Ten Commandments from the hands of God.

Harry had marked Bir Hathour as accurately as he could, relying on the diagram from the article in the *Journal of Egyptian Archaeology*. He'd located it about five miles from a spot marked as a permanent Bedouin settlement. But, in the wilderness of the southern Sinai, that still meant he could be out by miles.

He had turned for help to Russell Pasha, whose knowledge of the area was second to none. Russell had confirmed the existence of the Bedouin settlement, which he said provided guides to pilgrims to St Catherine's Monastery further inland. He had also promised one of his Egyptian constables to the expedition, a man with experience of tracking heroin smugglers in the region. The officer would drive the small Renault truck that Russell Pasha had also promised, because, as the police chief had explained, only someone with a death wish would drive into the mountains without a decent supply of water and food, spare tyres, a medical kit, a rifle and ammunition… The man would also prove handy if an arrest had to be made.

'This policeman, does he speak English?' Harry had asked. 'Because I don't have any Arabic.'

'I very much doubt it.'

It was Prim who came up with the answer later, at the Villa Narcisse.

'It's obvious, Harry. We take Tarek with us.'

Harry had looked doubtful. 'It might be best if we kept this private.'

'Tarek *is* private. He and Daddy are friends. They used to have man-to-man talks; Tarek told me that himself. Tarek's presence will reassure him; it's bound to. He's hardly going to feel safe if he comes face-to-face with you – a man he doesn't know from Adam – and an Egyptian policeman, who will presumably be armed.'

In the end Harry had acquiesced. Now, some thirty hours after he had called her with the news of Monsieur Drioton's discovery in the museum archives, they were well on their way.

Tarek engaged the handbrake and began an animated conversation with the ferry's engineer. The goats began to surround the Citroën, inquisitively snuffling at the doors. The shepherd went on chewing his *khat*, eyeing the Europeans with studied apathy.

When the Renault truck was safely aboard, the pontoon's engine began to rumble. They waited for a small freighter to steam past and then the chain ferry inched out into the Canal. Once they had gained the other side, Harry reckoned, all that remained would be ninety miles of often-unmade road and track to Abu Zenima further down the coast, before they turned off over open country to the Bedouin settlement. That was the easy part.

The quartermaster at the British garrison at Abbassia had refused to issue desert tyres to the embassy without written orders from his general, who was off shooting ibex on the Libyan border and wasn't expected back for five days. At some point they would have to abandon the vehicles and hike into the hinterland. Even if they enlisted the help of a Bedouin guide, that could take many hours. The mountains would set a daunting test, and Harry wasn't sure they were up to it. He closed his eyes and wished vehemently that he was back in Vienna, sitting in the Café Central and listening to the string quartet playing Strauss waltzes. He had little expectation of reaching Turquoise – if they could even locate it – until tomorrow. Still, there was no hurry. If Archie bloody Nevendon hadn't already succumbed to its tribulations, he wasn't about to bolt from his hiding place in the wildness of the Sinai mountains any time soon.

Mike Luzzatto had chosen the table on the terrace of Shepheard's carefully. It was set beneath an established palm tree well away from the entrance and isolated enough for the three men who sat around it to speak without fear of being overheard. Their desire for privacy was helped by the noise of the traffic on the adjacent boulevard.

Luzzatto was the host. The other two were younger, barely in their twenties, sun-browned and lithe. Whereas Luzzatto was dressed in neatly pressed slacks and a crisp white shirt, his companions, though still bearing the appearance of young executives like Gamil and el-Madani at Anglo-Levantine, were, at least this morning, somewhat less spruce. They had been awake most of the night. They had not shaved. They were sore-eyed and irritated and they had good cause to be, though as they sipped their coffee they did their best not to draw attention to themselves by raising their voices.

'We've been spinning the goddamn sling for twenty-four hours, and just when we're ready to let the rock fly and let

Goliath have it right between the eyes, you say it's all off,' said the youngest, a dark-haired boy whose name was Chaim. 'What the hell gives, Mike?'

'It's all over, that's what gives. Bachmann's called a halt.'

As Luzzatto spooned sugar into his coffee and began stirring it, he thought back to the conversation he'd had in the small hours with his old friend in Palestine. It hadn't been solely Bachmann's decision to abandon the hunt for Archibald Nevendon, though from the start the change of heart was evident in his voice. All Luzzatto had done was to foster it, help it grow. He'd never been comfortable with the violence that some members of the cause were eager to espouse. Self-defence was one thing; extrajudicial murder was quite another. And the thought of being complicit in the death of Prim Nevendon's father was more than he could stomach.

She had got to him; there was no denying it. And wherever that led, there were going to be some secrets he could never reveal to her.

'I don't get it, Mike,' said Getzel, who was Chaim's brother. Both young men ostensibly worked for an import–export business in Port Said, whose owner was a Luzzatto family friend. In their spare time the brothers were committed to helping recently arrived Jews fleeing persecution in Europe. Luzzatto had enlisted them for his endeavours in Cairo, paying for their temporary replacements from his own pocket.

Chaim shook his head, refusing to accept what Luzzatto had told him. 'With respect, Mike,' he said, keeping his voice deferential because Luzzatto was a man of importance, and Rabbi Bachmann even more so, 'from the moment Rockefeller's daughter arrived back from Palestine it's been clear something is brewing. She and her English friend – well, all I can say is it's been like watching termites when the nest's been poked with a stick.'

'He's right,' Getzel said. 'You told us to keep watch on the Villa Narcisse. And that's what we've been doing, one on and one off, day and night. You think we're going to stop, now that something's buzzing?'

They were good boys, Luzzatto knew. Dedicated. He hated having to slap them down. It was like putting good hunting dogs on the leash the very moment they'd caught a scent. 'It's not my decision,' he told them.

'All we had to do was follow them,' said Getzel pleadingly. 'Look, before first light – *long* before – the villa gates opened and out comes Rockefeller's green Citroën. In the darkness it's hard to be sure, but I reckon it's Shalaby, his driver, at the wheel.' He moved his coffee saucer an inch or two across the tablecloth to indicate the scene. 'What the hell is he up to at a time like this? I ask myself. It's way before morning prayers, so he's not driving to the mosque – not that I ever saw him do *that*. And *way* too early for a work meeting. So, being a dutiful boy, what do I do?'

Luzzatto said robotically, 'You follow.'

'I sure did, Mike. And we end up downtown, at the back of the Anglo-Levantine building. There's only a low wall, so I can see Shalaby filling the tank from the company pump. Then he sticks the hose in two gasoline cans and puts them in the back. Well, now it's obvious to me that he's planning a long journey. So I keep on following. On the way back Shalaby stops for a while at a house in Buraq and goes inside. I know the place, because I've been keeping tabs on Shalaby pretty much since Rockefeller went missing. It's his brother's place. He's only there a few minutes. Then it's back to the Villa Narcisse, where all the lights are on. The place is lit up like Jerusalem at Hanukkah. How much more evidence do I need that they've found out where Rockefeller's hiding? So I stop by my uncle Simon's shop, wake him up – he's pissed as hell – and I use his telephone to call *you*.' Getzel stared hard into Mike Luzzatto's face. 'And do I hear, "Get your running shoes, Getzel, the chase is on"? No! Screw that. Instead I hear, "Stand down, Getzel. Join me for breakfast, Getzel." The only thing I didn't hear is: "Getzel, go back to bed and catch up on two days' lost sleep." So what the fuck happened?'

Luzzatto looked at Chaim, whose head was down because of his brother's insurrection, and then back to Getzel. 'Bachmann had a change of heart,' he said softly.

From the boulevard came a squeal of tyres and a tirade of Arabic. Then the voice of the Shepheard's doorman bringing some order, in French.

'A change of heart?' repeated Getzel, squinting as if he was trying to peep through a letterbox. 'After all the effort we've put in?'

'I spoke to him on the telephone a few hours ago,' Luzzatto said. 'He's talked Rachel and our young friends across the border out of it. There's no point any more. Rockefeller is a distraction.'

'I don't understand, Mike,' said Chaim hotly. 'Bachmann lost his own son in the attack on al-Sarhan. His own *son*. If I'd suffered a loss like that, I'd hunt down the bastard responsible even if it took me until I was toothless and riven with arthritis. And even then I wouldn't stop. I'd crawl after him on all fours, if I had to.'

Luzzatto hated having to frustrate two such good boys. But in his heart he was grateful for Bachmann's order. 'Which makes his decision all the more admirable,' he said evenly to Getzel. 'The supply of explosives has been cut off, and if we want Rockefeller to pay for his part, well, he's lost the woman he was in love with – Jabour's sister. When all's said and done, Bachmann considers that a price he can live with. It was his son. It's his call.'

Getzel put his hands over his head. 'I just don't get it, Mike. After all the work we've put in—'

'And Bachmann's grateful, he really is,' Luzzatto said. 'But he's right. Fixing Rockefeller gives us nothing. Absolutely nothing. It's a waste of resources, when things are hotting up in Palestine.'

Getzel said, 'I'll tell you what it gives, Mike. It gives *me* a good feeling, knowing that the guy who supplied cookies to Kazem Jabour to blow up Jews has been held to account. Get me a gun, Mike. I'll do it. Chaim, you'd be with me, wouldn't you?'

'I don't know,' replied Chaim. 'Maybe Bachmann's right.'

'It's settled,' said Luzzatto firmly. 'Rockefeller is off the menu. Period. Now, let's order breakfast. You guys must be starving. If you're so concerned about Rockefeller, let Kazem Jabour do the work for you. I doubt he's as forgiving as Lev Bachmann.'

The windows were down, but the smell of gasoline still lingered inside the Citroën. It was making Prim nauseous. About eight miles from Ras Sudr, at a point where the road ran close to the shoreline, she could bear it no longer. Tarek pulled over, the Citroën's tyres rasping on the dusty scree beside the tarmac. She climbed out and took deep breaths of hot air. Harry followed her and together they waited in silence for the truck to catch up. Prim could just make it out in the distance, seemingly trapped in the heat haze that boiled off the surface of the road. She looked around at the arid emptiness. Inland, it lifted towards a line of low hills, blistered by aeons of merciless sun and scoured by desert winds. Half a mile away across the road, the waters of the Gulf of Suez glinted in the sunlight. Two freighters were making their ponderous way north towards the Canal, thin plumes of oily smoke rising from their funnels like distress signals. Suddenly Prim had a desperate longing to be back in Cairo with Mike Luzzatto. And that only made her feel guilty because Archie needed her, and how could a daughter abandon her father at a time like this?

She glanced at Harry, reluctantly allowing him back onto the surface of this alien world she inhabited. If Archie needed her, then she needed Harry Taverner, though she hated to admit it. In the car he'd hinted there might be some sort of deal on offer. The authorities in Palestine might be amenable to overlooking Archie's transgressions if he provided intelligence on the Arab rebels. In Egypt, testifying against Shakir Hamad might keep him out of prison. The fact that he was coerced might work in his favour. Nothing could be promised, of course. It would all depend on Archie's cooperation.

When the truck arrived, Tarek took the two fuel cans from the Citroën and loaded them onto the flatbed. The Egyptian policeman looked down from the cab, watching Prim with a stony face. She hadn't seen him smile since they left Cairo. To break the ice, she hopped onto the running board and offered him her water bottle through the open window. He shook his head and said something in Arabic. Prim shrugged. 'Please yourself,' she replied and stepped back onto the gravel. But not before she'd had the opportunity to glance past him to the truck's passenger seat. Which left her with a troubling question: if Harry Taverner was expecting Archie's cooperation, why did the policeman have a rifle propped in the footwell of his cab?

They reached Abu Zenima at noon, though Tarek could have been forgiven for driving straight on because the cluster of sandy mud-brick single-storey buildings were all but indistinguishable from the rest of the barren landscape. Whether they had been constructed recently or in the time of the Ottoman Turks was almost impossible to judge. The place had a forlorn, listless air, as if it knew it had no choice but to wait for the day when the desert and the mountains rising in the distance subsumed it. Only the cluster of fishing boats pulled up on the shingle beach offered hope of escape.

At the centre of the town stood the battered minaret of a mosque, its arched door faded and pitted by centuries of attack from the sun and woodworm. Nearby, in the shade of a scrawny acacia tree, a huddle of old men sat in timeless discourse. From their hunched postures and dark, deeply lined faces, Harry reckoned they were engaged in an argument that might have had its origins around the time Napoleon came to Egypt, and was equally distant from resolution. Tarek stopped the car and went over to them, the Anglo-Levantine map flapping lethargically from his hand, caught by the faint but torrid breeze coming off the Gulf.

Prim and Harry got out to stretch their legs. 'Bit like Tunbridge Wells,' she said drily as a scrawny dog padded past in search of a cooler place to sleep.

Harry said, 'How are you bearing up?'

Prim shrugged. 'I'll be better when we get to Bir Hathour.'

'If we find it.'

'We'll find it,' she said, looking back out at the Gulf and the disappearing freighters. 'We'll find *him*. I know we will.'

Tarek returned and settled himself behind the steering wheel. Harry and Prim got back in and Tarek passed Harry the map. 'It is a good map,' he said. 'Outside the town, we go left. There is a track through a wadi, up into the hills. Ten miles. Then we find the Bedouin settlement. After that, no more road. We walk.'

'They know about Bir Hathour?' Harry asked.

'They say there are many ruins in the area – and old turquoise mines from the times of Rameses. But they have not heard of Bir Hathour.'

Prim cast Harry a worried look.

'I wouldn't draw anything from that,' he said, seeking to reassure her. 'They've probably never even been as far as Cairo, and I doubt the *Journal of Egyptian Archaeology* has a particularly large readership around here. Maybe it has another, local name.'

Prim said to Tarek, 'Did you ask if they'd seen my father?'

'Of course, Miss Archie. But they tell me no.'

Prim sighed despondently.

'Don't lose heart,' continued Harry as the Citroën's engine started up again. 'Archie knows the area. He had no reason to stop here; he would have driven straight through.'

As Tarek put the car into gear, he called over his shoulder, 'The Bedouin may know. Those elders, they say the Bedouin sometimes work as guides for the Christians who make the pilgrimage to the monastery at St Catherine's. Maybe they see Mr Archie. Maybe they know where is this place called "the well of the goddess Hathor".'

'Is that what Bir Hathour means?' Prim asked. Flashes of memory came back to her: she and Archie playing at digging up pretend clay artefacts in the garden at Bevern Lodge; the smell of his Harris Tweed jacket and the smoke from his pipe curling between them like incense on an altar; his voice as he read to her from one of his archaeology books…

'She is most important goddess,' said Tarek, as though he knew her personally and much admired her. 'The mines here are sacred to her. Sometimes she is called the Lady of Amethyst. Other times we call her the Lady of Turquoise.'

From Abu Zenima the road became little more than a series of tyre marks in the gritty sand. There were runnels and scourings to show where wheels had lost their grip, spinning and digging deeper into the surface. It was less a road and more a fossilized record of the vehicles that had passed along it. The Renault truck was better suited to the ground here, so Tarek allowed it to take the lead. He followed at a good distance because sometimes it would slide like a skittish horse and he didn't want to get side-swiped, or run into it broadside. Besides, Tarek had his own battle to fight: the Citroën's steering wheel had taken on a life of its own. It could only be subdued by constant wrestling, accompanied by frequent and voluble cursing in Arabic.

They were beginning to climb now. A slow, bone-crunching ascent towards jagged hills and narrow defiles. The terrain ahead had turned from stultifyingly monotonous to threatening. But not even the Sinai's brooding menace could dampen Prim's new-found conviction that they were on the right track. She was already rehearsing how she would greet her father, refusing even to consider the possibility that this unforgiving landscape might have already extinguished his spirit. It would have to be portentous, something befitting two explorers meeting in the remoteness of *terra incognita*. Yet try as she might, she couldn't find the right words, and even thinking about it brought tears to her eyes. And she didn't want Harry to see that.

By the time they reached the Bedouin settlement the only thing Prim could think about was getting out of the car; she had spent much of the lurching ride since Abu Zenima being cannoned around the rear seat. As she flexed her legs and looked about her, she felt as though she'd been worked over by a thug with a baseball bat.

They had arrived in a small, circular dip in the now-stony landscape. Ahead of her was a daunting curtain of fiercely jagged peaks, cut with narrow glaciers made not of ice, but of sand. The earth had a reddish tinge to it, as though it was smouldering, though the temperature here was cooler than down on the coast.

The settlement comprised a few low-roofed tents with no sides, barely more than large sunshades, beneath which Prim could see figures sitting. The men were all robed in dark gowns. The women and children wore bib necklaces made of overlapping discs of cut metal, draped with bead pendants. No one seemed overly interested in the arrival of two vehicles containing Europeans, which surprised Prim, because she was pretty sure the odds on coming across *anyone* in this empty place were about as high as finding your next-door neighbour waiting to greet you after you'd trekked to the South Pole.

Behind the tents were a few makeshift huts with wattle walls and brushwood roofs, though where anyone found building materials around here was something beyond Prim's comprehension; the only greenery in sight was a sparse cluster of almond and hawthorn trees and, behind that, a patch of something that might possibly have been vegetation, where three camels stood lazily mouthing the ground. And then there were the goats. Just as at al-Sarhan, they grubbed about with grand nonchalance as if they, and not the humans, were the masters here.

The settlement's sheikh was a flint-faced man of indeterminate age. His beard was white, yet his eyes had the vigorous sparkle of a mischievous child. He exchanged a few words with Tarek, glancing often at Harry.

'What's he saying?' Prim asked.

Tarek looked at her with barely suppressed satisfaction. 'He says if the European has come here to purchase the motorcar, he's wasted his time. He says it's not for sale.'

Barely two minutes later Prim and Harry were peering through a gap in the wattle wall of the largest of the makeshift huts. Inside, deep in the shadows and covered by a thin film of dust, was a pale-blue Vauxhall Light Six, sitting – with the unconscious serenity of a duchess taking a nap – on its desert tyres.

In Major Courtney's office at the British residence in Cairo, Mrs Fulready-Laycock was tidying her desk in preparation for leaving early. The diplomatic wives had arranged a fundraising event that evening at the Gezira Sporting Club, in support of the embassy's pack of foxhounds. Her attendance was vital; there wasn't a man in Cairo who dared to keep his wallet closed when Mrs Fulready-Laycock was at full gallop. When the phone rang, she was less diplomatic than was her custom, passing the receiver to Major Courtney without comment when the man on the line gave a work name that immediately alerted her to the fact that he was one of the major's intelligence sources. Her fear was that something was about to break that would delay her from her important duties, namely ensuring the ambassador's continued enjoyment of riding to hounds.

She need not have worried.

Courtney listened in silence to the voice on the other end of the line before handing back the receiver with an unadorned 'That is very good to know. Thank you for calling.'

Mrs Fulready-Laycock gave Courtney a quizzical look. 'Nothing to detain me, sir?' she asked.

'No, Hilda. All is in order,' he replied. Then, because Harry Taverner wasn't around to tell, he said in an earnest whisper as if divulging a great secret, 'That was my source who spotted the housekeeper at the Villa Narcisse, Madame Sauvier, having a cosy lunch with a Syrian diplomat. I asked him to dig a little deeper. It appears he was mistaken; the man she met wasn't who he thought. Shame young Taverner is out of contact. I'm sure he'd be pleased to know that he can rule out any sharp practice in *that* quarter.'

Thirty-Five

It was only five miles from the Bedouin settlement to the spot Harry had marked on the map. On the flat ground around Abu Zenima, keeping the speed down to protect the exhaust and suspension, the Citroën could have done it in maybe half an hour. But up here a car was worse than useless. Even Archie hadn't risked it, and his Vauxhall had desert tyres.

By now it was too late to hike up to the site; the headman had told Tarek it would be a three-hour trip, even for those hardy souls accustomed to the mountains. Darkness would be falling by the time they reached Bir Hathour. Even Prim, feeling now so close to Archie and desperate to press on, could see the sense in accepting the offer of Bedouin hospitality for the night.

She ate with the women and girls, a ragout with meat in it that she assumed was goat. They were kind to her in an amused way, as if she were a novelty toy someone had brought them. Her ineptitude at eating with her fingers caused them great hilarity. She slept beside them, though only fitfully. But their acceptance and the proximity of their warm bodies provided a sense of security that both surprised and comforted her. When she went outside the tent to relieve herself, she didn't know which to marvel at most: the utter darkness around her or the blaze of stars above. But she didn't linger. The wild howls coming out of

353

the mountains chilled her blood. She imagined monsters hunting amongst the peaks – monsters hunting for Archie. 'Jackals,' explained Tarek when they assembled at dawn for a breakfast of syrupy date pudding and green tea.

The plan was to set off early, to reach Bir Hathour before the heat became a problem. The settlement's sheikh offered them a camel to carry water and food taken from the Renault; and one of the young men, a teenager really, whose name was Mehedi, to lead the way. He was a toothy, shy lad, but the sheikh assured them he knew the mountains and could spot a *nashîr haye* – a cobra – better than a grown man with three times his experience. Prim was not wholly reassured. Of all the tribulations she had considered, and she'd considered many, snakes hadn't been one of them.

They followed the dried riverbed as it coiled away into the mountains, maintaining a steady, efficient pace. Through Tarek, the young guide entertained them with a mix of youthful boasting and wildly inapposite questions: *How many camels does the king of England own? How wide are the deserts in Europe?* Prim felt an almost joyous sense of adventure, an echo she remembered from holiday trips with Archie and Celestina to Camber Sands. The stout walking boots she had brought with her to Egypt, on the advice of Granny Grace, were serving her well; they were the pair she used for walking in Ashdown Forest and on the South Downs. You could march across half the world in a pair like these and not get a single blister. She grinned as she recalled what Archie had told her, aged nine, when he'd bought her first set: *Primmy, my girl, wear them with pride. The Empire will never fall while its servants have a decent pair of boots on their trotters.* Sometimes, though, she rode the camel, which took a while to master, but had her laughing like a child at the funfair.

Her ebullient mood lasted almost until the wadi they were following entered the lower peaks. Then the land became serrated, dragon's teeth rising on either side; only the height of tall buildings at first, but becoming progressively higher until they soared like the New York skyscrapers she'd seen on the Pathé newsreels at the cinema. They were the colour of fossilized bone and just as ancient, just as silent. Wherever the jackals were, they were keeping out of sight.

Two and half hours into the march, deep into the Sinai massif, they stopped for a rest and took water from the bladders slung over the camel's saddle.

'How far?' Harry asked the young guide.

Tarek translated and received the answer. 'Is not far, maybe a mile. At the head of this wadi there is a track between two great boulders. It leads into the next valley. That is where is Bir Hathour.'

Prim splashed water on her face and felt a thin slurry of dust slide down one cheek. 'I don't want it to be like this,' she said suddenly, voicing a fear that had been slowly growing on her since they had left Cairo.

Harry looked at her. 'Like what? I don't follow.'

'Like an arrest.'

'Well, that's sort of the truth, isn't it?'

His words only made her determination grow. 'No, Harry. It's not going to be my truth. Or Archie's. I want to go to him alone. He'll need coaxing out. You can all wait a little way off. If he sees us all together, what's he going to think? What if he takes us for Kazem Jabour's people, or Hamad's, or the Jews?'

'You can't possibly go to him alone, Prim. That's crazy.'

'Look around, Harry,' Prim replied, doing it for him. 'There's the constable with his rifle... there's Tarek... there's the guide.

There's a whole bloody posse of us, and my father's going to think he's the outlaw we've come to lynch.'

Harry thought about simply taking over, but he could see the sense in what she'd said. And if Archie Nevendon was armed, what state would his mind be in, after weeks in hiding? 'Okay,' he said reluctantly. 'But I'm coming with you. I have a job to do. My Service threw a fit when one Nevendon went missing. I'm not going to be the man who has to tell them we've lost another one.'

The track led between two almost-sheer cliffs that Prim judged to be five hundred feet high, over a gravelly saddleback and down into a defile perhaps two hundred yards across. On each side, the valley floor rose gently at first before steeping into a rockface scarred with deep vertical fissures. Not a single sign of human presence, now or in ages past.

'This can't be it,' she observed, overawed by the silence and the crushing sense of desolation. 'There's nothing here.'

'Look, there,' said Harry, his arm outstretched. He seemed to be pointing at a random part of the valley's slope, about sixty yards away.

And then she saw it. A broken pattern in the landscape. A cluster of weathered stone walls barely shoulder-high, almost indistinguishable from the scattered remnants of ancient rock-falls. With Harry close at her heels, she went nearer.

She tried to conjure *TURQUOISE, 1913* out of this des-olate place, but couldn't. The walls, if they even were walls, refused to fit the photograph of Nim and Archie at their dig. 'We've got it all wrong,' she mouthed to the stones, to Harry, to Archie, to Hathor, to God himself if only he would listen. 'We're in the wrong place. I'm sure of it.' The desolation of the mountains entered her body and made her weak. She sank to her knees, crouching as if she was waiting for the vastness to fall in and crush her to atoms.

And then she heard the scrape of gravel moving. She knew instinctively it wasn't coming from behind her, where Harry was. Rising, Prim turned towards an outcrop of wall – and saw him.

He looked so utterly unlike the man she had known that for a moment she thought she was hallucinating, imagining some crazed Old Testament prophet had materialized before her. The setting was right; the matted beard and the wild, frenzied stare were right; the staff in his right hand… All he needed to complete the picture was a stone tablet of God's Commandments tucked under his other arm. But it was him all right. Then her heart took over as she saw the red wheals of sunburn on his heavy bald head, the filth on his ragged clothes and the complete ruination in his eyes.

How could Archie have become the creature standing before her? He looked worse than the tramps who had sometimes come to Bevern Lodge seeking bread from the kitchen, and God knew she pitied them enough to filch leftovers and leave them by the gates, though it was only the foxes that really benefited. She began to weep. 'Daddy! Dear God in heaven – Daddy… Daddy…'

And then she realized that the staff he was pointing in her direction was a rifle.

'Go away! Get out of my head!' he shouted, his voice rasping and uncertain, as if he'd half-forgotten how to use it. 'It's not you. You're not here. You're an illusion. Leave me alone.'

Fighting back the tears, Prim moved closer.

The rifle swayed as Archie sought to hold it level. 'This cannot be real. It's not you. You're not here.'

357

'I promise you, Daddy; it's me. It really *is* me. It's Primmy.'

Archie turned his head towards Harry. 'Nim,' he said, 'make her go away. I can't bear it any more. I don't want to see her. For God's sake, Nim, make Celestina take her back inside.'

Harry, having never previously been mistaken for a ghost, said nothing. He stayed very still, wondering how much control Archie Nevendon had over his trigger finger. He was glad he'd refused Major Courtney's offer of the office revolver. There was no knowing how Nevendon might respond to an armed man. Grudgingly he knew Prim had been right to leave the others behind.

But Prim had no such inhibitions. She stepped closer to her father. 'Daddy, you're not well. I've come to take you home.'

To her relief, she saw a flicker of comprehension in his eyes. He had stepped out of his world and – almost – into hers.

But not quite.

Archie was peering at her as if there was a gauze curtain between them. She feared he might decide it was too much effort to see through it.

'Is it really you, Primmy?' he said in a voice so quiet she might have imagined it.

'Yes, Daddy. It's me. I've come all the way from England – just for you. I've come to make you safe again.'

She smiled at him and waited for him to smile back. He didn't. Now there was fear in his eyes. 'It's *them*,' he said, his glaze darting from Prim to Harry and then around the valley, and for a moment Prim thought Tarek and the others had followed them. 'They've sent you to make me drop my guard. Who was it who betrayed me?' Archie went on, as his eyes settled once more on Prim.

'Daddy, there's no one else here. It's only me and—'

He cut her off with a snarl. 'Was it Hamad? Was it Jabour? Was it the Jews? Who told you to come? They're devils! *Devils*, all of them.'

Prim saw in Archie's eyes that he was slipping away from her. 'No!' she insisted. 'It's not like that. Look, it doesn't matter what you've done. I'm here because you're my father and I love you.'

He kept staring at her, as if he thought she might be a mirage. Why wasn't he asking her how she'd found him? Was he indifferent to the struggle she'd gone through? Terrified he would retreat into whatever unreachable place the mountains and his own mind had offered him as a refuge, she began to plead. 'You have to believe me, Daddy; I've come all the way from Bevern to find you. We had happy times there, didn't we? – at least for a while. Remember when I was a little girl: how you used to let me play at being an archaeologist, just like you and Uncle Nim. You'd bury Celestina's little statues in the earth and then help me dig them up.' To her relief, she saw in Archie's stare a flicker of his once-rational self. 'That was *me*,' she told him earnestly. 'That was Primmy. Primmy wouldn't ever betray you.'

His reply was utterly unexpected. 'I never did that,' he said brutally.

For an instant Prim didn't understand what he meant.

Then, in a throwaway voice, he shattered every careful memory she had constructed for herself in the years since he'd walked out on her and Celestina. 'I never played those silly games with you,' he sneered. 'It wasn't me. It was old Elwyn, the gardener at Bevern. He used to let you sit on his tractor, remember? And he took you around, digging up those stupid bits of clay your mother wasted her time on. I had better things to do with my time.'

Prim fought to drag the words out of her reeling mind. 'That's not true! I remember how bristly your tweed jacket was… and the smell of your pipe – everything.'

'It's all in your head, Primmy,' he said, almost contemptuously. 'You had plenty of time without me around to build a fantasy. You've invented it all, child. It's just a lie you've been telling yourself for your own comfort.'

'But… but I *remember* it.'

'You imagined it. I told old Elwyn to do it because I couldn't bear your constant infantile interruptions while I was working in my study. I never wanted a child. I was never able to love; not even you. I didn't know what love was until I met Ifaya.'

'Daddy, being here in this place, it's made you unwell. You're talking nonsense. Remember all the letters you sent me… the birthday and Christmas cards…'

He stared at her, and in his eyes she could see something that was far worse than hate. It was disinterest. 'What letters? I stopped sending letters years ago.'

Even in her distracted state, the awful truth seared itself across Prim's understanding. Archie's priceless letters and cards: never handwritten, always typed. Changing when she was about twelve, as if he no longer quite knew her. Those hadn't come from him at all. They must have been Granny G's work, to protect her from her son's heartlessness. He's hit me in the face, she thought. I can feel the pain of it. I can feel my cracked jaw dropping. Yet there he is, still standing with the rifle, out of reach. Perhaps that's what he always has been for me: *out of reach.*

'I know all about Ifaya, Daddy,' she managed, because it was the only way she could think of touching him. 'I can guess how much you loved her. So it's not true. You *can* love.'

'It doesn't matter. It's too late now,' Archie replied, raising the barrel of the rifle until it was pointing directly at her chest. 'Go away. I don't want you here. I don't want you in my study, wittering your childish nonsense when I've work to do.'

Prim was having trouble keeping up with his fitful jumps in time and place. 'Come back with us, Daddy,' she said. 'Harry can help us sort things out.'

Archie cast Harry no more than a glance, but it was clear to Prim that it wasn't Harry he was seeing. 'There's no going back, Primrose,' he said. 'Not from this place. Not after what I did. I have to stay here with Nim and Ifaya.'

'That's not what Ifaya would want – for you to die out here in this awful place, alone.'

The aggressive bravado fractured. Archie almost spat out his words. 'You don't understand, child. I *killed* her. I killed the only woman I've ever loved. That's why I must stay here – with her.'

How do you reason with a man whose mind has been destroyed first by guilt and then by the wilderness that he takes himself into for penance? wondered Prim. It was beyond anything she knew how to deal with. 'I know you did some bad things, Daddy,' she said gently, 'but that's not one of them. You can't blame yourself.'

She had thought that might ease his pain. But she was wrong. 'Ifaya shouldn't have been at al-Sarhan,' Archie shouted, his voice rasping like a rusty hinge. 'If she'd told me she was going, I'd have found a way to stop her. She was never going to persuade her brother. Never!'

'Then you have nothing to blame yourself for. It was a tragic case of being in the wrong place at the wrong time. You weren't responsible.'

Archie looked at her as if she was stupid. 'Don't you under-stand, you idiot girl? I'm the guilty one. It was me. I was the one who told the Jews about her brother Kazem and the explosives. *I* told them. I told them so that they could kill him. I told them so that we'd be free of Kazem Jabour. Then we could truly be together. How could I have known that Ifaya would take a taxi up from Tiberias on the very day of their attack? How could I have known that Bachmann's boy would be one of the Irgun fighters, that he'd be killed? None of it was meant to *happen* like that! But *I* told them to attack al-Sarhan.'

Prim stared at her father. In his eyes there was now a misery that scared her with its black intensity. To her horror, he raised the barrel of the rifle until it was pointing straight up beneath his chin. 'Now get out of here,' he shouted, 'before I put an end to this once and for all.'

Archie pulled the trigger. The gun went off. It was over.

But the gun was silent. Archie hadn't pulled the trigger. Nothing had changed.

Prim almost screamed, because now it was her mind sparking between reality and fantasy. She stepped forward, ready to plead with her father to lower the rifle, to accept the comfort she'd come all this way to offer him. To make everything all right again, the way she'd believed *he* had done when she was little, but which he was now denying.

She felt Harry's hand on her arm. 'I think it's time to go,' he said softly. She didn't turn her head because she didn't want to look at him. The reasonableness in his voice, the very fact that he was right, only made her hate him more. 'You've done everything you can,' he whispered, though in this empty place it sounded like a bellow. 'Archie's made his choice. Don't take that away from him. It's all he's got left.'

———

Prim had almost no memory of the walk back from Bir Hathour. She spent the return journey to the Bedouin settlement sitting astride the camel while Harry and the young guide led the animal by the reins. At times she wondered if she'd fallen and was suffering from some sort of concussion, because her senses and her memories were all jumbled up and chasing each other round and round in her head. Noise and smell. Places and moments. Fragments and shards. Truth and lies. After Archie's rejection, she could not tell which were real and which she had invented. Her father wasn't who she thought he was. Her childhood wasn't what she remembered it to be. She couldn't even be sure, then, that Primrose Nevendon was not in fact a fiction to herself.

At one point she was conscious of a persistent buzzing in her ear. She thought it was a fly; there were plenty of them here and they settled on you if you stayed still. Then she realized it was Tarek's voice – Tarek asking questions. He was pressing her for details about her encounter with Archie, until Harry told him to shut up and mind his own business.

At the Bedouin settlement the sheikh announced that she was suffering from the malady that often afflicted those who entered the mountains for the first time, especially Europeans. She was given a restorative tea with herbs in it. It did nothing for her at all, because standing amongst the ruins of Bir Hathour she'd learned there were some things that cannot be restored – even by a glass of tea.

I've abandoned him, she thought, as Harry eased her into the Citroën, the light softening as evening came on. But then he wasn't mine to abandon.

She told herself that Archie had been delirious, that he hadn't realized what he was saying. That it was the mountains that had changed him. But that brought no consolation; it was clear now she hadn't really known Archie at all – Granny G's cards and letters were the physical proof of that. And all the time his rejection of her roared around inside her mind like a bad migraine.

Harry said he wanted to reach the road at Abu Zenima before dusk, and Tarek was all in agreement, volubly so. Harry asked to buy a couple of the rugs that the Bedouin rested upon beneath the spread of their tents, but the sheikh would accept no payment and made a gift of them. Maybe it wasn't the mountain malady, he said, revising his opinion. Maybe it was exhaustion, or heatstroke. But Prim knew what it was. It was the reaction of a child digging excitedly in the grounds of Bevern, only to learn there was nothing there to unearth but an adult's deception.

On the rear passenger seat, Harry made a comfy nest of the rugs and Prim climbed in. He sat up front and they set off back down the wadi towards Abu Zenima.

Of the night journey back to Cairo, Prim remembered little. Her mind tumbled wildly between fitful dreams and semi-wakefulness, a state that was neither asleep nor fully conscious, but a vague no-man's-land of distorted perception. Which is why her awareness of the event – one that she later judged to have occurred some miles out of Abu Zenima on the road up to the Canal – was, at the time, muddled and disconcerting.

Opening her eyes, she perceived the Citroën was stationary. Night had fallen, but the interior of the car seemed lit by a bright light. Maybe the sun had come out at night, a concept that in her present state of mind seemed as likely as any of the other strange inversions she'd experienced over the previous exhausting hours. Or maybe it was the headlamps of what she took to be another car, alongside the Citroën, facing in the opposite direction. The front side-windows of both cars were down, and Tarek was having a conversation with the other driver, in Arabic. Harry, too, had been asleep and was only now coming awake. Prim raised herself a little and looked across into the second car. She was sure she recognized the man to whom Tarek was speaking, but couldn't place him. Similarly, the passenger beside him seemed oddly familiar – a huge man with a scowling face and a thick beard. She caught a glimpse of two other men in the back. They looked almost as threatening as the passenger in the front. Was she awake or was this a dream? Was it a distorted replaying of the time when she'd been passing through the Buraq slums in this very car, Tarek at the wheel, when the boy on the motorcycle had raised his gun at her? Was the driver about to do the same?

Then she heard Tarek say to Harry, 'They're mechanics. They go down to Abu Rudeis for a steamer with engine problem. Is arriving at dawn. They ask if this is correct road.' He recited this in Arabic for the benefit of the men in the other car, who laughed uproariously, even though Prim couldn't think of anything remotely funny about a ship with a defective engine, or why they might be asking if this was the right coastal road, when even she knew by now there was only one.

It's dark, Nim, old boy. The house-lights are down. It's the moment before curtain up.

I love these last few minutes before the show begins, peeking out into the blackness of the house. Beyond the footlights, the audience has taken their seats, eager, expectant. Waiting for the magic to start.

I can hear footsteps in the first row: four latecomers – men. They're only just in time. Madame Nasoul won't abide tardiness.

If you're not sitting by the time the overture has ended, you'll have to wait for the first act to close, and you've only yourself to blame.

Old Moussa's worked his magic again, getting it all in place and ready to go. He's given the call: Act One beginners to the stage! The cast is buzzing. Ifaya's in the wings, always a bag of nerves before she goes on. But the moment she's onstage – well, she takes my breath away.

So, here we are, Nim, old fellow. You, me, Ifaya and another night at the Nimrod Theatre. Break a leg. Curtain up. Let the show commence!

Thirty-Six

The answer came to Prim the following day, late in the afternoon, when she awoke in her bed at the Villa Narcisse, and then not before she'd spent a good hour taking every punch she could throw at herself. She was the worst daughter in the world. She had abandoned Archie in his darkest moment, left him to die. Worst of all, she had failed to make him see that his rejection of her was nothing but his misguided attempt at protecting her. And when all that was washed away in a flood of tears that soaked the expensive cotton pillow that Anglo-Levantine Oil had so thoughtfully provided, she counter-attacked. Archie was exactly the cold, heartless bastard that Celestina had always said he was. He had thrown aside his own daughter with breathtaking cruelty. And Granny G had been his accomplice. Then Prim pummelled the soggy pillow with her fists, before spilling even more tears.

Exhausted, she lay back and stared at the slowly turning ceiling fan, the wooden blades tipping her from anger to grief to confusion, feeling as liquid and passive as if she was a stream flowing over the blades of a water mill.

It was during this period that she replayed in her mind the night return to Cairo. And suddenly she knew it hadn't been a dream. She *had* recognized the driver who'd been speaking to

Tarek. He was one of Shakir Hamad's smooth young men, the very one who had picked her up at the Qasr el Nil Bridge the day she tried to enlist the gangster in her search for Archie.

Dressing and sorting out her make-up – she hadn't bothered to remove it on her return to the villa – Prim went down to the study. It felt like entering a crypt. She half-expected to see an open coffin and Archie lying in it, his arms crossed over the breast of his tweed jacket. Then the tears threatened to come again. She fought them off, because after what she'd learned at Bir Hathour she wasn't sure he'd want them.

Opening his desk drawer, she took out the theatre programme that had Ifaya Jabour's photo in it. Flicking to the right page, she studied the image. It wasn't easy to spot any similarities between Ifaya's image and the face of the man she'd seen sitting beside Hamad's smooth young assassin in that car. But there was at least *something* about the shape of the eyes that made her believe she'd been looking into the face of Kazem Jabour.

At six p.m. Harry telephoned to ask how she was. Prim didn't want to lie because she'd had her fill of lies – more than a decade of them. The only answer she could give him was, 'I don't know, Harry. Truly, I don't know.'

He asked if she wanted him to come round. He said he quite understood when she told him no. 'You've had a shock, Prim, a bad one,' he reminded her gently – as if she didn't know it. 'Don't try to be brave. If you need me, you know where I am. Anything at all. Just pick up the phone.'

She thanked him and, after he'd rung off, dialled a now-familiar number. The switchboard operator put her through.

'Hey, Miss Primrose, you're back? Is all well? Did you find him?'

Hearing Mike Luzzatto's voice gave her the courage she needed. 'I found *someone*,' she said. And when he didn't immediately reply, she added, 'I have to get out of this place, Mike. Can I come and stay with you for a few days, until I decide what to do?'

'Of course.'

'If I ask you a question, will you answer it honestly? I'll know if you're lying to me.'

'Ask away,' he said in a slightly tentative voice, which worried her.

'When I told you I thought I'd found out where Archie was hiding, did you tell Shakir Hamad?'

'Why on earth would I do that?' he replied. He sounded almost offended. 'You made me promise on my mother's grave not to tell anyone. So I didn't. As God is my witness.'

'Do you swear that's the truth.'

'Happy to.'

'Say it, Mike. I'll know if you're lying.'

On the line, she could hear Mike draw breath. 'Primrose Nevendon, I swear by everything I hold dear that I did *not* tell your secret to Shakir Hamad.'

And she knew Luzzatto was telling the truth, because suddenly she'd remembered how Hamad's messenger had found her so easily when she'd been hiding at Tarek's brother's house in the Bulaq district. Hamad knew where she was because Tarek had told him. Archie's driver hadn't been the friend he'd pretended to be.

Prim took the programme and Uncle Nim's army paybook that contained the photo of him and Archie at Turquoise and walked out of the study without even closing the desk drawer.

'Is Tarek here?' she called to Madame Sauvier.

'No, Mademoiselle. He went out. He didn't say where.'

That, at least, was a relief. She wasn't frightened of him. She just wasn't sure she could face the man who had betrayed Archie, without trying to stab him in the eye with the revolting Turkish cigarette he was always smoking.

Prim returned to the bedroom and pitched her now very dusty walking boots out of the open window. She never wanted to have them on her feet again, because of where they'd carried her. Then she threw the rest of her things into her suitcase, placed the theatre programme and the paybook on top and closed the case. Trying not to run, she went down to the hall and telephoned for a taxi to take her to Shepheard's Hotel.

Cairo did not extend to the luxury of a cipher clerk, so Harry encrypted his brief cable to London by himself. Nor was he going to wait for Major Courtney's approval to send it – the head of station was attending a polo match at the Gezira Sporting Club. It didn't take him long, couching the end of his investigation in the vaguest terms he could, while still reassuring London there was no reason for them to assume Nevendon had given Berlin information that was prejudicial to British interests, or for Harry himself to remain in Egypt:

Subject Nevendon: Correction to earlier assessment + Almost certainly dead + Body unrecoverable + Unwitting victim of dispute with local criminals + No further action required or possible + Cairo police aware.

As for the incident on the road back from Bir Hathour, he was prepared to keep an open mind about that. Perhaps Tarek Shalaby had told him the truth: that the four men in the car that had flashed them down had indeed been engineers heading to Abu Rudeis. But he doubted it. There was only one road between the Canal and the port, so they must have known where they were heading. And though at the time Harry had only just come awake, and Tarek had done his best to hide it, it had been obvious that the two drivers knew each other. But what could have been done? The policeman in the slower Renault truck had been a couple of miles back. Outnumbered, a shootout would have ended only one way. Still, it was all academic now. He'd given Shalaby's name to Russell Pasha as one to watch.

As for forcing Prim to leave Bir Hathour without her father, Harry had justified his actions to himself and felt at ease. If Nevendon had shot himself in front of his daughter, as he was threatening to do, he couldn't begin to imagine what it would have done to her. Besides, Archie Nevendon had made his choice. Even if he was still alive, which Harry doubted, sending the police into the Sinai – assuming Russell Pasha had agreed – would change nothing. It was all far too late. The man had chosen his own way of atoning for what he had done. It was to be admired. And Harry believed that eventually even Prim would come to that conclusion.

But that didn't stop him worrying about her. He knew enough about running agents to know that a shock like that could set off all sorts of unexpected responses. He thought of the agent he was running in Vienna – Anna: she'd thrown him a few surprises. He missed her, he realized with a shock. What would the Service have to say about *that*? Dreadfully unprofessional, probably. But he couldn't help it. The fact that Primrose Nevendon possessed the same sort of courage made him smile. They'd like each other, he was sure of it.

It was almost midnight when the reply from London arrived:

Consider assignment completed + Proceed Vienna Station by steamer soonest.

That was London all over, Harry thought. Now that his job was done, the Service was having one of its idiosyncratic fits of parsimony, closing the departmental purse with a snap. No more Imperial Airways flying boats for young Taverner; put him on a slow steamer.

Turning out the office lights, Harry headed for his single bed in the embassy's domestic quarters.

It began as a game of Truth or Consequences. Lying in the spacious bed, a plate of smoked salmon set beside the champagne on a room-service silver platter resting between them, Mike used a die he'd picked up after a winning streak at the Casino de Paris on Emad al-Din Street. Low numbers meant a minor embarrassment; a six demanded a bared soul.

Prim went first and threw a two. She confessed to quoting a terrible review to a director who'd once propositioned her. 'It was cruel. I should have been kinder,' she said.

Three turns later, Mike threw a six. He regarded the die in silence for a moment, as if it was his nemesis. As he turned to her, she saw real fear in his eyes.

'Oh dear. Should I brace myself?'

Tentatively he said, 'We have something going here, you and me. Am I right?'

It was the first time she'd seen him uncertain about anything. 'I think so, yes,' she said.

'Then this one is going to put it to the test.'

Prim took a deep breath. 'Truth and Consequences, Mike: that's what we're playing, isn't it? I've had enough of lies to last me a lifetime.'

'It's about your father.'

Prim could see he was floundering. She laid one hand on his. It seemed to calm him.

'You already know I'm a Jew,' he said. 'Well, I do some work for certain people in Palestine. I was part of the hunt for Archie Nevendon.'

Prim's mouth opened, but no sound spilled out.

'I recruited the guys who were going to kill him. They were going to follow your friend Tarek Shalaby, once you'd located where he was. In the end a guy named Bachmann called it off. It was supposed to be in revenge for getting his son killed.'

Prim tilted her face to the ceiling and closed her eyes. 'I've heard of Bachmann,' she replied softly. 'A woman I met, who called herself Rachel, said he was a good man.'

'Oh, he is. One of the best. And he loved his only son so much that he wanted retribution. I don't know what changed his mind. I guess he decided too many decent people had already died. So he took the pain and turned it into something good. It's a lesson for us all.'

'So you were just using me to find Archie?'

'At first, yes. Now – well, that's a whole new ballpark. I'll understand if that doesn't cut it with you, but it's God's honest truth.'

Looking directly into Mike's eyes, Prim said, 'If Bachmann hadn't called it off, would you have gone ahead?'

Mike paused, holding her gaze. Then he said, 'Yes.'

'Thank you. It would have been so easy for you to have lied.'

Letting his breath out in a slow sluice of relief, Mike went on, 'Well, I guess it's your turn.'

Prim picked up the die. Without throwing it, she found the six and held it towards him.

'Oh God, you're going to tell me you're married.'

Prim laughed. 'No, silly. But I did once do a bad thing. And given how the Nazis in Germany are treating your people right now, I really don't think you're going to like it.'

'Try me.'

Prim gave him the same apologia she'd given Harry at the Cleopatra Club when he'd brought up the subject of her brief membership of the British Union of Fascists. Mike listened without giving her the slightest hint of what he was thinking.

'Well?' she said anxiously.

'Aw, what the hell,' he said, with a weary rumble of mirth. 'We've all been fooled into something stupid. When I was six my older sister made me an honorary mascot of the local Girl Scouts troop. You wouldn't believe the fights I got into about *that* later.' He took a sliver of smoked salmon from the plate and popped it in his mouth. 'Shall we stop this game before one of us has to confess to drowning kittens?'

'You *haven't?*' Prim said, appalled.

'No, of course I haven't!'

Prim, too, helped herself to a slice of fish. 'On a set once, a friend and I put a whoopee cushion on the seat of a rather pompous actor during a rehearsal of *King Lear*. He was playing Gloucester – it was the scene where his eyes are put out. He was furious.'

Mike leaned across and kissed her on the nose. 'Yeah,' he said, 'that's just the kind of bad behaviour that got you all kicked out of the Thirteen Colonies back in 1776.'

———

Early next morning, before Major Courtney or Mrs Fulready-Laycock were at their desks, Harry made a call to the British military headquarters at the King David Hotel in Jerusalem. His luck was in: Captain Orde Wingate was also an early riser.

'What can I do for you, Harry?'

'It's about Archie Nevendon.'

'Have you found him?'

'In a manner of speaking.'

A gruff bark of laughter came down the line. 'I assume by that you mean he's dead.'

Briefly but succinctly, Harry recounted what had happened following the flight back from Palestine. In closing, he said, 'I've informed Russell of the Egyptian police, but it's probable Kazem Jabour is already back on your side of the border. You might want to keep an extra eye open for him.'

'Thank you, Harry. I appreciate that. I can't offer more than a titbit in return, I'm afraid. But some knowledge is better than none, eh?'

'Indeed it is. What have you got for me?'

'There's an American chappie,' Wingate continued. 'A Jew. Goes by the name of Michael Luzzatto. Works for the Jewish Agency, buying up land here in Palestine from the Arabs. In my book that's no crime, but the Mandate government threw him out a while back. They're trying to hang on to what little peace we've got left here. Last heard of in Athens, according to my informants, buying a ticket on the Imperial Airways flight to Alexandria. He was observed boarding, so he could still be in Egypt. He might be useful to your people. There again, he might be a source of friction with the Egyptians. Nothing criminal recorded against him, but at least you now know about him. Do with that information what you will. Cheerio, and keep up the good work.'

'I've got business meetings downtown,' Mike told Prim over a late breakfast on Shepheard's terrace beneath the sun awning. 'They'll go on till around four. Will you be okay on your own? I'll postpone them if you want. How about I take you to Santi's afterwards?'

Touched by his concern, Prim assured him she'd be fine. When he'd gone, she went to the concierge desk to enquire about the international call to England she had requested. 'Perhaps later this morning, *Inshallah*,' the concierge told her with a hopeful smile; it was not in his professional nature to disappoint. He laid the blame on business and diplomatic traffic taking priority because of all the political uncertainty in Europe.

Returning to the terrace, Prim spent the next hour reading the newspapers and watching the hotel guests come and go in a procession of shiny limousines and taxis. She began a game in which she tried to invent exotic backstories for the men and women the doormen greeted or bade farewell to. But then she began to doubt her motives and stopped. Hadn't she had her fill of invented lives?

Another taxi pulled up at the kerb. The Shepheard's doorman stepped forward and opened the passenger door. Even if she hadn't dismissed the stupid game she'd been playing, this time there was no need of invention. She recognized only too clearly the young man who stepped out.

Spotting her almost immediately, Harry raised a hand in greeting and came towards her. He was wearing grey Oxford bags and a cream shirt, collar loose, no tie. Unofficial business then, she hoped. But by his face she could see she was wrong. He asked if he might join her and when she said, 'Of course', he came straight to the point.

'I thought you'd want to know, Prim – I've just taken a call from Thomas Russell at Cairo police headquarters. I rang the Villa Narcisse, but the housekeeper said you'd left. So I played a hunch.'

'And here you are. Go on.'

'It's about your father.'

'I thought it might be.'

Harry cleared his throat with a cough. A waiter took it as a summons and hurried over. Harry ordered coffee. Prim said she was fine.

'The Bedouin went up to Bir Hathour the morning after we left,' Harry said solemnly when the waiter had gone. 'They found Archie's body there.'

For a while there was only the sound of the traffic and the murmur of conversation from the other occupants of the terrace. Prim stared at her fingers splayed on the tabletop. They seemed to belong to someone else. Then she asked, 'Where is he now? What have they done with him.'

'They buried him straight away. Partly custom, mostly due to the heat.'

'That was kind of them.'

'Do you want me to explore the possibility of having him disinterred and buried here in Cairo?'

Prim shook her head. 'No, Harry. I think it best if he's left alone now.' Harry's coffee arrived. Prim waited until they were alone again before speaking. 'I think we already know, but any news on how he died?'

'Gunshot apparently.'

'His gun or someone else's?'

'Impossible to tell.'

'I think it was Kazem Jabour, and Shakir Hamad's people. Remember the car that stopped us on the way back?'

'Yes, that's my guess too. I'm sorry.'

They made small talk while Harry finished his coffee. Prim noticed that he hadn't once mentioned Mike Luzzatto. Nor had he asked when she might be going home. As he rose to leave, she took his hand. 'I'm sorry I got you into this, Harry. It can't have been pleasant for you.'

'You didn't get me into anything, Prim. But before I go, I need to know how you're bearing up. Remember, I was there too. I heard everything Archie told you. Every word. That must have hurt like hell.'

She smiled. 'I'm fine. Honestly. Mike is being a sweetheart.'

'I'm glad to hear it. But may I say something?'

'After what we've been through together? I should think so.'

'Yes, well...' He took a deep breath. 'Please, Prim, be careful. You're in a vulnerable state. Maybe it's a little early to be putting all your trust in Mike Luzzatto.'

'Is that the spy talking or the friend?'

'Bit of both really. But mostly as a friend.'

Prim laughed knowingly. 'You really *are* jealous, aren't you?'

Standing beside her, he patted her shoulder. 'Primrose Nevendon, you are a dreadful judge of character.'

She looked up and him and nodded. 'And haven't I learned *that* the hard way.'

It was past noon when the boy from the concierge desk brought her news that the international operators had at last connected her call to England. Prim hurried to the public phone kiosk and closed the door. After swallowing hard a couple of times, because her mouth had suddenly become dry, she lifted the receiver.

'I'm really sorry to tell you, but I've got some bad news about Daddy,' she said when Celestina's scratchy voice came on the line, sounding as distant as if she was answering the call on the moon.

'He's dead, isn't he? I can tell by your tone, Primmy.'

'I'm afraid so.'

The line was only noise for a moment, and Prim was expecting the operator to announce that the connection to England had been lost when her mother spoke again. 'Well, he was never going to pop his clogs in a rest home in Brighton, darling, was he?' The weariness in Celestina's voice was the one thing Prim could hear clearly over the miles.

'Aren't you just a little bit sad?'

'Of course I am,' she said. 'Do you think I'm made of stone? He was a swine, but he *was* your father. At least I have that to thank him for. How did it happen?'

Prim thought of making up a fib about Archie dying in the desert on a dig, but she'd made a promise to herself about lies. 'He got mixed up in a fight between the Arabs and the Jews.'

'Always sticking his nose into things that he shouldn't have – that was Archie all over. Where is he buried?'

'At the place where he and Uncle Nim used to dig. You must remember the photo: Turquoise.'

'Oh yes, I remember. Where is that?'

'It's in the Sinai mountains.'

'That sounds remote.'

'It is – very.'

'Well, if you should go there, say a little prayer on my behalf. We did have a few good times, at the start. When will you be home?'

'Well, Mummy, that's the point, you see. I won't – at least, not yet.'

When Celestina came down off the ceiling, Prim said she'd write with more details. She told her mother she loved her and rang off. Then she found a table beneath one of the huge palm trees in the lobby, ordered a lemonade and penned a letter to Grace Nevendon. It took her a while even to know how to begin, but eventually she settled on:

> *Darling Granny G, I'm most dreadfully sorry to be the bearer of bad news…*

Prim revealed what she felt she could about Archie's death. When it came to the subject of his letters and cards, she hesitated. What was the point? It would only cause her grandmother even more pain. And Granny G, she had come to realize, had only ever sought to soften her granddaughter's abandonment. Besides, Prim remembered the warning Grace had given in the flat at Lennox Square: *What happens if you don't like what you find? Have you thought of that?*

Trust a grandmother to be wiser than you gave her credit for, she thought. Prim signed off, handed the envelope to the concierge for posting and took herself to the Cairo Museum until Mike was due to return from his meetings.

He picked up the phone on the second ring. From the bathroom came the sluicing rumble of running water as Prim opened the taps. The door was half open and, as he held the receiver to his ear, he watched her slip out of her robe. 'This is Luzzatto,' he said distractedly.

'I have a gentleman here who wishes to speak to you, Mr Mike.'

Immediately Luzzatto recognized the voice of one of the concierge boys. 'Put him on, Magdi.'

The next voice on the line was even more familiar to him. 'Before you say a word, Luzzatto, I don't want you to speak my name, understood? Prim mustn't know you're talking to me.'

A pause, during which Prim moved out of view and left him with only the crumpled robe on the floor to admire. '*Oka-a-ay*,' he said slowly. 'What is this all about?'

'It concerns your real-estate interests. Especially those in Palestine.'

Luzzatto picked up the telephone set and stepped back from the bathroom door as far as the cable would permit. 'You have my full attention… Mustafa,' he said, still keeping his eyes on the half-open bathroom door.

'I need to see you, right now.'

'Where do you suggest?'

'Your room overlooks the street, doesn't it?'

'Yes.'

'In that case, meet me outside the Thomas Cook office just up the road. Ten minutes. Don't even think of standing me up.'

'Wouldn't dream of it.'

When Harry had rung off, Luzzatto returned the phone to the table and went into the bathroom.

'Just what I need – someone to scrub my back for me,' Prim said from amidst the bubbles, turning her head across one gleaming shoulder.

'Honey, I need to go out for a moment,' Mike said regretfully. 'A difficult client.'

'I wondered who that was on the phone,' Prim replied, wiping soap bubbles from her chin. 'We're not going to miss Santi's, are we, Mike?'

Mike kissed the top of Prim's head. 'No chance. I won't be long, I promise.'

She looked up at him and smiled. 'Hurry back. Cairo and hot water have an uncertain relationship.'

It was dusk, but in the desert air the buildings stood sharp against a salmon sky. The street lamps and shop fronts were already lit. Harry was studying the displays in the Thomas Cook window when Luzzatto joined him, playing the inquisitive traveller for the benefit of the crowd. Would it be a steamship cruise of the Mediterranean... Ceylon and Australia with P&O... New York with Hamburg–America?

'Okay, I'm here,' Luzzatto said, a little breathless from his brief but brisk trot from the hotel. 'Shoot.'

As if addressing the smart couple drinking cocktails in St Mark's Square who beamed at him from the show-card on the other side of the glass, Harry said softly, 'Forgive me if this sounds rather Edwardian, but if you don't behave honourably towards Prim Nevendon there will be consequences.'

Luzzatto let out a full-bellied laugh and slapped his thighs. 'What are you, Harry, her guardian? Have I got to ask you for her hand?'

Only now did Harry turn his head to look directly into Luzzatto's eyes. 'I'm her friend,' he said firmly. 'She's been through a lot. I'm not going to delve into personal details, but—'

'I know all about it, Harry. She told me everything.'

Harry seemed surprised. 'About what happened at Bir Hathour?'

'Didn't you hear what I said? *Everything.*'

'You're really serious about her?'

'What is this, Harry? She's a grown woman. Prim doesn't need you to behave like some goddamn second-rate knight in shining armour. She'll make up her own mind.'

Harry considered this statement and seemed to find it convincing. He replied, 'If you know how Archie Nevendon was towards her at the end, then you'll know she's in a parlous state. She's been hurt enough, Mike.'

Luzzatto folded his arms across his chest. The shop lights glinted on a gold wristwatch that Harry reckoned he'd never be able to afford even if the Service kept him employed into his nineties. 'Look, I know what people think of me,' the American said. 'They guess that because I got born with good bones and into money, I must be some kind of shallow pond. A playboy. A heartbreaker. A cad. Well, let me tell you this real straight, Harry: right now my heart is brimful of feelings I never ever had before. If you must know, it's brimful of Primrose Nevendon, and I'd really like to keep it that way.'

Harry returned to studying the promises of sun, sea and adventure, all at reasonable rates, for a moment or two before speaking again. When he did, his voice had a smooth hardness to it. 'We know all about you, Michael Luzzatto – what you were doing in Palestine, who you work for...'

'I should have guessed this was coming.'

'So making progress should be nice and easy, shouldn't it?'

'Look, I haven't broken any laws, Harry,' Luzzatto said. 'There's no crime in paying someone a fair price if they want to sell you their land.'

'No, there isn't. But my guess is that you'll want to return there some day. And I can make that easier for you.'

For an instant Luzzatto had no answer. 'Are you trying to *recruit* me, Harry?'

Harry smiled into the glass. 'Not at all, old boy. But my sources in Tel Aviv tell me things could get much worse there before they get better. Someone like you could help save a lot of lives, on all sides. Does that appeal to your sense of humanity at all?'

Luzzatto considered this for a while, his eyes fixed on the vacationing couple in Venice, because if he turned to Harry he would have to talk to the side of his head and that would make him feel foolish. 'You British will be gone from Palestine one day, Harry,' he said at length. 'Then I can just walk back in.'

'That's true,' Harry replied. 'But if there was peace, my government would probably be all the more willing to hand back the mandate to the League of Nations, and your people have already agreed to a partition. Whereas if the fighting goes on, we could be there for decades.'

'What are you proposing?'

'I'm just taking soundings, Mike. That's all. You help us, I'll do what I can to make my friends in Jerusalem reconsider their prohibition on your return.'

Luzzatto's chest heaved in a lurch of silent laughter. 'Well, I've got to hand it to you: you like to play for stakes, don't you? Let me think about it.'

'Don't take too long. I leave in a few days,' Harry responded, turning to Luzzatto once more. 'One other thing.'

'What?'

'Shakir Hamad.'

'What about him?'

'I have it on good authority he's going to take a bit of a fall quite soon. If I should hear you've messed around with Prim Nevendon's heart, I'll make it my business to ensure that you keep him company on the way down. Clear?'

Luzzatto gave a slow, accepting nod. 'You know, from the moment I first met you, I figured there was more to Harry Taverner than met the eye.'

'Nonsense, old chap. I'm just a minion of the British Council. But I'll make sure the right people know you're on the side of the angels.'

They shook hands and went their separate ways, Mike Luzzatto to his room at Shepheard's and Prim Nevendon, Harry in the direction of the British embassy – to anyone who might have observed their brief conversation, they were just a couple of acquaintances who'd looked in a travel agent's window and decided on a pleasant break away from the heat and bustle of Cairo.

Harry Taverner saw Prim Nevendon only once more before he left Egypt. It was three days later, and Major Courtney was standing him a farewell drink at the Long Bar in Shepheard's. Harry was packed and ready to leave for Alexandria.

'Isn't that your girl over there?' The chatter and the clink of glasses almost drowned out Courtney's drawl. 'Looks like she's doing well for herself.'

Harry followed the other man's gaze and saw Prim and Mike Luzzatto walking into the Long Bar together. It was the first time he'd seen her in a cocktail dress. They looked like a movie couple at a premiere. He recalled how she'd accused him of being jealous. Unfair, he thought. You've been though a lot; I'm just happy for you.

Harry watched as the pair settled into wicker chairs beneath a potted palm tree. As Luzzatto waved for a waiter, Prim looked in his direction. Catching sight of him, she checked herself for an instant, said something to the American and came over.

'Hello, Harry,' she said. 'I wondered if I might bump into you.'

'It's good to see you,' Harry replied as he rose to greet her. 'Are you all right?'

'For a girl who's had her childhood memories pulled out from underneath her, I'm doing okay. I've told myself it's no worse than going to the dentist and having a tooth out.'

Harry looked down at his shoes, a little humbled by her bravery. 'I'm sorry,' he said. 'I truly am. I wish it could have turned out differently.'

When he looked up, she smiled briefly. 'Oh, it wasn't your fault, Harry. I should have listened to Celestina and Granny Grace. They warned me not to come here. That's my problem, you see: I'm not very good at listening to people.'

'I'm going back tomorrow,' he said lamely, not really knowing what else to say.

'To England?'

'To Vienna.'

'Ah, that *someone* you mentioned.'

Harry laughed, but only to hide his blushes. 'It's not really like that. Not yet anyway.'

Prim gave a toss of her head, as if to say *your loss*, but there was humour in the gesture, not triumph. 'Well, I wish you all the luck in the world,' she went on. 'You did me a real favour, Harry Taverner. And it's not often a girl can say that when she gets turned down.'

'A favour?'

Prim glanced back to where Luzzatto was signing the bill for the drinks that had arrived at their table. 'Mike has found an interest in the theatre. He has hidden depths, you know. He's going to help me get the Nimrod back on its feet.'

'You're going to stay in Cairo?'

'For a while. I'll see how things turn out. I mean, who wants to go back to Europe with all the nastiness that's brewing?'

'In my case, it rather comes with the job,' Harry said.

'Talking of favours, would it be awfully off-form to beg for a final one?'

Seeing the sudden trepidation in her eyes, Harry responded, 'You don't have to beg for anything, Prim. Just ask. If I can help, I will. You know that.'

She stiffened, as if the occasion required a formality she hadn't planned on. 'You have contacts, Harry. You work for the government. Do you think it might be possible to have Uncle Nim's remains disinterred and buried at Bir Hathour, beside my father? I'd like to think of them together.'

For a moment Harry didn't know what to say. Then he nodded in understanding. 'I don't know if it's at all possible, but I can ask the ambassador to speak to the high commissioner in Jerusalem. I'll do it today. Maybe they can arrange something.'

'You're one of a rare breed, Harry Taverner,' Prim said. And with that, she kissed him on the cheek and returned to her companion.

Major Courtney suggested another round. Harry agreed, reluctantly. He pretended to listen to the major's rendering of Cairo gossip, embassy gossip, Service gossip... It all seemed painfully parochial. When at last Courtney shook his hand and announced that he was going back to the office to dictate to Hilda Fulready-Laycock a briefing for the ambassador, Harry felt nothing but the relief of being left alone. He looked across the Long Bar and saw the two chairs under the palm were now empty.

He walked down the busy street, past the vendors in their white robes haggling with Europeans, past the middle-class Cairenes in their business suits, past the coachmen in their *galabeyas*, past the shoeshine boys and the women in dark robes with clay water jugs balanced on their shoulders, past the parked cars, the strolling British soldiers in their khaki shorts, the whole crazy bustle of Cairo, until he came to the riverbank. Out on the water a fleet of white-sailed feluccas was making its stately way towards the Qasr el Nil Bridge, heeling with the wind. He lit a cigarette and watched them for a while, transported by the timelessness of the view, oblivious to the modern city at his back. He thought of Prim and wondered how you dealt with a blow like the one Archie had delivered in that little valley. He thought of Archie himself, a man he barely knew. He wondered how brave you had to be – for all your faults – to seek sanctuary from a hell of your own making in a place that was even worse. Perhaps that was why Archie Nevendon had chosen Bir Hathour in the first place: as a punishment. Perhaps, right from the start, he had never intended to leave. Unless, of course, he hadn't seen Bir Hathour as a place of punishment at all. Maybe he'd thought he was going home to his brother.

When he had watched the river long enough, Harry ground the cigarette butt beneath his heel, removed his jacket and tie, rolled up his shirtsleeves and – having violated all the conventions of the British diplomatic classes abroad in hot climes – set off back into the city to collect his steamship ticket.

Author's Note

Of the real-life characters featured in this story:

Miles Wedderburn Lampson continued in post as British ambassador to Egypt until his retirement in 1946.

In Palestine, later in 1938, Orde Wingate trained Special Night Squads to counter Arab attacks on Jewish villages and on the oil pipeline. Many of those he recruited and tutored went on to build the Israeli Defence Force, which reveres him to this day. His methods were criticized at the time by several of his contemporaries. While the events described in this book – the human shields on the train journey from Haifa and the assault on the Galilee village – are fictitious, they are based on similar documented instances. Wingate would later go on to lead the famous Chindits during the campaign in Burma during the Second World War. He was killed in a plane crash in 1944.

Major G. W. Courtney's tenure as Cairo head of station ended not long after Harry Taverner departed. His career in the Secret Intelligence Service, and in the diplomatic service, continued. His son, Nicholas, became an actor, playing the part of Brigadier Lethbridge-Stewart in the *Doctor Who* TV series.

After four decades of service in the Egyptian Civil Service, Thomas Wentworth Russell – Russell Pasha – retired in 1946. He returned to England and died in 1954.

By the time the Arab revolt against the British Mandate government in Palestine ended in 1939, more than 5,000 Arabs had been killed, and possibly many more. A significant number – perhaps one-fifth – were slain by their own side in blood feuds and retribution. Around 500 Jews were killed, and about half that number of British troops and police. The end of the uprising did not mean the cessation of attacks on Arabs or the British authorities by the Irgun and Haganah, which became increasingly terroristic. In May 1948, with civil war raging, Britain relinquished the mandate to govern Palestine, and the State of Israel was declared. The following day the armies of Egypt, Iraq, Transjordan and Syria crossed the border of the newborn nation. During the fighting that followed, around 700,000 Palestinian Arabs fled their homes, never to return. In subsequent years a broadly similar number of Jews were either forcibly expelled or left their homes in the surrounding Arab lands.

My gratitude is due to the redoubtable Helen Lieberman, whose warning to a friend about the dangers of searching for a missing father gave me the first spark of an idea that ultimately led to this novel. I must also thank my superb editor at Corvus, Sarah Hodgson, and her team for bringing it to life. Also my agent, Jane Judd. Mandy Greenfield, my copy editor, has once again saved me from embarrassments too numerous to list, for which I am both grateful and chastened. Finally, I must acknowledge the thoughtful and wise counsel of my wife, Jane, and her seemingly inexhaustible well of tolerance and forbearance.